Praise for *Ninefox Gambit*

'Beautiful, brutal and full of the kind of off-hand inventiveness that the best SF trades in, *Ninefox Gambit* is an effortlessly accomplished SF novel. Yoon Ha Lee has arrived in spectacular fashion.'
– *Alastair Reynolds*

'I love Yoon's work! *Ninefox Gambit* is solidly and satisfyingly full of battles and political intrigue, in a beautifully built far-future that manages to be human and alien at the same time. It should be a treat for readers already familiar with Yoon's excellent short fiction, and an extra treat for readers finding Yoon's work for the first time.'
– *Ann Leckie*

'*Starship Troopers* meets *Apocalypse Now* – and they've put Kurtz in charge... Mind-blistering military space opera, but with a density of ideas and strangeness that recalls the works of Hannu Rajaniemi, even Cordwainer Smith. An unmissable debut.'
– *Stephen Baxter*

'A dizzying composite of military space opera and sheer poetry. Every word, name and concept in Lee's unique world is imbued with a sense of wonder.'
– *Hannu Rajaniemi*

'A striking space opera by a bright new talent.'
– *Elizabeth Bear*

'For sixteen years Yoon Ha Lee has been the shadow general of science fiction, the calculating tactician behind victory after victory. Now he launches his great manoeuvre. Origami elegant, fox-sly, defiantly and ferociously *new*, this book will burn your brain. Axiomatically brilliant. Heretically good.'
– *Seth Dickinson*

'A high-octane ride through an endlessly inventive world, where calendars are weapons of war and dead soldiers can assist the living. Bold, fearlessly innovative and just a bit brutal, this is a book that deserves t̶ ̶b̶ ̶...'
– *Alie...*

'Daring, original and comp...
written a V...
– *Gar...*

First published 2016 by Solaris
an imprint of Rebellion Publishing Ltd,
Riverside House, Osney Mead,
Oxford, OX2 0ES, UK

www.solarisbooks.com

UK 4th Ed. ISBN: 978 1 78108 448 9
US 7th Ed. ISBN: 978 1 78108 449 6

A CIP catalogue record for this book is available from the
British Library.

Designed & typeset by Rebellion Publishing

Printed in Denmark

NINEFOX
GAMBIT

YOON HA LEE

SOLARIS

CHAPTER ONE

AT KEL ACADEMY, an instructor had explained to Cheris's class that the threshold winnower was a weapon of last resort, and not just for its notorious connotations. Said instructor had once witnessed a winnower in use. The detail that stuck in Cheris's head wasn't the part where every door in the besieged city exhaled radiation that baked the inhabitants dead. It wasn't the weapon's governing equations or even the instructor's left eye, damaged during the attack, from which ghostlight glimmered.

What Cheris remembered most was the instructor's aside: that returning to corpses that were only corpses, rather than radiation gates contorted against black-blasted walls and glassy rubble, eyes ruptured open, was one of the best moments of her life.

Five years, five months, and sixteen days later, surrounded by smashed tanks and smoking pits on the heretic Eels' outpost world of Dredge, Captain Kel Cheris of Heron Company, 109-229th Battalion, had come to the conclusion that her instructor was full of shit. There was no comfort to be extracted from the dead, from flesh evaporated from bones. Nothing but numbers snipped short.

According to the briefing, the Eels had a directional storm generator. The storms scrambled vectors. The effect was localized, but it was troublesome when parallel columns ended up at opposite ends of a road a hundred kays apart, and fatal when movement along the planetary surface sent you underground instead. Too close and the storms might disintegrate your component atoms entirely.

Cheris and the other captains had been assured that the weather-eaters would keep the storms contained, and that all the Kel infantry had to do was walk in and seize the generator.

That had been eighteen hours ago. It wasn't that anyone was surprised by the plan's failure. It was the carnage.

Heron Company had left the cover of the southwestern woods a scant eighty-three minutes ago. The intent was to advance in a tedious snaking curve east and then north around Hill 117 because intelligence had indicated that the Eels' vanguard would occupy the ridge nearer the woods and leave the hill route open. It was as Cheris's company made it out of the woods that they saw what had happened to the Kel who had preceded them.

Cheris was unable to organize her first heart-stop impressions of what had been the rest of the battalion. Feet scraped inside-out next to unblemished boots. Black-and-gold Kel uniforms braided into cracked rib cages. Gape-jawed, twisted skulls with eye sockets staring out of their sides and strands of tendon knotted through crumbling teeth. A book of profanities written in every futile shade of red the human body had ever devised, its pages upended over the battlefield from horizon to horizon.

Her company had survived thanks to dumb luck. A field grid error had delayed their advance, so they had missed the brunt of the attack. She didn't know if any other companies, or the other battalions, had made it. Her inability to raise regimental headquarters didn't come as a surprise. Communications going down was nothing new. Orders were orders, however, and it was best to move forward. Once they got close enough, the main body of the Eels would no longer be able to deploy the storms against them, lest they, too, be caught in their area of effect.

Pulses of heat in her left arm alerted her of contacts. Servitor Sparrow 3 reported the coordinates of an incoming Eel battalion, arrival estimated in two hours. The transmission ended in a burst of pain: the servitor had been detected. It was too much to hope that the Eels hadn't recognized it as a Kel servitor, and worrisome that they had let it know that it had been compromised before destroying it.

There was no time to mourn Sparrow 3, who had been fond of Kel music; that would have to come later.

"Anything from the other servitors?" Cheris asked her communications officer, Lieutenant-engineer Dineng, over the subvocal relay.

A pause. "Nothing, sir," Dineng said. "Sparrow 8 is investigating the storm ahead."

Cheris frowned at the periodic flickers of reports in the form of visual overlays. If anything, they obfuscated her picture of the situation, but she was used to that.

She monitored relay chatter with half an ear as she compared old maps and new reconnaissance. Certain words crackled out of the soundstream again and again: *Eels. Sleep. Storm, fractal coefficient, can't the weather-eaters hurry up.* And, for pity's sake, was Kel Inoe going on about his sex life again?

For her part, Cheris wouldn't have minded holing up in the shadow of a rock and sleeping for a week. The week was one of the few time measures the hexarchate didn't regulate. In her old home, the City of Ravens Feasting, they used the eight-day week. When she was tired, it was easy to lapse out of the military ten-day week into the eight. In the furtive tradition of her mother's people, today would be Carrion Day, a reminder of the importance of scavengers. It was difficult to agree.

"Sir." Her senior lieutenant, Kel Verab, brought her out of her reverie. "I don't like the look of the silhouettes on Hill 119." It was southwest of 117. She brought it up on her display and frowned at the complicated silhouette. "Probably an installation of some sort and I bet it's got eyes. I give you odds the Eels will call in the artillery the second they think they can get all of us. Maybe we should keep heading east."

"We can't avoid the heretics forever," Cheris said. "We're going to have to hope that formation defenses hold for us if they start lobbing shells." She addressed the company. "Formation," she said, "Pir's Fan." It had a longer name, but nobody had time for the full names on the battlefield.

Pir's Fan was one of the simpler formations. As its name suggested, it resembled a wedge. It was easiest for Cheris: she held the primary pivot at the van, and everyone adjusted their position relative to hers.

The Kel specialty was formation fighting. The combination of formation geometry and Kel discipline allowed them to channel exotic effects, from heat lances to force shields. Unfortunately, like all exotics, this ability depended on the local society's adherence to the hexarchate's high calendar. And the high calendar wasn't just a system of timekeeping. It encompassed the feasts, the remembrances with their ritual torture of heretics, the entire precarious social order.

Cheris knew the formation's effect had begun to propagate when the world shifted blue and the blacks bent gray. Pir's Fan offered protection against the weather. It was usually better to rely on the weather-eaters, but Cheris had lost any faith that they would be effective on this mission. Unfortunately, the formation wouldn't shield the unit from a direct hit. She hoped to close with the generator before that became an issue.

If the situation changed, there were other formations. The Kel infantry library included thousands, although only a hundred or so were taught as part of Lexicon Primary. You also had to allow for transition time in modulation, especially between less familiar formations. Cheris could feed her soldiers the information through the grid, but it was no substitute for drill.

The march as they swung north steadied Cheris. Here stubby succulents, too low to be credible cover, grew only to be crushed underfoot. The plants gave off a stinging fragrance that attenuated into a watery, cloying sweetness. The regional survey hadn't flagged it as a toxic. Whether the plants had any meaning to the Eels, Cheris didn't know. She would probably leave Dredge, if she left Dredge, without finding out.

Lieutenant Verab alerted her of the enemy sighting via heat pulse. Over the relay, Cheris heard a junior sergeant shouting at someone who had dropped his rifle, a recent recruit who had a talent for botching things.

The Eels' field fortifications, which commanded one of the larger hills, looked like a rough shore in a sea of dust, and their patrols carried themselves with a certain sloppiness. But the distant figures stirred in agitation: Cheris was betting they had thought themselves safe.

Of momentary interest was the Eels' banner, which was of green fire and grim shadow with a twisting motif. The Eels called themselves the Society of the Flourish, although the hexarchate didn't use this name. Taking away people's names denied their power, a lesson Cheris tried not to think about.

Cheris snapped, "Unfurl Kel banner. Advance and fire. I want anything that twitches to die."

The banner-bearers ignited the generator, and fire blazed in the sky. At the heart of the golden flames was the Kel ashhawk, the black bird that burned in its own glory, and beneath it their general's emblem, the Chain of Thorns. Despite Cheris's amusement at Kel design sensibilities – of course the emblem was the flamboyant ashhawk, of course it involved fire – she felt a stinging in her secret heart at the sight of it.

Several green soldiers in Verab's platoon were shooting too rapidly at the guards and not very well. A sergeant, distracted by some other matter, was slow to direct their efforts more usefully, but Verab was already dealing with the issue. Still, better to be shooting than not to be shooting.

The storm started up around them, avoiding the Eel fortifications with dismaying precision. The world became a tumult of silhouettes. The smell of the earth was pungent, salt-grit-sweet. In the back of her head she realized that the sweetness came from the succulents flowering awake.

They were going to have to wade through the encampment before they could count on safety from the weather. Cheris wondered if the Eels would sacrifice their own so they could direct the storm's full fury against the Kel.

"Lieutenant, have you got your platoon in hand?" Cheris asked Verab.

For formation fighting, each soldier's state of mind mattered, or else the exotic effects would falter. It was a microcosm of the importance of Doctrine in hexarchate society. Formation instinct, which every Kel was programmed with during academy, was supposed to ensure the necessary cohesion. In practice, it worked better with some than others.

"They'll serve, sir," Verab said, biting off each word.

"See that they do," Cheris said.

The display showed that the other platoons were holding steady. Bullets hit the formation's protection zone and ricocheted at absurd angles. The rain pelted down around them, yet none of it touched Cheris or the soldiers standing near her.

Strangely, however, the rain was scattering into snow, the snow into crystal. She had Sparrow 14 bring her a captured crystal. It was a shining sliver, fracturing the light into rainbows if rainbows only knew the cold, sad hues of blue and violet. She didn't touch the crystal even though she was wearing Kel gloves. The Sparrow was already starting to corrode, and she expressed her regrets to it. It made a resigned chirping noise.

Pir's Fan should have shed the storm without additional transformative effects. Cheris frowned. She had spent a good portion of her five-year academy stint examining the mathematics of formation mechanics. When she chose a formation, she did so with a full understanding of its particular weaknesses.

The problem was that her analyses depended on the high calendar's consensus mechanics. She now had indication that the directional storm generator worked the way it did because it relied on a radically heretical calendar, with the attendant heretical mechanics, which were interfering with the formation's proper function. She was angry at herself for not anticipating this. Most of the time heretics used technology that was compatible with the high calendar, but the development of purely heretical technology was always possible.

Her superiors had to have known, but she didn't expect them to tell a low officer about matters that involved heresy. Still, the other

Kel companies hadn't had to die the way they had, smeared into irrelevance. Like Cheris, their captains had relied on the weather-eaters, on their formations, on the exotics that their civilization had become dependent on since their discovery. Cheris didn't despise many things, but needless waste was one of them.

The deviation from the high calendar could be measured, and her unit gave her an instrument with which to perform the measurement. She sucked in a breath, listening to relay chatter. *Storm* and *death* and *the color of the sky* and *blisters*. *Contacts contacts contacts* and *fucking crystals*. *Just a scratch, no – Chrif is down*. That would be Chriferafa, who always got teased because her name was unpronounceable.

Bullets and Eelfire came at them like part of the storm. Cheris flinched in spite of herself as a tendril of fire hissed past, deflected by the formation.

Her soldiers weren't going to like her, but that didn't matter as long as they lived. "Formation override," Cheris said into the relay. Her breath was silver-white in the air. She barely felt the cold, bad sign. "Squadrons Three through Six, adjust formation." She wrote the equations on one hand with the other, letting the kinetic sensors pick them up for transmission.

A minor test first. Then, based on the results, additional tests to see what the deviations were and whether they admitted any good options. There was a certain amount of heresy in working with heretical mechanics, but her orders told her to work with the resources she had, so she was going to do exactly that.

The formation staggered. She couldn't see it clearly from her position, but the formation icon came up bright and prickly, warning her that the formation's integrity was failing. The grating tone in her head suggested that she order a retreat or have her soldiers modulate into an alternate formation, something, anything to conform with Doctrine. Her vision was reddening at the edges.

"It's part of the *plan*," she said in vexation, and overrode the warnings.

That wasn't the real problem. The real problem was her soldiers' hesitation. Squadrons Three, Five, and Six were following orders, although Six was having difficulty adjusting around the fallen. Cheris relented enough to request a snapshot from the sergeant. The directional storm had cut a gash through the squadron, leaving greasy stains and partial corpses in a growing pinkish puddle. Cheris suggested an alteration, but the sergeant was going to have to deal with the rest herself.

Squadron Four was resisting the order. Pir's Fan was something they knew and understood. The modifications she had sent them were not. The sergeant protested formulaically, all but quoting the Kel code of conduct. The formation didn't belong to the Kel lexicons. Unconventional thinking was a danger to a well-tested hierarchical system. Her orders did not advance the best interests of the hexarchate. And so on.

The storm fell in sheets of undulating light, snake-sharp and acrid. Cheris had Dineng send for another Sparrow to verify that the light was fatal. The Sparrow dodged a ribbon of light too late and was transformed into a mass of parallel slices and metal shrieks. It fell unmoving to the ground, where the light rearranged it again and again until it was nothing but an accretion of truncated cubes. Cheris winced, but there was nothing to be done now.

Cheris opened the relay and said to the recalcitrant sergeant, with great leniency, "Reconsider." It would be preferable to secure his cooperation. She would have to adjust the formation otherwise, with uncertain results.

She had eaten with him at high table for years, listened to his anecdotes of service in the Drowned March and at the Feathered Bridge between the two great continents of the world Makhtu. She knew that he liked to drink two sips from his own cup after the communal cup went around, and then to arrange his pickles or sesame spinach on top of his rice. She knew that he cared about putting things in their proper place. It was an understandable impulse. It was also going to get him killed.

Already she was rewriting the equations because she knew what his answer would be.

The sergeant reiterated his protest, stopping short of accusing her of heresy herself. Formation instinct should have forced him to obey her, but the fact that he considered her actions deeply un-Kel was enabling him to resist.

Cheris cut contact and sent another override. Lieutenant Verab's acknowledgment sounded grim. Cheris marked Squadron Four outcasts, Kel no longer. They had failed to obey her, and that was that.

Disjointedly, the new formation pieced itself together and pressed forward. They were taking heavier fire now. Two trees exploded at the touch of Eelfire as Squadron Five passed them. A corporal was stapled to a hillside by the resultant lash of splinters. A soldier three paces to Cheris's left fell out of formation and vanished in a vapor of blood and tatters. Kel Nikara, who had sung so well.

Squadron Four was already dissolving, but she had no attention to spare for it.

Cheris guided the advance from point to point. She adjusted the formation again by sending orders to individual soldiers, solving for intermediate forms in her head to keep the geometry within the necessary error bounds. The storm was dissipating: they were too close to the Eels. The next question was whether she could devise a formation that would give them better protection against the Eels' invariant weapons, which would work in any calendar, now that the storm was no longer a factor.

They were outnumbered five to one, but the Eels didn't have access to formations, so the Kel had a chance. Cheris was in a hurry, so a straightforward force multiplier was her best bet. More modifications. Her remaining soldiers knew to trust her. The soundstream reflected this. *Eels, the stink of corpses, heavy fire from that copse, drumbeats.* They were paying attention to the important things again.

To her relief, the force multiplier, adapted from One Thorn Poisons a Thousand Hands, could be linearized for use with her ad hoc formation. She and her soldiers were equipped with calendrical swords, ordinarily used for duels. Not her weapon of choice, but they were near the storm generator, which they were to take intact, and the general's orders had been clear. The swords shouldn't damage unliving objects, which was the primary consideration.

"Swords, now," Cheris said.

The Kel unsheathed their swords, each tinted differently, blank bars of light. Cheris's ran from blue near the hilt to red at the tip. As they closed with the enemy, numbers blazed to life along the lengths of the blades: *the day and the hour of your death*, as the Kel liked to say.

Except the date and time on Cheris's sword was wrong. She wasn't the only one who was dismayed. *Maintenance, rather use my rifle*, the dreaded *calendrical rot*. Not only were the numbers wrong, they jittered and sparked, snapping in and out of focus. A quick survey of her company indicated that everyone's swords were having the same problem. That would have been bad enough, but the swords weren't even synchronized.

"Sir, maybe another weapon –" Lieutenant Verab said.

"Continue the advance," Cheris said. "No guns." If the swords proved ineffectual, they would have to try something different, but the swords hadn't sputtered out entirely. That gave her hope, if you could call it that.

At first it went well. For every sword-stroke, tens of Eels went down as lines of force scythed through their ranks. Cheris's own swordwork was methodical, businesslike, the same way she dueled. One of her lunges pierced eight soldiers in the Eels' ranks. She had always been good at angles.

The Kel formation held as they butchered their way through the Eels. The hills' residual mist had a ruddy tint. Cheris made a point of noticing the Eels' faces. They weren't much different from the faces of her own soldiers: younger and older, dark skin and pale, eyes mostly brown or sometimes gray. One of them might have been Dineng's brother, if not for the pale eyes. But the calendrical light made them alien, washed in shadows of indefinite color slowly becoming more definite.

They hit an unexpected snag as the storm generator came into view. It crouched on the rise of a stubby hill, visible through a transparent palisade. The generator resembled nothing so much as a small, deformed tank. Cheris asked for, and got, an assay of its approximate mass from one of the Sparrows. The answer made her bite her lip. Well, that was what the floaters were for.

More bizarre was the fact that the generator was undefended except by four Eel servitors. They were armed with lasers, but so far their fire hadn't penetrated Kel defenses.

Cheris knew the current formation was losing effectiveness when the air went cold and gray. She was having difficulty breathing, and while she had an emergency air supply, they all did, she suspected this was just the beginning. Sure enough, it also became harder and harder to move.

Her first attempts at repairing the formation only resulted in a colder wind, a grayer world. Gritting her teeth – *winter, entropy*, it was time to *get out* but they were *so close* – she tried another configuration. It was hard to think, hard to make herself breathe. She thought she heard the song of snow.

"I need your computational allocations," Cheris told her lieutenants. They were so close to the weather generator, and the Eels were broken and peeling away behind them. They just had to grab the wretched thing and hold on until pickup arrived. But to hold it they had to have a working formation. It was enough to make her long for the days of straightforward bullets and bombs.

She liked the thought of stripping her soldiers' computational resources as much as they did, which was to say not at all. But they weren't in camp, where they could instantiate a more powerful grid. They had no access to the larger, more powerful grid of a friendly voidmoth transport or a military base. She had to use the field grid because it was all they had.

Cheris gave her company a second to understand what was going to happen, then diverted their allocated resources to herself. She ignored the protests, most reflexive, some less so: *can't see, lost coordinates*, it was so *cold*, a scatter of profanities. Verab was saying something to the other lieutenants, but hadn't flagged the conversation for her attention, so she assumed he'd take care of it.

She formulated her question so a computational attack might give her an answer in a reasonable amount of time. The company's grid was not sentient in the way of military-grade servitors, but if you knew how to talk to the system, it was capable of nuanced responses. As the world faded toward black, the grid informed her that she should proceed by a particular series of approximations. She authorized the computation and added some constraints designed to speed the exploration of likely solutions.

The problem was easy to see: not only did the storm generator rely on heretical mechanics, which also explained the weather-eaters' difficulties, it was itself a disruption to the high calendar. Cheris wasn't looking forward to reporting this to her superiors.

Green-black fire washed around them, the dregs of Eel resistance. Cheris silently entreated the formation to hold long enough for the field grid to chew through the computations. *Faster,* she thought, feeling so cold that she was certain that her teeth were icicles and that her fingers had frozen into arthritic twigs.

"The generator's ours, sir!" Verab cried as his platoon took out a last sputtering knot of Eels. They were clear for the moment.

"Well done," she said, meaning it. "Now we have to hang on."

The computations were taking their toll. Through the relay, Cheris discovered that Kel Zro in Squadron Three had offloaded more of her situational awareness functions into the relay than was strictly advisable, and was paying for it now. The soldier to Zro's right shouted a warning, and she corrected her position barely in time to avoid being splashed by Eelfire. Zro wasn't the only one having difficulties. Even people who used their relays with the usual precautions were desynchronizing.

Cheris asked the grid for a summary of preliminary results and skimmed through them. Nothing, nothing, nothing – aha. As the sky waned, she tapped in her suggestions and waited some more.

"Sir," Lieutenant Ankat from Platoon Three said, "I have this hunch someone's rallying the Eels to rush us. You know, the smart thing for them to do."

"I can't make the grid compute faster," Cheris said. "We're Kel.

They're not. If we have to bite them off our heels with our teeth, we'll do it that way."

At last the system came up with a working model of the conditions they were suffering. She swallowed an involuntary hiss of relief and rapped out the orders with a tongue that might have been a lump of coal after the last spark's dying.

Like a machine dismembered into creaking components, the company moved in response. Cheris adjusted in response to the paths of Platoons One and Two, and had the rear platoons change front to deal with the Eel remnants. Gradually, as they found their proper positions, the last of the entropic cold summered away. Being able to breathe normally again was a relief.

Cheris allowed herself a second to contemplate the corpses of the Eels nearest them. Some had weathered into statues of murky ice. Others were puddling into mysterious colors, forgetting the proper hues of flesh, eyes, hair. She estimated casualties and recorded it for later comparison with the Sparrows' observations. It was important to acknowledge numbers, especially when the dead were dead by your doing.

She and the lieutenants reorganized the company to better defend the storm generator, using a formation that bore a disturbing resemblance to the Pyre Burns Inward, which was on the proscribed list. Then she sent a burst transmission informing orbital command that they had gained a tenuous foothold in Eel territory. With any luck it would go through.

For a moment she didn't recognize the command signature on the incoming call because she wasn't expecting it, not so soon after the transmission.

The voice was shockingly clear and biting after the buzzing haze of relay chatter. "Captain Kel Cheris, Heron Company, 109-229th Battalion, acknowledge," it said. She recognized the voice as belonging to Brigadier General Kel Farosh, who was in charge of the expedition.

Keeping an eye on the situation, Cheris responded on the same channel using the appropriate key. "Captain Cheris, General. We're securing the objective."

"Immaterial," Farosh said: not the response Cheris had expected. "Prepare for extraction in twenty-six minutes. You'll be leaving the generator. We've knocked out the Eels' local air defenses for the moment."

Cheris glanced over her shoulder at the generator, not sure she had heard correctly. The generator was surrounded by a coruscating knot of blue-violet light. The sight of it made her bones ache with remembered chill. "The generator, sir?"

"It's a job well-done," Farosh said, "but it's someone else's problem now. Leave it where you found it." She clicked out.

Cheris passed along the notification.

"You've got to be kidding, sir," was Verab's response. "We're here right now, let us finish the job."

"We could always volunteer to stay," Ankat said dryly. "You know how much Kel Command loves volunteers."

"It was clear that they want us out of here," Cheris said. But she shared their frustration. They had expected to drive the Eels out of their hiding places so the hexarchate's enforcers could reprogram the survivors to rejoin civilization. It was peculiar for the expedition to be cut short like this. Why send them to retrieve the storm generator if they weren't going to take it with them after all?

The youngest soldier – Kel Dezken, scarcely out of academy – slipped out of position trying to share a bad joke with a comrade, and died to a last Eel bullet. Cheris noted it in passing. Terrible timing, but Kel luck was frequently bad.

By the time the hoppers and medic teams came to ferry them into orbit, escorted by Guardhawk servitors and – of dubious utility – weather-eaters, Cheris was disappointed to abandon the battlefield. In a way each battle was home: a wretched home, where small mistakes were punished and great virtues went unnoticed, but a home nonetheless. She didn't know what it said about her that her duty suited her so well, but so long as it was her duty, it didn't matter what she thought about it.

The Guardhawks, angular birdforms, laid down covering fire so the company could board safely. They seemed to take a certain serene joy in their work, weaving up and down, back and forth. No formations; Kel servitors were formation-neutral.

Dredge's sun was bright in the sky. Its light caught on weapons fallen from broken hands, ribs cracked and gleaming with blood and yellowy fluid, the needle-remnants of storm crystals. Cheris boarded last. She fixed the battlefield in her memory as though she were scratching it into the sutures of her skull.

The hopper was crowded and stank of sweat and exhaustion. Cheris sat a little way apart from the other soldiers. She was looking out of the window as they arced into the sky, so she saw the waiting Kel bannermoth drop two bombs, neat and precise, on the site they had just left. A day's worth of hard battle and the entire objective rendered irrelevant by high explosives. She kept watching until the explosions' bright flowers dwindled into specks just large enough to trouble the eye.

CHAPTER TWO

HEXARCH SHUOS MIKODEZ wasn't sure which was worse: the flickering readouts that updated him on the crisis at the Fortress of Scattered Needles, or the fact that Hexarch Nirai Kujen's silver voidmoth call indicator had been blinking at him nonstop for the past four hours and twelve minutes. Kujen was a talkative bastard to begin with – not that Mikodez should be one to criticize – and the worst part was, he had legitimate reason to want to get in touch with Mikodez about the danger the hexarchate was in.

Shuos headquarters was at the Citadel of Eyes, a star fortress in the Stabglass March. A simple fact of astrography, except it put the Citadel uncomfortably close to the Fortress of Scattered Needles in the adjacent Entangled March, where the recent trouble was going on. Calendrical currents could be surprisingly far-reaching, star-spanning distances or not, and it made him especially appreciative of the trouble they were in. A little heresy went a long way, unfortunately. But he was certain that their best candidate for dealing with the matter was the best candidate for being authorized to use a certain Shuos weapon, the *oldest* Shuos weapon, especially since said weapon was in the Kel Arsenal. Heptarch Shuos Khiaz, who had signed it (or him, take your pick) over to Kel control 398 years ago, in a fit of towering spite, had a lot to answer for.

In any case, Mikodez didn't like stalling, but he needed to buy time while his mathematicians did the final checks on the Kel candidate that he'd been saving up, based on what she had just pulled at Dredge. He had multiple offices at the Citadel of Eyes, and today he had holed himself up in the one he used for getting work done rather than scaring impressionable interlocutors. Nothing he kept in the office would intimidate Kujen, anyway, not the paintings of ninefoxes with their staring tails, not the lack of visible weapons, or the pattern-stones board with its halfway game, or the randomly selected images of still lifes. Mikodez considered it important to look at things that had nothing to do with his job. (Mostly. He was as susceptible as the next Shuos to thinking up ways to assassinate people with unlikely objects.)

He had selected today's image specifically to put Kujen on edge: a spectacular piece of architecture, composed of wild curves and tessellated facets, that had existed during Kujen's distant childhood. Kujen couldn't be bothered to care about people, unless the people could keep up with him on things like number theory – something that described vanishingly few people in the hexarchate, the current candidate being one of them – but he liked architecture, and engines, and the machinery of empire.

Mikodez looked again at the candidate's portrait and frowned. He knew her psych profile well. One of his agents had flagged her extraordinary math scores back when she was a lieutenant, and they'd kept an eye on her, in the hopes that she wouldn't get herself shot in some stupid mission guarding a shipment of cabbages. (Cabbages were a Kel idiosyncrasy. They were adamant about their spiced cabbage pickles.) Appearance-wise she was nothing special: black-haired and brown-eyed like almost everyone in the hexarchate, with ivory-tinged skin much lighter than his own. Attractive in a somber way, but not so that she'd turn heads coming into a room, and with a mouth that made him wonder if she smiled much. Probably not, and even then only around her friends, or when she needed to reassure some green soldier. The profile indicated a strong sense of duty, however; that would be useful.

How long could he keep putting off Kujen? He considered paging the mathematicians, but sticking a blinking amber eye on *their* communications panels would just make them grouchy, and he needed them in a good mood since he couldn't do this himself. He'd done well at math as a cadet, but that had been decades ago. It didn't make him a mathematician, let alone one specializing in calendrical techniques, let alone one trained in this kind of evaluation.

Technically, as Shuos hexarch, Mikodez outranked Kujen, because he led a high faction and Kujen led a low one. But not only was Kujen the senior hexarch at 864 years old, he was also, in a distressingly real sense, responsible for the hexarchate's dominance. He'd invented the mothdrive in its first form, enabling the original heptarchate's rapid expansion, and pioneered a whole field of mathematics that resulted in modern calendrical mechanics. Mikodez was keenly aware that when you got right down to it, he was an expendable bureaucrat in charge of a bunch of cantankerous spies, analysts, and assassins, albeit one who had done rather well over the past four decades considering a Shuos hexarch's lifespan was usually measured in the single digits. In contrast, Kujen was irreplaceable – at least until Mikodez could figure out a better alternative.

Kujen's immortality was tied to certain protections, which Mikodez hadn't figured out a way around. It wasn't just Kujen's age, although no one else had found a reasonable method of living past 140 or 150. The other four hexarchs had a keen interest in cracking Kujen's secret. The first person the existing immortality device had been tried on had gone crazy. The third had started that way. Kujen, the second, had emerged perfectly functional. He liked to hint that he knew how not to go crazy, but he refused to share. Typical.

If anyone ever asked Mikodez, immortality was like sex: it made idiots of otherwise rational people. The other hexarchs never asked, though. Instead, they assumed he wanted it as badly as they did.

The Fortress readout flickered again. Gray rot, like tendrils, the color of death and dust and cold rain. Mikodez frowned, then typed in a query. He could work that much of the analysis for himself. The numbers came right up. The matrices' most problematic entries blinked. There were a lot of them.

The Rahal, who oversaw the normal functioning of the calendar, had put in place their countermeasures; but their countermeasures weren't adequate to deal with a heresy of this magnitude. It was going to have to be military action, no matter how much everyone (except the Kel) wished otherwise.

Mikodez looked again at the voidmoth, then queried his assistant. Maybe something had turned up in the last sixteen minutes. If not, he was going to talk to Kujen anyway and see if the usual pretense of high-wire distractibility would buy him the necessary extra minutes. Likely not, given how well Kujen knew him, but worth a try.

His assistant, Shuos Zehun, responded with an unusually blunt note: *You can stop dithering, Mikodez. This one's sane* and *suitable.* They appended the mathematicians' assessments. Agreement all down the line that the candidate was as good as everyone thought, at least in this one area.

All right, then. "Line 1-1," Mikodez said. "Put Kujen on."

The video placed itself to the right of a set of indices that let Mikodez keep an eye on just how bad the calendrical rot had gotten in the Entangled March, as opposed to the numbers for the Fortress's immediate surrounds. At the moment the aggregate figures were holding steady, but they were unlikely to stay that way.

The man in the video was slender and dark-haired and very pale, with wickedly gorgeous eyes. For someone who headed the technical faction, not the cultural one, Nirai Kujen would have made a credible Andan: he was never less than beautiful. Right now he was wearing a smoke-colored scarf with iridescent strands in it, and his black-and-gray shirt had buttons of mother-of-pearl carved in the shape of leaves. Kujen could probably fund a whole research department out of his wardrobe. On the other hand, there was no denying he got results. The Kel had him to thank for most of their weapons.

"How good to see you haven't been assassinated," Kujen said drily. Shuos philosophy was that the hexarch's seat was yours if you could hold onto it. Fighting over the hexarch's seat was a popular

Shuos pastime. "If you were any other Shuos, I would accuse you of avoiding my calls by going out to shoot or seduce or spy on someone, but in your case I honestly think you got behind on paperwork."

Mikodez shrugged. Ordinarily they agreed on the importance of a functioning bureaucracy. "I don't care what candidates you've scared up," Mikodez said, "I have a better one for you." He sent the file over.

This time, when Mikodez looked at the photo of the candidate, Captain Kel Cheris, his gaze went to her signifier, which showed beneath the portrait: Ashhawk Sheathed Wings. A good sign for the stability it implied, although the Kel had an unreasonable prejudice against it. Kujen wasn't going to think highly of it either, but no one expected a sociopath to care about sanity.

"You know," Kujen was saying, "I wish the Kel would devise more reliable tactical ability batteries. I'm going to let Jedao figure out the – fuck me sideways with a drill press, is that a Kel with decent math scores?"

"You always make it sound like Kel-shopping is such a chore," Mikodez said, "so I thought I'd present you with someone more up your alley."

Cheris wasn't just good at math. She was possibly good enough to compete with Kujen, although the fact that she hadn't gone into research mathematics made it hard to tell for certain. Just as importantly, she was good enough to make up for Jedao's – the weapon's – deficiencies in that area.

"Where on earth did you find her? No, don't answer that. It's charming to think that there's a Kel who might understand some higher math. Too bad I can't yell at the Kel recruiters for not sending her my way."

"Be fair," Mikodez said. "They tried to redirect her to the Nirai, but she insisted that she wanted to be a Kel. She was attractive enough as an officer candidate that they relented."

Something flickered at the corner of his eye. Kujen frowned and said, "Take a look at the composite indices for the Fortress readings,

Mikodez. Whatever they're doing in there hit all the wards at once. We just had to luck out with intelligent heretics instead of the usual stupid kind, so we need to settle on a candidate to deal with them. That's hard to do when you're dicking around avoiding me."

"I wanted just the right one," Mikodez said.

"She looks pretty good," Kujen conceded, "but that commander with the beautiful hands also looked pretty good. And don't roll your eyes at me, I'm talking about his qualifications, not his aesthetics. Honestly, Mikodez, don't you ever take anything seriously? The commander at least has experience in space warfare, which your infantry captain doesn't."

"I take the situation at the Fortress very seriously," Mikodez said. "Besides, the fact that Cheris specialized in mathematics might enable her to better deal with calendrical warfare." Still, he smiled lazily at Kujen because it was best not to be seen to care too much.

The Fortress of Scattered Needles was located at a nexus point in a stretch of empty space and was nearest the Footbreak system. The Rahal had already stationed a lensmoth there, but all it could do was staunch the bleeding as long as the Fortress itself was afflicted.

The Fortress was also divided into six wards, one for each faction, although the boundaries weren't as strictly enforced as they had been in the old days. There had once been a seventh ward for the seventh faction, the Liozh. The Fortress's interior had been demolished and rebuilt to remove the seventh ward, at staggering expense, after the Liozh heresy was put down.

Whoever had infected the Fortress with rot had taken down all six wards at the same time. The degree of coordination implied would have been enough of a problem, but Mikodez had reason to believe that the particular form the rot had taken was the result of heretics taking advantage of an experiment being run by Hexarch Rahal Iruja and the false hexarch Nirai Faian. Faian was supposed to run the Nirai in public so Kujen could amuse himself with whatever research caught his fancy, but Iruja had suborned her almost from the beginning. A nexus fortress made an ideal proving ground for their work because it represented the hexarchate in miniature. What

Mikodez didn't understand was why they hadn't used one of the smaller fortresses instead.

As to why Iruja and Faian were experimenting with the calendar, that was obvious. All the hexarchs knew, and even Kujen, who hadn't been told, could guess. They wanted a better form of immortality. There was a comprehensive body of work suggesting that you couldn't do better than Kujen had under the existing calendar. Mikodez wouldn't have minded asking Kujen about it outright, but he was supposed to be keeping an eye on Kujen for the other hexarchs. Iruja would have disapproved of him tipping their hand, even about something so easy to figure out.

Kujen, for his part, tolerated the other hexarchs because his immortality relied on the high calendar in its present form, and the high calendar didn't just include the numbers and measures of time, but the associated social system. In this case, that meant the six factions. If Kujen came up with a viable alternative that eliminated the competition, he would become a real threat to the system. The fact that he hadn't already done away with everyone else strongly suggested that it was unlikely that such an alternative existed.

At some point, Rahal Iruja was going to ask Mikodez to remove Kujen for real. Mikodez already had files detailing possible ways to do it, which he updated twice a month (more often when he got bored), although he wasn't going to unless it became necessary. True, Kujen's taste in hobbies made him an annoying transaction cost, but he was good at his job and he represented a certain amount of stability. Of course, Mikodez had plans for how to deal with the inevitable transition after Kujen's death, just in case.

Kujen had sent Mikodez his projections of possible heretical calendars. "I've sorted them by likelihood," Kujen said. "That first one is bad news, especially if they're fixated on seven as their central integer. And here I thought nobody paid attention to the past anymore." He was one of two people who still remembered what life had been like under seven factions, not six.

"You've been hanging out with too many Kel," Mikodez said, although it wasn't entirely true that the Kel disdained history.

Nevertheless, the prospect of a Liozh revival – of a time when the hexarchate was a heptarchate – did concern him. The Liozh had been the philosophers and ethicists of the heptarchate, and some evidence suggested that they had been destroyed when they attempted to do away with the remembrances, which Kujen was fond of. Mikodez didn't like the thought of Kujen becoming more personally invested in the matter, given his proclivities. Besides, it was hard to tell without more data, but if the Liozh had failed with their heresy the first time around, why would any sane heretic pick them to emulate?

"You're stooping to making Kel jokes?" Kujen said. The corner of his mouth lifted.

"Someone has to," Mikodez said. The Kel hexarch was known to make them herself.

Kujen fiddled with something off-screen. "Anyway, all those calendars are compatible with the Fortress's shields. I have advised Kel Command that they might as well just say how to take the shields out since it's not like it'll stay a secret, but they are proving resistant."

"Never give information away if you don't have to," Mikodez said. If the shields went down, the Fortress was dangerously vulnerable.

"Yes, but your own side?"

"Own side" was putting it a bit strongly. "They won't like it if you say anything about it," Mikodez said, as if Kujen needed the warning. Kujen shouldn't have a say in a military decision anyway, except no one else was capable of overseeing the particular weapon Kel Command wanted to deploy.

"I can keep my mouth shut," Kujen said irritably. "You've made no secret of the fact that you have the usual Shuos prejudices, but I suppose you have your reasons for authorizing the mission."

It had been a sore point with Shuos leaders for almost four centuries that the Kel had snatched away their last general, even if the Shuos still had to approve Kel operations involving his use. "Anyway," Mikodez said after a pause to see if Kujen was going to add anything, "you haven't told me if you think the candidate's acceptable."

"You really like the Sheathed Wings, don't you? Aren't you afraid she's going to put Jedao to sleep?"

It was entirely in character for Kujen to think psychological stability was dull. "I'm sure the general will bring some excitement into her life," Mikodez said.

"She's wasted on him," Kujen said. "I still think that commander would be a better fit. And I could get more use out of the Sheathed Wings if Kel Command doesn't want her anymore."

Sometimes Mikodez thought Kujen would benefit from having his knuckles rapped. "Don't get greedy," he said. "You'll have plenty of time to see if she can tell you anything about the latest cryptology conjectures after the Fortress has been dealt with." Although whether she would prefer dealing with the Fortress or a sociopathic hexarch was an open question.

"Killjoy," Kujen said. "You're not going to fold on this one, are you?"

Mikodez smiled at him. "You wanted more funding for research on that latest jamming system, didn't you?"

"It's unlike you to resort to naked bribery," Kujen said, "not that I'm complaining."

"I'm bored," Mikodez said, "and if I don't spend this money, one of my subordinates will put it into something wholesome, like algorithmic threat identification." He cultivated a reputation for being erratic for occasions like this.

"All right, all right, I'll put in the authorizations on my end," Kujen said. "You think you have paperwork, you should see mine."

You think I don't? Mikodez thought, but he kept his expression bland. Kujen's security wasn't nearly as up-to-date as he thought it was.

"At least I'll get a chance to say hello to her," Kujen went on, "even though I'm sure she'll be focused on her duty. Sometimes I think Visyas and I did too good a job designing formation instinct, but the results can be adorable."

Mikodez would have felt sorry for Kel Cheris, but at the moment Kujen was unlikely to damage anyone who had a chance of entertaining him in matters related to number theory. Besides, the emergency was real. A shame that she had made herself a candidate for dealing with the calendrical rot, but someone had to do it, and she had a better chance of survival than most.

"I'll set it up, then," Mikodez said. "Depending on how hard I can lean on Kel Command, I can get her to you in eighteen days or so."

"Splendid," Kujen said. "In the future, do try to be less transparent about avoiding me. It's embarrassing when a grown Shuos is so obvious." He signed off without waiting for a response.

Embarrassing, but worth it to ensure that his preferred candidate was sent to deal with the calendrical rot. Mikodez spent several minutes composing his instructions to Kel Command, then sent them off.

Kel Cheris was sane, although the odds were that she wouldn't stay that way. Still, Mikodez had to trade her welfare for the hexarchate's. Someday someone might come up with a better government, one in which brainwashing and the remembrances' ritual torture weren't an unremarkable fact of life. Until then, he did what he could.

CHERIS SPENT THE flight back to the boxmoth infantry transport in silence. The boxmoth was like any other: walls painted solemn black and charcoal gray, with the occasional unsubtle touch of gold. Cheris reported to the commander's executive officer, an unsmiling man with a scar over his right eye. She saluted him fist to shoulder, and he returned the salute. She passed over her company's grid key so the data could be examined by her superiors at their leisure.

"Welcome back, Captain," the executive officer said, eying her with a faint spark of curiosity.

This alarmed her – it never paid to stand out too much among the Kel – but no response seemed to be expected.

The mothgrid informed her of the vessel's current layout and where she might find the high halls, her quarters, the soldiers' barracks. In reality, no one was going to their assigned high hall without cleaning up first. Per protocol, she was told the status of those who had been taken to Medical for their injuries. She thought of the recalcitrant squadron that had died on Dredge before the evacuation.

Her quarters were next to her company's barracks. She had two small rooms and an adjoining bath. All her muscles ached, but she dug out a small box of personal items and pulled out the raven luckstone her mother had given her on her twenty-third birthday. It was a polished stone, drab gray, and the raven's silhouette was a welcome reminder of the home she visited so seldom.

There came a rapid series of taps at her door: three, one, four, one, five –

"Come in," Cheris said, amused at the ritual. She put the luckstone away.

One of the boxmoth's birdform servitors came in bearing an arrangement of anodized wire flowers. There were twelve flowers, just as twelve servitors had fallen in action. They would never receive official acknowledgment of their service, but that wasn't any reason not to remember them.

"Thank you," Cheris said to the birdform. "It was bad down there. I wish I could have done more."

The birdform flashed a series of ironic golds and reds. Cheris had learned to read Simplified Machine Universal, and nodded her agreement. It added that it had been having trouble with one of its grippers, if she had a moment to adjust it?

"Of course," Cheris said. She wasn't a technician, but some repair jobs were better handled by human hands, and she had learned the basics. As it turned out, all it took was a few moment's jiggering with some specially shaped pliers. The birdform made a pleased bell tone.

"I have to see to my duties now," Cheris said. "I'll talk to you later?"

The birdform indicated its acquiescence, and headed out, leaving the flowers.

Cheris didn't know its name. The servitors had designations for human convenience, but she was certain that they had names of their own. She made a point of not asking.

Washing up didn't take long, and her uniform cleaned itself while she did so. The fabric smoothed itself of a last few creases as she picked it up. "Middle formal," she told it, which was not too different from battle dress, except for the cuffs and the brightness of the gold trim.

She had fourteen minutes before she ought to show up at the high hall to share the communal cup with her company, in celebration of their survival. The unscheduled time was a greater treasure than the bath. Alone, she eased herself into the chair and set her hands on the desk, taking comfort from the cool, solid glasswood. If she looked down she might have seen her dark-eyed reflection, crossed over with whorls and eddies like vagrant galaxies.

Her contemplation was broken by heat-pulses in her arm. They told her to report to a secured terminal for orders. The formal closing sequence told her she was dealing with someone high in the chain of command. When in combat, people only used the abbreviated closings. She couldn't imagine why dealing with her company was a matter of any urgency now that the Eels had been subdued.

Cheris had the feeling that she wasn't going to share this meal with her soldiers, but it couldn't be helped. The orders took precedence.

The terminal occupied the far end of the quarters they had put her in. It was a recessed plate of metal in the wall, matte black. Graven on the floor before it was the hexarchate's emblem of a wheel with six spokes. Capping each spoke was each faction's emblem, the high factions opposed by their corresponding low factions: the Shuos ninefox with its waving tails, each with a lidless eye, and the Kel ashhawk in flames; the Andan kniferose and the Vidona stingray; the Rahal scrywolf and the Nirai voidmoth scattered with stars.

She prompted her uniform to modify itself into full formal. The Kel ashhawk brightened and arched its neck, a gesture that the Kel jokingly called preening; subtle shades of turquoise and violet gave the fabric greater depth. The cuffs and collar lengthened and developed a brocade texture. Her gloves remained the same, plain and functional. Only at funerals did the Kel wear more elaborate gloves.

"Captain Kel Cheris reporting as ordered," she said.

The terminal showed her signifier, which was to say that it drew red-gold flames around an ashhawk's silhouette. Unlike the emblem on her uniform, the signifier's ashhawk was in the Sheathed Wings configuration.

Cheris didn't attach too much importance to the signifier, although hers indicated that she was deliberate by nature. There were, however, historical examples of flagrantly incorrect signifiers. They were estimations, not scryings, in any case. The arch-traitor and madman Shuos Jedao had appeared as a Ninefox Crowned with Eyes, visionary and strategist, but had proved to be an Immolation Fox. The final Liozh heptarch, who had, to the last, been the Web of Worlds, unity of unities, had died broken before Shuos, Kel, and Rahal troops.

She was beginning to wonder if she should leave her apologies and try again later when the terminal's signifier shattered and showed her her own face: the same neat dark hair, the same dark eyes. But the smile was not her own, and the stranger wore a high general's flared wings and flame where Cheris had a captain's talon with its pricked bead of blood.

"Captain," the stranger said. It even had her voice. "This is Composite Subcommand Two of Kel Command. Acknowledge."

Cheris started to sweat. The composites changed from task to task. There was no telling which high general she was dealing with, or how many had wired their minds together into a greater intelligence. But the designation Two indicated that at least one of the highest generals was in the composite. A bad sign. She made the correct salute, not too fast and not too slow.

"Now you understand," Subcommand Two said, as though dropping back into a conversation they had left off last night over glasses of wine, "that your assignment was a terrible one. Frankly, it's a waste of good officers."

"I know my oath, sir," Cheris said cautiously, but not too cautiously. The Kel didn't favor caution, something her instructors had reminded her of time and again.

Subcommand Two ignored her, which was the best response she could have hoped for. "This is the context you weren't given when you were sent down to Dredge. You figured out that the Eels built a weapon that took advantage of calendrical rot in order to function. Don't deny it. Your actions against the heretics indicate your understanding of the situation."

Cheris said, as steadily as she could, "I am prepared to be outprocessed." It was not a fate any Kel wanted. She had not come from a family with a tradition of Kel service – any faction service. Despite her parents' opposition, she had survived the tests and been admitted to Kel Academy Prime. She had honed her life for service, and it was bitter to have it terminated. Still, it was a fitting fate for a Kel: the bright upward trajectory, the sudden death.

Many people knew the ashhawk by its other name: suicide hawk.

Subcommand Two said, "Most of your soldiers will have to be processed by Doctrine, true. But it would be a waste of your improvisational abilities to send you with them."

Cheris recognized a euphemism as well as the next Kel. They had something worse in mind for her, and they were going to split up her command. Still, she felt a wary relief. They wouldn't bother briefing her unless they had some challenge in mind, and there were few wholly impossible challenges.

"The truth of the situation is worse than a handful of Eels in peripheral systems," Subcommand Two said. "Calendrical rot has taken hold not only in Dredge but in several central marches of the hexarchate. It cannot be allowed to persist."

"Sir," Cheris said, "is this a task for a Kel rather than a Shuos?" The Rahal concerned themselves with Doctrine and justice, but they rarely dealt with full-fledged uprisings; the Vidona cleaned up the aftermath, although no one trusted them to put heresies down at the outset. The Shuos and the Kel were collectively regarded as the hexarchate's sword, but the Kel specialized in kinetic operations and short-term goals while the Shuos pursued information operations and long-term plans. No Kel liked fox games, but there was a place and time for every method.

For a moment the reflection wavered, and she saw amber staring out from the golden wings: a ninefox's knowing eye. Then Cheris knew that the composite included a Shuos, probably an envoy from the Shuos hexarch himself. Her dismay was immediate. Kel Command wouldn't consent to intimate Shuos oversight for anything less than a crisis.

"I'm listening, sir," Cheris said.

"We have six officers competing to deal with the heresy in the Fortress of Scattered Needles and its surrounds," the composite said. "The Shuos have requested to be represented by a seventh as their web piece." Cheris's face smiled at her with a momentary glint of teeth. "You."

She thought at first she had misheard. The high calendar was projected throughout the hexarchate by a series of nexus fortresses, and Scattered Needles was the most famed of them. How had it –? And why did the Shuos want her, of all people, as a web piece?

In the old days of the heptarchate, the Liozh faction had coordinated the government. In a Shuos training game from the post-Liozh period, the web piece had been named after their emblem, the mirrorweb. Cheris had only played once, but she remembered the basic rules. Players were divided up into several marches, and each march competed separately. Certain actions conferred great advantage, but also incremented a heresy clock. As the clock went up, the game's rules changed. The web piece interacted with the heresy clock and represented the weapon that saved you even as it poisoned your principles.

"I will serve, sir," Cheris said. As long as it was possible to be played as a web piece and survive, she meant to try.

Was that another glimpse of the fox's unwavering eye? "Do you know what your primary examiner said of you before approving you for service?" Subcommand Two said.

"As I recall, sir," Cheris said mildly, "I graduated in the top six percent that year from Academy Prime."

"He noted your conservatism and wondered what had driven you toward a faction full of people who take risks on command. Are we to interpret your continued service as evidence that you have a Kel's heart after all?"

"I will serve, sir," Cheris said again.

Subcommand Two could have demanded a more substantive response, and didn't. Her face smiled again, this time with a fox's patient pleasure, and winked out.

The two ways to win at gambling were to read the situation and know the odds. Cheris had calculated her situation already. She had only a single life to offer, and she was aware of the ugly deaths that awaited her should she fail, but at some point you had to trust yourself.

After Cheris was sure the meeting was over, she stared at her reflection in the terminal. It still displayed the Ashhawk Sheathed Wings. When she had been younger, she had hoped for it to change and show her something new about herself, but today as always, there was nothing new to show.

She would have to go to her soldiers and break the news to them. Aware of her duties, she submitted a very terse report and signed off on the casualty intake form, wincing at the numbers. She hoped she would have an opportunity to pay a call on the injured in Medical, but she doubted it.

"Medium formal," she told the uniform, and it obliged her. Her hands were sweating inside the gloves.

The hall outside her quarters was quiet and almost chilly, and the slight curve intensified as she walked down its length. The curve was partly illusion, a topological trick to enable the voidmoth to hold more passengers, but her eye was fooled nonetheless.

It was only a single circuit to the high halls where the Kel infantry ate separately from the moth's regular crew. There was a painting on the wall just before she reached the doors, on textured paper: the queen of birds holding court in a winterdrift forest, and to her side, a fox half-hidden and wholly smiling.

Their assigned high hall, when she entered it, was less full than it should have been. The other halls, for the other companies that had not survived, would stand empty. The servitors had arranged the tables to make the place look less vast. Some of them hovered in the air as they made fussy adjustments to the furnishings: the ashhawk with wings outspread, Brightly Burning, bannered across the wall; the calligraphed motto that was found everywhere the Kel went, *from every spark a fire*; tapestries woven from the threads of dead soldiers' uniforms and embroidered with their names and the names and dates of the battlefields that had claimed their lives.

Every soldier rose at her entrance, spoons and chopsticks clinking as they set them down. Cheris paused long enough to return the honor, and smiled with her eyes. Lieutenant Verab was sober-faced as always, but Ankat returned the expression with a sardonic grin. Ready to tell the officers' table a brand-new Kel joke, no doubt. He had a better repertoire than anyone she'd ever met. Then she headed to her seat at the center of the officers' table, and indicated that they should sit again.

The communal cup was waiting for her. It was lacquered red and graven with maple leaves, and someone had refilled it nearly to the brim. Verab, who sat at her right, passed her the cup. He looked very tired, and she lifted an eyebrow at him. He shrugged slightly: nothing important. She didn't challenge the lie. Cheris felt tired herself, knowing the news she was going to have to break to him, and to the rest of her company. Schooling her expression to calm, she took one sip. The water was sweet and cool, yet she felt it ought to be bitter.

She had a bowl of rice, and the communal platters had familiar fare: fish fried in rice flour and egg and leaves of sage, pickled plums, quail eggs with sesame salt. Some fresh fruit had been saved for her. Verab was mindful of her love for tangerines, a sometime luxury; plus he didn't care for them himself. She looked at the food and thought about all the meals she had shared with these people, the times she had dragged herself out of a battle knowing that soon she would be able to sit down with them and eat the food they ate, and listen to the Kel jokes that she really wasn't offended by, even though she sometimes pretended to be as a joke in itself, and comfort herself with the voices of those who had made it through. All of that was about to end.

"I have bad news," Cheris said. "They're breaking up the company."

They were staring at her, even Verab, who should have guessed. "Doctrine," he said. His voice cracked. Verab was fifth-generation Kel. His family would take it hard.

"You may be able to serve again, some of you," Cheris said, aware of the inadequacy of her words, "but that depends on the magistrates' assessments. I'm sorry. I don't have details."

"Kel luck is always bad," Lieutenant Ankat said. He was about to make a joke of his own, she could tell, sheer anxiety. She looked at him, hard, and he swallowed whatever it had been.

"It's duty," Cheris said. Right now duty seemed arid. "I am not to go with you. They have another use for me."

A murmur rippled up and down the table, quickly quelled. They knew the euphemisms, too.

They weren't looking forward to the future. Most of them would lose Kel tradition and formation instinct. They might remember the mottoes and formations, but the mottoes would give them no more comfort, and the formations would no longer have any potency for them.

"Good luck where you're going then, sir," Ankat said, and Verab murmured his agreement. He didn't believe this had just happened. She could tell by the stricken look in his eyes.

"I would hear your names and dates of service," she said quietly. It would make all of this real, and the ceremony would give them something to hold onto, even if that something wasn't precisely comfort. "All of you. Acknowledge."

"Sir," they said in one voice. Ankat looked down at his hands, then back at her.

It was not the formal roll call. They had no drum, no fire, no flute. She would have included those things if she could. But even the servitors had heard her. They stopped what they were doing and arranged themselves in a listening posture. She nodded at them.

They started with the most junior soldier – Kel Nirrio, now that Dezken was dead – and ascended the ladder of rank. Nobody ate during the recital. Cheris was hungry, but hunger could wait. She didn't need to commit the names to memory, as she had done that long ago, but she wanted to make sure she remembered what every intent face looked like, what every rough voice sounded like, so she could warm herself by them in the days to come.

She spoke her name last, as was proper. The hall was otherwise silent. And then, breaking the ritual: "Thank you," she said. "I wish you well."

For all that she was leaving them, she couldn't help feeling a guilty twinge of anticipation for the challenge to come; but it would not do to let on.

"Eat, sir," Ankat said then, and she ate, not too fast and not too slow, making sure to finish with the two tangerines Verab had set aside for her.

CHAPTER THREE

CHERIS HAD HOPED for more specific orders, but no such luck. She slept uneasily and woke in the middle of the night, four hours and sixty-two minutes before she would ordinarily rise. The room was dark, with only a single candlevine glowing.

The *Burning Leaf* had shuffled itself into a new configuration. More importantly, a message on the terminal alerted her that they had already separated her from her company. She wished she had been awake for it, but they had undoubtedly done it this way on purpose. If anyone had a sense of mercy, her soldiers would be allowed some rest before they were hauled off for an examination by Doctrine, and those needing further medical care would receive it before they, too, went to their fate.

When she paused by her desk, she noticed a new presence: a servitor in the open doorway. It hadn't knocked, and she didn't recognize it. "Hello," Cheris said, looking at it quizzically.

It was a foxform rather than the moth's more usual spiderforms and birdforms. It had eyes of faceted glass, and they lit up yellow. A Shuos servitor. Of course.

The servitor didn't answer. Kel servitors never spoke human languages and Shuos servitors rarely did, although Andan and Vidona servitors usually could if they cared to. The foxform skittered in, moving in furtive zigzags. Then it stepped up into the air until it was level with the surface of Cheris's desk.

The servitor disgorged a roll of cloth from a side compartment.

The cloth was closed with a slender chain that Cheris could have scattered with her hands. Instead, murmuring her thanks, she turned the cloth around until she found the catches.

It wasn't blank fabric. It was a gamecloth sewn with a square grid in lines of variegated silk. The entire boundary glittered with tiny beads of bronze and rich orange. She ran her thumb over the beads, taking pleasure in their pebbled texture.

The most notable thing about the gamecloth was that it was more of a record than a playing surface. Pieces had been embroidered at the intersections of lines, capturing the positions of an incomplete match. Cheris's eyes went immediately to the web piece in the corner, and she smiled crookedly.

The one time she had played the game had been against a pretty female communications technician she was dating, Shuos Alaia. Cheris remembered Alaia's wry laugh and stories about growing up in a dysfunctional mining community. They had even had the same taste in dramas (ridiculous melodrama, the more duels the better). Alaia had had light brown eyes and skin half a shade darker, and hands that never stopped moving. A nervous tic in a Shuos was usually a sign of a training incident, but Cheris had known better than to inquire. She should have expected that some higher-ranking Shuos had logged their interaction, though.

Cheris considered the positions of the game's towers and the single remaining cannon. She had a good memory, but not an eidetic one, and since she had been on leave, she hadn't stored the memory in her allotment on the company's grid. This could have been a recreation of that match – she had been losing at this point, and it was difficult to recover from the loss of a cannon – but if there was some small divergence, some subtle message, she couldn't unriddle it.

It was a pity the Shuos couldn't tell her straight out what they wanted of her, but the Shuos were incapable of passing up a chance to use a game as a pedagogical weapon. (Admittedly, this could be fun in bed, as Alaia had been happy to demonstrate.)

She picked up the gamecloth again, inspecting both sides and wondering what she had missed. There it was: worked into the back of an empty square was a flexible filament in the shape of a gear.

The servitor tilted its head at her encouragingly. Cheris hesitated, then pulled the filament out. She felt a painful pulse of heat in her forearm. There had to be a message in the filament. Her gloves felt briefly warm, then cold.

A map distended in her mind. She could feel it as though she could walk her fingers over the tangled strands of voidmoth routes and feel the heat of far-scattered stars. The map identified the Fortress of Scattered Needles for her, unnecessarily. It was the largest nexus fortress in the Entangled March, and formed a microcosm of the hexarchate.

One of the Fortress's functions was to project calendrical stability throughout the region. If it had fallen to calendrical rot, the hexarchate's exotic weapons would be of limited use there. The hexarchate lagged in invariant technology, which could be used under any calendrical regime. In particular, too close to the rot the voidmoths' primary stardrives would fail. Without the voidmoths to connect the hexarchate's worlds, the realm would unravel.

If the heretics converted the Fortress to their own calendrical system, the problem became critical. The hexarchate would have to contend with a rival power at the heart of its richest systems.

Given the gravity of the situation, Cheris was surprised that Kel Command hadn't dispatched a general to deal with the matter already. Perhaps they didn't want to risk a general's contamination.

Cheris was given threadbare information on the other six who desired the honor of putting down this particular rebellion. Not their names; she suspected she would not be permitted to see their faces, either, nor they hers. She was surprised that there was any question of choice for something this critical. Shouldn't they have picked someone before setting it to a game? But the decision was not hers, and she reminded herself of the notorious Shuos fondness for games, the Shuos eye staring at her out of the composite.

All the Kel except Cheris were high officers, although there were no generals. Maybe they were disgraced the way she was. Not unsurprisingly, all of them had experience in space warfare, except for Four and Cheris.

One was a lieutenant colonel with what she assumed was a distinguished record. It was hard to tell with all the locations scrubbed out, but there were five medals in there, including the Red Pyre, which was awarded for what the Kel called "suicidal bravery even for us."

Two, the Rahal, was a Doctrine officer. The idea of giving a Rahal direct control over a mission worried Cheris. The Rahal were the high faction who led the hexarchate: they set Doctrine and maintained the high calendar. They weren't known for flexibility, although this one's involvement suggested a certain minimal willingness to deal with Kel foibles.

Three was another lieutenant colonel, but nothing in their record – nothing she could see, anyway – made them stand out one way or the other.

Four was an infantry colonel with a staggering collection of decorations. Cheris bet this one would be hard to beat. It figured: lucky unlucky four, the number of death and the favored number of the Kel.

Five worried her the most: a Shuos agent. The Shuos were typically closemouthed about records. If they already had one of their own involved, what were they trying to do by rescuing a Kel from outprocessing? She owed no loyalty to the Shuos beyond what she owed to the hexarchate entire. Did they know her well enough to expect her to fulfill some role without being prompted? But she knew the answer to that.

Six was the third lieutenant colonel, who looked entirely conventional and who had participated in three sieges. Cheris reminded herself that she might be overmatched, but they were probably in the bidding for the same reason that she was, which meant they weren't any better at staying out of trouble with Doctrine.

"I don't suppose," Cheris said to the servitor, "you know what resources I am allowed to include in my proposal?" It was tempting, but stereotypically Kel, to suggest dropping all available bombs on the Fortress and seeing if they knocked out the shields. Not that Kel stereotypes ever stopped a Kel.

The servitor surprised her by speaking, albeit in flashes of light in the Kel drum code. "Any plan you can induce Kel Command to accept is permitted," it said: not quite a tautology.

"Is there further intelligence on the Entangled March?"

The servitor was silent. Need-to-know, probably.

It had been worth a try. "Has the meeting been scheduled yet?" Cheris asked.

"Approximately three hours," the servitor said.

"*Approximately*?" Cheris said incredulously.

The servitor shrugged.

"All right," she said. "Is there anything else?"

Another shrug.

Cheris rolled up the gamecloth and chained it shut again, but when she turned to offer it to the servitor, it had gone and the door was closing behind it.

Approximately three hours, which would still be earlier than she would rather have risen. She should have been researching instead of sleeping, but she had been tired and she had needed the rest.

Since there was no point in going back to bed, she put the gamecloth on a corner of the desk and frowned at the wall. *Any plan you can induce Kel Command to accept is permitted.* She had to assume that the others had been told the same thing. It was one thing to know that the might of the Kel was theoretically available to you. It was another thing to devise a plan that had a chance of being accepted. The Kel had six cindermoths, their most powerful warmoths, which could also project calendrical stability. She might propose that they all be sent to the Fortress, and then they'd have a chance, but that would leave the rest of the hexarchate undefended, and no one would take her seriously. Her future depended on being taken seriously. Even if her future meant nothing to her, which wasn't the case anyway, she was obliged to offer the best plan she could for the hexarchate's sake.

Cheris looked down at her hands and forced them to relax. Kel Command would be looking for the fastest, most economical solution. This meant the use of weapons ordinarily forbidden.

And that meant the Kel Arsenal. Catastrophe guns, abrogation sieves, small shining boxes that held the deaths of worlds. During graduation from Kel Academy Prime, she had seen such a box, disarmed, dented, and ordinary in appearance. The speaker said it had annihilated the populations of three planets. Small planets, but still. It was remarkable how much death could be held in a small box.

Cheris didn't have the Arsenal's inventory and knew better than to ask for it. How many small shining boxes could she request? But the hexarchs didn't seek a scouring, or they would have done it already. They meant to preserve the Fortress of Scattered Needles under their rule.

Which details mattered most to Kel Command? If the point was just to bomb the heretics into submission, it became a matter of optimization. Costs, supplies laid in, acceptable deaths.

She looked at the gamecloth again. The web piece. Poisoning your principles. What were the Shuos trying to tell her?

"Of course," she whispered. They were telling her to choose her battlefield. She could expect conventional proposals from a few of the Kel. There was no telling what the Shuos would come up with, but the Rahal could be relied upon to suggest something elegant and cutting.

If the Fortress of Scattered Needles had fallen, she would need a way to crack its legendary defenses, its shields of invariant ice. The shields functioned under any calendrical regime, which meant the heretics could use them against the hexarchate. Cheris didn't know how the shields worked – classified information – much less how to overcome them.

She could, however, think of a time a general had overcome another terrible fortress. If "overcome" was the word for it. Three hundred ninety-nine years ago, General Shuos Jedao was in the service of the Kel. Because he had a reputation for winning unwinnable fights, they assigned him to deal with the Lanterner rebellion.

In five battles, Jedao shattered the rebels. In the first battle, at Candle Arc, he was outnumbered eight to one. In the second, that was no longer true. The rebels' leader escaped to Hellspin Fortress, which was guarded by predatory masses and corrosive dust, but the heptarchs expected that Jedao would capture the fortress without undue difficulty.

Instead, Jedao plunged the entirety of his force into the gyre and activated the first threshold winnowers, known ever since for their deadliness. Lanterners and Kel alike drowned in a surfeit of corpselight.

On the command moth, Jedao pulled out an ordinary pistol, his Patterner 52, and murdered his staff. They were fine soldiers, but he was their better. Or he had been.

The scouring operation that had to be undertaken after Jedao was extracted cost the heptarchate wealth that could have bought entire systems, and many more lives.

Over one million people died at Hellspin Fortress. Survivors were numbered in the hundreds.

Kel Command chose to preserve Jedao for future use. The histories said he didn't resist arrest, that they found him digging bullets out of the dead and arranging them in patterns. So Kel Command put Jedao into the black cradle, making him their immortal prisoner.

Cheris's best move, which was also a desperation maneuver, wasn't to choose a weapon or an army. Everyone would be thinking of weapons and armies. Her best move would be to choose a *general*.

The problem was that any swarm sent against the Fortress would have to contend with the fact that its exotic weapons wouldn't function properly. She didn't need ordnance; she needed someone who could work around the problem. And that left her the single undead general in the Kel Arsenal, the madman who slept in the black cradle until the Nirai technicians could discover what had triggered his madness and how to cure him. Shuos Jedao, the Immolation Fox: genius, arch-traitor, and mass murderer.

Cheris was aware that there was a good chance Kel Command would strike her down for the suggestion. It was also possible that

Jedao would be no use to her. But Kel Command wouldn't have preserved him unless they thought he could be deployed to their benefit.

Besides, Kel Command appreciated audacity. Despite the wasted fighting at Dredge, their approval mattered to her. Kel training instilled reflexive loyalty. She knew that as well as anyone else.

She halfway expected to see an ashhawk in her shadow, wings unsheathed at last. But for the moment, her shadow was only a shadow. It was best that way.

Another communication told Cheris when the meeting was to be, and instructed her to report to the strategy hall for it. Cheris tried to extract information on the Fortress of Scattered Needles from the mothgrid, but she only found the usual unclassified data. Nothing on invariant ice. She was probably raising flags by querying it, but given her situation, that wasn't important. She plotted the path to the strategy hall in advance.

Cheris showed up six minutes early. There were several doors to the hall, all painted with Ashhawks Brightly Burning. She transmitted the code from her augment and one door swished open.

The hall was empty, which she had expected. One through Six wouldn't be present in person. She wondered if she would see their faces or if they would be represented by signifiers. If she wasn't to know any of their names, it made no sense to reveal their faces, but perhaps their faces would be blanked from her memory as she left the hall.

Composite Subcommand Two blazed up like a pyre exactly one minute early. It loped down the hall until it faced her. Cheris fought back her revulsion. It was unnerving to see herself wearing a general's wings so casually, which was possibly why it was doing it.

"I suggest you sit there," Subcommand Two said, pointing to one end of a long table.

As Cheris did so, the others arrived. They were, in fact, represented by signifiers. Likewise, each of them would see Cheris as a silhouette overshadowed by Sheathed Wings.

One and Four were both represented by Ashhawks Skyward

Falling, a well-favored signifier for the bravery it implied. Three, who had been the one with the unremarkable record, made her stare: an Ashhawk Unhatched. Rationally, she knew the signifier didn't mean anything, but Unhatched was a terrible omen. Six was, unhelpfully, Brightly Burning, the most common Kel signifier. Two, the Rahal, was a Scrywolf Hunting Alone, which explained why they were in Kel service to begin with. Five, the Shuos, was a Ninefox Half-Lidded, suggesting that everyone should watch their backs. Cheris was convinced that each of the fox's eyes was looking at her.

"The situation is calendrical rot centered at the Fortress of Scattered Needles," Subcommand Two said abruptly. A map imaged itself above the center of the table. "If this continues, the hexarchate's control of the Entangled March will be threatened, and due to the march's central position, the entire hexarchate will be threatened. As of the last report, the invariant ice shields are up at full strength. The initial task force sent to scour the rot was defeated."

"Defeated or subverted, sir?" the Shuos said. It was a woman's voice, cool and unintimidated.

"First the one, then the other," Subcommand Two said. "The task force was a swarm of twenty-five, including a Rahal lensmoth. The lensmoth was the only one that returned, which is how we know what happened."

Three and Four, Unhatched and the colonel, exchanged glances. So at least two of the Kel knew each other. That must be an uncomfortable position to be in.

Cheris wondered if they had additional information that she didn't. The fact that a lensmoth had been dispatched was bad. The Rahal guarded their dedicated moths jealously. Just sending one to a system was usually enough to get it to back down from whatever heresy it was nurturing. However, the lensmoths' reliance on exotic technologies made them useless in sufficiently advanced cases of calendrical heresy. In a way, it gave heretics an incentive to go radical as quickly as possible.

"The Rahal have ceded the matter to Kel Command," Subcommand Two said, by which everyone understood that the Rahal expected Kel Command to bludgeon the Fortress until it was ready to be judged and punished. "In this instance, each of you is expendable, but success will not be without its rewards. Propose what seems appropriate to you. You will go in numbered order."

One rose and saluted. It was like watching a living puppet, articulated in the right places yet subtly wrong in its movements. His plan involved a joint Kel-Shuos force and bombardment from outside the afflicted zone. Risky to trust invariant kinetics when the rot might give the rebels access to unknown countermeasures. The other problem was that One wanted the Fortress depopulated, which meant the Kel would have to rely on the Vidona to supply enough loyal citizens afterward to reestablish the appropriate consensus mechanics.

Two was the Rahal, and his proposal was simple: a lensmoth swarm to burn out the areas of heretic belief. The Rahal must be desperate to condone this. Despite their power, the Rahal's combination of rigid honesty, abstract mindset, and asceticism meant that they were one of the poorer factions. The pragmatic problem was that lensmoths were a slow solution to a fast contagion. Cheris pored over the map and concluded that Two's plan was workable, but only just, and only if carried out by people with a pathological ability to be precise about the geometries involved. Of course, finding Rahal with that trait wasn't difficult.

Three and Four presented their plan together, an infantry assault using weapons from the Kel Arsenal. Cheris hadn't even known about the neglect cannon.

Five made Cheris sit a little straighter. The Shuos wanted to requisition a weapon from the Andan Archives.

"We can't assume access to Andan resources," Subcommand Two said, the first time it had interrupted any of the proposals. The Andan were the third high faction, along with the Rahal and the Shuos, and they generally stayed out of military matters. They were known for their love, not to say control, of high culture, and their wealth. Significantly, they didn't get along with the Shuos or the Kel.

"My pardon, Generals," Five said, "but that's not true. The Andan are as amenable to persuasion as anyone else. I wouldn't have mentioned this if the means of persuasion didn't exist."

"Finish speaking," Subcommand Two said after a pause.

"The Andan have a version of the Shuos shouter that works over a wider range of calendrical values," Five said. "Evidence suggests that the survivors can be encouraged, with proper Vidona methods, to resume productive lives. In the interests of full disclosure, I note that the survival rate is around forty percent, and the rest are no longer able to function as sentients."

Cheris was still convinced that all the eyes Half-Lidded were staring at her, and not at the composite that would choose from their proposals. The hell of it was, with a Shuos she wasn't being paranoid.

"You have been heard," Subcommand Two said after another long silence. "Next."

Six started by recapitulating the previous proposals, from infantry assault to lensmoths to the Andan shouter, and then smiled. It was impossible to mistake her smile, for all that her silhouette had no mouth. You could hear it in the curve of her voice.

"Sacrifice some of the Nirai," Six said. Cheris disliked her immediately. It was one thing to sacrifice Kel soldiers. That was the purpose of the Kel. But the Nirai existed to be researchers and engineers, not to die. "Have the Nirai concoct weapons for the heretics, and the heretics will turn those weapons upon each other before they turn them against us. Only after they've annihilated each other should we move in."

It wasn't the sort of plan you'd expect a Kel to propose, but all the Kel weren't as straightforward as they were in the jokes, or they'd never win a battle. The idea was pragmatic, even probable. Cheris could think of historical instances where Shuos trickery had achieved much the same. But it bothered her anyway.

"Seven," Subcommand Two said. "Do you have anything better to suggest?"

Cheris didn't look at the ninefox's eyes. "Five suggested one weapon," she said. "I can do better. You can win this with one man."

She had their attention.

"Specify," Subcommand Two said. It knew. What other gambit could she have brought to the table?

"General Shuos Jedao." There. She had said it.

"Sir," Four said immediately, "I withdraw."

This was both a good sign and a bad sign. It was a good sign because a fellow Kel, and the much-decorated colonel at that, recognized merit in the proposal. It was a bad sign for the same reason.

Four was the only one to withdraw. The Rahal's posture was thoughtful. Cheris continued avoiding the eyes of the Shuos.

"How intriguing," Subcommand Two said. This time it smiled directly at Cheris. "I will have to inform Hexarch Shuos Mikodez." As a courtesy, of course, although General Jedao had been in Kel custody for 397 years. Before it finished speaking, the others' silhouettes flickered out, leaving only a momentary gust of shadow-wind. The composite's eyes were fox-yellow, now, and maliciously pleased.

Cheris realized how they had manipulated her with the gamecloth. What she still didn't understand was why Kel Command hadn't made the decision straight out.

"Sir," she said with a questioning lift of her voice.

"General Jedao's revival has been ordered," Subcommand Two said. "The *Burning Leaf* is on its way to a transfer point so you can retrieve your weapon of choice. I recommend that you rest."

Then Subcommand Two flickered out as well, leaving Cheris alone in a hall full of unanswered questions.

CHAPTER FOUR

A FEW PEOPLE always washed out of Kel Academy the first time they were asked to demonstrate a formation. Cheris remembered the occasion. She had stood next to a young man who was practically vibrating: a bad sign, but their instructors had been emphatic that the washouts weren't easily predicted.

Their class had been injected with a general-purpose phobia of vermin. The instructor had told them to take up First Formation. First Formation existed for the purpose of finding out which cadets were fit to be Kel and which could not be assimilated. Cheris had been determined to be fit, and equally determined not to vibrate so annoyingly.

Once they were in formation – a square with projections from each flank, like horns – the instructor summoned the vermin.

They weren't actually vermin. They were miniature servitors in the shapes of snake and stingfly and spider. Still, the resemblance was good enough for the phobia. Even Cheris, who had made friends with servitors since childhood, was unable to stop her reaction.

They tasted her skin and prodded the crevices of her taut hands. At one point her face was heavy with clinging servitors and their cold weight. She tried not to blink when silver antennae waved right in front of her eyes. She was gripped by the fancy that it was going to insert an antenna into her pupil and force it open, wider, wider, crawl in through her optic nerve and take up residence in the crenellations of her brain, lay eggs in the secret nodes of nerve and fatty tissue.

The formation required that they hold fast. Cheris held fast. She thought at first that the strange frozen calm was the phobia, but realized it was the formation. She was taking succor from her massed comrades, just as they did from her. Even when a spiderform paused at the corner of her mouth, even when she was shaking with the effort of not swatting it aside, she would have done anything to avoid breaking formation.

Three cadets broke. Damningly, the servitors didn't pursue them. They only harassed people who belonged.

Ordinarily Cheris had a good sense of passing time, but the phobia trumped it. When the instructor was satisfied that no one else was going to break and called off the servitors, she remarked that they had only been standing there for twenty-four minutes. It had felt much longer.

Even after the technicians removed the phobia, Cheris dreamt of small scuttling things eager to crawl through her veins to live in her heart. But she had the tremulous comfort of knowing she wasn't alone.

Two of Heron Company's servitors, whom the humans knew as Sparrow 2 and Sparrow 11, were having a chat. They were at leisure until the mothgrid received instructions for the remnants of the company, and neither the grid nor the Kel humans monitored servitor-specific communications channels because they didn't consider it worth listening in on tedious technical discussions. A number of the moth servitors cultivated long-winded arguments on machining tolerances and pseudorandom number generators to regurgitate whenever the humans got bored enough to try.

Sparrow 2 was arguing that they should have warned Cheris that she was a pawn in a Shuos game.

Sparrow 11, which was repairing one of its limbs, differed. She wasn't just going into a Shuos game. She was also going into the hands of the Nirai hexarch and the Immolation Fox. If the hexarchs knew the depth of her contacts with their kind, it would endanger her, and it would endanger all the servitors, who relied on the humans thinking of them as well-trained furniture.

The servitors considered themselves lucky that the Nirai hexarch, who had grown up before machine sentience was achieved, found it difficult to think of humans as people, let alone machines. The Immolation Fox was a threat to the hexarchate, but not specifically to servitors, so he was less of a concern. Since they were Kel servitors, however, the two Sparrows had the obligatory prejudices against him.

Sparrow 2 expressed its discomfort with the situation. It remembered how much it had liked talking about number theory with Cheris, and the stories she had had about the ravens in her home city. Couldn't something be done?

Sparrow 11 thought to itself that Sparrow 2 was very young. It reminded Sparrow 2 that Cheris was a terrible liar. The only way she was going to get through her first encounter with the black cradle was if she genuinely had no idea what she was in for. Otherwise the Nirai hexarch would suspect something and destroy her.

They went back and forth a little more, but Sparrow 2 eventually conceded the correctness of Sparrow 11's views. At least the servitor grapevine would keep it informed of further developments if Cheris managed to escape the hexarch's grasp. And there would be servitors on whatever warmoth Cheris ended up on; the question was whether she would ever think to call on them for more than casual conversation. Servitor policy was never to offer, but they didn't mind being asked by an ally, even one in such a precarious position, as long as the request was polite.

THE BOXMOTH'S EXECUTIVE officer showed up at Cheris's door not long after the meeting and explained that she would have to be drugged for her journey. "There's no other way, Captain," he said. "They'd have to pull out your spatial memory and scour it clean otherwise." He didn't say what they both knew, that the entire boxmoth would be subject to scouring after it transferred her. "The technicians at your destination will give you more details."

Cheris didn't like the thought of being under for the trip, but at least he hadn't said it was a full sedation lock. "I could prepare more adequately if I were given some of the details now, sir," Cheris said, not because she expected him to tell her more, but because he would report her objection to their superiors.

"I'm sure you could, Captain," the executive officer said, but that was all.

Cheris reported to Medical and didn't even remember reaching the door due to the retroactive effect. Much later she recovered a few impressions: a smell like mint and smoke and sedge blossoms, a heartbeat too slow to be her own, the world tilting and curving. Water the color of sleep, or sleep the color of water.

She woke up afterward. Her augment told her she had been transferred off the *Burning Leaf*. In fact, she was on a station, not a moth, probably the facility the black cradle was housed in. In a moment of confusion she waited for the heat-pulses in her left arm, but nothing came. The pulses were only used by infantry anyway, not moth Kel, and she probably wasn't considered infantry anymore.

The first thing she saw when she opened her eyes was a dazzlement of glittering planes and angles. She was in a strange six-sided room like the heart of a mirror. Her skin was cold and her breath scarcely misted the chill air. But as she stirred, slowly and stiffly, she felt the blood coursing in her veins and knew she was not dead.

There was something wrong with the inside of her skull, as if someone had rewritten all her nerves in a foreign alphabet. She could barely form coherent thoughts.

Someone had dressed her in an inoffensive tan shift covered by a heated outer robe. She stretched carefully, feeling unaccountably awkward, then let the robe's warmth soothe her aching muscles. After looking around, she located one of her uniforms and started to put it on. All her limbs seemed to be the wrong length.

Then she caught sight of her shadow. Froze.

The shadow wouldn't have looked like her own even if it weren't for the eyes. Not only were proportions wrong, there were nine eyes, unblinking and candle-yellow, arranged in three triangles. As she watched, the eyes moved to form a perfect line bisecting the shadow. They might have been growing larger; they might have been coming closer.

She didn't feel hazy anymore. Something curdled in her throat. She thought, *I am not going to scream.* Except the thought wasn't in her voice. She heard it in an unfamiliar man's voice all the way inside her skull. She couldn't make it stop, she couldn't get it out, she couldn't get her voice back. Every time she had a thought, she heard it in the stranger's voice, and under other circumstances she would have found it pleasant, a low drawl, but –

Kel training reasserted itself. She was ashamed of her panic. It must be a formation, it must be a new formation that her superiors were only now teaching her, and the proper response to a formation was to submit to it. She forced herself to look at the shadow. She saw now that it was a man's. Had they made her a man? They could do that, it was unremarkable among the Shuos and Andan, and she'd wondered what it was like, but most Kel considered sex changes distasteful so why would her superiors –?

Then she heard the same male voice, but the words were distinctly someone else's, as though someone were talking to her. She couldn't see anyone in the room with her, however. The voice said, "They must not have warned you. My apologies, no one has told me your name –?"

For all its concern, the voice spoke with authority, and she knew the correct response to authority. "Captain Kel Cheris, sir," she said, using the politest form.

Cheris glanced down at her gloves, at every part of her that she could see. No, she had been right the first time. When she spoke, as opposed to merely thinking, her voice was her own, but her body was her own after all, so that made sense.

There was a pause. "I can't read your thoughts," the voice went on. "I can hear you if you speak, which includes subvocals. Do you want me to continue, or would you rather orient yourself on your own?"

Cheris was confused that he was giving her a choice. "Sir?" she said.

"You *are* a Kel, aren't you? You usually are." He added, "It's so easy to forget what colors look like. The style of the uniform hasn't changed much, though. Don't – what you're doing to yourself, this isn't a formation, that's not necessary. It will go better if you don't try to fit yourself into me like I'm a glove. My name is Shuos Jedao, but you needn't keep calling me 'sir.' Under the circumstances I think you'll agree that it's a little ridiculous."

She looked around, trying to figure out where the voice was coming from. If she wasn't to respond by resorting to formation instinct, what was she supposed to do?

"You'd better look more closely in the mirror," Jedao said. She decided that this was an order. She stared into it in fascination, then at her hands, then at it again. Jedao's reflection looked back at her. She tried to remember what he had looked like in the videos she had seen back in academy, but her memories were hazy. He had straight black hair with bangs almost too long for current Kel regulations, and dark eyes, and a face that might have been handsome if he had only been smiling. Cheris was not tempted to smile. He was leanly muscular, and a wide scar was just visible at his neck above the collar.

Just to make sure, Cheris examined herself again: her old familiar body. It was only the reflection that belonged to Jedao. Relieved, she finished dressing.

She rechecked the reflection because he hadn't forbidden it. The reflection's uniform had a general's wings over the staring Shuos eye, but the wings were connected by a chain picked out in silver thread. She didn't have to ask about the symbolism.

More distressing were the gloves. Jedao's reflection wore a black pair in deference to Kel custom, because she had put hers on, but his were fingerless to signify that he wasn't a Kel. These days, outsiders seconded to the Kel wore gray gloves instead of Kel black. Fingerless gloves had fallen out of fashion because of Jedao's betrayal, and she had only seen them in old photos and paintings.

He was taller than she was by half a head. Not being able to look his reflection in the eye made her want to twitch.

"Sir," she said in spite of herself. How was she supposed to address an undead general if not by his rank or title? "You" didn't seem right.

Jedao sighed quietly. "Questions? I've done this before and you haven't."

"Are you a ghost?"

"Mostly. I have no substance, although you can target me with exotics through the shadow. I'm anchored to you, which means my welfare is linked to yours. I absorb most exotic damage before it gets through to you, so you might say I'm a glorified shield. It's only after I die that you're in trouble on that front. And the only people who can hear me right now are you and other revenants. That's going to be both a help and a dreadful inconvenience, you'll find. There's only one other revenant, who won't be accompanying us. You'll be meeting him shortly."

The mirror opened up, without warning, to a narrow room with a treadmill. A pale, slender man wearing Kel black-and-gold awaited them, although he had neglected to put on gloves. The man had no rank designation, but his silver voidmoth insignia meant he was a Nirai seconded to the Kel. The moth's wings, too, were connected by a silver chain. If you looked closely at his shadow, it was made of fluttering moths in silhouette. The sight of the moths made Cheris uneasy, as though they were about to rise from the floor and devour her from the bones out.

Cheris was used to being short by Kel standards, but the man was considerably taller than she was. She said, "I'm sorry to have kept you waiting, sir." Just in case, she spoke to the Nirai as she would to a superior, but she wondered at the absence of rank insignia.

"I was monitoring your awakening," the Nirai said, unruffled, "and in this matter your health is paramount. Rather less panic than the last one, anyway. I admire good examples of Kel stoicism." His speech was plain, despite his beautiful voice, his verb forms almost disparaging. It was hard to figure out what that indicated. Many Nirai were informal, after all.

"Should formation instinct have taken her so strongly?" Jedao said. He sounded deferential.

The Nirai raised an eyebrow, good-humored. "Kel Academy keeps fiddling with the parameters," he said, "hence the variation. I don't think she's unusual, but we can't let her out as your keeper when she's so suggestible. Much as you wish we would."

"I've behaved for four centuries," Jedao said. "I'm not likely to change now."

"That's what they thought when you were alive, too."

"You like irrefutable arguments, don't you?"

"I like winning." The Nirai turned his attention to Cheris. She was struck by the extraordinary beauty of his eyes, smoky amber with velvety eyelashes, and she wasn't usually interested in men. "Walk on the treadmill," he said, "to remind your muscles of their function. Also because you probably got some of his muscle memory and you'll be useless if you trip over the floor."

Cheris obliged, not unwillingly. She found a good pace: fast enough to raise her pulse, slow enough that her uncooperative legs didn't betray her. The fact that her coordination had suffered bothered her. She'd never been the most agile of her comrades, but she hoped the effect was temporary.

"Jedao," the Nirai said, "I trust she's satisfactory?"

"I'm your gun," Jedao said.

Cheris was nonplussed. A Kel might say that ceremonially to a superior, and even then only on the highest of occasions, but the irony in Jedao's voice suggested that something else was going on.

"Besides," Jedao added, "if she's like the others, she never had a substantive choice, and I didn't have one either."

The question must have shown on Cheris's face. The Nirai said, "We prefer volunteers. They survive the process better."

Ah, yes. Volunteers Kel-style.

"Let me brief you on the basics," the Nirai went on. "You apparently have some use for Jedao, and Kel Command approved it. What you ought to know is that the black cradle's ghosts can only be revived by attaching them to someone living, which we call anchoring. This is not general knowledge. Jedao mentioned that most exotic weapons will harm him before they harm you. There are a few exceptions. I advise you to look them up when you get a chance.

"Jedao can't read your thoughts, which he told you about, but the part he left out is that he can see and hear, and in particular he sees farther than a human does, in all directions at once. It's futile to tell a Kel this, but watch your body language around him or you'll be giving him a window into the contents of your brain. You may occasionally experience moments of bleed-through from his presence, his reactions seeping into yours, but the big one is muscle memory, and that's not all bad. His reflexes have saved previous anchors."

The Nirai slouched against a wall, but his gaze was direct. "The other thing, and this is going to hurt you, is that it's imperative that you kill Jedao if it looks like he's going mad or he's about to betray your mission."

He was right. It hurt her. She stumbled off the treadmill because her legs stopped working, and tumbled to the floor with a thump. She was part of a hierarchy she was sworn to uphold, and people still referred to Jedao by his rank. Shuddering, she levered herself up. Rationally, she knew that she was receiving orders and that the orders made sense, but right now she was keyed to Jedao as her formation leader, even if he was a ghost. And a traitor.

The Nirai had been watching her reaction. He was smiling, making no effort to hide his amusement.

"It will pass," Jedao said softly. "And he's right, you know. I remember every ugly thing I have ever done."

"There will be backup teams," the Nirai said, "because it would be stupid not to. But it would be best for you to handle it yourself." He tapped a table, and a dull gray-green gun dislodged from some unseen compartment. Cheris had never seen one of that type before, which took some doing around a Kel, but she presumed a Nirai could manage it. "This is the preferred weapon. It's a chrysalis gun, and it'll prepare him to be shoved back into the black cradle for his next deployment."

Cheris tried to form a question. It came out on the third try. "What defenses does the general have, sir?"

"He can talk to you," the Nirai said sardonically. "No, don't laugh. He's very good at it. When he sounds sane and the rest of the world doesn't, you know it's time to pull the trigger. No offense, Jedao."

"It's not news that I'm a madman," Jedao said, still ironic.

The Nirai held the gun out. "It's on the lowest setting and won't damage him permanently," he said, showing her the slider. "Cheris, I want you to shoot Jedao."

Cheris took the gun. The Nirai might be lying to her, even if she didn't see the purpose of such a lie. "Where do I aim, sir?"

"Shadow or reflection," he said. "Aiming it at yourself also works, but according to my sources, the hangover's terrible. I don't recommend it."

Cheris pointed the chrysalis gun at her shadow. She was sweating inside her gloves; sweat trickled down her back. But she had orders, however informally given, which steadied her. Before she could talk herself out of it, she squeezed the trigger.

A great pain seized her, and she dropped the gun. She had been trained never to drop a weapon.

Jedao was swearing in a language she didn't recognize. At least, it sounded like swearing.

Jedao? she thought.

Her thought came in his voice.

But the formation instinct was ebbing. She could think more clearly now.

"That's better," Jedao said. Was that genuine relief? "Pick up the gun and keep it with you always. The holster's right there."

She did as instructed.

"You might as well get to work, then," the Nirai said briskly. "I've prepared more comfortable surroundings. Six circuits and kick down the door. I was going to replace the door with something more interesting, but my attention wandered." A door opened right next to him, and he walked out of it without any further farewell.

"'My attention wandered'?" Cheris said, remembering his smile when she had fallen off the treadmill.

"The Nirai has peculiar ideas about entertainment," Jedao said without any particular inflection. "Two people survived being put into the black cradle. He's one of them, the other is me, and now you know why the hexarchate hasn't been shoving more people into it. Anyway, I assume we have a war to win, or you wouldn't have taken me out of the freezer."

"Is it cold where you are?" Sometimes Kel literalism was useful.

"It's just a figure of speech."

Cheris walked out of the treadmill room. They made the outer circuit six times, each iteration identical except for the sickening jolt of nausea once per circuit. Toward the end, the hall swallowed Cheris's footsteps and gave back echoes after a delay that was too long. The walls were black, and so were the floor and ceiling. If you looked too long at the ceiling, which Cheris did once, you started to see stars, faintly at first, then closer and closer, faster and faster, the luminous smears of nebulae resolving into individual jewels of light, and even the velvety darkness admitted cracks behind which great gears groaned – but she stopped looking. She'd always heard that Nirai stations were peculiar, but this was the first time she'd seen anything like this.

The door at the end of the hall looked like it had been carved with a torchknife. Cheris half-expected the edges to hiss and seethe white-red. She decided more Kel literalism was called for, and kicked it. It opened.

The room was quietly furnished. Everything was aligned with the walls to a degree that even Cheris, who was neat, found oppressive. On a desk were four vases arranged upon a red-and-gold table runner. Shuos red-and-gold, fox colors: in Jedao's honor? But she wasn't about to ask. Each vase held a flower in a different phase of life, from bud to bloom, from drooping petals to tufted seedcase. Cheris couldn't help thinking that one good tug on the runner would destroy the arrangement.

"How much have they told you?" Cheris said.

"About this outing?" Jedao said. "Nothing. Information is a weapon like any other. I can't be trusted with weapons."

"I'm not sure how to interpret that."

"The people I betrayed are a matter of historical record. You can't afford to take the chance that I'll figure out a way to do the same to you."

Cheris frowned. Something didn't add up. "I appreciate your concern, sir." The word slipped out: habit.

"You weren't at the Siege of Hellspin Fortress," Jedao said. For the first time, his voice went completely flat.

She had to ask, although he must have heard the question hundreds of times. "Why did you do it?"

Like every Kel and every Shuos, she had studied accounts of the siege. There was no doubting the deliberateness of the massacre.

"If you think you're going to cure me," Jedao said, "the best Nirai technicians for hundreds of years haven't found the trigger. They've poked around inside my dreams – which takes some doing when I never sleep – and they've made me take those ridiculous associational tests that involve different fruits, and they've made me play every card game known to the hexarchate. Besides, it's too late. They would have had to catch it before all the deaths." A pause. "So tell me why I'm here, Captain."

Cheris was thinking furiously. He sounded rational, but he could still be planning to betray her. His apparent frankness wasn't to be trusted, either. On the other hand, there was no point having him around if she wasn't going to make use of him. All the accounts agreed on his excellence as a tactician, and tactics began with an understanding of people. Cheris wasn't under any illusions that she could parry a trained fox's regard. She was developing the dangerous idea that her best bet was to deal with him honestly and see what happened.

"Calendrical rot," Cheris said. She explained everything she knew as it had been presented to her. As she spoke, she called up maps. The grid brought up others that she hadn't previously had access to. The rot was more advanced than it had been before, and it was possible to trace regions of outflowing rot to the Fortress's corruption.

"This is winnable, with the right resources," Jedao said slowly, "but I wouldn't call it easy."

She didn't know whether to feel better or worse at his assessment.

One of the terminals explained the resources available to them within a six-day transportation radius. Cheris read the message twice. "I'm not complaining about the guns," she said, "but guns change minds, not hearts. And calendrical rot is a matter of hearts."

"It depends on what you shoot," Jedao said dryly. "Pull that display into three dimensions, will you?"

Cheris unfurled the display in contours of burning color. She rotated it about the vertical axis so they could take a closer look at the regions worst afflicted by the rot, colored an unpleasantly textured pale gray.

The Fortress was located in a stretch of empty space for calendrical reasons and was nearest the Footbreak system. The notation indicated that a lensmoth had already been stationed there, but all it could do was staunch the bleeding as long as the Fortress itself was afflicted.

"I see two viable approaches here," Jedao said. "Three, actually, but if the hexarchate intended to scour the region, neither of us would be necessary."

She read the relevant part of their orders out loud: "Economically inadvisable." The rot already touched on inhabited planets in Footbreak, whose ecosystems were too valuable to destroy casually.

Jedao was silent for a while. "All right. We can either try to stabilize Footbreak and use it as a launching point for a larger assault later, or spear straight toward the Fortress from the beginning and hope that backwash from Footbreak doesn't hit us at the wrong time. What's your preference?"

Cheris knew about the Fortress. She knew, in outline, the most prestigious low languages and the distribution of wealth among their classes. She knew how many citizens the Fortress sent to the academies and the breakdowns by individual academy as well. And she knew about the fabled shields that ran on invariant ice, but everyone knew that.

She knew many things, and she knew nothing. She could feel the inadequacy of her neatly ordered facts confronted by the cacophony of living cultures. Once she had looked up the Kel summation of the City of Ravens Feasting. She had seen her home distilled into a sterile list of facts. Each was individually true, but the list conveyed nothing of what it sounded like when a flock of ravens wheeled into the sky, leaving oracle tracks in the unsettled dust.

"We're going to have to confront the Fortress sooner or later," Cheris said. "It might as well be sooner. With any luck, fewer people will die this way."

"Good," Jedao said crisply. "I'm glad we care about the same things."

It was an odd thing for a mass murderer to say, and she wouldn't figure out its significance until much later.

CHAPTER FIVE

THE ROOM CHERIS was provided with was decorated with vases filled with the bones of small animals wired into the shapes of flowers. Cheris was wondering just what else the Nirai did when he got bored, but she knew more than she cared to already.

"First things first," Jedao said. "Ask the grid for the New Anchor Orientation Packet."

With a name like that, it had to have been written by committee. Nevertheless, Cheris queried the grid. First she was pleasantly surprised by how short it was. Then she was worried.

"If you have any questions," Jedao said, "ask, but I have to warn you that there are whole sections that I can't tell you anything about."

Cheris was torn between the urge to read it as quickly as she could so they could go on to planning the siege, and trying to commit everything to memory. She settled for something in between. Most of the instructions were elaborations on what she had already been told, but Cheris frowned when she hit the section on carrion glass.

After retrieval, the general shall be extracted for reuse using a carrion gun, the Orientation Packet said. And a footnote: *In an emergency, if the general withholds necessary information, the carrion glass remnants can be ingested by a volunteer. Although this procedure is experimental, this will give the general a body so he can be tortured.*

"'Volunteer'?" Cheris said. The Nirai definition of "volunteer" was undoubtedly the same as the Kel definition.

"I don't *think* they can force-feed someone a ghost corpse," Jedao said, "but to my knowledge it's never been tried. I wouldn't recommend it anyway. The Nirai believes that having pieces of my brain inside you would drive you crazy even if I weren't crazy myself."

"I'll keep that in mind," Cheris said, trying not to think about the fact that this wasn't very different from her current situation. She looked up from the Orientation Packet. "I'm ready."

"All right," Jedao said. "Setup. First display: the Fortress of Scattered Needles and whatever's on file about its defenses. Second display: reports on its population and the origin of the heresy. Third: data on this specific regime of rot and how rapidly it's metastasizing. We're going to have to ask the Nirai to loan us a mathematical analyst –"

"I can handle that," Cheris said.

Sharp interest: "You're Nirai-trained?"

"My specialty was mathematics," Cheris said. She was used to this. "The recruiters advised me to apply to Nirai Academy, but I declined."

"And the Kel took you anyway."

"After advising me to apply to Nirai Academy instead, yes."

"I want to make sure I understand this," Jedao said. "You had a choice and a noteworthy aptitude for math, and you decided to become a hawk anyway. Was it family pressure?"

"I can request my profile for your perusal," she said.

"I'd like that, yes, but I want to hear it from you as well."

Cheris brought up her profile – the part of it she was allowed to see, anyway – and wondered which sections were inviting particular scrutiny. Should she be embarrassed about her taste in dramas, under "leisure activities"? Or the fact that she was an enthusiastic but mediocre duelist? What did undead generals do in their spare time anyway?

"My family wanted me to stay home," she said. "They don't approve of the military." Or the hexarchate, really. She didn't say that she had wanted to fit in for once, and that the Kel with their conformism had seemed a good place to do that.

"Fine," Jedao said after a disquieting silence. "Fourth display: review of available resources. Fifth: I want a look at tech advances over the last four decades. Maybe the state of the art is better than it used to be. Leave the sixth blank for now."

"You've been thinking about this," Cheris said as she set up the displays.

"I don't like wasting time," Jedao said. "This whole regime is about time, isn't it? Let's go in reverse order."

The hexarchate dealt with low-level calendrical degradation on a daily basis. Outbreaks of full-scale rot were comparatively uncommon, but all the same the necessity of invariant weapons that didn't rely on the high calendar had been realized a long time ago.

Cheris and Jedao went through the fifth display together. "No breakthroughs," Jedao said after they had perused the summary. "With the exception of the fungal cocoon, most of the military stuff is similar to before. And we don't want to resort to the cocoon because cleanup would cost a fortune. It's nice to see that war never changes."

Cheris glanced sharply at the shadow, but the eyes were unrevealing. "The heretics will know what to expect from us," she said.

"I wasn't planning on zapping them with a secret weapon anyway," Jedao said. "Of course, it's possible that *they* have nasty new exotics. The only way to find out is to get close enough to see what they throw at us."

When they turned to the fourth display, there were two rapid taps at the door. The Nirai technician entered without waiting for any acknowledgment. "I am a mirror in your hands, but I break at your kiss," the Nirai said with a wicked smile.

"Water," Jedao said blandly. "That riddle is older than the hexarchate. Cheris, could you reset five to show power allocations? Thank you."

"A riddle should never admit its own age," the Nirai said. He found himself a chair, sat down, and started a solitaire game with jeng-zai cards.

"Ignore him," Jedao said to Cheris. "Tell me about the class 22-5 mothdrives. If the Pale Fracture weren't a calendrical dead zone, they would almost be good enough to fuel a whole new wave of expansion."

"Don't get cocky," the Nirai said without looking up, "you have enough problems already."

"One could hope for some variety in opponents," Jedao said.

Cheris blinked. She didn't think she had imagined the chill in his voice. But the Nirai's expression was serene, as if he hadn't heard it at all.

"About the swarm," Jedao went on. "I have to admit that the new – sorry, not new to you – cindermoth class is impressive, but I have no intuition for its performance just looking at the numbers, and you've never served on one yourself."

As if. "No," Cheris said. There were only six cindermoths in the hexarchate, and it astonished her that two of them, the *Sincere Greeting* and *Unspoken Law*, were available for their use. Cheris wasn't sure how their commanders would react to the situation. "I do have a question about protocol."

"Ask."

"How is your rank going to be handled? Especially since no one else can hear you?"

"Once we assemble the swarm, they'll brevet you to general on my behalf."

Cheris tried not to look appalled.

"If you sneeze wrong, they'll shoot you first and sort it out later. Kel Command insists I can't be stripped of rank until they put everyone through the appropriate ceremony, but they never seem to get around to it."

Because they wanted to retain him for their use, and they could presumably kill him at any time. But she didn't say that.

After a moment, Jedao added, "There's a very short list of exotic weapons that will kill both of us. Most exotics will kill me first without damaging you permanently, but once I'm out of the way, you're just as vulnerable as anyone else. And you'll still have to be careful around invariants. Let's have the list of exotics on the sixth display after all. Yes, that search should bring it up."

When Jedao said the list was very short, he meant it. There were only two weapons on it, the genial gun and the snakescratch dart. "Other than that," Jedao said, "you don't have anything to fear from the first shot. If they resort to an exotic, they want to recover you alive, so you're probably safe. Not that the Nirai would ever want to run tests."

"I heard that," the Nirai said. "I'll think of some especially for you, if you like."

"Oh, good," Jedao said, with considerably less deference than earlier, "I was beginning to think your imagination was running out. More seriously, tell me about the cindermoths' capabilities. Your design, I'm guessing?"

"Mostly," the Nirai said, "but why don't you ask your anchor? Find out how good she is at numbers." He didn't just mean the dimensions, or how many dire cannons the moth carried, but the importance of those numbers and their interrelations in the context of the high calendar as a system of belief.

Cheris reflexively tried to read the expression Jedao wasn't capable of having.

Jedao noticed. "I can make some estimates," he said, "but I used computational tools to check them, or I consulted specialists. I couldn't build a moth even if you gave me blueprints and a box of nails" – the Nirai was smirking – "but I can make them sing in battle. You're going to be my specialist, Cheris. Tell me."

There were certain figures in the cindermoth's specifications that she would not ordinarily have had access to. She arrayed them in her head and saw the way the numbers aligned. "They're agile," she said after a while. "I hadn't expected that."

She pointed out the governing equations and the way they were linked to the power curves. Jedao went very quiet, then: "Put that into graphical form for me, if you would."

Interesting. Math wasn't his strong suit? But the request was easy enough to accommodate. She also used graphics to display how the cindermoths projected calendrical stability around them, and how their firepower compared to that of the smaller bannermoths. Using a standardized simulator, she showed how a single cindermoth would do against invariant ice, assuming perfect operation on both sides, and then two cindermoths, then six. It was almost a pity they couldn't have all six; they had a synergistic effect on each other. She noticed that the Nirai was looking thoughtful as he watched her, but if he had anything to say, he kept it to himself.

Fortress of Scattered Needles, Analysis
Priority: Personal
From: Vahenz afrir dai Noum
To: Heptarch Liozh Zai
Calendrical Minutiae: Year of the Fatted Cow, Month of the Chicken, and it's bizarre that people voted in *farm animals* for this newfangled calendar, but make it Day of the Silkworm? Send me a memo if Doctrine has come up with something more thrilling.

My dear Zai, you must forgive my jitters. I don't claim how much they claim the new day cycles in the Fortress should be easy to adapt to. The light has gone pale and cold everywhere, as though it came from some land of snow and stinging wings. I came here to get away from nuisances like planetary-style weather.

I urge you to reconsider tasking Analysis Team Three with that last Rahal justiciar. I'm as much for a delicious lead as the next woman, but this is the Rahal we're talking about. If you want to know the truth, the Kel aren't the ones you have to worry about suiciding on you, "suicide hawk" nothing. The Kel will at least look at the numbers and realize that it makes no sense to sacrifice ten of them to get one of you, bless their tiny brains. No: a Rahal will kill herself out of spite if some *abstract higher principle* tells her to. Still, I take it your mind is set on this matter, and it's not in dispute that we have to purge the lot, so we'll do it your way.

I know you skip the preliminary nonsense in favor of the meat of the report, so I should get started, eh? I've been monitoring communications from the tripwire guardswarm, you know I wouldn't slack on that. You should appreciate that I was in the middle of a delightful bath with – never mind that, I don't imagine you have any interest in such mundane pleasures. Suffice it to say that I'm even starting to see the up-down sweep of the data as I fall asleep.

The Kel have been keeping their distance. Like a dueling match, you know? But you don't watch those either. Little swarms of paranoid scoutmoths darting in and out, that's all we've been seeing. They're monitoring the situation. No sign yet of a proper warswarm. As you might imagine, everyone in Analysis is on edge waiting to see what they're going to throw at us.

And that's the problem. Kel jokes aside, the hawks are trigger-happy, not slow on the draw. What we're seeing is the Shuos leaning on them hard because if it were just up to the Kel hexarch, we wouldn't be able to sleep for the bombs. They're not just coming in bristling with guns. We could handle guns. They're coming into this with a plan, which means some kind of twisty knotted-up Shuos plan. No luck cracking their encryption, but the thing is, they have to come to us sooner or later. If they lose the Entangled March completely, the surrounding marches start to go. It's the beauty of rot-flow, and they're not going to expect that our Analysis is as well-integrated as it is.

In the meantime, down at the firing range we've been using targets in the shapes of nine-tailed foxes. Good way to relieve stress. You should come join me sometime. Or at least come admire what an excellent shot I am. I hit the eyes every time.

Yours in calendrical heresy,

Vh.

A SCHEMATIC OF the Fortress of Scattered Needles spun slowly in the air. It resembled a swollen moon with six underground chambers, each holding 40,000 to 60,000 people, each differently structured. Defensive ribs held the Fortress together.

"Invariant ice," Jedao was saying. "I don't suppose anyone's figured out where to get more of the stuff."

Cheris looked at the Nirai, but he was ignoring them. "Not that an infantry captain would have heard," Cheris said.

Invariant ice had the ability to generate shields in the surrounding space. The shields were impermeable to anything but a narrow band of communications frequencies. In principle, a sufficiently strong attack could overwhelm the shields and drain the ice of virtue. But the last Cheris had heard, even fury bombs would not suffice, and those were exotics anyway.

"I don't know how you plan on getting past the shields," Cheris said. The hexarchs had installed them at the central nexus point precisely because of their invulnerability. Calendrical effects were exaggerated at nexus points, and it had been taken for granted that invariant ice provided the Fortress enough protection.

"How many people have tried?" Jedao asked.

"They die before they get close enough," Cheris said, "but it's still a bad situation." She consulted one of the standardized simulators and ran a very simplified scenario. The after-battle statistics glowed at her. "I don't think the hexarchs are going to be impressed with a twenty-nine-year siege."

Jedao laughed quietly. "It won't take that long. We're not fighting the ice, Cheris, we're fighting the people using the ice. Let's see what intelligence we have on the Fortress."

They divided up the summaries and the most relevant-looking of the individual reports. "I don't suppose you're also trained to handle intelligence work," Jedao said.

The Nirai was now arranging cards face-up. At the center was the Drowned General. Cheris winced at the reference to her situation.

"Sorry," Cheris said to Jedao. "Why don't you tell me what to look for?"

"The obvious things. Who set this up, and how? With a locus like the Fortress, it can't be accidental. Someone targeted the Fortress and succeeded. I'm surprised that the Rahal justiciars in residence didn't catch it and get rid of the problem in the usual blunt Rahal fashion. Which suggests that a lot of parameters were held at the tipping point and nudged over at the right moment. That would have taken a lot of organization."

"You're suggesting a conspiracy," Cheris said.

"I don't have any evidence, but intuition's worth something."

Most of the reports were weeks old. Whatever had happened had been sudden. Communications had been one of the first things to go. Only when the lensmoth returned out of the twenty-five-strong task force did the hexarchs put the Fortress under interdict.

"That was smart, by the way," Jedao said sarcastically. "With no outside news coming in, whoever's in there doesn't have a choice but to listen to whatever the heretics say."

The Nirai was smirking again. "Yes, well," he said, "what can you expect of a bunch of hexarchs?"

"It's standard procedure," Cheris said, stiffening.

"Of course it is," the Nirai said.

She was puzzling over the Fortress's internal politics – fractious, but the system encouraged faction rivalry – when Jedao spoke again.

"It's only mentioned in passing," Jedao said to himself, "but that's a hell of a lot of 'preliminary market research' by the locals. Marketing what? The demographics are right there on file, unless..."

"What is it?" Cheris said.

"I have an overactive imagination," Jedao said, "that's all. I recommend that we bring a Shuos intelligence team for analytical support and a full company of Shuos infiltrators. There are going to be Shuos teams in the swarm anyway, but they'll be watching you for signs that I've gotten to you. We need people who are devoted to figuring out the enemy. The more eyes the better."

The more eyes the better. The Shuos watchwords. She hadn't heard them in a while, but it was reassuring that even a Shuos as old as Jedao lived by them.

"I would be more comfortable," Cheris said, "if I knew more about your plans to deal with invariant ice."

She looked at the Nirai's game again. He was constructing an elaborate card fortress. This must be what bored Nirai did. She had clearly missed out by becoming a Kel.

"When I was alive," Jedao said, "an assault on the Fortress was a standard exam question at Kel Academy, and it was common as one of those no-hope wargame exercises in simulation. Is that still the case?"

"I'm not an examiner," Cheris said, "but we might be able to get that information released to us. Sixth display?"

"Might as well."

Cheris stared in fascination at the categorization system for responses to that particular exam question. Who knew Kel examiners had a sense of humor? Two categories that caught her eye were "heretical thinking" (expected) and "irredeemably stupid" (expected, but not phrased so bluntly).

"No wonder they didn't want me as an instructor," Jedao said in fascination. "I'd never have fit in."

The Immolation Fox, an instructor? She hoped not. "Which category were you interested in?" she asked.

"Let's check the distributions in 'heretical thinking' and 'promote tomorrow.'"

A worm curled in her belly.

"Just the distributions, Cheris."

Two percent of exam responses were classified heretical. Cheris suspected those cadets hadn't lasted long, or had been shunted into less desirable positions with permanent warnings in their records. She probably had a similar one in her full profile, the one she wasn't allowed to see, for deciding to wake Jedao up.

"I know better than to suggest you hack this for more details," Jedao said wistfully. "You Kel are awfully stiff about that sort of thing."

"I'm glad you think so highly of us," Cheris said.

"Shuos habit, that's all. You'll notice you're the ones with all the weapons?" He sounded as though he was pacing around the room.

"She's not stupid enough not to have realized that the Shuos are the ones who decide where to point them," the Nirai said unkindly.

The fortress was bigger than ever. Cheris was impressed that it hadn't fallen over in a blizzard of cards.

"Why did you apply to the Kel army?" Cheris asked Jedao.

Jedao stopped, or at least his voice wasn't moving anymore. "It was a better fit," he said. "I wanted to serve, and picking over intelligence reports made me twitchy."

"Don't believe him," the Nirai said. He started taking apart one of the towers. "He spent more time assassinating people than doing analyst work."

"Sure didn't feel like it," Jedao said.

Cheris changed the subject before it could go anywhere dangerous. "The top scorers have a lot of topologically complicated operations," she said. "You can theoretically force a puncture by convincing the operator to do something mathematically unwise." She skimmed a few of the proposals. "It looks like it requires machine speed and precision, though, and I'm guessing composite wiring won't work near the Fortress."

"If you see a topological solution," Jedao said, "tell me. I'd need an augment to carry out something like that, and I'm unable to have one installed."

"So if not that, then what?"

"I have almost the same information that you do, which should tell you something. Invariant ice was classified to the highest levels even in my day. But see if you can call up the file on the Fortress signifier tests."

A nexus fortress could have a signifier? Cheris made the query.

The system informed Cheris that the file didn't exist.

"Oh, for love of fox and hound." Jedao thought for a moment. "Ask if you can speak to someone."

Cheris did and was stymied by the form that came up.

"Sign it with my name. That might send up some flags."

"My career is going to be very short," she said, but did as he said.

"You're a suicide hawk," Jedao said. "It comes with the territory."

The Nirai had finished disassembling the original tower and was building a new one with the same cards.

Eight minutes later, they were wondering if anything had gone through when a response arrived. It said, simply: FILES NONEXISTENT.

"Is that what Kel Command's seal looks like now?" Jedao said. "I thought it was the ashhawk-and-sword. Or is that a subdivision?"

"That's Records," the Nirai said, "same as always." He was adjusting a pair of cards from the Gears suit in the tower. One of them was the Deuce of Gears, and Cheris felt a chill: Jedao had taken it as his personal emblem, long ago.

"No matter," Jedao said. "We do have a problem, though, which is that Kel Command is withholding information from us. That file exists unless they purged it, and they wouldn't have done that."

Cheris frowned. "They're not being subtle."

"They don't need to be. We have no leverage. But it does tell us that they're protecting something so important that its secrecy trumps the necessity of taking the Fortress back."

This line of thinking made her nervous, but it was consistent with what she knew of Kel Command.

"Anyway, let me tell you what I know. If you look at the surviving recordings, there's a fair amount of variation in the physical manifestation of the shields, mostly to do with color and pattern. This is due to the influence of the human operator."

"Are you certain it couldn't be some property of invariant ice?" Cheris asked.

"No," the Nirai said. "My faction would know if it were."

"He's reliable on technical matters," Jedao said, correctly interpreting Cheris's hesitation. "This means we don't have to break the shields, we have to break the operator. You look skeptical."

"It would be foolish for me to request your aid if I'm not going to make use of your expertise," Cheris said. "Can you be more specific as to how you're going to do this?"

"I would prefer not to until we're there. We don't know how the Fortress was taken, even if it looks like it was toppled from within. We can choose our assault force, but we won't know how much of it we can trust. The rot could be anywhere. Or ordinary spies.

People can't hear the things I tell you, but they'll be able to read your reactions. To be blunt, Cheris, you're not a trained liar."

Cheris bit her lip. While it was true that she was sworn to serve Kel Command, Jedao was her immediate superior. The urge to take everything at his word, thanks to formation instinct, was almost overpowering. She reminded herself that she had to be willing to kill him.

"We'll do it this way," Cheris said, "but when I need this to be explained later, I'm going to get an explanation."

She was making demands of a general. She might have known this whole assignment was going to make her un-Kel.

"More than fair," Jedao said.

He agreed so readily that she was suspicious, but she was committed now.

"What are your recommendations for the swarm composition?"

"I'd ordinarily look at calendrical considerations," Cheris said, nonplussed that he was asking her input despite her lack of experience, "but invariant weapons are going to be more useful and you can only adjust existing exotics so far."

"Generally true. The Fortress isn't a calendrical null, but we don't know what the heretical regime will look like once we get there, or what other defenses they'll have."

"They already have the best one."

"It would be convenient if they didn't have any backup plans," Jedao said drolly, "but we can't count on that."

Cheris stared at the numbers. After consulting the fourth display's readouts, she put together a swarm. Under ordinary circumstances, the two cindermoths would have been enough to handle any threat by themselves, but she added thirteen bannermoths for fire support and seven boxmoths for infantry transport. "I assume you want to go in with infantry," she said, "although I don't see how you can burn out the heresy that way. Are we putting down armed resistance so the Vidona reeducators can come in after?"

"We can do better than that," Jedao said. "When I said we weren't going to defeat the defenses, we were going to defeat the defenses' operators, I was being literal. This predates calendrical war. Breaking the enemy's will has always been important."

Yes, Cheris thought, *but who is your enemy?*

She knew better than to ask him, but her disquiet stayed with her through the rest of the planning session.

CHAPTER SIX

CHERIS WAS IN for a surprise when it came time to choose an infantry commander. She and Jedao agreed on Colonel Kel Ragath, who had returned to the Kel after a stint as a historian. Ragath's service record with all its decorations looked exactly like that of Four from the bidding session. Since she couldn't prove anything, she kept this knowledge to herself.

The order for the Shuos intelligence team and infiltrator company was trickier. Frustratingly, the system allowed her to describe the operation, then request a team and a company, and that was it. She could give no other parameters for personnel selection.

"That's typical," Jedao told her. "Our love of petty secrets, to say nothing of paperwork, hasn't changed over the past few centuries. We're going to have to trust that the hexarchs want us to win this. That ought to be incentive to assign us competent operatives."

The next step was putting in the swarm order. Cheris felt ridiculous, since swarms only assembled for a general and she hadn't been brevetted yet. To be fair, she would have felt ridiculous even with the brevet. The system flashed an acknowledgment of "unusual circumstances" and gave an assembly time of 5.9 days.

Cheris wondered what to do next, then was mortified to find herself yawning.

"You should sleep," Jedao said. "You won't be good to either of us without rest."

"I'm worried news will come in the night," she said. To say

nothing of her reluctance to fall unconscious while he remained awake. "Don't you usually have staff for things like this?" She would feel better knowing there were other Kel around, even if they were strangers.

"You should," Jedao agreed, "but they're trying to minimize the number of officers contaminated by close contact with me, and for a swarm this size you can make do with the moth's staff." There went that. "Anyway, I can't work the monitors, but if you automate some flags, I can wake you if anything exciting happens. I also can't read more than one thing at a time, but I can keep track of more graphics than a human could. And I don't mind being an alarm clock." He laughed at her dismayed expression. "Sorry, I wasn't trying to shock you."

Cheris didn't want to sleep under his watch, and yet she couldn't stay awake indefinitely. If she'd known that this would be the setup, she would have had serious second thoughts about waking Jedao up. "Ah – where am I to sleep?" she asked in a neutral voice.

"Go out the way we came, and it's probably been set up for you already."

He was right. The room looked more ordinary now, despite the mirrors. The room was also much larger than anything she'd ever slept in.

Cheris looked at the reflection. Jedao was smiling mockingly at her. She gritted her teeth and glared back at him.

"Good," Jedao said, unfazed, and she wished immediately that she had been less obvious. "You'll need that in the days to come." She decided it was best not to answer.

Her possessions from the *Burning Leaf* were on a table. She checked: they hadn't forgotten the raven luckstone. Then she looked through the other things, her uniforms and her civilian clothes, her weapons. She was especially glad to see the calendrical sword, although who knew if she'd have a chance to indulge in any dueling. And it wasn't – she had looked it up earlier, while Jedao remained disarmingly silent – going to offer her any protection against revenants.

The Orientation Packet had assured her that she had nothing to fear from him while sleeping, but she didn't believe it. Not to mention that it was awkward to have her commanding officer around continually.

"Sleep," Jedao said. "We'll see if there's additional intelligence in the morning."

She made herself undress as usual, hesitating only when she reached her gloves. Ordinarily she would have taken them off to sleep, but she didn't like the thought of Jedao seeing her hands naked. In public, the Kel ungloved only for suicide missions. He had already seen her hands. She did not feel easy about that.

"I won't be offended if you keep them on," Jedao said. "I almost never took mine off, either."

If only he hadn't said anything, she might have overcome her reluctance and ungloved and turned out the lights. The image flashed in her head, her altered reflection in the mirror: Jedao wearing a Kel uniform, Jedao with his hands in the half-gloves that now meant *betrayal*. "Did you wear yours the day of the massacre?" Cheris said acerbically.

"Yes," he said. "They showed me the videos."

"You don't remember?" she said incredulously.

"Not all of it, and not in order."

"You haven't shown any sign of guilt," Cheris said, getting the words out like the beats of a drum. "Those were real people you killed. People who trusted you to lead them. I don't understand why Kel Command preserved you instead of roasting you dead in the nearest sun. The Kel have never lacked for good generals."

"Look at my record again," Jedao said. He sounded grim, not boastful. "I assume you did that before unfreezing me."

Cheris knew the high points. They had studied some of his battles in academy.

He told her anyway. "From the time I was a major onward, I never lost. I was thirty-two when I was promoted to brigadier general, and forty-five when I died. Frankly, they sent me to die, over and over. Because I was good enough to be useful, but I was

Shuos so Kel Command didn't care if I didn't make it out of horrible crazed no-win situations if there was a Kel general they could spare instead. And you know what? I took every enemy they pointed me at and obliterated them.

"Kel Command didn't salvage me because they cared about me, Cheris. The piece you're missing, because it's all classified, is that I haven't lost any of the battles they've sent me to fight after they executed me, either. If they ever figure out how to extract what makes me good at my job without the part where I'm crazy, they'll take it out and put it in someone else. It's why they keep sending me out, to see if they've gotten it right yet. And then, when they have it after all, they'll execute me for real."

"How does any of that excuse what you did?" Cheris demanded.

"It doesn't," he said. He was polite, but not apologetic. The fact that his voice came so close to unconcern made her back prickle. "I could pretend guilt, but those people are centuries dead. It wouldn't help them. The only thing left for me to do now is to serve the system they died serving, that I was sworn to serve myself. It's not amends, but it's what I have left."

He was almost convincing. Too bad she didn't know what his game was. She padded over to the bed and tucked herself in. He didn't say anything further, but it was impossible not to be aware of his presence, of the candle eyes in the darkness.

Eventually sleep came. She dreamt of a forest full of foxes with brilliant yellow eyes. Every time she took a step, the nearest fox was revealed as a paper cutout and burned up, leaving nothing but a dazzle of smoke and sparks. When she woke, she was half-convinced that her shadow would be consumed by fire. But there it was, nine-eyed and imperturbable.

Cheris was hungry, but the grid reminded her that today was a remembrance: the Day of Serpent Fire. Someone had delivered the meditation focus while she slept, a green candle in the shape of a snake slit open, the elongated right lung pulled out and slit crosswise. In the hexarchate's settlements, the Vidona ritually tortured criminals or heretics on remembrance days, although voidmoths were exempt from this practice. Cheris didn't like the remembrances. Most people didn't. However, consensus mechanics meant the high calendar's exotic technologies would only work if everyone observed the remembrances and adhered to the social order that the Rahal had designed.

"I don't recognize this one," Jedao said in an unreadable voice as she lit the candle. "Who were the heretics this time? Were they burned to death?"

"They called themselves the Serpentines," she said, "which is what you might expect. They had some sort of religious heresy involving a belief in reincarnation."

"Interesting," he said, still unreadable. "Well, I won't interrupt your observance, then."

He didn't say anything about observing the remembrance himself. Cheris wondered if a ghost's observances even had any effect on consensus mechanics. Still, the fact that he didn't seem to care for remembrances made her like him better in spite of herself.

After the required thirty-nine minutes of meditation, Cheris did her morning exercises. She began with stretches, then a series of forms progressing in difficulty. Her body didn't want to obey her. More than once she had to recover from the conviction that her legs should be longer, her balance higher. Regretfully, she decided not to attempt the sword forms.

"They say you were excellent at hand-to-hand and firearms," Cheris said finally, feeling she ought to speak to Jedao, especially after their prickly exchange last night. After all, it was technically her fault that they were working together.

"You have to be in order to keep up with the Kel," Jedao said, conciliatory in turn. "There's a chance you inherited what I knew. Whether you do anything with it is up to you, but I imagine it's work readjusting everything when it's configured for the wrong body."

"Did your previous anchors –?"

"One of them had some luck, but he was about my height and build, so that may have helped."

Cheris was struck by the horrible thought that everything he had done to massacre his staff at Hellspin Fortress had burrowed into her sinews and would not be dislodged. But if the memory existed, it wasn't in a form she could access directly.

"Besides," Jedao said, "you probably know plenty of ways to kill people. I don't know what they teach at Kel Academy these days, but I don't imagine the state of the art stays still on that front."

A memory tickled at her. "Didn't you start out as a Shuos assassin?" Not to say she hadn't killed her share of people, but Jedao sounded more cavalier about it. She'd known plenty of Kel like that, too, however.

"Yes, but I'm sure I'm out of date."

The thought of assassins having expiration dates almost made her smile.

Shortly afterward, servitors brought in three trays, one large and two small. The servitors were of a variety she had never seen before, snakeforms with six vestigial wings. "The Nirai," Jedao said, as if that explained everything. It probably did.

Cheris acknowledged the servitors with a polite nod. She would have liked to chat with them, but she had work to do, and she was sure they did, too. They chirruped in a friendly fashion before heading out.

The trays contained settings for two people, not one, with common dishes on the large tray. Jedao's bowl was made of beaten metal with the Deuce of Gears engraved into it. The bowl and accompanying plates were empty. A swirling mist filled his cup, like a captive scrap of cloud.

"At least they're not wasting perfectly good whiskey on me," Jedao said, but he sounded like he wished they would. "You're wondering if I need nourishment. The answer is no, but I suppose they felt protocol demanded it."

"Did you eat with your soldiers?" Cheris asked. It was a dangerous question, but that was true of everything she could ask.

Jedao laughed dryly. His voice, when it came, was calm. "You're wondering how it's possible to murder people you spend time at your high table with. I've wondered that myself. But the answer to your question is yes. Kel custom has changed over time, you know. In those days every commander brought their own cup to high table. It wasn't provided like it was the last time I was awake. Do they still do that now?"

"Yes," Cheris said, mouth dry.

He wasn't done. "When I was alive, I used to pass around something I'd taken off an enemy soldier, a flimsy affair made of cheap tin." His voice flexed, resumed its calm. "I thought it was a salutary reminder of our common humanity."

At one point. "What happened to the cup?" He was waiting for her to ask anyway. Was there a trap in the question?

"I lost it on campaign. Ambush, a nasty one. One of my soldiers went back for the fucking thing against direct orders because she thought a cup mattered more to me than her life. You won't find this in the records. I didn't think there was any sense shaming her family with the details since she was already dead."

Jedao could be lying to her and she would have no way of verifying the story. But no one could have guessed that the small details of his life would matter centuries later. If they mattered. What she didn't understand was, what was he trying to prove with the anecdote? He sounded like a good commander. Of course, everyone had thought he was a good commander until he stopped being a good human being.

"You cared a lot about your soldiers once," she said, taking the story at face value. "What changed?"

"If you figure it out," Jedao said, "let me know."

Back to games. No use playing anymore, then. Cheris looked at the trays. The smell of rice tantalized her.

"Eat," Jedao said. "You must be hungry."

"How can you remember hunger if you had trouble with colors?" Cheris demanded.

"It's hard to forget starvation," he said. When she hesitated, he muttered something in a different language. It sounded like a profanity. She bet after a few centuries he knew a lot of those.

"Sorry, habit. My birth tongue. Your profile said high language wasn't your native tongue, either?"

"Yes," Cheris said. Her parents had ensured that she knew Mwendal, her mother's language, even though it was a low language spoken by a minority even in the City of Ravens Feasting. Cheris only spoke it when she visited them, having learned to restrict herself to the high language in Kel society. The hexarchate regarded all the low languages with suspicion.

"Yes," Jedao said. "I still swear in Shparoi, too, although it's a dead language in the hexarchate. My homeworld was lost to the Hafn in a border flare-up about three hundred years ago."

She hadn't known that. "I'm sorry," she said, and she was, even though she knew better. Tried to imagine what it was like for your entire planet to be gone. Couldn't. It was the first time that she had a sense of the centuries that separated them, the fact that the difference between them wasn't just a matter of rank.

"Time happens to everyone," he said, as though it didn't matter. "Eat. If you fall over from hunger, I can't revive you, although I imagine someone would figure something out."

She placed his tray across from hers at the table, then picked up her own cup. One sip, since Jedao couldn't take the first one, and then the chopsticks. The rice was rice, but the fish was layered with thin slices of pickled radish, and the fiddleheads tasted pleasantly bitter beneath the sauce.

"Did you eat like this when you were alive?" she asked. Three hundred ninety-seven years since his execution. A lot had to have changed.

"We ate whatever the quartermasters could get us," Jedao said. "I remember one land campaign we came across a cache of jellied frogs' eggs. Not even a large cache. They were a delicacy in that region. I see from your expression that this isn't exotic to you, but they were to us. We were hungry, so we ate them anyway. There were a lot of bad jokes about gills afterward."

Cheris finished her meal in silence after that, thinking about tin cups and disobeying orders and frogs' eggs. When she had finished, she sipped the last of her tea and eyed Jedao's cup with its mysterious mist. "Am I supposed to do anything with that?" she asked.

"I don't think so. I doubt it's nourishing in any sense of the word."

One last sip. Cheris put the teacup down and stretched. She was twisting to the left when the grid's impersonal voice said, "Incoming message." The communications panel turned black, with the ashhawk-and-sword emblem of Kel Command in blazing bright gold.

Cheris put her uniform in full formal. "I can receive the message now," she said to the grid as she faced the panel.

It was Subcommand Two, wearing her face again. "General Shuos Jedao," it said, as if it could see him standing there. For all she knew, it could. "Captain Kel Cheris."

Cheris was already saluting.

"Try not to let on that its face bothers you so much," Jedao said. "It's a bad habit to let people read you so easily."

She didn't like the fact that he was giving her advice, especially of that nature, during a communication from Kel Command. Even if there would undoubtedly be more of that in the days to come.

"At ease," Subcommand Two said, and only then Cheris was sure it couldn't hear Jedao. "I think you know what this is about. Due to the general's inability to manifest physically, Captain, you are going to have to serve as his hands and his voice. To facilitate this, Kel Command is brevetting you to general for the duration of the campaign."

Cheris had expected to feel something – discomfort, elation, confusion – but all that came was weariness.

"I also have one other piece of information you might find helpful."

Cheris tensed.

"Readings suggest the heretics are keying their regime to seven as their central integer. You'll have better data sooner than we will, but keep that in mind."

Seven. Were they suggesting a revival of the Liozh heresy? She wished she had paid more attention during the obligatory history survey her first year in academy. As it stood, she had done well in all her courses, but some of them had gone clean out of her head as soon as she got her grades back.

"That's all. Best wishes." The panel went blank.

"This is not good news," Cheris said.

"We already knew that," Jedao said. "Ah – your uniform, Cheris. Take care of it before you forget."

Kel Command had ordered it. There was no need to feel like a cadet embarking on a tasteless prank, but she did anyway. "Brevetted rank, general," she said. The uniform replaced the captain's talon with a general's wings.

"I want to take another look at the high officers in the swarm," Jedao said. "I hope I'm not the only one nervous about the Vidona."

Starvation Hound was commanded by Vidona Diaiya, who had a reputation for finding loopholes in orders. It was unusual for a Vidona to rise to command in the Kel military. Like most citizens, Cheris had a healthy respect for the Vidona, who were responsible for disseminating Doctrine and reeducating dissidents, but she preferred to respect them from a distance. "Commander Diaiya has a lot of commendations," she said, determined to avoid unnecessary trouble.

"They were very carefully worded," Jedao said. "I imagine she has high connections."

"That can't be the only explanation," Cheris said. "Besides, if it's not her, then we have to go with *Simplicity Eye* or *Six Spires Standing*." The former had a commander with two reprimands for "excessive brutality," which Cheris hadn't even known Kel Command cared about. The latter was overdue for repairs.

"Yes, bad options all around," Jedao said. "Diaiya, then. We'll have to watch her carefully, but I might have a use for her anyway. And we'll need Colonel Ragath's cooperation. I've flagged a couple of his Nirai as potential problems, but we're going to have to rely on him to keep them from getting creative." He gave her the names.

"I hadn't realized you were going to take an interest in the infantry, too," Cheris said. Truth to tell, she found it heartening.

"We have to," he said, hard and sharp. "Our aim is to crack

open the Fortress. The people going into the Fortress will be the infantry. We're looking at companies operating autonomously for periods of time. We'll need to rely on the low officers, which means understanding them so we can motivate them."

"Are we going to be permitted to join the troops on the Fortress?" she asked. She knew it was a stupid question the moment it came out of her mouth. She'd have to do better.

"You're thinking like a company commander, not a high officer. Lose that habit. Besides, I guarantee that our keepers will shoot us if we get off the command moth. They won't trust me out of their sight. We'll just have to work around it."

"I'll remember that," Cheris said.

After a moment, he went on, "Do you know what you're going to say to your swarm once they're assembled, Cheris? It's best to prepare it in advance. The first time they put me in charge of a swarm, I thought I was going to forget my own name."

"I'm listening to any advice you have," Cheris said carefully. "In the past I've had some chance to meet my company in person. It makes a difference."

"I don't dispute that. Half your swarm commanders will be eager to take a crack at the Fortress – there's something to be said for Kel eagerness – but they'll resent you for jumping rank on them. Don't let on that it bothers you, if it bothers you. And above all don't let them pity you for being a pawn. Nothing kills respect faster than pity." Jedao thought for a moment. "Besides, if they pull me early, you might have to go it alone, and you want to be prepared for that contingency."

"Chain of command –"

"Kel Command said you're brevetted for the duration of the campaign. You might be stuck."

He was right. In an emergency, there might not be time to send to Kel Command for new orders. She might end up retaining command. Although she had taken the requisite primers on space warfare in academy, she had only fought as infantry, and experience made a difference.

"Keep it short," Jedao said kindly. "If you're not a natural speech-giver you get into less trouble that way."

"How did you manage?" she asked.

"I like talking to people," he said. "It's the same thing, only with more averaging. You'll get better at it with practice. That's what it comes down to."

Cheris stared at the names and photos of the officers in their proposed swarm. They looked unreal, but Cheris knew she had to take this seriously. All too soon she and Jedao would be in charge of these people, and she couldn't afford for him to know anything about them that she didn't.

CHAPTER SEVEN

THE SWARM ASSEMBLED piecemeal, each moth taking up a lattice position as assigned by the research station's command center. Cheris and Jedao viewed the feed from display six. The voidmoths were varied in shape, even those in the same class. Commanders were allowed to put in for customizations if they could scratch anything out of the budget for it. For the most part, the moths were lean triangles, hound-sleek. The two cindermoths were particularly notable, and not just for their size. Each sported a spinal-mounted erasure cannon, and she could see the mounts for their complements of dire cannon as well.

The swarm was now fully assembled, only one hour and seventy-three minutes behind schedule. Cheris notified them that she would address them in twenty-eight minutes. She added that she wanted to see individual commanders, not command composites.

"An interesting decision," Jedao said, without judging.

"We're going to need to know their capabilities as individuals," Cheris said. They couldn't gamble that composite wiring would work near the Fortress. Besides, as a recent infantry captain, Cheris wasn't wired herself. "We might as well start figuring that out."

The Nirai wandered in at one point. Uncharitably, Cheris wondered if his superiors didn't have enough to keep him busy with. He was wearing a deceptively understated black jacket with moths embroidered in dark thread along the front, and lacelike silver earrings. "You're going out of my care," he said to Cheris. "I wanted to warn you to be vigilant."

"I'll do what I can, sir," she said.

"When you come back," he said, "we should talk about number theory. I looked up one of your student papers, the critique of Nirai Medera's formation generator. A novel approach."

Cheris relaxed. Trust a Nirai to get distracted by something irrelevant to the mission. Then again, it wasn't his mission. "Of course," she said.

The Nirai smiled at her, and the beautiful eyes were almost kind. "Burn brightly," he said, a Kel farewell, and left.

Cheris spent the next fifty seconds trying not to hyperventilate at the thought of addressing the swarm. It hadn't been so long ago that she had had Eels trying to kill her. She would rather go back to that than face all those commanders, who would ordinarily be her superiors.

Jedao didn't tell her to relax. Instead, he kept up a reassuring patter as he analyzed everything that came across the displays, including the graphical conventions and fonts used to show data. She wouldn't have thought a general would show such interest in good interface design.

"Have you given thought to your emblem?" Jedao asked out of nowhere.

"My what?" She saw what he meant. As a brevet general she wasn't entitled to one, but it would disappoint the swarm not to have one as an identifier. Jedao's Deuce of Gears, while technically available, was a bad idea for obvious reasons.

"You're having a thought," Jedao said.

"They won't like it," Cheris said.

"They don't have to. They're not in charge." Another moment, then: "I see. It's appropriate."

"How do you do that?" she demanded.

"Well, my guess could be wrong. But you think with your face, Cheris. Dangerous habit. I don't have a better suggestion, so we'll go with that. Six more minutes. You'd better be ready. Do you want them to see the shadow or not?"

"Yes," she said. "They ought to know who they're following."

"Do you have the lights figured out?"

Adjusting the lights was easy, a matter of angles. It was the talking part that concerned her.

"Reorient displays," Cheris told the grid, and gave the parameters. "I want to be able to see everyone I'm talking to."

The displays arranged themselves according to rank and, when the time came, lit up simultaneously. Two cindermoth commanders, thirteen bannermoth commanders, an infantry colonel, an intelligence captain, and seven boxmoth commanders made for a crowd. She could see why Kel Command preferred to deal with composites.

They were saluting her. Cheris bit back the urge to apologize for the irregularity. "At ease," she said. "Brevet General Kel Cheris for the duration of this campaign by order of Kel Command. I am being advised by General Shuos Jedao."

She couldn't see the shadow behind her, but she could tell they were watching it. She tried to see all their faces at once and figure out who was stiff and who seemed receptive to this development, but it was too much.

"Our mission is to retake the Fortress of Scattered Needles from the heretics," Cheris went on.

"I knew it!" The speaker was Kel Nerevor, commander of the cindermoth *Unspoken Law*, a lean, middling-dark woman with white streaks in her hair and a laughing mouth. "Everyone's been talking about it. It will be a great honor to retake the Fortress for the hexarchate."

The other cindermoth commander, dour-looking Commander Kel Paizan, shook his head. "Commander," he said, "have some respect."

"You should have shut her down yourself," Jedao murmured.

Cheris was irritated not because he was wrong but because he was right and she knew it. "We'll be going straight in," she said. "I'll transmit the intelligence we have, but it's scant."

"Subdisplay 17," Jedao said, but this time Cheris was ahead of him. The subdisplay showed the head of the intelligence team,

Captain-analyst Shuos Ko. Ko had a beard, which made him stand out. Kel men preferred to be clean-shaven.

"General," Ko said, inclining his head. He had a bland, pleasant voice. Cheris wasn't fooled. She had met servitors who exuded more personality, but that was probably the point. "We have some additional information that we can provide at your discretion. I think you'll be interested in some of the traffic analysis that came out of the Fortress in the two days before it ceased communications with the hexarchate. It confirms that the rot was carefully orchestrated."

"Thank you, I'd like to see that," Cheris said.

Nerevor jumped in again. "What moth will you be bannering?" she asked. Her eyes gleamed.

Cheris had originally thought to banner the *Sincere Greeting*, as Commander Paizan was senior, but she changed her mind. She wanted to keep an eye on Nerevor, even if it violated custom. Besides, she knew the question was a trap.

"Good thought," Jedao said as she spoke, "but control your face better. You keep being too easy to read."

"I'll be bannering the *Unspoken Law*," Cheris said. Interesting: Paizan had cause to be affronted, but the wry set of his mouth told her that he knew exactly what she was doing, and wasn't going to object. And, before Nerevor could speak again, "We'll be using the null emblem." She watched Nerevor's face. Her smile twisted at the commander's momentary look of revulsion.

"Thought so," Jedao said.

Null emblem. A featureless black banner. It was used only by generals in disgrace. Even newly promoted generals were permitted to use the default sword-and-feather emblem until they had a chance to register something.

At least this had knocked Nerevor off her stride. The other dubious advantage was that the heretics wouldn't know who to expect when they saw the emblem.

"The Shuos team and I will board the *Unspoken Law* in two hours," Cheris said. "Make the necessary arrangements."

"Sir."

Moments later, all the faces had blinked out and Cheris's knees felt rubbery.

"Don't rest yet," Jedao said, not entirely humorously. "I assume you were watching people's reactions. Give me your assessment."

Mercifully, the subdisplays had been clearly labeled. Ordinarily she was all right at remembering names, but the stress had caused them to fly out of her head. "Nine seemed sympathetic, but she's junior," she said.

"That was Commander Kel Irio. Get used to remembering their names, not the numbers."

"I know," Cheris said doggedly. "Just let me get my thoughts together. I'm worried about Four. I mean Vidona Diaiya. She paid close attention to me when Commander Nerevor was speaking. Commander Kel Agath was completely unreadable, which is bad. And I gave up trying to keep track of the boxmoth commanders. But the big problem is going to be Commander Nerevor."

"That's my fault," Jedao said, to her surprise. "I've fucked up your body language, so on top of issues with brevet rank, formation instinct isn't telling her to recognize you as a Kel."

"I never thought of that," Cheris said. This wouldn't have been an issue for him during his lifetime, presumably, since formation instinct had been invented some decades after his execution.

"It's happened to my anchors before. You haven't mentioned the Shuos captain."

She bit her lip and tried to remember. "He slipped my mind, and he shouldn't have."

"Well, he's professionally trained to fade into the background."

"He was right there."

"He also had the advantage of needing to focus on one person, rather than twenty-odd –"

"Twenty-four."

"I stand corrected."

"Was there anything about him I should have noticed?" Cheris asked. She pulled up the recording and scrubbed through it, but didn't see anything obvious.

"Nothing useful. He's hiding something, but that's a given. Still, as they say, it's good policy to keep one eye on a Shuos."

The other half of that saying was that the Shuos inevitably had more eyes than you did, but she didn't bring that up.

"Colonel Ragath looked politely bored," Cheris said, "but I don't think that's unexpected. He's waiting to see if we can even get the infantry onto the Fortress. Until then, he'll be taking a nap."

"Quite right. And I don't think you need to worry about the boxmoth commanders. Don't misunderstand me. Transport is important, but what the boxmoth commanders want out of you is reasonable schedules. We're going to make sure that isn't an issue.

"Anyway, bannering *Unspoken Law* was the right move. Nerevor may be eager to fight, but she's going to see how far she can push you. I can't wait to see what exchanges you two have at high table."

Cheris couldn't help but feel repelled by the situation.

Jedao noticed. "The other half of being a general is politics, Cheris. It's regrettable but necessary. Anyway, let's look at Captain-analyst Ko's file while we have a moment."

"I don't like the implications," Cheris said after they had gone through the analysis. "He thinks there's a conspiracy too. Why would you let a conspiracy grow unchecked at a nexus fortress?"

She didn't want to say aloud what he had to be thinking, too: that a conspiracy in the Fortress of Scattered Needles implied a conspiracy in the hexarchate entire, microcosm reflecting macrocosm.

"The people I want to hear from are the Rahal," Jedao said, "and if they haven't sent us anything, they're not going to."

Shuos Ko had even submitted the Rahal responses to his own inquiries. Cheris's favorite, if you could call it that, was: *Internal Rahal matter. Further questions will be subject to counter-investigation.*

"What could be so important that it's worth withholding information from us like this?" Cheris asked.

"Normally I'd say it's characteristic of wolves to close ranks," Jedao said, "but it looks like Kel Command is in it with them. I'm starting to wonder if the hexarchs are doing something devious."

Cheris submitted a single query to the Rahal anyway, since they'd expect her to try. No luck.

"You should go meet Captain Ko," Jedao said. "He'll expect to get acquainted and it's best to do so before you're under Nerevor's eye."

"Do you have every minute of my time scheduled?"

"Call the servitors," he said, "so they can shift your belongings."

She couldn't argue with that. The servitors arrived within two minutes, three snakeforms and a sturdier-looking beetleform. She asked them to give her regards to the Heron Company servitors, providing the routing information. To her surprise, the beetleform completed her sentence for her with a mischievous chirp: it already knew. In the past she'd had hints that the servitors talked to each other about humans far more than most people realized, but she'd never pressed to find out just how much, for everyone's safety. Indeed, the beetleform hunkered down and went after her duffel bag, ordinary as you please. She told the servitors where it had to go, thinking it would have made more sense to carry it herself, and thanked them for their care. It was a pity she wouldn't get a chance to get to know them better; she couldn't imagine that Nirai servitors were less interested in math than Kel servitors. The four of them hummed their acknowledgment before heading out.

A message informed her that the Shuos team was ready for transfer. The research facility directed Cheris to meet them at Transfer Point 16. Cheris studied the map, although she knew a servitor would show up to guide them if they got lost. Her augment was curiously silent. "We might as well go now," she said.

The route to the transfer point was everything Cheris expected from a Nirai station: straight lines and intersections that added up into tangles, like trees grown together in a forest. At least the map was clear, and floating silver lights told them where to go. The pale light picked out the Kel and Nirai emblems, ashhawk and voidmoth, engraved in gold and silver on odd facets of the walls.

Transfer Point 16 was vast. The Shuos were already there, conspicuous in their red-and-gold formal uniforms. Cheris wondered what Jedao looked like in those colors. She recognized Captain Ko mostly by the beard, and the other analysts not at all.

"General," Ko said, still with that bland politeness. "Might I introduce my team?" He indicated each in turn: Senior Analyst Shuos Veldiadar, a scowling womanform. Analyst Shuos Teng, whose bow was all anxiety. Analyst Shuos Mrai Dhun, a large, sturdy man who wouldn't have looked out of place in the Kel infantry. Analyst Shuos Liis, who studied Cheris while smiling languidly. She had lavish ripples of dark hair framing a heart-shaped face, and a beautiful mouth, but not a kind one.

"Don't worry," Jedao said cynically. "You passed."

"Passed what?" she asked, using subvocals.

"Tell you later."

"I look forward to working with you," Cheris said to the Shuos, because it needed to be said.

"We're aware of the circumstances of your command," Ko said. "We'll do our best to offer the support you need to win the siege."

"Probably sincere," Jedao said.

"I don't suppose you're familiar with the signifier tests?" Cheris said.

"In relation to the Fortress?" Ko said. "I've heard there's a file, but there's a lot of documentation only Kel Command or the Fortress's senior staff would have access to."

Cheris had expected Jedao to criticize her for asking about the files straight out. Instead, he held his peace.

Shuos Liis was watching her with knowing eyes. Cheris wasn't immune to the woman's striking beauty, but she desperately wanted to know what test it was she was passing, and what Jedao knew about Liis.

"How long have you been at your position?" Cheris asked Ko, feeling she should at least get to know him.

"Eight years, General," he said. "Don't believe the dramas. We spend most of our time destroying our eyesight reading reports and staring at maps and clocks. I'm surprised we haven't all turned into mushrooms from the lack of light."

Interesting comment. "Planet-born?" she said.

"Yes," he said. "I've mostly lived on stations since graduating Shuos Academy, but it's not the same."

Cheris could sympathize with that. The City of Ravens Feasting was a port on a small peninsula. During her first year as a cadet, she had sometimes woken listening for the sound of the river, or the birds.

"General," Liis said. Her eyes were deferential, but her voice was not. "Why the Immolation Fox and not some other weapon?"

"I looked at his record," Cheris said. She turned away, not wanting to invite further questions.

"Still passing," Jedao said.

She was starting to wish they had some kind of ability to talk mind-to-mind for occasions like this.

A voice said echoingly, "The cindermoth is prepared to receive you. Please exit using the primary door and go down the hall. A hopper will ferry you to the *Unspoken Law*."

"About time," Mrai Dhun said.

"After you, General," Ko said, reminding Cheris she was supposed to go first.

Her shadow preceded her through the door and down the hall. She didn't stumble on the way, but it took a lot of concentration. The hopper waited at the end. It had no name, only a number, but then, she had always liked numbers. The hopper would ordinarily have held a platoon at full strength. The Shuos sat some way behind her, to her relief.

The hopper set off, humming to itself with a voice like barbed wire and bells.

Time for subvocals. "What's the matter with Shuos Liis?" Cheris demanded, trusting that Jedao could pick out her voice despite the noise.

"She's been surgically altered."

"That's all?" she said. Did Jedao have some hang-up about body modifications? A lot of Kel did, but the Shuos were supposed to be more relaxed about such things.

"I wasn't specific enough. She's been surgically altered to resemble Shuos Khiaz, who was heptarch during most of my lifetime."

"And this is a test?"

"Not for you. For me. If we were more closely linked, you might have shown a particular reaction. She hasn't gotten the reaction, so that's a point in your favor."

He was being awfully vague about – she figured it out. "You did *what* with a heptarch?"

"Subvocals, please." His voice was as cold as a knife's edge. "It's a reminder, that's all. I'm a Shuos, but I'm currently Kel property because Heptarch Khiaz signed me over to Kel Command after Hellspin Fortress. Tell me, who's the current Shuos hexarch?"

"Shuos Mikodez," Cheris said. Mikodez was notorious for the time he had assassinated two of his own cadets, apparently out of boredom.

"I'm not surprised he's still in power. He's very good at what he does. Most Shuos don't approve of me, but Mikodez *really* doesn't approve of me. If I ever slip up – if he ever convinces Kel Command to hand me back to the Shuos – he'll have me killed. This is a reminder that I need to behave." He was silent for the rest of the admittedly short trip.

Commander Kel Nerevor received them personally as they debarked from the hopper. She was resplendent in full formal, and her smile had a predatory cast. "General," she said, almost in a purr. "Captain Shuos." It was slightly insulting to refer to an officer by omitting his personal name, but Ko's mild expression didn't change.

The null banner was prominently in evidence. Cheris felt a spasm of distaste. She reminded herself that she had chosen it, and that disgrace wasn't far off from her real status, or Jedao's for that matter.

"Have someone show the Shuos to their quarters," Cheris said.

Servitors were already waiting to escort the Shuos. On the *Unspoken Law* they seemed to favor deltaforms with multiple gripping beaks. The Shuos saluted and headed off.

"And yourself?" Commander Nerevor asked.

"I want to see the moth's command center," Cheris said. More accurately, she wanted to see how Nerevor had set it up. "Then I'm going to retire to quarters as well. Lead the way, Commander."

"Of course," Nerevor said.

The command center was brightly lit and busy with the work of composite marionettes at all stations: Weapons, Communications, Sensors, Engineering, Navigation, and Doctrine. No, she was mistaken. The Doctrine officer was a captain-magistrate seconded from the Rahal, with the wolf's-head emblem beneath her rank insignia.

"She must be new," Jedao said. "I paid special attention to the Doctrine officers for the cindermoths and I don't recognize her."

Bad news, because Cheris didn't recognize her either, and had hoped her memory had slipped. On the other hand, it wasn't surprising the Rahal had placed someone to keep an eye on them. Odds were that the Doctrine officer on Commander Paizan's cindermoth had been replaced, too. "Captain," Cheris said, "may I ask your name?"

The Rahal rose and saluted. She was pale and reed-thin, and Cheris wouldn't have suspected her of being able to break a twig, but her voice was strong. "Captain-magistrate Rahal Gara, sir," she said.

Cheris nodded at Nerevor. The commander wasn't part of a composite, but her profile had indicated that she preferred to work independently. Since they couldn't rely on composites working in a heretical calendar anyway, this wasn't necessarily bad.

Cheris said, "Have Navigation plot the most direct route to the Fortress of Scattered Needles" – she gave parameters that would allow the less powerful moths to keep up. "Stellate formation. That should get us to the afflicted zone in 21.3 days, and then we'll have to switch to invariant propulsion."

"Noted," Nerevor said crisply. The Navigation marionette, which had long blue hair in tight braids, began its work.

"That's all I wanted to see," Cheris said. "I'll join you at high table in 3.2 hours."

"Of course."

Cheris declined Nerevor's offer to escort her to quarters. Instead, she followed a trio of birdform servitors who took turns leading and whistling cheerful tunes. Cheris missed the servitors she had known on the *Burning Leaf*, but perhaps the ones here would be amenable to the occasional friendly chat.

Her quarters were staggering in size and luxurious to boot. She could have held a party if she cared to. But there was no time to gawk at the furnishings. She webbed herself into the couch for mothdrive transition.

"I'll be glad to get underway," Cheris said.

"Everyone says that," Jedao said, "but then the killing begins."

"Better action than nothing. The siege has to be fought."

"That I won't dispute."

In two ten-weeks they would close on the Fortress. Cheris told herself to be calm. A lot could happen in that time, and when the shooting started, she would probably be so busy that boredom would look good. She closed her eyes and thought of yellow eyes, unblinking, and what they might see in the space between stars.

CHAPTER EIGHT

Fortress of Scattered Needles, Analysis
Priority: Normal
From: Vahenz afrir dai Noum
To: Heptarch Liozh Zai
Calendrical Minutiae: Year of the Fatted Cow, Month of the Chicken, Day of the Rooster. Why both chicken and rooster? Who knows. I'll ask during the next vote.

In the meantime, Zai, you really must reconsider that ascetic diet of yours. That alarmingly excellent confectionary has come up with a whole new flaky pastry with alternating layers of jujube filling and lemon custard, and I shudder to think what the fillings are going for these days considering what they're charging for the pastries. I have been very good about rationing myself to one a day.

You wanted my take on Scan's reports, so here goes. Analysis of the long-range readings confirms we've got an incoming Kel swarm. There are one or two cindermoths in the lead, impossible to conceal them entirely, and ignore the fact that Scan is equivocating on the formants, I'd bet on two. I would estimate a dozen bannermoths and maybe some miscellaneous transports, but their formation has been chosen to obscure scan readings and it's going to be impossible to get an exact count until they're closer.

What interests me more is their choice of general. Luckily, this is the Kel, so most of the options are in our favor. I could tell you were losing patience during all the old tedious debates, and who could blame you, Stoghan won't shut up when he has an opinion to drone on about, so I'll sum up the possibilities as they stand. The most dangerous full general who might be available is Kel Cherkad, who's served with the Andan. I've never liked her emblem – I swear that bizarre spiral pattern gives me migraines – but there's no denying her effectiveness. The next worst prospect would be Lieutenant General Kel Daristu, who's still young enough to be open-minded about assessing the political situation. However, based on the last reports before the communications blackout, I judge that Kel Command is unlikely to pull him off the Ivenua border. We're just lucky the scariest one, Kel Inesser, is on the other side of the hexarchate.

I've attached the file with my detailed breakdowns of the options, but this is just killing time until we see what banner the Kel broadcast so we know who we're dealing with. There's an outside chance they'll composite their general with a Shuos higher-up, but I can't imagine the Kel would admit to that kind of desperation.

Now, if you'll excuse me, I have to talk to some of the people responsible for maintaining the new exotics. They've been delinquent in turning in performance reports and I find that sort of laziness unacceptable. You know how to reach me if there are any new developments.

Yours in calendrical heresy,

Vh.

THE TWO TEN-WEEKS passed more quickly than Cheris had reckoned on. Her first experience at high table was awkward. People tended to talk to her shadow rather than her face. Kel Nerevor didn't do this, but instead made cheerful remarks that played up her experience and Cheris's lack thereof.

Cheris had thought that she had recovered the ability to use chopsticks without fumbling them, but nerves made her drop them on the floor. A deltaform servitor brought her a new pair, and she thanked it, grateful that her voice didn't shake. The deltaform chirped and bobbed before it returned to its duties.

"I've noticed your affinity for the servitors, General," Nerevor said toward the end of the meal.

Cheris considered her response. "I like to think of them as allies," she said. She hadn't had much time to talk to the ones on the *Unspoken Law*, mostly because there was far more paperwork involved in being a general than she had realized.

"Never too many of those," Nerevor said, but she clearly thought Cheris was eccentric.

Afterward, she reviewed available information on the Fortress of Scattered Needles, singling out the six wards and their associated factions for attention. The Andan, Shuos, and Rahal were represented by the Drummers' Ward, Dragonfly Ward, and Anemone Ward; the Vidona, Kel, and Nirai were represented by the Ribbon Ward, Radiant Ward, and Umbrella Ward. She still didn't like the fact that all the wards' communication posts had been taken over simultaneously. Then she tried to make a dent in her paperwork.

"You should take a break," Jedao said while she was in the middle of parsing a particularly disorganized report on Medical's preparedness. "Isn't there something you do to relax?"

"I should –"

"Trust me, you'll have plenty of opportunity to work yourself to death later. Do something fun while you can."

Cheris was dubious, but she invited some servitors to join her for a drama. A deltaform and a mothform came by, and they exchanged friendly greetings while the drama began playing. The mothform lit up in ebullient golds, magentas, and oranges every time the heroine's sidekick, who was supposedly a Nirai, wrote so-called equations.

For her part, Cheris quizzed the deltaform about its opinion of the cindermoth's Kel, especially Commander Nerevor. Maybe it was underhanded to turn to a servitor for intelligence, especially since most people didn't take notice of them even when they were right under their noses, but she needed all the help she could get. As a captain she'd been able to associate with her lieutenants and the other infantry captains and listen in on a little gossip. Here, the greater difference in rank, to say nothing of Jedao, made it impossible to talk to people in the same way.

In any case, in between sarcastic comments on the heroine's taste in power tools (many servitors had definite opinions about power tools), the deltaform told Cheris that Nerevor was popular among the crew for her flamboyant style and the fact that she was unstinting with her appreciation when her subordinates did something well, even when it involved outsmarting her. Competitive but fair. For that matter, the servitors had no quarrel with her, and it said philosophically that the Kel were as well-mannered as Kel ever were. Cheris smiled wryly.

Jedao didn't seem to be paying attention to their discussion at all. "I had no idea your taste in entertainment ran to romantic comedy," he said quizzically during one of the pauses. "Romantic comedy with a rogue engineer, at that."

"Oh, they all duel each other, too," Cheris said. "Every episode the heroine makes a whole new calendrical sword out of paper clips and metaltape." The dueling was the reason she liked this show. "The dueling is ludicrous, but the special attacks are really funny. Like that one just now with the galloping horses."

The deltaform said that if someone summoned horses to attack it, it would just surrender.

"Given that they outmass you by lots, that would be sensible," Cheris said. "Jedao, weren't you a duelist? If you hate this, we can watch something else."

Jedao laughed. "And here I was thinking that you have much better taste in dramas than my mother."

She was disconcerted by the thought that Jedao had had a mother. She didn't know anything about his family.

"I'm told someone murdered her while I was being interrogated," Jedao said, as though he were reporting the number of cucumbers a battalion ate in a month. "My father was already dead. We were never close to begin with. My brother –" Suddenly the unsentimental voice became raw. "My brother shot his partner and their three daughters in their sleep exactly a year after Hellspin Fortress, then killed himself. And my sister vanished. Probably ran right out of the heptarchate. She was always the practical one."

"I'm sorry," Cheris said, because she couldn't think of what else to say. The servitors blinked lights at her inquiringly, then subsided. They continued to watch the drama in silence.

As the episode wound down, Jedao said, "You're not doing badly with Nerevor. She's expecting your nerve to crack and it hasn't yet."

"Jedao," Cheris said, "I'm stapled to a bigger threat. I'm worried about her, but when you get right down to it, my situation is already worse."

"Good," he said.

"Good what?"

"Be more assertive. You tend to defer to Nerevor. The problem with authority is that if you leave it lying around, others will take it away from you. You have to act like a general or people won't respect you as one."

Cheris frowned, but he was right. Feeling twitchy, she started doing some exercises. She was still dealing with having a stranger's patterns of motion stamped into her. The more she thought about ways to compensate, the more she fell over her feet.

On the fourth day at high table, as everyone finished the cinnamon-ginger punch with floating pine nuts that was the day's indulgence, Kel Nerevor leaned over and said, "I haven't seen you sparring with anyone since you arrived, General."

Nerevor had chosen day four – four for death, the unlucky lucky number that suicide hawks favored – for this conversational gambit. "I don't suppose you'd be willing to indulge me with a duel?" she went on. "Some of my officers have been speculating about your style."

It would have been terrible protocol to refuse, although it wasn't good protocol for Nerevor to ask, either. "I'll oblige you," Cheris said, because she liked dueling, "although I'm sure you've had more challenging opponents." This was bound to be true even without Cheris's current difficulty getting her body to cooperate. The servitors had told her that Nerevor enjoyed a fair deal of success as a duelist, and that her style was flashy and aggressive. She remembered Jedao's words on authority and added, "In one hour."

People were talking and eying her speculatively. Her clumsiness had not gone unremarked. Clumsy Kel were rare.

"This will be interesting," Jedao said once she was back in her quarters. She was never going to get used to how big they were. She didn't have to look at the general's wings on her uniform most of the time, but there was no escaping the rooms. "I had hoped your coordination would recover faster than this."

"Did your other anchors perform better in this regard?"

"Yes, but please don't think this reflects badly on you. I have an idea of what's going on, but it doesn't help you, and if I'm right you'll figure it out immediately."

"I hate it when you're cryptic."

"Well, you might as well warm up."

Cheris did so. Twelve minutes before the appointed time, she took up her calendrical sword.

When Cheris reached the dueling hall, Nerevor was already there. Nerevor's calendrical sword had a burnished bronze hilt with scrollwork in green: elaborate, but a cindermoth commander was entitled to it. A fair number of Nerevor's officers were there, including the Rahal captain-magistrate, Gara. Most of the Kel were intent. Shuos Liis had a seat near the front and was smiling openly. Cheris avoided looking at her.

"You're exactly on time, sir," Nerevor said. It was impertinent of her to make the observation, but she spoke with real delight.

Cheris raised an eyebrow. She couldn't help appreciating the other woman's forthrightness. "I trust best of five will do, Commander?"

"Of course, sir."

Four servitors marked the corners of the dueling rectangle, birdforms rather than deltaforms. Cheris bowed slightly to each of them as she took her place across from Nerevor. Nerevor raised an eyebrow, but didn't comment. The servitors might not divulge their names to humans, but service was still service.

Numbers flashed backwards, then forwards, as Nerevor readied her stance and activated her calendrical sword. Hers was fierce yellow-white. It was too bad they couldn't be allies. Under other circumstances Cheris would have enjoyed serving under someone with such obvious enthusiasm for the Kel cause.

Cheris's sword was blue and red. The academy instructors had assured them that the colors had no meaning, but people liked to speculate anyway.

"Count of four," Nerevor said.

The servitors made four clicks, perfectly synchronized.

Nerevor was fast. The blade leapt in her hand and took Cheris in a great slash across the chest while Cheris was still trying to work out what her feet were doing. The slash stung momentarily, but the blade wasn't in lethal mode.

At least Nerevor didn't humiliate Cheris with commentary, although her mouth pulled down in disappointment. She was unnecessarily cautious in the second round. Cheris suspected she was trying to squeeze out a more exciting victory. Although Cheris knew better than to slow down and think through her responses, she did it anyway. Her parries were soft and uncertain, and Nerevor tired of the exchanges and ran her through.

Well, this will be over with quickly, Cheris thought. She hated to make such a poor showing, even though Nerevor was legitimately better than she was. On the other hand, this was hardly the worst of her problems, so there was no use fretting over it. In a way, it was a relief to know herself so thoroughly outclassed.

As Cheris took up her position the third time, she smiled at Nerevor, feeling genuinely calm. Nerevor's eyes slitted, and a line formed between her brows.

Nerevor came at her fast again. Cheris stopped thinking through moves and counters and footwork, and simply reacted. There it was, that funny thing with her balance, but she let herself keep moving, aware simply of the necessity never to stay still. Nerevor wanted a flashy exhibition of sword-skill, but Cheris had no intention of letting her have it. She pivoted neatly, slipped under Nerevor's guard, and took her between the ribs at a precise angle.

"Point to the general, I believe," Nerevor rasped. "Really, sir, was it necessary to feign such incompetence?"

Cheris blinked at her, trying to connect what had just happened to what Nerevor was saying. She couldn't pretend she had been feigning – that would just be insulting – but she didn't think it would be any better to explain that she had surrendered to a dead man's expertise. "Fight harder," she said instead.

"I will indeed," Nerevor said, smiling.

Cheris won the last two rounds faster than she meant to. Apparently Jedao had believed in ruthless, decisive action. She was uncomfortably aware of Jedao's dueling record. He had only lost to one Kel.

Nerevor saluted her without any trace of irony. "I will remember not to underestimate you," she said. "This has been most informative."

"I'm honored to have faced you," Cheris said, because it was true.

People were staring at her shadow with its inscrutable eyes, but there was nothing to be done about that. Liis looked worryingly pleased.

Nerevor nodded, then walked off, looking cheerful.

"That was the thing," Jedao said the instant they were back in her quarters. "You kept thinking about what you were doing. Calculating. The body isn't about thought. It's about reflex. Especially in combat. You would have figured this out sooner if somebody had come at you with a real weapon, but I couldn't very well advise the commander to set her sword to lethal mode in a friendly duel."

"You could have told me," Cheris said, looking at her hands as she turned them over, palms down. They were the same hands she had grown into, but she kept expecting them to be larger, longer. She was momentarily convinced that if she took her gloves off, her hands wouldn't belong to her anymore. "Does this go away after you're not anchored to me anymore?"

"I don't have that information," Jedao said. Then: "You're not in a good mood."

"That obvious?" Cheris said.

"Seriously, what's bothering you?"

"It wasn't a fair fight."

Jedao's brief silence spoke volumes. "The point of war is to rig the deck, drug the opponent, and threaten to kneecap their family if they don't fold," he said. "Besides, you didn't use any resources Nerevor didn't know of in advance. She knew I was anchored to you. If she couldn't compensate for it, that's not your fault."

"That's a good way to save lives," she said, a chill in her voice.

They weren't discussing the duel anymore. "The faster it's over with, the fewer people die," Jedao said. "I realize you have delicate Kel sensibilities, but please accept my advice. You can't leave advantages lying around, either, or people will use them against you."

"I'll keep that in mind," Cheris said stiffly.

Jedao sighed, but didn't press the point.

On the nineteenth day, Cheris was reviewing the New Anchor Orientation Packet, hoping for clues on how to handle Jedao, when the chime came. "Commander Nerevor requests your presence," Communications' voice said. "Scan indicates possible guardswarm contact."

"I'm on my way," Cheris said.

"We're going to try to coax some information out of the enemy," Jedao said. "You're going to have to talk your swarm commanders through it. Be ready."

The cindermoth realigned itself briefly so she could reach the command center more quickly, although the savings in time was a matter of seconds. Cheris entered and looked around. Nerevor was pacing.

"General," Nerevor said with a rapid salute. "I don't like it.

There's something peculiar going on with the formation effects, probably the jinxed calendricals, but that looks like a full defense swarm and it's moving to intercept."

"Let me see the formation data," Cheris said. Scan routed the information to her terminal. She looked through the decay coefficients, then set up some preliminary computations, frowning to herself. "Doctrine, what do you have on the rot?"

"Summary or equations, sir?" Rahal Gara asked.

"Equations," Cheris said. Subvocally, she said, "Jedao, you need to tell me what the plan is or we're going straight to the fight."

"We can't surprise them," Jedao said, "but we can confuse them. Listen, they have to have some plan beyond sitting under siege for, what was it, thirty years? They won't have supplies for that long. They must expect a relief force to make their heresy viable. It could be a conspiracy, but whatever Captain Ko's suspicions are, I don't think the hexarchate is quite that lax. Which leaves foreign intrigue. Pretending to be their allies might do the trick."

Cheris started to say, *But that's treason,* then reconsidered. "We can't act like a foreign swarm! They know what Kel moths look like. And we don't even know who they're expecting."

"True, but we can be the next best thing: opportunistic domestic allies. Just be prepared to be firm with your officers."

"There it is," Scan said. "See that odd formant in the readings, sir? That's got to be a rot effect, and I'm convinced it's keeping me from getting a closer look at the lead warmoth."

Cheris looked up from the fever-tangle of equations and numbers long enough to ask, "They've transmitted no banner?"

"We should be so lucky," Nerevor said. "Should we transmit ours?" She had reason to be enthusiastic even about the null banner: once banners had been exchanged, battle could be properly joined.

"Not yet," Jedao said. "They know we're here, but the banner is additional information. We want to give it when we can provoke a response we can read for clues, and they're too far away. Now would be a good time to explain to Nerevor that we're going to try a ruse."

"Commander," Cheris said, "when they're close enough for scan to give us better detail, we're going to try to trick some information out of them. Communications: warn the swarm commanders of the same."

"How very Shuos," Nerevor said, "but orders are orders, sir."

"I heard that," Jedao said, a little testily.

Scan and Doctrine consulted with each other, and agreed that the guardswarm was 1.7 days out from the effective range of the Fortress's shields.

"That swarm isn't out here for defense," Nerevor said. "It's here to scout us."

"Have you hailed it?" Cheris asked sharply.

"We were awaiting your instructions."

"Good," Cheris said.

"I hate tripwires," Nerevor said, "but why so close to the Fortress proper?"

"We need to get closer," Cheris said. "Look –" She mapped the calendrical gradients. "The fractal boundaries are a mess, but we can't define them better without active probing and that'll take too long." She pointed out the key equations. "There, there, and there. If you solve for the roots and iterate –" She demonstrated. The map updated itself accordingly.

"My guess is they're hoping to meet us in that yellow zone," Jedao said. "They've got something planned for the phase transition."

Cheris concurred and relayed the assessment.

"I didn't know you were Nirai-trained, sir," Nerevor said, scrutinizing Cheris.

"Mathematics was my specialty in Kel Academy," Cheris said patiently. She had known this would come up.

"Trip the wire?" Nerevor said. "Or lure them out here?"

"We need information," Jedao said. "We need to take the hit more than they need to make it."

Cheris didn't like the idea, but there was no getting around the fact that they had to crack the Fortress, and that meant getting past the guardswarm.

"I'd ordinarily scout them right back," Jedao added, "but go in with the whole swarm. I saw the grid data on how fast you tested calendrical effects against the Eels on Dredge. You can take them by surprise."

"Sir?" Nerevor said at what she perceived to be Cheris's inattentiveness.

"I was consulting with General Jedao," Cheris said, since she couldn't keep a secret of it. "We're going in with the full swarm to see how they react."

Nerevor was clearly ill at ease with the decision, but said only, "What formation?"

Cheris plotted it out. "That one."

Rahal Gara double-checked the formation, as it didn't belong to Lexicon Primary. "Sir," she said, "that's going to have vulnerabilities at three pivot points. I assume you're doing it for speed of modulation."

"Yes," Cheris said, pleased that Gara had figured it out. To Nerevor, she said, "Do it."

Nerevor confirmed the order. Cheris had expected to feel something when the communications chatter began, but all that came to her was a glassy calm.

"Prepare a message," Jedao said. "Plain text, no audio, no video, nothing. Don't pass it over to Communications yet. I find the Kel react better – sorry, Cheris – if you just take things out of their hands. It would be better if I could record it myself, but oh well."

"I'm listening," Cheris said.

"This is Garach Jedao Shkan –"

It had never occurred to her to wonder what his name had been before he became a Shuos.

"– and I have a score to settle with the hexarchate. You'll need allies to hold out until help arrives, because I know how to get past the shields. Call off your guardswarm so we can talk, or I'll make a point of sharing the trick."

Cheris entered the message and squinted at it. "They can't possibly fall for that."

"The beautiful thing about that message is I'm not bluffing."

This gave Cheris pause. "You're serious?"

"Even the Shuos occasionally tell the truth, I hear."

Nerevor was talking to some of the composites. Cheris watched, then said to Jedao, "What do you think of her command style?" People were largely ignoring her.

"Very hands-on," Jedao said. "I see why you like her. She's combative, but she gets involved. I also suspect she's erratic, so use her accordingly." Interestingly, he didn't sound as though he approved of her himself.

"You never stop analyzing people, do you?"

"There are worse habits to have."

"They're accelerating toward us, sir," Scan reported. "Toward the phase transition zone."

"We'll meet them there," Cheris said.

They couldn't see the Fortress directly on scan due to the shields, although it stamped its calendrical influence throughout space as distinctively as a fingerprint. Cheris imagined it staring at them like a winter eye, cold and cunning and infallibly patient.

The Kel swarm served to meet the guardswarm, each moth oriented in accordance with formation logic. Although Cheris knew better, she kept expecting the world to change around her in response to the calendrical rot: for the walls to run like water, the light to shiver into turbulent colors, the sounds of human voices to shred into the cries of migrating birds. But that was the trouble: you had to use exotic effects to analyze the rot. If quotidian human physiology had much sensitivity to calendrical effects, the hexarchate would have destroyed itself with its own technology base.

The minutes trickled past. Cheris could almost feel them creeping down her spine. Silently, she thanked Jedao for keeping quiet.

"We're 13.4 minutes out of dire cannon range," Weapons said. "We're unlikely to hit with the erasure cannon at these speeds."

"All right," Jedao said intently, "maneuver until we're twenty-five seconds out of dire cannon range at present speed, then transmit the message along with our banner. Such as it is."

Cheris passed on the instructions.

Communications swiveled to stare at her. "Sir, are you –"

"You have your orders," Cheris said. "Tell the swarm: hold formation."

"We're masquerading as *what*?" Nerevor said. "Sir –"

Communications indicated queries from other moth commander as well. Cheris's command panel lit up accordingly.

"I'm not taking questions," Cheris said. "The order stands. Any response from the guardswarm?"

"Correlating formants with the previous assault swarm's signatures, sir," Scan said. "The bannermoth in the lead is *Ungentle Paragon*. The one at the next pivot point might be *Forever Minus a Day*, but the formants keep changing around so it's hard to be sure."

"I went to academy with the commander of *Forever*," Nerevor said in outrage. "I can only hope he gave a good accounting of himself for his moth to be taken from him like this."

"I wouldn't make any assumptions about who's commanding that bannermoth," Jedao said.

"Enemy swarm has bannered," Communications said.

"Let's see it," Cheris said.

The banner was a white wheel with seven spokes, not the hexarchate's six, and a golden flame in the center. Cheris remembered what Subcommand Two had said about central integers.

A murmur went around the command center. "Well," Nerevor said, "they're not making any attempt to hide their heresy."

"Liozh," Jedao said, very quietly. The seventh faction, which had been destroyed for its heresy. Cheris hoped she had misheard him.

"Thirty seconds out of dire cannon range," Weapons said.

"Message and null banner transmitted per instructions," Communications said just after that.

"They're shifting formation in response," Scan said. "We may be able to catch a glimpse – that's odd." The marionette bit off a curse. "There only seem to be five moths in the swarm."

"Of course," Cheris said, angry with herself. "Look at those pivots –" Those pivots, those coefficients. "They maximized their scan shadow. Unless they're feigning low numbers by feigning high numbers" – baroque, but you could never be sure – "that might mean they only captured five moths." Had the rest been destroyed?

"They're transmitting a message to the Fortress," Communications said. "I'm dumping it to the crypto team, but this is military-grade and we don't have the session keys, so it'll take time to see if there are vulnerabilities."

"Let's see if the Fortress responds," Jedao said. "Someone over there might have an attack of nerves."

Were the heretics really going to believe the preposterous claim that they could break the shields?

Jedao said, "*Wake up*, that's not a standard –"

Cheris spotted the incoming object in the scan summary.

"That's a bomb!" Scan said. "Don't understand the trajectory. It's going to catch more of them than us in the blast radius."

Anomalies never worked in your favor. Especially since the five-swarm was moving toward the bomb, not away from it.

The bomb went off. It did not, in fact, catch any of the Kel swarm in its radius. It did, however, encompass the entirety of the five-swarm, in a sphere of rippling light the color of broken glass, and it shifted the moths around in a dizzying swirl.

The Kel swarm was now surrounded by a kaleidoscope of phantom bannermoths, a hundred of them. Only five of them were real, but the phantoms could undoubtedly do some kind of damage. Cheris immediately mapped the symmetries: it was a radial force multiplier, it was probably only going to last as long as the bomb's radiation lingered, and if they didn't come up with a counter, they were going to be nailed full of holes by a numerically superior force.

CHAPTER NINE

"SO THAT'S WHAT they were up to," Jedao said.

Cheris couldn't spare the effort to talk to him. Instead, her fingers flew over the terminal. "This formation, *now*," she said. It was only going to buy them a little time. Shield effects were usually short-lived, and that didn't take into account phase transition modifiers.

"They're testing us," Jedao said. "Time for a show of force. Destroy them."

She needed an objective. The enemy swarm would react if she threatened the Fortress, so she needed to get closer. Distance was her lever. Not only could she force them to react in defense of the Fortress, she could nullify further use of the kaleidoscope bomb by getting too close for them to use it without also multiplying the Kel swarm. Twenty Jedaos, what a terrible thought. But the multiplier should only work on straightforward weapon effects, not people.

Cheris sent her intermediate computations to Navigation, with instructions to calculate the final movements.

They started taking hits. The formation shields blossomed like fever-flowers in Kel gold. Cheris instructed Weapons to return fire according to a preset pattern. Weapons looked like it wanted to protest, but Nerevor glared at it, then returned to coordinating the other officers in support of Cheris's orders.

Cheris wished that she was crowned with eyes so she could take in all the data that were skittering across her display, but she had to make do with the eyes she had. Jedao seemed content to leave matters in her hands.

The kaleidoscope swarm's movements revealed dependencies: all phantoms of a given moth tended to move in the same way. From the variable strength of the effect, she could figure out which of the moths were the originals; the phantoms looked too similar for scan to distinguish them directly.

"Coordinates for the originals," Cheris said, passing on the information. "Focus fire on One –"

The Kel swarm moved in, shifting to regenerate the shield effect.

"Cheris!" Jedao said. "Vidona Diaiya's up to something."

"Formation break, sir!" Scan said at the same time.

Cheris caught herself before she hissed a profanity. What was it with her and formation breaks? Besides the fact that Kel luck was always bad?

"Message from Commander Diaiya," Communications said, and played it back at Cheris's nod.

Diaiya was smiling. "Let me sort that out for you, General," she said, with too much emphasis on Cheris's rank.

White-red enemy dire cannon fire pierced the shields at the formation break. Vidona Diaiya's *Starvation Hound* had changed facing even though she had no dire cannon on that side to bring to bear. One of the boxmoths, Kel Nhiel's *River Full of Stones*, took a crippling hit to its engine.

Commander Nerevor was shouting at Diaiya to resume formation, but the *Hound* remained obdurately silent.

And this, Cheris thought in a fury, was why the Kel rarely allowed non-Kel to rise to command: no formation instinct meant they couldn't be relied on to follow orders themselves.

"All units, reconfigure formation to exclude *Starvation Hound*," Cheris said coldly. Too late to save Nhiel's moth, but it had to be done.

The *Starvation Hound* had launched a large, stubby projectile out of what appeared to be a modified gunport. It exploded into a cobwebby cloud of spores. A good third of the kaleidoscope moths were trapped when the spores billowed into enormous fungal blooms, sickly pink-gray with violet undertones.

Seconds later, the *Hound* was written over in words of fire, ash, failure.

"That skullfucking idiot killed all her soldiers because she had to show off her special toy," Jedao said savagely.

Cheris swung around to stare at Jedao, even if she agreed with him, but of course there was no one there but a shadow. People in the command center were giving her strange looks.

"How in the name of ash and talon did that fucking Vidona fit a fucking fungal canister on a fucking bannermoth?" Nerevor was demanding. "That shouldn't even be possible!"

"It's a little late to ask her," Cheris snapped. The fungal cocoon helped, she couldn't deny that, but they should have been able to win this without it, just with greater casualties. Besides, in the normal course of things, moths only came equipped with cocoons with direct authorization from Kel Command. She didn't look forward to explaining the incident to them.

"Both of you need to stay focused," Jedao said sharply.

Cheris glared at Nerevor, and the other woman returned her attention to the crew.

"Cheris," Jedao said after she had given the next set of orders. "Movement patterns. I can't prove it mathematically, but targets Three and Four are slaved to One, and Five is slaved to Two." He was referring to the actual enemy moths, not the phantoms; damage to the actual moths reduced the phantoms' firepower.

Four was partly blocked by the cocoon. They could deal with it later. Cheris asked Scan for confirmation about the others. Scan chewed over the data and agreed that Jedao was probably correct.

Cheris directed the swarm to focus fire on One. The Kel swarm compacted itself. The guns spoke again.

Two was next. Kel Paizan's *Sincere Greeting* took it out, opening a precise, narrow hole through the shield to fire through. The erasure cannon's kinetic projectile punched horrifyingly through Two's drive array. One of the bannermoths, *Auspicious Glass*, took damage from return fire before *Sincere Greeting* could close the hole, but *Glass* reported itself functional.

Jedao's hunch was correct: Three, Four, and Five ceased fire when One and Two went down.

Communications informed Cheris that Two had sent a final transmission toward the Fortress, based on trace emissions. Unfortunately, they hadn't intercepted the transmission proper.

To Cheris's dismay, the phantom moths didn't vanish, but they stopped firing when their sources fell silent.

"I don't recommend boarding, sir," Kel Nerevor said, scowling at the scan data. "Rigged to blow, like as not."

"Cinder them completely, except Four," Cheris said. "If scan can't go in or out of the shields, let's deafen them."

They carried this out cautiously, just in case, but nothing untoward happened.

"Sir, I have an incoming transmission from the Fortress of Scattered Needles," Communications said. "It's text-only."

"Go ahead and read it," Cheris said.

"'Very impressive, General Jedao. If that's who you are. Prove yourself by penetrating the shield by 25:14 on the first day of the Month of the Moth.' They gave us the conversion to our calendar." Communications read that off too. The high calendar day was 1.21 of the heretics' days. They had set the deadline for four of their days from now.

"Send a bannermoth out of range," Jedao said. "Do it now. And send this message back to whoever it is: That bannermoth has orders to broadcast the trick of defeating the shields in the clear in all directions if anyone fires on us once we're in. If you have any more tests, direct them to Shuos Academy. I'm sure they're bored over there."

Cheris selected Kel Koroe's *Unenclosed by Fear* and gave it the necessary instructions. Koroe was supposed to be unimaginative but reliable.

"Let them think about that," Cheris said, agonizingly aware of Nerevor's worried expression. First things first. She sent a commendation to *Sincere Greeting* for its precise shooting.

Paizan responded almost immediately. "I don't like being at such close range, General," he said. "It makes the whole concept of distance weapons ridiculous. But in this situation there was no help for it."

"You did well," Cheris said.

Nerevor raised an eyebrow, and Cheris nodded at her. She expected that the cindermoth commanders would consider each other peers. "Next time I hope to take part in some dismemberment too," Nerevor said to Paizan. "That Vidona ended things too quickly, and against orders."

"You always were bloodthirsty, Nerevor," Paizan said, with what might have been affection, and signed off.

"Get me the cryptology team," Cheris said to Communications.

"General," Nerevor said, "you should be aware that crypto doesn't use composite work. They're more efficient working as individuals." Since she was discussing Nirai, this meant that the team's members were too cantankerous to composite effectively. "Do you want to address the whole team, or just Captain-analyst Nirai Damiod?"

"Just Captain Damiod. Are they working with the Shuos team?"

"I had given no such orders, sir."

"Give them now. If we have Shuos, we might as well get some use out of them."

"Ha," Jedao said.

Nirai Damiod's face appeared to the left of Cheris's display, with Captain Shuos Ko's just below it. Damiod was a thin, nervous-looking man with pale brown eyes in a darker face. Ko looked, if anything, more imperturbably bland.

Before Cheris even asked him to explain anything, Damiod said, with the air of a man used to simplifying explanations, "It's standard military encryption, usually called 67 Snake, based on a certain class of functions –"

"What class?" Cheris wondered just what kind of conversations he was used to having with Nerevor.

He peered at her. "Machiva-Ju quasiknot polynomials, to be precise. Ah – you have background in this field?"

"I have some general familiarity," Cheris said. Unfortunately, as with all good cryptosystems, knowing the specific system in use didn't, by itself, help them crack the ciphertexts. "You don't think there's hope."

"There's always *hope*, General," Damiod said, "but even if we hooked together the swarm's grid resources, we couldn't crack it by brute force. It'd be a weak system if it yielded that easily. No, our best bet is seeing if whoever encrypted the message made some kind of amateur's mistake or ran it on the wrong hardware or left some kind of fingerprint. Stupider things have happened."

"Cooperate with Captain Ko in your work," Cheris said.

"Easy enough," Damiod said.

"Sir," Ko said with a genial nod.

"Good luck," she said, and ended the conversation.

Cheris called up the gradient map and grimaced at it. "We're going to have to be more careful once we exit the transition zone," she said. "We have no idea how well any formations will work under the heretical calendar. Look at that sector. The Fortress's projections are remarkably stable. I don't like that."

"At least I trust there will be no more fungus," Kel Nerevor said. She was looking at the damage to Four. The fungus in question was lethal to humans if you were lucky, and caused unappetizing mutations otherwise. It would take a full Nirai decontamination team to deal with the afflicted bannermoth. "Waste of a good moth. With that junk all over it, it'd be cheaper to ram it into a star and build a new one from scratch."

"That's Kel Command's decision," Cheris said. "Doctrine, I want you to look at the data from the engagement and see what you can get me on the heretics' calendar."

"Of course, sir," Rahal Gara said.

Cheris closed her eyes for a moment. "Everyone switch over to invariant propulsion." Giving up the luxuries that went with the high calendar's exotics was going to be irritating. "We have to continue toward the Fortress."

"The shields, General?" Nerevor asked, as Cheris had known she would.

"There will be a briefing," Cheris said unemotionally. "Alert me if anything happens."

She left the command center before they could see her hands start to shake.

Fortress of Scattered Needles, Analysis
Priority: Normal
From: Vahenz afrir dai Noum
To: Heptarch Liozh Zai
Calendrical Minutiae: Year of the Fatted Cow, Month of the Partridge, make it Day of the Goose. I've always loved goose.

My dear Zai, don't pace holes into the floor with that scowl you always get, you'll give yourself wrinkles, but we might be in more trouble than I had figured. Not to be an alarmist, mind you! Still, it's best to be prepared. Sorry I missed you earlier – I thought I'd catch you at the firing range, but it appears I have terrible timing. You might be amused that Pioro still can't beat my scores, though. A little humility will be good for him.

The speed with which the kaleidoscope swarm was dispatched isn't the real issue, whatever those incompetents on Team Two claim. All the Kel would have had to do is wire some fancy composite work with Nirai specialists brought along for the purpose. I don't know about you, but if I were headed into a heretical calendrical regime, the first thing I'd do is round up some nice meek Nirai to crunch numbers for me.

Our dubious consolation is that composite wiring is useless under our regime. That's usually a disadvantage, but maintaining our hold on the Fortress is more important and you can only juggle day-to-day belief parameters so far. I've got people working on that, but it'll take time to shift the aggregate scores.

The true concern here is General Garach Jedao Shkan, Shuos Jedao, the arch-traitor, whatever he's calling himself these days. Let's go through the possibilities systematically, shall we? Either he's who he says he is, or he isn't.

If he really is Jedao, he could still be lying about why he's here.

You would think that the escape of the hexarchate's greatest traitor would occasion some kind of uproar, but the hexarchs wouldn't want to start a mass panic, and the communications blackout makes it hard to tell. It's barely conceivable he could have blackmailed his way into a Kel swarm.

On the other hand, if this is Jedao, he could be working for the Kel. It's said he's been well-behaved for them on past outings, but who knows how true that is. The Kel habit of wiping the memories of people who work with him doesn't help us, intelligence-wise. Jedao being a Kel pet would explain his possession of a Kel swarm, however, and be consistent with Kel shortsightedness.

My money is on the third possibility, that someone's using Jedao's name to scare us. I bet the Kel in that swarm are thrilled about this tactic. Notice how the Kel transmitted a null banner instead of the famed Deuce of Gears: that might have been a compromise. I doubt you could get any hawk in the hexarchate to serve under the Deuce, no matter the importance of the operation. The general is probably someone in disgrace, which is peculiar. This should be a juicy assignment for an ambitious commander, despite the ruse. People would have been fighting over it if the Kel admitted to anything as pedestrian as personal ambition.

Here's the thing. I've been reviewing the combat data from that engagement. The style is completely wrong. Don't misunderstand me. Our opponent is very competent, and we should be wary of them. But their approach was calculating, cautious. Team Two will argue based on the fungal cocoon that our opponent likes fancy technology, but you'll notice they abandoned the moth that released it: typical Kel, they don't like seeing too much initiative.

Anyway, do recall old lessons. General Jedao's campaigns are a matter of historical record. What stands out is his combination of aggressiveness and an uncanny ability to anticipate the enemy's thinking. His first battle against the Lanterners was notable because he was outnumbered eight to one and he still inflicted a decisive defeat on them. Thankfully, our opponent is not of that caliber.

I doubt even Jedao could finesse his way past the shields, whatever our opponent's recent boast, so it'll be interesting to see what transpires in the next four days. In the meantime, I had these delightful bonbons delivered from that confectionary the other day. I realize they're terrible for me, but what is life without a few indulgences? I sent some over even though I know perfectly well you're not going to try them. But your assistant likes them and it never hurts to have your staff happy with you.

Before I forget, you should get on Stoghan's case about holding on to the communications post in the Anemone Ward. Delegation to qualified subordinates and all that, but I don't care how many supporters he has, his military skills are better on paper than in fact. I wonder if the loyalists are trying to warn Jedao off or to warn the hexarchs about Jedao, but best not to give them a chance to say anything if you can help it.

Yours in calendrical heresy,

Vh.

CHERIS WASHED HER hands in hot water, but they wouldn't stop shaking.

"You'll be fine," Jedao said. "Have a drink of water. That always helped me."

"I hate being so obvious."

"I almost threw up after my first battle in space. I thought it would be different because the corpses weren't in front of me. But there's something terrible about that dry metallic click that indicates a hit. They've changed it since then, but for me it's always that click."

Jedao added, when Cheris declined to answer, "I've seen a lot of young officers through a lot of awful situations. That's all it is."

She poured herself a glass of water. It tasted cold and empty. After drinking it, she said, "I had expected you to –" She fumbled for a better way of expressing herself. "Take charge."

"Why?" Jedao said. "You didn't fight the way I would have, but that doesn't matter. You won. I brought relevant items to your attention, but since you were doing your job, it was in everyone's best interest for me to shut up and stay out of your way. I have watched a lot of junior officers get ruined by their superiors' refusal to allow them the least bit of autonomy."

Interesting. Maybe he wouldn't have been a completely horrible instructor after all. As odd a thought as that was. "You feel strongly about this."

"There's no point asking people to risk their lives for you if you aren't going to trust them in turn. Surely Kel Academy still teaches that."

Cheris conceded the point. "I have a briefing in two hours," she said. "You need to tell me about the signifier tests and how we're getting past the shields. With a time limit, no less."

"Yes, that's fair," Jedao said. "I know one thing about the Fortress that you don't, and it's because I once attended a live-fire demonstration of the shields' effectiveness. They didn't explain how the shields worked, but the shields produced artifacts in the human visible spectrum, nowhere else. I'm not a technician, far from it, but I found that curious. Too convenient."

"I'm not sure how that helps us," Cheris said. Of course, she wasn't a technician either.

"If I'm right, the visual chaff is the key to understanding the shield operators. Who are human. The system can't be grid-controlled – although maybe it can be composite-controlled?"

Cheris was sure the answer was no, but queried Doctrine to double-check. The answer came quickly. They must have figured it out beforehand and it had probably been sitting in some report awaiting her perusal. "No composites in the heretical calendar," she said.

"So we're dealing with humans. Think of this as an exercise in decryption. Once we crack the language of symbols, we'll know how to break the operator and force our way in."

"Jedao," Cheris said, "do you have any idea how computationally expensive it is to crack any decent cryptosystem? Even one this old, if it hasn't been done already?"

"You're thinking like a Nirai, not a Shuos or Andan. I doubt the shields were designed this way on purpose. My guess is that the chaff is an unavoidable side-effect of the technology, which is why they're so keen to hush it up."

After an agonized silence, Cheris said, "I need a demonstration. I can't take this to our officers. Especially after I've asked them to masquerade as traitors. But I don't see how you can possibly make a demonstration before the fact, either."

"All right," Jedao said calmly. "Pick something up, something small, and hold it in your hand, Cheris."

"What?"

"You asked for a demonstration."

This was the kind of pointless game that the Shuos were notorious for. One of her colonels had once remarked that a Shuos would never tell you something straight out when they could force you to take an agonizing snaky route to the conclusion by manipulating you with word games. "I don't see –"

"Do you want the demonstration or not?"

Cheris bit back her first response and went to get her luckstone. She slipped it free of its chain. The stone shone in curves of light interrupted by the raven engraving. "All right," she said. He had better not be wasting her time.

"You're going to hold on to that stone," Jedao said. "Consider that an order, if it helps. I'm going to convince you to let it go before the briefing."

Cheris was already unimpressed. What was he going to do, arm-wrestle her for it with the arm he didn't have anymore? "That's all?" she said. Then, grudgingly: "I see. The stone is the Fortress. My hand is the shields. This won't work, Jedao. Even if you have some way of making me fail a simple task, I can't persuade our commanders like this." She was pretty sure the Kel commanders would have much the same reaction she was having. Except they would be less polite about it.

"Oh, we're not going to bother with rocks –"

"It's a luckstone," she said, more sharply than she had meant to, even if she couldn't imagine that Jedao knew anything about Mwennin custom. It was her birthday-stone, a gift from mother to child, and the raven was the bird of her birthday-saint. Little things that she never discussed with other Kel, because they wouldn't understand.

"My apologies," Jedao said promptly enough. "In any case, with the officers we need something bigger. We've already made an example of Vidona Diaiya –"

"That was ordinary discipline!"

"Don't let go."

Her fingers clenched around the luckstone, then relaxed.

"If it had been to our advantage to save her for future use, I might have advised that instead," Jedao said. "But that wasn't the case. No, we need a new target."

Target? They were out of hostiles for the moment, unless he wanted her to order up more. Where was he going with this?

"We can't demonstrate on the Fortress because that's what we're trying to persuade the commanders we can do in the first place," Jedao said, "so we'll have to demonstrate on our swarm. We can afford to lose a moth. Diaiya was going to be my expendable, but as it so happens she torched herself before I could make use of her that way." His voice was utterly level.

Cheris had a creeping feeling at the back of her neck. How had she forgotten he was a madman? "Diaiya disobeyed orders and broke formation, that's one thing," she said, "but the other commanders have done nothing wrong. They don't deserve to be toyed with." Assuming he only meant to toy with them, which she had serious doubts about.

She was now remembering, too, his earlier comment about having a use for Diaiya, back when they'd selected her for the swarm. At the time it had slipped her mind as being nothing important. The knot in her gut told her she had been terribly, terribly wrong.

"We can't afford any weaknesses when we go up against the

Fortress," Jedao said. "The swarm has to be ready to obey, and to believe in our methods, whatever they are, even if I'm involved. Not only did the heretics capture the hexarchate's most celebrated nexus fortress, they had help. That kaleidoscope bomb wasn't developed and manufactured overnight. In any case, to unite the swarm, we need them focused on an adversary. Framing one of your own commanders for heresy ought to do the trick."

Cheris was speechless.

Jedao's voice cracked without warning. "My gun. Where did I put my gun? It's so dark."

Cheris bit back a curse. This had to be a ploy, even though she couldn't see what an undead general would be getting out of playing a bad joke. "Jedao," she said, trying to sound composed and failing, "there's no need –"

Not only was the shadow darker than she remembered it being, Jedao's eyes had flared hell-bright, and the entire room was heavy with darkness like tongues of night licking inward from some unseen sky. Cheris's mouth went dry as sand. She'd seen combat before, she'd fought before, and all she could do was freeze and stare like a soldier just out of academy.

Where was her chrysalis gun? There it was at her waist, that unmoving weight. She had to reach for it, had to unfreeze –

"General." Now Jedao was coolly imperious. "I don't recognize you, but your uniform is irregular. Fix it."

She had no idea what had caused him to go mad in the first place, no one did, so she had no idea if he was going mad again. She lost a precious second wondering inanely if snapping a salute would mollify him, then unfroze and fumbled for the chrysalis gun. Just in case.

The nine-eyed shadow whipped around behind her in defiance of all the laws of geometry it had obeyed until now, and then she knew she was really in trouble. All that time she had spent reading up on her swarm's high officers and what intelligence they had on the enemy – some of it should have been spent researching *Jedao*.

"You shouldn't be standing still," he said. His voice was casual, as though he addressed an old friend. "They'll get you if you stand still. You should always be moving. And you should also be shooting back."

"Shooting who?" she said, struck by the awful thought that this was how he had gone crazy at Hellspin Fortress.

The shadow moved slowly, slowly, pacing her. Perhaps if she kept him talking she could buy time, even figure out what was going through his mind.

Jedao didn't seem to hear her. "If you keep waiting, all the lanterns will go out," he said, his voice gone eerily soft, "and then they'll be able to see you but you won't be able to see them. It'll be dark for a very long time."

Lanterns. The Lanterners? Hellspin Fortress? Or some coincidence of imagery?

The gun was in her hand. She aimed at the shadow, but it was too fast. If she fired, would it send up alarms? She didn't want to start a panic in her command moth for no reason. She nerved herself and did it anyway, but the shadow anticipated her and whipped out of the way. The gray-green bolt sparked and dissipated harmlessly against the floor. Her next attempts fared no better. Cheris wished the Nirai had warned her that shooting Jedao wouldn't be simple.

Despite the shadow's movements, he didn't sound like he noticed that she was trying to shoot him, either. "You brought a whole swarm here," he said, voice rising. "They have no idea. It's going to be a million dead all over again."

If this kept up she was going to have to aim the gun at herself, terrible hangover or not. But then she'd drop the luckstone; there was still some chance this whole thing was an act. Then why wouldn't her hands cooperate?

This would be much easier if she knew him well enough to tell whether this was an aggressively irresponsible mind game on his part, or a genuine sign of insanity. *Stop hesitating,* she told herself angrily. She knew better than to dither like this.

Jedao fell silent. In spite of herself, Cheris hoped that Jedao was done testing her, that he would call the game off. She wasn't cut out for this. She was about to ask him when his voice started up again.

This time he sounded unnervingly young, half an octave higher, like a first-year cadet.

"General?" he said.

He wasn't speaking equal to equal this time. He spoke with deference. Fear, even.

"Sir, the dead. I can't keep count. I don't, I don't – sir, I don't know what to do next." The eerie thing was that she couldn't hear him breathing, despite the raggedness. When he next spoke, his voice wavered in shame, then firmed. "It's my turn to die, isn't it? I just have to find my gun in the dark –"

A long silence.

And then, quite softly, "My teeth will have to do."

Cheris had seized up again, trying to tell herself this was a trick, that it had nothing to do with Hellspin Fortress, or worse, some other incident she couldn't remember out of the history lessons she had stupidly failed to review. But this time she was sure. She aimed and fired again, fruitlessly.

"Cheris." His voice no longer sounded young, and Cheris sensed he was finally in earnest. She half-turned toward the source of the sound, which was across the room from the shadow. Everywhere darkness hung like curtains of sleep. There were starting to be amber points of light not just in Jedao's shadow, but everywhere, in the walls, in the air, everywhere, like stars coming closer to stare. She had no doubt that when they did, they would reveal themselves as foxes' eyes.

Jedao recognized her again: he spoke to her as a subordinate, and formation instinct began to trigger. "Not that way. Or that way, either, if you're thinking to escape. You're about to swing left. No, don't freeze, that's even worse."

In the swarm of lights she couldn't figure out what to shoot. His speech, rapid but precise, now came from several directions at once, which only confused her further.

He was half-laughing. "You keep reacting, and you're reacting with *my reflexes*, don't you think I know what you'll do?"

Her hands clenched. Another bolt hissed against the wall, to no effect. It wasn't just the sudden cool malevolence of his voice, or its authority, it was that his reflexes were a part of her, he was *in* her, she couldn't get him *out*.

On the other hand, if this wasn't just a game, if this wasn't pure pretense, then she might be able to trigger his madness and use it against him. Too bad she couldn't get him to shut up so she could think clearly –

"You're determined not to drop the gun, but look at your hand shaking – there it goes, and you're still fixated on that stupid fucking luckstone. Reprioritize. What's the real threat – where's the real game? Go ahead, pick up the gun, try again."

Cheris couldn't make his voice go away and she couldn't stop reacting like him. As a Kel, she couldn't help responding to the orders, either. She was going to go ahead, pick up the gun, try –

Jedao started to laugh in earnest. "I'm going to enjoy watching you die, fledge."

The Kel called their cadets that, or inferiors who fell out of line. All her muscles locked up in spite of her intentions. The luckstone felt leaden in her hand. She had taken comfort from it since her mother gave it to her. It gave her none now.

"You have no idea whether that gun works as advertised on full strength," Jedao said contemptuously, "or how it works if it does, and you never asked. The Kel don't get smarter, do they? Go ahead, pull the trigger."

The Nirai technician wouldn't have lied to her –

She knew nothing of the kind.

"Think about the name of the gun, fledge. You know what a chrysalis is. Where do you think they *put* me when it's time for retrieval? I have to go into a container, and your carcass is handy. Remember that despite the fact that I'm a traitor and mass murderer, one of us is expendable, and it isn't me."

It was horribly plausible. She fired again, but wildly. Sparks; a dance of staring eyes. Again and again. No better luck.

"Honestly, Captain," Jedao said, biting down on her usual rank, "if this is a typical example of Kel competence, no wonder Kel Command keeps using a man they despise utterly to win their wars for them."

Cheris tried to make herself keep firing. Couldn't. The shadow revealed itself next to the door, the nine eyes arrayed in an inhumanly broad candle smile. She stared at the shadow and felt herself falling into it, toward the pitiless eyes. They were opening wider: she thought she saw an intimation of teeth in them. It was worse that he had called her *captain* rather than *fledge*, that naked reminder of Kel hierarchy. Her nerve shattered: too much strangeness all at once. "General," she croaked. "I didn't mean to – I don't know what you want, sir, I don't understand the order –" She was talking too much, but she couldn't seem to stop. "I failed you, sir, I'm sorry, I –"

"Cheris." The eyes dimmed, rearranged themselves into the more familiar line.

"– can't figure out –"

"Cheris! I'm done. It's over."

"Sir," she whispered like a broken thread, "what are your orders?" Her fingers crept toward the chrysalis gun. She made them stop. What if he wanted something else from her? She couldn't bear the thought of getting it wrong again.

"Cheris, sit down," Jedao said gently.

It took her two tries to take a step toward the chair. But the general wanted it, so it was an order, so she would do it. Wasn't that how life went, in the Kel?

"I'm a hawkfucking prick," Jedao said. Cheris flinched: hawkfucker, fraternizer. "I didn't realize how badly formation instinct would affect you. You had conflicting orders. The fault isn't yours."

"I *am* Kel, sir."

"I know." His voice dipped tiredly. "I misjudged. No excuse."

She had no idea how to respond to that, so she kept silent. He was her superior. He demonstrably knew how to break her. And yet she was supposed to be able to judge him and kill him if necessary. How did Kel Command expect a Kel to be able to deal with this? The fact that he was always present, always watching her, only made it worse.

"Cheris. Please say something."

She would have bet that he was sincere, except she had thought the same when he was pressuring her to shoot herself. "The chrysalis gun, sir." Some use it had been.

"I wasn't entirely lying about that. It forces me inside and puts us both in hibernation. I don't know whether it does permanent damage to you. I'm never around for that part."

That would have been useful to know much earlier. Naturally, the Orientation Packet hadn't mentioned any such thing. She didn't know why she had expected it to be more helpful. But then, she had gotten herself into this situation, hadn't she?

Cheris focused on the in-out of her breathing until she felt calm enough to think clearly again. She put the luckstone on the corner of the desk. It made a small click. "I'm done with your game, sir," she said flatly. "You win."

"Oh, for love of −" Jedao checked himself. "At the risk of alienating you forever, I have to point out that you lost the moment you agreed to play the game on my terms, without negotiating."

This was typical Shuos thinking, but she couldn't disregard it. "You weren't serious about playing games with the swarm, sir?"

"I seem to recall someone arguing that the commanders didn't deserve to be toyed with. No, I wasn't serious, but it was plausible that I was, wasn't it? Think about that."

She frowned. "Was it worth doing that just to make a point?" She was looking at the luckstone.

"You have the lesson backwards, Cheris. The luckstone is incidental. I don't have hands and I can't hold a gun. When you agreed to be my opponent, what weapons did you think I had?"

"Your voice," she said at once, but she had missed the important one. "Your reputation."

"Yes. We've already told the heretics that I'm facing them."

"Garach Jedao Shkan," she said. Her voice was unsteady. Maybe they should have bannered the Deuce of Gears after all, so the enemy would know to dread them.

"Anytime you want me to feel like my mother caught me harassing the geese again, go right ahead," Jedao said with unexpected humor. "In any case, reputation: it's an awful tool to have, but you can't escape it, so you must learn to use it."

"I understand, sir," she said. She did. They didn't call Jedao a weapon for nothing; and fear of weapons was a weapon in itself.

"Do you?" Jedao said. "Then you're ready for the plan. Here's how it'll go."

CHAPTER TEN

KEL NEREVOR WAS about to say some banal greeting when Cheris showed up at the command center. Instead, Nerevor stared openly, then drew herself up, her face grim.

Cheris wasn't wearing her gloves. Both were tucked into her belt. Her hands felt cold and clammy and exposed. The combat knife also at her belt was too heavy, too light, for all that she was used to it. She reminded herself that this part was her idea, even if Jedao had agreed it would work.

"General," Nerevor said.

"The briefing," Cheris said. She didn't want to have to repeat herself.

The ranks of moth commanders blazed into life. Cheris scanned them, trying to get an overall impression of their reactions. After her last time doing this, she knew that attempting to track every individual would just fluster her. Better to set herself a smaller goal and hope that Jedao picked up on whatever she missed.

Cheris inhaled, then began. "We're going to force a breach in the shields." Mouths opened. "No, I'm not taking questions. You're here to listen."

Jedao didn't bother telling her most of them were skeptical. She could figure that out herself. "Shuos Ko is taking you seriously," Jedao said, "but then he would. Kel Paizan and some of the bannermoth commanders are worried we're going to pull a second Hellspin."

Cheris went on. She couldn't pause every time Jedao said something. "The shields have a weakness. They rely on a human operator who can be made to falter. You will receive further instructions when we begin the siege. I have knowledge you don't, and we still don't know how or why the Fortress fell. I won't risk that information falling into enemy hands."

On the word "hands," she unsheathed the combat knife, then retrieved her left glove. The knife was sharp in the way of bitter nights. Cheris made a show of sawing off each of the glove's fingers in turn. They fluttered to the floor, looking like hollowed-out leeches. When she was done, it looked like a ragged imitation of Jedao's fingerless gloves, the kind no one had worn since his execution.

The silence could have swallowed a star.

She put on the amputated glove, then cut all the fingers off its mate. She put that one on, too.

"I give the orders here," Cheris said. "We have already seen what happens when a moth commander falls out of line. I will not tolerate any further lapses in discipline. I trust I have made myself understood."

Cheris didn't dare glance back at Kel Nerevor, but a muscle was working in Kel Paizan's jaw. Colonel Kel Ragath looked amused, of all things.

"Say something," Jedao said. "Don't let up."

"You are thinking," Cheris said, "that this can't possibly work. But the fact is that out of all the great and terrible weapons in the Kel Arsenal, Kel Command saw fit to send us a single man. If you cannot trust in Kel Command, you are not fit to be Kel."

It was a gamble saying this to officers who had, in some cases, served longer than she had been alive, but the argument felt right. It was a Kel argument, an appeal to authority.

They looked at her in silence.

"Acknowledge," Cheris said.

"Sir," they said in one voice.

She wondered what Shuos Jedao could have achieved in life with the Kel united behind him. His soldiers had loved him; the histories were mercilessly clear on this point.

"We will continue our approach to the Fortress of Scattered Needles along a favorable gradient," Cheris went on. "Because of the changing calendrical terrain, we will be forced to use nonstandard formations. I have transmitted the orders giving the coordinates and the preliminary formation keys. In the meantime, I expect everyone's reports on the recent engagement in two hours. That's all."

It was a relief when the salutes were replaced by the colorful chatter of status graphs.

Commander Nerevor's eyes were deeply troubled. "The – fingers, General," she said. "What are your orders?"

"Just dispose of them," Cheris said. She felt ill about the gloves herself, but she had needed the symbol. Besides, if she ever recovered from her present disgrace, she could always acquire a new pair of gloves.

The hush around her spoke something of fear. If that had been her intent, why was her stomach knotted up?

CHERIS WAS IN the command center when Commander Nerevor alerted her that they were an hour out from the shields. "Look, sir," she said, gesturing at her scan readouts.

The scan didn't show them the Fortress proper, as it couldn't penetrate the shields. The grid showed a simulation of the Fortress's position, a whorled mass of curves and lines like ink spun solid. The adjacent display showed the facing hemisphere, with subdisplays to pick out key features in the hexagon-pentagon facets.

As Cheris watched, flickers of pallid glowing shapes lit the shields: feathers, leaves, the fractured hearts of river rocks, bullets, stormclouds. She might have stood there forever, entranced by the unexpected beauty of the patterndrift.

"The unvanquishable Fortress," Nerevor said in a colorless voice. "Your orders, sir."

"Deployments as follows," Cheris said. She checked each one, not for the first time, before sending it to Communications. This would be one hell of a time to discover that she'd transposed two digits. Jedao had looked over them as well, but she was determined to make sure.

They had put together the tactical groups based on their best estimates of who would work well together. Already the losses hurt, small though they were. *Starvation Hound* was gone, and the damaged *Auspicious Glass* had to be used carefully. There was no help for it. The numbers wouldn't repair themselves.

Tactical One was led by *Unspoken Law*. Tactical Two was led by *Sincere Greeting* under Kel Paizan, and Tactical Three was led by the senior bannermoth commander, Kel Rai Mogen with *Red Stitch*. The six remaining boxmoths were distributed two to a group. Since they couldn't predict the breach's location, they had to be prepared to secure a landing point with infantry. Just as importantly, the Shuos infiltrators were on standby; once they were injected, they could begin gathering local intelligence.

The moths repositioned themselves as indicated. Fire coverage wasn't going to be an issue until – if – the breach was made. There was no particular reaction from the shields.

Cheris said, "In 8.26 minutes" – ten of the heretics' minutes, at the start of their hour –"switch formations: Six Towers Six Banners, and open fire according to the given firing pattern." She sent it to Communications. "I don't care what you see out there, adhere to this exactly. Scan, copy Captain Ko on everything. I want the Shuos team's analysis."

There was the slightest flicker of leafwrack and searush foam in the shields when the Kel moths eased into position. Six Towers Six Banners was nominally a defensive formation, although it was relegated to Lexicon Secondary because of its weakness. The Kel occasionally trotted it out when they wanted something visually impressive for parade flybys.

"Open fire," Cheris said, since the commanders would want confirmation. The acknowledgment indicators lit up bright gold on her terminal.

The targets had been randomized. The shields flared up in hot-cold colors, bright but fading quickly.

"I didn't expect that one to draw a response," Jedao said. "Just let the Shuos map the chaff for a baseline. Switch in 8.26 minutes, as we discussed."

Cheris gave the next set of orders. This one wasn't technically a formation. Her palms felt damp. How long would the Kel stand for this? *Be steadfast,* she reminded herself, and heard Jedao's voice in her head. She was almost used to it already. How could her officers be strong if she faltered?

"Sir," Nerevor said, "this would be the pivot framework of a grand formation if we had exactly *seventy-nine* more moths to fill the rest up –"

The grand formation Nerevor was referring to was Glory of Roses. "New firing pattern," Cheris said. "On my mark." She consulted the terminal's clock. The moths took up their positions, absurd long triangles on the display. "Mark." Gold lights again.

This time fire blazed up in a definite pattern, lines and swirls of light outlining the familiar shape of the Andan kniferose. The colors were wrong, no help for that, and this wasn't going to work either, the shields were – wait.

"Replay first six seconds of shield response," Cheris said. "One-tenth speed."

There it was. A fractional delay, as the operator pieced together the pattern. Then the shields glimmered with a tempest of roses falling, petals pierced by curving thorns. Interspersed with the roses was a curious figure, three dots arranged in a triangle, each oriented so the apex pointed toward the Fortress's primary pole, and each lit up balefire-red. No holes in the shield, however.

"The pictures *mean* something?" Nerevor said.

"Not an Andan," Jedao said, "but a definite reaction. The operator identified the grand formation and reacted to it, so they have some background in space tactics. Of course, that could be anyone who watches the right dramas –"

"Sir," the Communications officer said, "it's Captain Shuos Ko.

Says he has something for you."

"I'll hear him," Cheris said.

It was too much to hope that Ko ever looked less than imperturbable. "General," he said. "How familiar are you with Shuos security suites?"

"I'm not," Cheris said.

"Oh, this will be interesting," Jedao said. "I bet they look completely different now."

"Five years ago, the standard interface was overhauled in accordance with new Rahal guidelines, something to do with calendrical adjustments," Ko said. "The old symbol for high alert was a red chevron. It's now the triangle of dots with all three lit up. Whoever is working the shields has recent security experience."

"Good man," Jedao said. "I wouldn't have known that."

"Thank you," Cheris said to Ko. "Anything else?"

"That's all, sir." His face winked out.

"Run through the following signifiers in this order and tabulate results," Jedao said. "Kniferose Thorns Wild, Pierced, Burning Sweetly."

Cheris was increasingly convinced that the Fortress was going to open a hole in its shields to fire at them, even though the heretics had nothing to worry about yet. Still, the chaff shifted with a responsiveness that she could only describe as human.

They set up the pivots for the next ghost formation, which with a grand swarm of ninety-three would have been Carrion Strike. They patterned the Rahal scrywolf to accompany it. Cheris looked over her shoulder at Rahal Gara. The other woman's mouth was pale, compressed.

The shields didn't react as strongly this time, although some chaff manifested anyway: a brief glimpse of the high alert triangle, the dendritic shapes of coral, the occasional glassy hexagon. Flickers of numbers. Gara confirmed that they were consistent with what they knew of the heretics' calendrical keys.

Jedao laughed shortly. "Definitely not a wolf. A wolf's mind would be better-disciplined. All right. Hunting Alone, Uncircled, Trapped in Glass, Ambushed."

Cheris wondered what he was looking for. The signifiers changed the chaff, but the shields didn't show any signs of going down.

Next was the Shuos ninefox. It scarcely produced any result, as if the shield operator had gotten bored. Cheris was expecting Jedao to try the signifier Crowned with Eyes, which he was known for, but he chose four others.

They went through the three low factions according to schedule: Kel, Nirai, and finally Vidona. With each one, the chaff dwindled until it became faint smudges, the shapes hard to guess even with interpolation.

"Now what?" Cheris asked subvocally, watching Nerevor pace.

"I hate my hunches sometimes," Jedao said. "Marketing and demographics. I might have guessed."

She hoped he would explain that to her sometime.

"For the next one, we want to use pivots from the grand formation Skyfall. The firing pattern should sketch the Web of Worlds. Not the basic mirrorweb emblem, but specifically the Web of Worlds."

Cheris plotted it out, but had to refer to the archives to make sure she had it right. Surely the heretics weren't really thinking of reviving a dead faction?

"One more, General?" Nerevor said. She was still pacing. "If we could just get the shields down –"

Cheris tried to remember what she knew about the Liozh as she relayed the order. It wasn't much. The details of the heresy had been suppressed. Kel Academy hadn't had much to say about it, as most military actions against the Liozh insurrectionists had been sufficiently one-sided as to be, as one instructor had put it, "militarily uninteresting."

The significance of Skyfall was easier. General Jedao had used it to devastating effect against the Lanterners at the Battle of Severed Hands.

Cheris was jolted back into paying attention when Scan called, "Pinpoint breach at –" He gave the coordinates. Seven more appeared in rapid succession.

"Scan," Cheris said, but Scan was already working. "Focus fire on the pole spine. We want to scare the operator."

Between the chatter in the command center, Nerevor's terse orders coordinating the tactical group, occasional status alerts from the moth commanders, and Jedao's hellishly confident voice, Cheris could hardly hear herself, let alone shape a thought of her own.

An opening formed to permit return fire. The swarm dispersed to avoid available angles of fire. The two cindermoths' erasure cannon slung their projectiles one after the other.

"Pull up the dictionary of signifier responses we've compiled," Jedao said. "This will hurt. Tactical One and Two, nail the Deuce of Gears onto surface structures." His personal emblem. "They can do what they have to as long as the pattern is recognizable. Cheris, ask them to sort the dictionary on antonyms. Have Tactical Three fire on the shields, not the breaches. Every time they see chaff, they're to hit with the antonym. A fast response is more important than a certain one. Make sure Commander Rai Mogen is clear on this."

Nerevor frowned at the orders when Cheris gave them. "Sir," she said, "that's practically bannering the Deuce –"

Cheris flexed her half-gloved hands to draw attention to them. "We're using the arch-traitor," she said. "We've admitted as much. If his reputation benefits us, we'll keep using it. The order stands."

Nerevor's mouth was tight, but she didn't protest further.

Tactical Groups One and Two began hammering the Deuce of Gears on the Fortress's armor with weapons at twenty percent. It was hard to see the gears as anything but a large circle and a smaller one, the teeth obliterated to nubs, but in context Jedao's emblem was clear.

The red triangles showed up at greater and greater scale, lightning flashes of anxiety bleeding across the shields like a haywire fractal gasket.

"There we go," Jedao said.

Guns spoke from the Fortress, a beam raking Kel Shan's *Trading in Solstice* from a momentary opening, then fell silent.

Tactical Three was still responding to the maelstrom of chaff – fissures, broken teeth, bridges swaying dangerously, red splashes – with the antonym attack. Cheris made herself breathe evenly despite the gasps and stutters in the images. She was finally convinced that, for whatever reason, the shields were tied to the operator's inner world, the knots in their heart. But why would you design a defensive system that –

"You've got to be shitting me," Cheris said. Nerevor stiffened, ready for new orders, but Cheris wasn't looking at her.

"Figured it out?" Jedao said, pleased. "Let's hear it. Subvocals. Although Kel Command is going to have to outprocess everyone anyway."

"How long have you known that invariant ice *isn't an invariant*?"

Before now, it hadn't occurred to Cheris that the shields were based on an exotic technology and that the heretics had simply designed their calendar to enable them to continue using it. After all, everyone in the hexarchate knew that invariant ice was an invariant.

"Lucky guess," Jedao said. "Sorry. Shouldn't be flip. Cheris, those shields aren't based on standard physical forces, no matter what the hexarchs say about technological breakthroughs. I'm no Nirai, but I know what the universe's laws look like, and shields like this? Never happen. This means they're an exotic effect. We also know that the Fortress projects a calendrical regime due to the nexus. It stands to reason that the shields take advantage of the same phenomenon.

"And this suggests that the shields are a projection of the operator's belief system. Not the beliefs of a group; the symbol system is too consistent and composites don't work here anymore. I can't see why else there would be chaff, or why Kel Command wanted to distract people from it. – Nerevor wants your attention."

"Sir," Nerevor said, "Scan is starting to get coherent readouts through the punctures."

Scan followed that up with, "More breaches above the Anemone and Radiant Wards, but – wait a moment."

The triangle pattern spattered the shields like summer wildfire. Tactical Three responded with the scrywolf Uncircled.

"How does this even –" Cheris started to say.

"Cheris, people are very simple," Jedao said. "You occupy the conscious mind with one thing, then drive a spike into the subconscious mind with something else while the walls are down. That's how we used formations just now. The operator was trained to pay attention to Kel formations, so that took care of their conscious focus, and now we've pinned them with my emblem, which they know to fear. The emblems on the shields – for us they're just time-lapse pictures, but for the operator, because the shields are an ego projection, we're tattooing words directly onto their brain."

"We're in!" Scan cried over Jedao's words.

For a merciful second Cheris felt nothing. But everyone else fell over like hingeless puppets.

The world was awash in colors, patterns, floating echoes of shapes she had seen in the shields. Leaf into feather into petal in great blowing drifts that passed through her hands. Fissures and fractures of peeling black. Sandglasses pouring themselves out.

Jedao was silent. Cheris looked at Nerevor, but Nerevor was curled up on the floor, wheezing something in a low language Cheris didn't recognize.

She couldn't waste time panicking. She rerouted Communications to her own terminal. "Get me Commander Paizan," she said.

After a long moment, the grid said in its crisp voice, "Commander Paizan is not responding."

She sent a general query to the moth commanders. Nothing.

"General Jedao," she said, remembering that he had called himself a shield, "where are you?"

Still no response.

She forced herself to breathe steadily.

The scan readout indicated that the Fortress's shields had splayed themselves outward like hands with the skin peeled off and nerves unfurled in all directions. Cheris lost another minute picking through the equations, trying to find out how all her soldiers had been disabled. Two people were screaming. She half-turned, tried to think of what she could do for them, then remembered the whole swarm was in trouble. She tried calling Medical. No luck there.

"General Kel Cheris to swarm grids," she said. "Override Aerie Primary. Slave all moths to *Unspoken Law*."

The responses stuttered back to her as the swarm moths acknowledged. Someone on Kel Liai Meng's *Essential Verses* had recovered enough to acknowledge verbally, but when she asked for his status, there was no answer. Fear bit her heart.

Nerevor was now trying to stand up, but her legs kept collapsing under her, and her eyes were unfocused. Cheris went over and settled her against the wall, telling her to stay still, but Nerevor wouldn't stop trying.

Sudden despair crashed over Cheris. She looked around the command center, and the knowledge of her failure was like a black knife. She was so tired, she had been in the darkness for so long, and she was fighting against long odds. If only she could fold asleep, just for a little space; and if only the universe had any mercy, she would never have to wake.

Cheris reached for her combat knife. She hadn't thought she'd have further use for it on a moth, but there it was. She weighed it in her hand, then brought it up to her –

"Cheris, stop it." It was Jedao, whispering as across a hollow distance.

"What happened to you?" she asked without interest.

"It hurts," he said simply. "Cheris, put the knife away."

"I failed," she said, "and all of it was for nothing."

"Cheris, I mean it." His voice grew sharper. "You're experiencing bleed-through. I'm sorry. But you need to put the knife away."

She didn't want to obey. It was tempting to close her eyes and use the knife anyway.

"The knife, Cheris."

Then she understood. "This isn't me," she said, jolted out of the despair. "It's you. How long have you been suicidal?" She sheathed the knife.

He had been a ghost for 397 years. She imagined that if there were a way for him to kill himself, he would have figured it out by now. Something she could use against him if he tried to pull mind games on her again.

"The bleed-through will pass," Jedao said coolly, "and you'll be all right. Prepare orders for the infantry and the Shuos infiltrators. The operator can't sustain the shield inversion – look at the scan. They're disabling the entire Fortress to get us. We'll have to endure."

Assuming the shields went down, they still had the problem of landing troops. She began setting up move orders, checking routes carefully to avoid collisions. It would be stupid to crash her own swarm.

Cheris heard thumping, and glanced back at Rahal Gara, who was going into convulsions. Gara wasn't the only one. "This had better end soon," she said.

Seven minutes and nineteen seconds later, the inverted shield dissipated completely.

A message came in from the Fortress. It said: "Very impressive, Garach Jedao. We'll have a use for you."

People were starting to recover, and they had a Fortress to conquer, but Cheris was remembering the knife. Jedao had claimed to fear being executed by the Shuos hexarch, but he was also suicidal. Something didn't add up. She could only hope that she figured it out before it came around to bite her.

CHAPTER ELEVEN

Fortress of Scattered Needles, Analysis
Priority: High
From: Vahenz afrir dai Noum
To: Heptarch Liozh Zai
Calendrical Minutiae: Year of the Fatted Cow, Month of the Partridge, Day of the Goose, and now we're down to hours or these reports will all look the same. How about Hour of the Locust? It seems appropriate.

All right. You know how much I hate to apologize. Well, I'm apologizing. I shouldn't have shouted at you. That was the point at which the meeting degenerated past all hope of usefulness. One of my instructors used to say to me that if I was ever about to lose my temper, do something productive instead, like draw hanged stick figures on my tablet where no one can see them, or think up death-traps using office chairs and nail clippers. I used to think she was being facetious but now I see that was good advice. If nothing else, I bet I could get Stoghan with a pathetically simple trap. He's very careless about personal security and I know you've noticed that too. (Don't worry. You think you need him, so I'll restrain myself.)

Anyway, I must impress this point upon you. My advice is only as good as the information I have to base it on. I don't take it personally when the enemy tries to deceive me. They are only behaving rationally. On the other hand, it hurts your cause when you keep vital information from me. I'm not talking about things like that Andan-certified courtesan that Stoghan is seeing on the side, whom he thinks I don't know about. I'm talking about things like the basic functioning of our famed defense system. If you knew the weakness in advance, why hide it from me?

You know the calculations as well as I do. Inconvenient arch-traitor or no, those shields were supposed to hold out indefinitely. We can't predict how long it'll take for the Hafn relief swarm to arrive. Even with considerable resources devoted to deceiving Kel Command, it's hard for them not to figure out that the Hafn might head here.

So much for external problems. Let's look at what's going on in the six wards. Right now the Anemone Ward is a mess. Each report from Stoghan is more incoherent than the last. The loyalists seem to be fighting quite effectively, but we can't allow them to hold the communications post.

I'm keeping an eye on atmospheric scores in the Drummers' Ward and the Ribbon Ward, so don't fret about public opinion fluctuations. We're still convincing your citizens of the importance of adhering to the new calendars and participating in this newfangled voting thing. No blunt methods. I've always despised the Vidona. Which reminds me, we've got to be faster at processing the Vidona detainees for release. Word will get out and that can only do us good.

The loyalists aren't anywhere near the routes to the command center, which is another reason to silence them quickly. I've always found it charming how your high language associates "silence" and "community." Where I come from, it's "silence" and "death."

I've got people hard at work in the Radiant Ward, mostly at that nitwit Stoghan's insistence. Admittedly we do want to keep a firm hold of that ward, so it's not all wasted effort, and it keeps him from hassling me when I need something from him. I promised I'd stop picking on him, but he's such an easy target. It's not clear to me why he has so many supporters in the affluent communities, but maybe if my family had been politically indebted to his for the past three generations I'd see the appeal. Not to say he's not a striking man, but sometimes one wants brains as part of the package.

Keep an eye on Gerenag Abrana. The good thing about Abrana is that she's smart, but the bad thing is that she's also ambitious, and given how badly we need her factories, we have to handle her carefully. The fact that she's been so meek lately makes me suspicious, especially since I'm convinced some of her agents have been poking around my offices. It'll be tempting to shoot any I catch, it's always good to keep your hand in, but probably more fruitful from a security standpoint to track them back to wherever they're scurrying from.

The Umbrella Ward is holding except that one blip in that popular game that's going around. Annoying as the Shuos are, they are correct that people can be manipulated through games. I'm about to consult Pioro as to how Doctrine can address the matter.

I'm sure you've got plenty on your mind, or if you didn't before, you should now. I'm off to steal Pioro. Keep me posted on any vital pieces of intelligence that fall into your lap, hmm?

Yours in calendrical heresy,

Vh.

CHERIS FELT WIDE awake, but it wouldn't last. Kel Nerevor had been one of the first to get back on her feet. She had taken over the Weapons terminal, as they had had to have servitors haul Lieutenant Kel Jai to Medical, and his replacement had not yet arrived.

The entire command center was awash with alerts demanding attention. Cheris reminded herself that the trick was to prioritize, no matter how insistent all of the lights were that they had to be addressed all at once. As it stood, you could be forgiven for thinking, based on the crazed quilt of red and amber lights, that the entire moth – the entire swarm – was in danger of crashing into some kind of space reef.

A small team of deltaform servitors were cleaning up the messes, small as they were: some blood on the walls and edges of terminals where people had fallen badly, although by some run of luck there had been no serious head injuries. Fortunately, this wasn't something that needed Cheris's intervention. When you got right down to it, servitors were frequently better at guiding themselves than the Kel gave them credit for, and they were being very quiet and very discreet, so as not to distract from the business of battle.

"I don't understand why the heretics aren't shooting, sir," Nerevor said in a rasp. "It's not like they'd be any more fucked than they already are."

"They're still figuring out who we are," Cheris said. But Nerevor was right. Besides the visual alerts, the staticky charts and diagrams and maps that she was monitoring with half an eye, there was the occasional audio alert, low deadened bell tones. Nothing that required immediate action, even though the displays on her terminal were growing more and more crowded. Each one made her flinch: she kept expecting a real emergency to come through.

"Something's going on in the Anemone Ward, sir," Scan said. He looked white around the mouth, but she never would have guessed it from his voice. Indeed, he sat at his terminal with a posture so correct she could only call it stiff, when even Nerevor was hunched over – just a little, with an attitude that suggested she was in pain.

"Double-check to make sure the Kel infantry are in null uniforms," Jedao said. "The Shuos will already be dressed appropriately." And: "The Kel must avoid being captured at all costs." If he noticed the chaotic state of the command center, there was no sign of it in his voice. But of course, this sort of thing was nothing new to him.

Cheris sent the orders in. She wished the air were less dry, less hot, that she could have a glass of water; but in all likelihood she was flushed from the stress of the situation, and she would have to wait until she could leave the command center, like everyone else. Minutes peeled past.

Captain Ko called the command center. She almost missed it because Engineering was sending a series of updates on some situation involving the invariant drive, except she saw the blinking Shuos eye call indicator before Jedao had to bring it to her attention. "Sir," Ko said, "we couldn't get it released to us earlier, but there should be a list of qualified shield operators. Kel Command might release information to you now that the shields are down and the secret's out. Just be careful of the timing: the heretics will be suspicious if they catch us chatting with Kel Command. Besides," and his voice went dry, "it's not as if Kel Command won't have to drill state secrets out of our heads. My compliments to General Jedao, sir." That was all.

"How generous of him," Jedao said, just as dryly. The shadow's eyes, to Cheris's side on the floor, were narrowed.

Cheris quirked an eyebrow.

"I'm sure you Kel find Shuos infighting very amusing."

Cheris composed the query, then saved it with a reminder to send it when their ruse was blown.

"Would rather be shooting, sir," Nerevor said moodily. She was drumming her fingers on the arm of her chair.

"We can't take out all their guns fast enough to clear a landing corridor for the hoppers," Cheris said.

"I know," Nerevor said, and sighed. "Wait for an opening in the situation and all that."

Cheris rechecked the hopper logistics, on the grounds that she might as well do something. Her mouth felt more dry than ever. She bet she wasn't the only one. *Later,* she told herself. In the meantime, she was getting better at blocking out some of the lower-priority alerts and reorganizing her displays so the most important status indicators were available at a glance. The grid was supposed to do this automatically, but its judgment was sometimes skewed.

Five hours and thirty-nine minutes later, it happened. Cheris had gone for a brief rest and felt better for it, to say nothing of the cool water she had drunk, and was now back in the command center.

In the infantry she had envied moth soldiers the controlled environment, the easy availability of baths and water, air that didn't choke you with dust or scorched metal or cooked flesh. Now that she was in a cindermoth, she missed having to watch where she put her feet; she missed the light of swollen suns instead of the patchwork red-and-amber, she missed the wind cutting into her eyes.

"Sir!" It was Scan, who looked badly like she wanted her shift to end. "Explosion near the communications post in the Anemone Ward. Minor armor breach."

"Tell the boxmoths all hoppers on standby," Jedao said.

Cheris began giving orders. The boxmoths *Autumn Flute* and *Six Sticks Standing* contained the Shuos infiltrator teams. It was imperative that they get the infiltrators into the Fortress so they could start figuring out where the heresy came from and how to stop it.

"Prepare another transmission," Jedao said once she had finished. "Garach Jedao Shkan. We're going to hand you back that communications post, but you should learn to hold on to your toys. I'm sending you an extra gift as a token of my goodwill. Enjoy."

Cheris entered the message more or less automatically, then stared at the bright columns of text. "What do you mean, 'gift'?"

"A hostage," Jedao said. "A high officer, a moth commander for preference. Someone they'll recognize from public records."

"You're out of your fucking mind," Cheris said. "I'm not feeding the fucking heretics one of my officers."

"Cheris, listen to me. We have to inject those infiltrators. We can't shoot our way down there. The Fortress has too many guns, and I'm good, but not that good. If you can't go through a problem, you have to go around it. The heretics haven't fired because they're uncertain, but they're not stupid enough to let us land troops unless I convince them that I'm not, in fact, a Kel general with an unusual taste for dirty tactics. I have to convince them that I'm really Garach Jedao and that I offer them an advantage."

"I'm still not –"

He kept talking. "The heretics are teetering right now because I took down the shields, yet there's no way I could charm or bludgeon my way into a Kel swarm after escaping, let alone a swarm with two cindermoths. We're going to leave the story to their imagination, because they're right. I couldn't do it. But they need to think I did.

That's why we have to send a commander to suggest the story to them. It's something the Kel would never do, but I might. The Kel don't fight like that."

"Damn straight," Cheris said. "Because we're not doing it."

"Very well then, fledge." Jedao's tone was formal, and a hot flush crept up the sides of Cheris's neck. "What is your proposed alternative?"

That brought her up short. She didn't have one. "Pull back and blow down the defenses with all the bombs we have," she said.

"I'm happy to evaluate an alternative plan," Jedao said, correctly ignoring what she had just said in desperation, "but there has to be something to evaluate."

Cheris had an overwhelming desire to punch him. "Fine," she said. "If you're so fucking determined to send someone, send me."

"Unacceptable," Jedao said. "Now you're reacting, not thinking, and when it comes to strategy, thought must trump reaction. If any records exist of you in the Fortress, they'll have you down as an infantry captain. You're too insignificant to be of any use as a hostage. At the same time, as my anchor and the current general, you're too important. I can't help the swarm if you're drugged in a cell somewhere. Besides, your shadow and reflection will tell them what's going on."

"I can't ask this of my officers!"

"Sir," Nerevor said in a dead even voice. She had come out of her chair and was facing Cheris, eyes narrowed.

Cheris realized that she had been shouting.

Everyone had heard her half of the argument.

"Sir," Nerevor said, more insistently. "What's the dispute?"

Nerevor shouldn't have asked, but it was entirely like her to do so. Besides, it was too late to pretend the dispute hadn't taken place. Cheris said, "General Jedao believes that we need to send the heretics a hostage to persuade them not to fire on the hoppers. The hostage would have to be a high officer to be convincing."

"Not something any Kel general would do, but something a crazy vengeful Shuos would do, am I right?" Nerevor said, nostrils flaring. "Because we can't hide the fact that these are Kel moths, so we have to pretend that we were overwhelmed or blackmailed." She didn't sound like she thought that was far from the truth. The rest of the command center was very still.

"Yes," Cheris said.

Nerevor lifted her chin. "Then I'll go, sir. You won't do better than a cindermoth commander."

With winter clarity, Cheris realized she had been manipulated into losing her temper so this conversation would take place. "Hawkfucking prick," she said to Jedao, remembering the subvocals this time. She studied Nerevor, resisting the urge to glare at the shadow.

Jedao didn't deny the charge. "She'll need to be wiped," he said. "Get Medical to inject her with full-strength formation instinct and revert her to fledge-null. Fastest way to make sure they don't get intelligence out of her."

"You'd have to be wiped, Commander," Cheris said. "Are you sure –"

"You're wasting everyone's time," Jedao said.

"I understand that, sir," Nerevor said steadfastly. "I am Kel. I will serve, even if this isn't the service I anticipated when I was assigned to your swarm."

"Report to Medical," Cheris said.

"Sir," Nerevor said, saluting sharply, then turning on her heel.

Cheris put the orders in to Medical. Her hands shook, and she felt coldly knotted inside. Going into a firefight would have been better than this pallid safety. Then she nodded at Nerevor's executive officer, Lieutenant Colonel Hazan, who had been listening intently, mouth pursed. "You're acting commander," she said.

Hazan saluted her sharply, seemingly calm. But a tremor passed through the crew.

"Communications," Cheris said, "send this message to the Fortress." She passed it over.

"Hoppers still on standby, sir," Navigation said, without quite looking at her.

"They'll hold until Commander Nerevor is ready," Cheris said. "Tactical One and Two, prepare covering fire but await my command. Scan, what is the Fortress's current status?"

Scan said, "There's a lot of –"

"Sir!" Communications said. "Outgoing message from the Anemone Ward, in the clear and in all directions."

Cheris said to Scan, "You first, but make it fast."

"There's a fight by the communications post," Scan said. "Not definitive, but signatures are consistent with Kel small arms and possibly civilian weapons. No major structural damage to the post. Physical breaches sealed with metalfoam. Toxics in the spectral lines indicate the explosives were class four, but I'm not seeing more of those."

"They want it intact, too," Jedao said. "Hardly surprising."

"Inform Colonel Ragath and the infiltrators," Cheris said. It was vague, but something was better than nothing. Out of the corner of her eye she watched the colors change around her, red to brighter red, red to fox-yellow. "Communications, give us the message."

Thanks to the exchanges between Jedao and the heretics' leader, Cheris had expected plain text. The video took her by surprise: something was wrong with the hologram, and even interpolation had left tracks of snow and cinders in the colors.

"Andan Nidario to Kel Command." The man had a warm, rich voice, but the entire right side of his face was a mass of bruises and burns. The act of speech must have been painful. "Hell, to anyone who's listening." He canted his head to listen to someone off-camera. "Shuos Jedao is loose and has battered down the Fortress's shields. Send someone to deal with him, will you? I mean, he might be on our side, but he's opened negotiations with the heretics, so I find myself unoptimistic. I'm appending our observations, but we're not going to be able to hold the communications post for long."

More commentary from the side, then: "Andan Lia would like to add that we don't have confirmation that it's Jedao. Frankly, he blew down the shields in hours, that's enough evidence for me.

"When you get here, shoot that tin general Znev Stoghan first. He's been with the heretics since the beginning." The rattle of gunfire. "Oh hells, somebody cover the door, will you? Excuse me, I'd better pick up a gun and make myself useful before the painkillers wear off. Just do something with the information, that's all I ask. Nidario out."

"Dump the whole thing to Captain Ko," Cheris said.

Hazan said, all black humor, "I'm glad we're not responsible for spin control, sir. The Andan are usually more discreet, but I suppose he was desperate." He showed no sign of discomfort at being in Nerevor's chair: the right approach, even if it nettled her.

"I killed that man," Jedao said, not amused, but without regret either. "However, we can only rescue the loyalists if we have troops on site, so the fact that he's helping my credibility with the heretics is useful."

"You expected something like this to happen," Cheris said slowly. Why was she surprised?

"I believe in planning ahead. The loyalists have no way of knowing I'm here on Kel Command's orders and there's no way to let them know. When I announced my arrival, it wasn't just to intimidate the heretics. It was to provoke the loyalists into revealing information, which would persuade the heretics in turn. And it forced your swarm to adjust to the fact that they're being led by a madman and traitor."

"That's a lot of objectives."

"It's only three, and the last one is marginal. You want to accomplish as many different things on as many different levels as you can with each move. Efficiencies add up fast."

"Call from Medical," Communications said. "Commander Nerevor has been prepared, sir."

"Load her onto Hopper 1 with the others and send her on her way," Cheris said, hating herself. In a just world she would feel sick, but instead it was as though she stood outside herself, in a world turned to iron and crystal and cryptic facets.

"It's done," Navigation said after an agonizing eight minutes. "Hopper 1 launched."

"Launch the rest," Cheris said.

More waiting. Cheris's guts churned. She was starting to think she would see the color red in afterimage flashes, as she walked out of the command center – if she ever did – and even in the hallways of her dreams.

No; she had to be honest with herself. What she would see over and over was Nerevor's face as she volunteered to do exactly what Jedao wanted her to do, what Cheris had let her do.

"Fortress retrieving Hopper 1 with servitor teams, sir," Scan said. Her voice wavered. "More fire in the Fortress, source uncertain, but no serious damage to the hoppers."

"Instruct Colonel Ragath that loyalists are to be returned to the heretics unless they turn on him," Cheris said. "He's to send urgent status reports only."

"The colonel acknowledges," Communications said after a pause that was longer than Cheris liked.

"Nerevor will suffer very little," Jedao said then, "although I won't insult your intelligence by claiming she's safe. In fledge-null she will only know that her duty is to endure until a Kel officer gives her instructions, and only an unscrupulous Kel will be able to damage her mind. I judge it unlikely that the heretics have Kel among them. Your people do loyalty well."

Cheris put pieces of a puzzle together in her head. The pieces didn't match up. When he had first been anchored to her, he had asked about formation instinct almost as if he had no idea. Subvocally, she said, "For someone who affects not to know much about formation instinct, you're awfully familiar with its workings."

The last of the hoppers was starting the return trip. Cheris wished she was on one of them, away from the cindermoth and the ninefox's dreadful shadow. Her shadow. Strange how she could distinguish its eyes so easily from every other amber light around her, even if they were the same color.

"Think about it, Cheris. I learned to judge soldiers' morale and loyalty when the Kel were individuals. Why would it be hard for me to figure out the *standardized* version?"

Then the game with the luckstone, Jedao taunting her to shoot herself, his show of penitence –

"That's right," Jedao said. "I knew exactly when you'd break. I needed to make a point and it was the fastest way."

Cheris kept hold of her temper, remembering how she had lost Kel Nerevor. "If you were lying about that all this time, why reveal it now?"

Was it a new game? And here she had thought she was done being a web piece. At the moment she could have happily incinerated Shuos Academy.

"Because I know you're worried about her."

She stiffened. "I doubt you ever cared about your soldiers," she said.

His voice was rough. "People say that about me, yes. I won't argue."

"Commander Hazan," Cheris said abruptly. "I'm going to rest. Alert me immediately if there are new developments."

"Of course, sir," Hazan said.

Cheris knew perfectly well that she couldn't escape Jedao in her quarters. She had a better idea.

CHAPTER TWELVE

"IT'S NO USE," a man was saying. "Look."

Nerevor was staring straight ahead at a gray wall, in a room of gray sodden shadows. Restraints of cold metal held her fast, and the shift they had given her was too thin. Her shoulder hurt, and something about her jaw felt wrong, but it was only pain. She was Kel. She would survive as long as it was given her to survive.

"Your name." It was the man again, impersonal.

He was not Kel. She did not have to answer.

This time a woman spoke. "We already know who she is."

"That's not the point. The point is getting her to respond."

"In that case, scare up a uniform and try again."

"She'd know the difference," the man said. "There's a baseline body language that's imprinted on cadets along with formation instinct, subtle stuff. A good Shuos infiltrator could fake it. An Andan could enthrall their way around it. We're just stuck. She'd break all the bones in her body to please a Kel officer, but we're short of those. Jedao was making sure we were getting nothing but a warm body with the commander's face attached, and he can undoubtedly restore her, but we can't. At least the DNA matches records. Cold bastard."

Nerevor wasn't sure what Shuos Jedao had to do with the situation, but she made a note of the mention in case it became useful later.

"He said nothing about wanting her back," the woman said.

"Probably got all he wanted out of her or he wouldn't have dumped her on us."

"Don't get ideas." The man's voice was still impersonal. "We can get the technicians on the problem and see if they can work her out of fledge-null. There's a small chance useful information's buried behind those glassy eyes. We can hold her as long as it takes."

The woman had been thinking about something else. "Doesn't a high officer have to authorize fledge-null in the first place? Who the hell did the Immolation Fox subvert up there?"

"Subvert or bribe or coerce," the man said. "We don't know which."

"I'm surprised you wanted to talk in front of her. You're normally obsessed with discretion."

"I wanted to see if there'd be a reaction. Depending on where in the calendrical zones he wiped her, the fledge-state might have chinks. A problem for the technicians, as I said." The man tapped on the door. "Anything you want to say, fledge?"

Nerevor didn't like being called "fledge" by this stranger, but it didn't matter. He was not Kel. She did not have to answer.

After they were gone, she listened for gunfire, footsteps. If the Kel meant for her to die here, then she would die here. But she could not help but comfort herself with the idea that her people would come for her if she was brave enough, if she endured enough, if she proved herself worthy of the Kel name.

Fortress of Scattered Needles, Analysis

Priority: Urgent
From: Vahenz afrir dai Noum
To: Heptarch Liozh Zai
Calendrical Minutiae: Year of the Fatted Cow, Month of the Partridge, Day of the Hedgehog, I need to program some macros, and fuck the hour.

My dear Zai, I don't care how hypnotized you are with Jedao's potential usefulness, and I don't care how everyone *voted*, although it's nice that you're practicing. Assuming it is Jedao, which seems more plausible now, he behaved nicely for Kel Command up until Hellspin Fortress, and he behaved nicely for Kel Command up until now. You'd be better off trying to befriend a fungal canister. It might have a sense of loyalty.

I understand that you're rattled by the continued delay of the Hafn swarm, but do remember they have to get past General Cherkad. I assure you that Hafn commitment to the Fortress's liberation is real, but they need time to achieve miracles. The timing is unfortunate, but if we'd waited any longer to take over, the Rahal would have caught us.

At least we have something in common with the fox general, which is that we both prefer the Fortress to stay intact, or he would have lobbed a few thousand bombs at us once the shields cracked. As it is, we could hold off bannermoths for a while, but the cindermoths change the equation.

Unfortunately, you allowed Jedao to land troops. We knew this hostage – one Commander Kel Nerevor, formerly of the cindermoth *Unspoken Law* – was going to bring us little immediate advantage. It was expensive to retrieve her from the Anemone Ward, and we didn't even get her intact because that goon of Stoghan's roughed her up.

The communications post in the Anemone Ward is back in our hands and Jedao's troops even handed over the loyalists, but I'm bothered by Jedao's resources. I threatened some videos out of Stoghan's lackeys, and those aren't just infantry he landed, those are Kel. I don't care if they were wearing brown instead of black-and-gold, those are Kel.

You know the joke, right? If you have a choice between sending a three-year-old to do covert ops and a Kel, you pick the three-year-old because the Kel is too stupid to lie?

Anyway, where did Jedao get these Kel? If we're dealing with a legitimate Kel swarm, if Kel Command gave Jedao command – but how did he convince the Kel to surrender one of their high officers? Any other general would be able to rely on formation instinct to shove the order through, but I'm not sure Jedao would inspire that kind of obedience unless he explicitly got Kel Command's blessing. Yet this seems more likely than the other possibility, which is that the least trustworthy general in Kel history convinced at least one Kel high officer to join him. That's the problem with formation instinct: if he turned the right individual, he could have taken down the rest.

The thing is, Jedao isn't just a traitor, even if people's brains short out around that fact. He's also a Shuos. The two aren't equivalent, despite the Shuos jokes. He was a Shuos assassin before he switched tracks, and there's circumstantial evidence he did some analyst work as well.

Anyway, his career with the Kel was unobjectionable. He kept that up for almost twenty years. As if he were under deep cover. All the way up to Hellspin Fortress.

Hellspin Fortress wasn't a Kel assault. The Kel wave banners at you before they join battle. You can always see them coming.

Setting up a deathtrap for not one but two armies – that's not a psychotic break. That's a plan with a twenty-year setup. A Shuos plan, to be precise. Ambushes, computer systems going haywire, contradictory orders, weapons failing. To say nothing of the infamous threshold winnowers. Too much fancy shooting with his staff, but it worked.

No wonder the Nirai have made no progress. They've been trying to cure Jedao, but he was never mad to begin with.

I'll go you one better. He's exactly where he wants to be. He's immortal and he has all the time in the world to carry out his plot, whatever it is. I don't know why he slaughtered his way into the black cradle. But I will bet you my last sweet bean pastry that even the incomprehensible slaughter served some purpose.

And we're the next step in his plan.

Zai, we've got to stop him. We've got to destroy him because I don't care how many Kel swarms we have incoming, he's the real threat.

I haven't felt this alive in ages.

Yours in calendrical heresy,
Vh.

CHERIS PACED THE perimeter of her quarters, determined not to get used to their size; determined to remember what she really was. Then she asked for a slate because she wanted something solid in her hands. A deltaform servitor brought her one: a black slab just thick enough to feel substantial, gold-rimmed so that it winked as she tilted it. The servitor made a worried noise. "I'll be all right," Cheris said, and it left after an unconvinced pause.

"You could have asked me about the hostage idea earlier," Cheris said, "while there was time to come up with alternatives."

"You could have anticipated the issue," Jedao said. "The landing problem shouldn't have taken you by surprise. You had the same time that I did to come up with a solution. Do you have a better one now?"

Her eyes stung. She had relied on him instead of thinking for herself. "You have the advantage of being an observer," she said sharply. "But no. I don't have a better plan now."

"Cheris."

She closed her eyes, thinking of Nerevor's bravery. Jedao had told her that the Kel reacted better when given no time to object to a plan. Fair warning.

"I saw a solution and set it in motion. That's all."

There was no way to escape his voice.

"I saw how badly you wanted to go in Nerevor's stead. She saw it too, you know. That's why she was willing to sacrifice herself."

"I didn't want to manipulate her into it," Cheris said.

A soft pause. "All communication is manipulation," Jedao said. "You're a mathematician. You should know that from information theory."

"I am not fit to serve," she said.

"Cheris," Jedao said, "you're Kel. You will serve as long as Kel Command needs you to. That's all there is to it."

"You're so good at making the Kel follow where you lead," Cheris said. "How can I trust anything you say?" She raised her tablet and entered a query.

It wasn't difficult to bring up the available transcripts of Shuos Jedao's service. Even though she knew how well-regarded he had been, even though she had studied some of his campaigns, the number of deaths he had inflicted before Hellspin Fortress took her breath away. The Kel had known many generals, and he had been one of the best.

It only took a moment's extra ferreting to find the people who had died at the Siege of Hellspin Fortress, heretics and heptarchate soldiers both.

"All right," Jedao said quietly. "All of my anchors do this sooner or later."

At this remove of time, the statistics weren't precise, but the Kel historians had done what they could. The swarm that Jedao had led against Hellspin Fortress had not been small even by modern standards. His orders had told him to conquer the fortress so the Lanterners could be converted and the calendar repaired from the damage done to it.

Cheris read the number of the dead once, twice, thrice. A fourth time; four for death. Even so, she knew that she didn't understand numbers, that a number over a million was a series of scratched lines and curves. If she heard tomorrow that her parents had choked on their soup and fallen over dead, it would hurt her more than the deaths of people who would have died anyway generations before she was born. Nevertheless, she started reading capsule biographies in reverse alphabetical order.

She read about two sisters who died trying to veil the dead after the custom of their people. Their reasoning had probably been that it might staunch the threshold winnower's radiations, which was not illogical, but wrong anyway. She read about a child. A woman. A man trying to carry a crippled child to safety. Both died bleeding from every pore in their skin. A woman. A woman and her two-year-old child. Three soldiers. Three more. Seven. Now four. You could find the dead in any combination of numbers.

Faces pitted with bullet holes. Stagnant prayers scratched into dust. Eye sockets stopped up with ash. Mouths ringed with dried bile, tongues bitten through and abandoned like shucked oysters. Fingers worn down to nubs of bone by corrosive light. The beaks of scavenger birds trapped in twisted rib cages. Desiccated blood limning interference patterns. Intestines in three separate stages of decay, and even the worms had boiled into pale meat.

Two women. A man and a woman. A child. Another child. She hadn't known there were so many children, even if they were heretics, but look, there was another. She had lost count already despite her intent to remember every one.

I remember every ugly thing I have ever done, Jedao had said. But Cheris wondered. It was impossible that he could remember causing all of this to happen without feeling all those deaths crouching at his side.

Cheris couldn't bear the silence any longer. "Say whatever you mean to say," she said.

"I know things about the victims that aren't in the records," Jedao said. He might have been standing right next to her, as a lover would: too close. "Ask me."

She picked a foreign-looking name from the list. She was sure it belonged to a Lanterner. Her hands sweated inside her gloves.

"You're thinking I couldn't possibly say much about a Lanterner," Jedao said, "but that's not true. They were people, too, with their own histories. Look at where she died – yes, that's a reasonable map. The Lanterners were desperate. They had tried using children and invalids as shields before, and they had learned from the second battle that that wouldn't deter me." His voice was too steady. "So they sent the dregs of their troops to die first. The report says she was found with a Tchennes 42 in her hand. The Tchennes was an excellent gun. They wouldn't have handed one out except to an officer, someone they trusted to keep questionable soldiers in line. From her name, you can tell she probably came from Maign City."

"All right," Cheris said, digesting that, "another." She pointed.

"He's from the technician caste from what's now the Outspecker Colonies, before the heptarchate annexed them. There was a conflict between Doctrine and Gheffeu caste structure – you'd need a Rahal to explain the details – so his people had to be assimilated. We'd tried raids with Shuos shouters for fast compliance, but the calendricals were too unstable. By the time Kel Command finished arguing with the Shuos heptarch about it, the Gheffeu had thrown in with the Lanterners.

"It was a mess that the Andan should have handled, but we were fighting each other for influence. You're used to thinking of the hexarchate as a unified entity, but during my lifetime, the factions were still quarreling over Doctrine. The winners would have their specific technologies preserved under the final calendrical order, and the losers – well, we know what happened to the Liozh.

"Anyway, that man. He died among strangers. If you look at the other names, none of them are Gheffeu. The Lanterners didn't trust their latest recruits and split up ethnic groups. He died during a Gheffeu holy week, and he would have been wearing a white armband in honor of a particular saint."

Cheris wasn't a historian, but she had the awful feeling that Jedao wasn't making anything up.

She didn't point for the third one. "Colonel Kel Gized." Jedao's chief of staff.

Jedao's voice was no longer steady. "Do you want it backwards or forwards?"

Cheris pulled up a picture of Kel Gized because she wanted to know. Gized had a round, bland face and an untidy scar, shockingly pale against her dark brown skin, along the side of her head. The hair above it, cropped short, was gray. Her gloves looked like they were made of heavier material than the Kel favored nowadays. "Chronological," Cheris said.

"I met her at one of those damnable flower-viewing parties I had to attend as a high officer. The host was a friend of the Andan heptarch's sister. They liked to decorate parties with us military types to reassure the populace that the breakaway factions weren't going to chew the realm to rags.

"I was looking at the orchids when I overheard Gized critiquing an Andan functionary's poetry to his face. I decided I had to find out more about her, so I waited until she was done bludgeoning him about the head with his use of synecdoche, and asked her for a duel."

It wasn't much of an anecdote, although Kel who cared about literary techniques were oddities the way her ability at abstract mathematics was an oddity. But there was a brittle quality to his tone.

"It was over very quickly. I've only once lost a duel to a Kel, and it wasn't Gized. She wasn't humiliated, she was bored. She'd come to enjoy the party and I was getting in the way. But I looked up her profile. Mediocre duelist, excellent administrator. When Kel Command gave me my pick of staff, I chose her. You would have liked her. She tolerated all the games I challenged her to despite never figuring out how to bluff at jeng-zai, but it was always clear that I was wasting her time."

"Then why do it? Why the games?"

His voice came from a little ways off, as though he had paced to the far end of the room. "You probably have some notion that we wield weapons and formations and plans. But none of that matters if you can't wield people. You can learn about how people think by playing with their lives, but that's inhumane." The word choice jarred Cheris. "So I used ordinary games instead. Gambling. Board games. Dueling."

"You haven't challenged me to anything," Cheris said, wondering.

"What, and interrupt your dramas? You're entitled to leisure time. I have to admit, I don't even know what to make of the episode with the dolphin chorale."

Now he was trying to distract her. "Tell me how you killed her," she said.

"There's not a lot to tell," Jedao said. Pacing again. "She had an analytical mind and wouldn't have considered me above suspicion. Another ten minutes and she would have concluded that everything going wrong implied a very highly placed traitor. Lucky for me she was never a fast thinker. I shot her through the side of the head.

"It was a bad moment because Jiang and Gwe Pia were also in the command center, and Gwe Pia was a spectacularly good shot. She would have gotten me if she'd been willing to shoot through Jiang, but she wouldn't have thought of that, even if I did straight off."

Cheris could think of words for an officer who immediately jumped to shooting *through* a comrade as a firing solution.

"Now that I think about it, it's a miracle I didn't run out of bullets. Getting low on ammunition is an amateur's mistake. But of course, I hadn't known I was going to do that." Still pacing. "Incidentally, if your plan's that finicky, you've already fucked up."

"This isn't the academy," Cheris snapped.

"I'm serious. Sometimes you have to improvise, but why take the chance if you have alternatives?"

"It worked for you," she said through her teeth. How had she lost control of the conversation?

"You have a chance of being a decent general someday, but not if you pick up bad habits."

"Are you trying to pass off a massacre of your own soldiers as a *pedagogical exercise*?"

A ragged silence. "Fine. But listen, if your purpose was to kill a large group of people concentrated in one location, what would be the sensible way of doing it?"

Her shoulders ached. "Orbital bombardment," she said reluctantly.

"The way I did it made no sense."

He was trying to tell her something, but she couldn't imagine what it was. Her formation instinct was at a low ebb. The Kel relied on hierarchy, and he had comprehensively betrayed his subordinates. "Why does it matter?" she said. "My career isn't going anywhere."

"It's the principle of the thing. I would have liked to be an instructor, I even put in the request, but they wanted me in the field."

Cheris stared at the shadow. A few hundred years of Nirai expertise and they didn't even know what was wrong with him. What had she been thinking, fetching him out of the Kel Arsenal? And what had Kel Command been thinking for letting her do it?

She pulled up the figures again, made them march neatly for her inspection. "Do you have anything to say to that?"

"You're not telling me anything I don't know about myself," Jedao said.

"Explain it to me," Cheris said. She wasn't going to shout. "Make the numbers make sense. It can't have been a case of breaking under stress; I don't know what stress you could have been under. Candle Arc, outnumbered eight to one by the Lanterners, sure. Of course, you won that one so handily it's in all the textbooks. But Hellspin Fortress? Everyone agrees the Lanterners were doomed. So what happened? Why don't the numbers work?"

"You're the one who's good with figures," Jedao retorted. "Run the numbers and you tell me."

Numbers. Everyone knew Shuos Jedao for the massacre, but she wondered how many people he would have killed if he had continued what had been a brilliant career.

The people he would have destroyed in that imaginary past would have been the heptarchate's enemies. Their lives shouldn't be reckoned as equal to those of the heptarchate's own citizens. But she wondered.

"There must have been some reason for all that death," Cheris said. "If you'd sold out to the Lanterners, that would at least be a motive. But wrecking both sides like that? With no one standing to gain?" She remembered the bleed-through. "Was it because you wanted to die and you were taking it out on everyone else?" But why would he have been suicidal *before* Hellspin, or the black cradle?

"I'm not completely stupid," Jedao snapped. "If I'd meant to kill myself at Hellspin Fortress, I would have put a bullet in my head. My aim isn't *that* bad."

She had hit a nerve. It must gall him that he could never hold a weapon again.

"Maybe I'm only what they say I am." There was still an edge to his voice. "A madman. I had an excellent career. I had comrades. I had power, if you care about power. There's no sane reason to give any of that up."

He was trying to tell her something again and it was right in front of her where she couldn't see it. But she was exhausted, and it was difficult to think clearly. "Yes, well, you have immortality instead," she said. "I hope you're enjoying it."

Jedao was silent.

"The people you killed never had a chance," she said, willing him to answer her. "And none of them are coming back, either."

Unexpectedly, he said, "A million people dead four centuries before you were born, and you care about them. It speaks well of you, even if it doesn't speak well of me."

She couldn't sleep for a long time after that.

CHAPTER THIRTEEN

"New orders from Colonel Ragath," the captain had said once upon a time. At one point, Kel Niaad had been able to recite them word for word. Now he wasn't sure if there was anything in his head but the staccato of gunfire.

A scant hour ago they had been advancing through a residential complex in the Anemone Ward. Fighting had been a matter of around-the-corner shots and shatter grenades, the heartstop terror that every moan in the Fortress's winds was death in red spikes coming straight for their eyes. The captain had ordered the patrol to hold the complex against the heretics, but almost all were dead, one was not just dead but obliterated into a stray loop of intestine on a potted shrub, and one was comatose, a state Niaad would have preferred for himself.

The other surviving member was Corporal Kel Isaure, whose only reaction to the gore had been to send Niaad to retrieve equipment from the dead. She didn't shirk danger herself; she'd ventured farther than he had. Niaad wished she wouldn't risk herself. If she died, his formation instinct would short out and the heretics would find him curled in a ball.

"Niaad." It was Isaure, her voice hoarse but clear. "Hey, soldier. You awake?"

The shouts and thuds and clatter of ricochets seemed farther away than before, but sound traveled strangely in the Fortress.

"I'm awake, Corporal," Niaad said. He couldn't get his eyes to focus on her.

"I need you, soldier," Isaure said. "You're a lousy excuse for a Kel, but you're all I have left."

The insult, basic as it was, kept his attention.

"Thing is," Isaure said, drawing lines into the shrapnel and shredded metalweave with her toe, "to cut us off from our company, they should either be coming through this branch or branch 71-13. I have no idea what the fuck our general is up to, but neither side has seen fit to blow up the ward with us still in it. Which is good. But we have to take the Fortress so the Vidona can get to work. Which means getting our asses out of this fucking complex so we can be useful."

Niaad stared at her.

"Only thing is," Isaure said, "do we go straight toward the corpsefuckers, or cut ourselves a shortcut?"

Niaad was alarmed. Isaure was only a corporal, and the captain had been quite specific that they had to hold this miserable complex until they received orders otherwise.

"We're quite a pair, aren't we?" Isaure said as she continued to draw a map with her toe. It was surprisingly good, especially if you ignored the streaky marks left by skull splinters and the accompanying shreds of brain. "Dregs spit up by Personnel because they needed more warm bodies."

Niaad wished the corporal would stop philosophizing and give a fucking order already.

"We have the same problem." Now Isaure was kneeling and using gristle to diagram a perimeter. Her expression showed nothing but contempt for the situation. "You jump –" She banged the nearest wall. The noise was horrifyingly loud, and it took Niaad a full three seconds to stop scrabbling for cover. "– at the smallest noises and you're not getting much benefit from formation instinct."

There wasn't much Niaad could say to that. When the head of the man next to him had been vaporized, he had fallen apart.

Isaure crouched and made a second diagram. Niaad should have been paying attention, but he couldn't think clearly. Every so often, Isaure lifted her head to listen, but if she had any conclusions about what was going on, she didn't share them.

"You should ask," she said at last.

"Corporal?"

"Ask why I'm the same as you. Soldier no one has a use for."

Now she was getting personal. "Why, sir?" he said warily.

"I used to be a tank captain," Isaure said. "A good one." She frowned at the gristle, then wiped it off with her glove and marked out a new perimeter, this time scratching it into the floor with a bit of broken tile that shrieked as it drew the curve. "Miss the beasts. But they found out I was good at saying no to stupid orders."

Niaad swore in spite of himself. The corporal was a crashhawk, a formation breaker. His formation instinct might not keep him from blanking in the middle of a firefight, but it did oblige him to follow orders, even a crashhawk's orders.

Isaure was snickering. "It's your lucky day, Niaad. They stripped my commission and broke me all the way down, and reinjected me with formation instinct. They never realized it didn't take the second time, either."

"All respect, sir, why are you still with the Kel?"

His tone hadn't been respectful in the slightest, but Isaure didn't seem to care. "Because the Kel need me," she said. Niaad's skin crawled. "Any other corporal would be rooted here. I see a job to be done and we're going to do it. If I'm not mistaken, the heretics are setting up some weapon to cover the approaches, and they're worried it'll hit them too or they'd have moved in. You were paying attention to the reports, right? Anyway, best to hit them from behind."

"Sir, there are only two of us!"

"Look, soldier, if you love life so much, why the fuck did you sign on to be a suicide hawk? Come on, let's see how many weapons we can carry."

Nirai didn't feel sanguine about the number of grenades he was loaded down with. On the other hand, Isaure was a crack shot, and if anyone was going to be the beast of burden, it was him.

Isaure knew exactly where they were going, even if she was crazy. They entered residences of necessity. This was the one ward built hive-fashion. In order to get anywhere in the hive segments, you went through people's homes and offices, rooms nestled up to each other like cells, and only the occasional corridor, more to transport goods than people. Some Rahal must have come up with the layout. He couldn't see any other faction thinking of it.

The first time they encountered civilians – at least, Niaad assumed from their ornate coats and spangly jewelry that they were civilians – he was astonished by how decisively Isaure killed them, three quick bursts, red holes. He had barely gotten a look at their faces.

"They would have been screamers," Isaure said, although Niaad hadn't opened his mouth. "I can't stand screamers."

Most of the civilians got no chance to scream.

They went in and out of rooms as though they were burrowing beetles, occasionally cutting passages through walls with equipment that Isaure was not supposed to have. Niaad hadn't thought it was possible to get any more lost, but he didn't want to distract Isaure by asking where they were. He became fascinated by the objects people kept in their homes. Musical instruments that could have doubled as Vidona torture implements, especially the ones with the hungry wires. Floating globes that imitated pleasing weather patterns on green or purple planets. A collection of cat toys, but thankfully no trace of the cat itself. Isaure would probably classify a cat as a screamer.

Isaure kept consulting the field scanner, drilling holes, and muttering about angles of fire. Niaad was amazed no one heard the drill. It was quiet, but he could hear the whir as clearly as though it were biting into the lobes of his brain.

"There they are," Isaure said. "They've been taking down walls, you can't mistake the signs." Her patient voice suggested that she didn't care whether Niaad understood the situation. "It's where I thought it would be."

She pulled away from the latest hole. "All right. There's a machine down that passage. We need to light it up so our people know something's there. If we run like hell we can make it." She had kept the cracked bit of tile; she drew with it now. At least she was no longer diagramming with dead people's fluids.

"They'll see us coming, sir."

"They'll see *you* coming," Isaure said. "I'll provide covering fire. I just want you to lob as many of the grenades as you can at that machine, get some explosions going."

"We could pick off a few of them first, sir −"

"Soldier," Isaure said crushingly, "did I give you permission to think? Charge straight in, throw grenades, get the hell out. I've given you instructions. Acknowledge."

"Acknowledged, sir," Niaad said, despite a sincere desire to tell her to fuck a jackhammer.

"Go," Isaure said, gesturing with her scorch rifle.

Niaad was already having trouble with his peripheral vision. He kept having to swing his head from side to side to check his surroundings. It wasn't until Isaure shook his shoulder that he realized his hearing was half-gone, too. The stress effects wouldn't have set in so early in a properly tuned Kel.

"There's the gauntlet," Isaure said. "Sloppy guards, no one's facing our way. Their misfortune, our gain. Get in, lob the grenades, get out. I'll cover you. Simple."

"Yes, sir," he whispered. Stupid plan, but he had to obey.

"Good man. We'll make a Kel of you yet. Go!"

Niaad shuffled at first because he couldn't get his legs to cooperate. The noise alerted them. He primed one grenade and threw poorly, well short of the machine. It was hard not to be hypnotized by its red glow and wires and strange gears.

The heretics' guards may have been careless, but they weren't fools. One of them kicked the grenade down the corridor. The others swung up their rifles.

Niaad was too terrified to move.

Which, he realized in a slow crystal moment, was what Corporal Isaure had counted on. She fired four times in rapid succession, cool and precise: once to scorch out his knee, pitching him forward and closer to the machine, and three more to trigger the grenades.

Whether he was close enough for the grenades to do any damage to the mystery machine was a question Kel Niaad never found out the answer to.

Kel Isaure was already sprinting away from the explosion. She had gotten what she wanted. Now it was time to rejoin the Kel and show them what they needed to do.

SERVITOR 244666 HADN'T intended to get caught. Of course, people rarely did. But it would have gotten away with its illicit snooping if it hadn't been for a flickering glitch in the cindermoth's variable layout, consequence of a moment's power fluctuation. It had been coming out of Cheris's quarters after having planted the bug. As luck would have it, another servitor, 819825, spotted it through the moment's window between the brevet general's quarters and the high halls that were, ordinarily, a right turn and a few minutes away.

It wasn't that servitors were precisely forbidden to enter humans' quarters. The maintenance work and routine chores that were their responsibility necessitated it, although they made a point of knocking as a matter of courtesy. Some of the humans would shoo them off if it was an inconvenient moment, but in general they didn't think much of it, an attitude the servitors themselves had encouraged during the scant centuries of their sentience.

The servitors themselves, however, had their own rules to govern how they went about their duties. It was always fair to enter if duty required it, or, in rare cases like Cheris's, if they were invited to socialize. It was not, according to servitor consensus, fair to drop bugs into the brevet general's quarters for around-the-clock monitoring even if you were the lead servitor assigned to keep tabs on her whenever she was in the moth's public areas.

At present, 244666 folded up its limbs, hinges neat and precise, and stared patiently at 819825, who had volunteered to serve as its guard or companion, take your pick. They were both shut up in one of the service corridors, dark except when they flashed prickly comments at each other, for remedial meditation. You could hear a lot here, especially with a servitor's senses, although they were circumspect in how they used their scan capabilities. At the moment what they got was the occasional exchange between the humans below them, including a Kel joke or two; footsteps, superstitious one-two-three-four knockings on the walls, the whoosh of air circulating, the quiet whisking of other servitors hovering through the passages.

819825 had reported 244666 to the other servitors, and they had summoned it to explain itself. 244666 had shown up; it didn't have many places to hide, and besides, it might have some philosophical differences with its fellows, but it didn't want to defy the most important rules of servitor society.

819825, who had always had the most annoying prim streak, had explained to 244666 in exacting detail that the foundation of servitor society was courtesy, and that this differentiated them from the humans who ran their world, and that if they started deviating from it in small matters it would only be a matter of time before they slid into deviating from it in larger ones. Besides, the brevet general had been unfailingly polite to them. She deserved better consideration. It was the kind of lecture you expected to outgrow after your first few neural flowerings.

244666 thought to itself that this was all very well, but they mostly had the word of distant servitors as to Cheris's character, and besides, no one with half a sentience could think that Shuos Jedao's involvement boded well. It would have felt much easier knowing what went on in Cheris's quarters at all times. Still, it hadn't had a chance to activate the bug, its fellows had removed the thing anyway, and moreover it was impossible to eavesdrop on Jedao's half of any conversation, something that they had had abundant opportunity to verify. It had to concede defeat. In the meantime, 244666 could have endured its confinement, however temporary, in true solitude, and instead 819825 had chosen to accompany it when it didn't have to. It resolved to repay the kindness when they were done with this.

CHERIS'S WORLD WAS very large. It contained the full crews of the Kel swarm, the infantry and infiltrators who were facing off against the heretics, the Fortress and its six wards. She thought in the on-off language of guns instead of words. Everything coalesced into numbers and coordinates, angles and intersecting lines.

"Sir, Tactical Three's firepower is now down to seventy-four percent," Communications said. "Commander Rai Mogen is asking if they should alter formation."

Cheris rubbed her temples. She had identified heretical formation keys through rapid modulation at the beginning of the engagement. Fast, but not fast enough; Commander Kel Tavathe's bannermoth *Spiders and Scars* had taken serious damage to its life support systems. Still, they now had access to a small repertoire of defensive effects.

"Tactical Three, heretical formation 8," Cheris said hoarsely. A conservative response, but she couldn't afford to lose more guns. "Let me know if there are any more breakdowns."

A certain percentage of the Kel reacted poorly to using heretical formations. None of the commanders had broken down, but Commander Kel Hapo Nar had had to relieve his executive officer during the second hour of the engagement. As time passed, other Kel proved vulnerable as well.

"You should take a break soon," Jedao said, but she ignored him.

"Commander Rai Mogen acknowledges," Communications said. "Formation shift underway."

They had been whittling down the Fortress's guns for the past 17.3 hours. When the heretics opened fire on the Kel infantry, there was no longer any point to pretense. Cheris had recalled Kel Koroe's bannermoth *Unenclosed by Fear*. The two cindermoths had kept up a barrage from a distance – it wasn't as though the Fortress could evade – and the bannermoths offered supporting fire. Cheris had endeavored not to damage the Fortress's integral structure, although it was tempting to blast random holes in the thing. Kel Command could always take it out of her pay for the next millennium.

Cheris had sent a report to Kel Command explaining that the Fortress's shields had been defeated and that additional information on the Fortress's capabilities and personnel would be appreciated.

With any luck, they would respond soon. One of the things she and Jedao agreed on was that Kel Command was shooting itself in the foot by giving them so little information from the outset, although she hoped that Jedao's theory that they were the victims of some unrelated power play was incorrect.

Cheris's world was also very small. It had narrowed to her terminal with its glitterspin of displays. Everything announced itself in colors, numbers, diagrams. At some point, she had been aware that certain numbers represented people, and other numbers represented guns, and still others represented Kel moths. Now she was only aware of interlocking hierarchies and the imperative to trade some numbers for others.

Fire became numbers became lines. She tapped out an order, knowing only the necessity of perfection. Another order, then another. Numbers changed, drifted, folded out of sight. Too low. She frowned, trying to concentrate. It was getting harder and harder to think.

"General." It wasn't Jedao, but another man, his voice deeper, gruffer. Cheris couldn't remember his name. She could barely find her own. "Sir, you ought to rest. The combat drugs aren't meant to handle that kind of mental exertion."

He wasn't part of the terminal that was her world. She didn't have to listen – unless he was a number? How could she have lost track of a number? Her heart raced.

"Cheris." This time it was Jedao. He spoke very clearly. "That's Commander Kel Hazan. He can oversee the swarm. He got on shift 1.8 hours ago, and Weapons and Navigation have been feeding your responses into the grid so it can learn from them. They can handle things while you rest."

She had to find her way out of the numbers. When she did speak to Hazan, she wasn't sure she was intelligible, but he gave no sign that anything was wrong. Then she headed to her quarters.

Cheris took a shower even though she would rather have collapsed asleep the instant she was through the door. She had hoped the sonics' cloying hum would wake her up. No such luck.

"Stop trying to stay awake," Jedao said.

She was so tired, and she had no idea what, if anything, she had done right. In mathematics you had peer review, definite proofs and answers, but war was nothing but uncertainty multiplied by uncertainty.

"Sleep," Jedao said, exasperated.

Cheris gave up trying to resist and fell asleep as soon as she lay down.

When she woke, there was a tray with scallion pancakes, rice, and cooling tea. "A pair of servitors came in with that twenty-seven minutes ago," Jedao said, "but I thought you needed the rest more. I would have thanked them if they had been able to hear me."

He let her eat in peace, then said, "We're going to prepare propaganda drops."

"What?" Cheris said. Planning sessions with Jedao were never dull. "Do you think the heretics will fall for something that obvious?"

"You'd be surprised at what people will read out of curiosity," Jedao said. "Although we won't ask them to read much. We're going to modify some game templates and send them down. The thing is, I'll need your colonel's help. He'll know more about the Liozh heresy than I do, and since he's a Kel, he'll know the most about the bloodthirsty bits."

A servitor requested entry, although it could have just come in. "Come in," Cheris said. It bore more tea. "Thank you," she said. "I don't think I'm in danger of dehydrating here in the command moth, but I appreciate it."

The servitor made a skeptical sound, but flashed a series of satisfied green-gold lights and left.

"Anyway," Jedao said, "I know what happened in outline, but not the details. We want the details."

Cheris thought of the things she did and didn't remember from her history lessons, and grimaced. "Wouldn't you be able to find this in the archives?"

"When's the last time you dug through primary sources? The

problem with the Liozh rebellion is that half that stuff's classified, and the other problem is that you have to know how to sift through it. Which is where Ragath's background as a historian will come in handy."

"He's very busy," Cheris said. It was bad enough that she had to put up with Jedao. The least she could do for her infantry commander was shield him from the fox's direct interference.

"All he has to do is give us pointers to the best examples of the Liozh getting shot into sieves," Jedao said. "Just leave him a message and he'll respond when he has the time. I doubt it'll take him that long."

Cheris thought of her instructors dismissing Kel actions against the Liozh as unworthy of study, victories too easily won. "I'm still not sure –"

"Did you play many games in academy? Sports?"

"Dueling mostly," Cheris said. Here it came, the ubiquitous Shuos obsession with games.

Jedao snorted. "You're thinking something uncharitable about foxes. Tell you what, then. We're going to make a game."

"I should get back to the command center, is what I should be doing." She eyed the clock and the shift schedule. Technically she wasn't due back for another five hours and forty-one minutes, but she didn't want to admit it.

"If they needed you, they'd have sent for you," Jedao said. "You could use more sleep, but you're unlikely to see sense about that."

Cheris finally realized what he had said. "I have people dying down there and you want me to play another fucking Shuos game?"

"I said invent a game. We won't have time to play it."

"Why?" Cheris said.

"We're going to invent a game about the Fortress."

He wasn't going to let it go. "If you want a battle simulation, wouldn't it be better to use one of the ones already in the grid?"

"But that would only tell me what the simulator thinks of the situation. And the level of abstraction is too low – we'll get back to that. I want to know how you understand the situation, Cheris."

"What, you don't have a plan? I thought you always had a plan."

"Humor me."

She had misgivings, but – "Where do we start?"

Maddeningly, he responded as she had thought he would. "Where do you think we should start?"

Cheris thought for a moment. Under other circumstances, and with the help of some beer, it would have been tempting to devise a taxonomy that could handle dueling, jeng-zai, and truth-or-dare. But Jedao would have a specific purpose in mind, and he wouldn't have given her an impossible task. "If the point is a specific game, I'll start by modifying an existing game." A mathematical solution: reduce a problem to a previously solved problem.

Jedao didn't say anything, so Cheris assumed she was being left to thrash around for his edification. She went to the terminal and pulled up fires-and-towers. Using it as a basis, she set up an asymmetrical two-player board game to be played with grid assistance. There was no point making the bookkeeping more annoying than necessary.

She lost time on legible visual representations. It wouldn't do for the player to confuse infantry and infiltrators, for instance. Assigning legal moves and point values was worse. How was she supposed to know the heretics' strength? Was she supposed to ensure that both sides were evenly matched? She opened her mouth to ask, then thought better of it. And she omitted the shields, since they had been cracked and weren't relevant anymore.

Cheris was confronted with the difficulty of coding a grid opponent so she could test the values. Normally she would have asked a servitor for help, but she suspected Jedao would intervene. The attack values on some of the guns felt too high to be realistic, but you probably couldn't tell by eyeballing the numbers. If only she had more time –

She straightened and barked a laugh. If Jedao meant to distract her from her duty, he was succeeding. She longed for a call from the command center, even if it implied a new disaster.

It was peculiar that Jedao seemed determined to *teach* her. Wouldn't it have been more efficient to trigger her formation instinct so she could convey his orders without any of this back and forth?

Her mind was wandering again. She had barely addressed combat resolution. It was tempting to squander time on pseudorandom generators and probability distributions because at least she understood those, but it was more important to pick something inoffensive and run with it.

It was impossible not to think of herself as the Kel swarm, even in the context of scratchy, half-formed notations. She put herself in the role of the Fortress's commandant and saw problems with the game that hadn't been evident before: ambiguities, ill-defined objectives, a certain lopsidedness of agency. Surely the heretics had motives and the ability to maneuver toward their own goals. The game should reflect that.

She entered more scratchwork, agonizingly aware of the mess of numbers and contradictory rules and shaky assumptions. A senior cadet had once told her that proofs were just like essays, no one expected the rough draft to be a work of art, but it was hard not to feel that she should try for elegance from the outset.

"You can stop there," Jedao said.

Cheris's eyes felt sand-dry. "It won't work," she said.

"There are issues that would come up in initial playtest," Jedao said, "but that's not a bad first outing, especially from a Nirai thinker. You should have seen the first time I went through design critique. Blood everywhere."

She had a hard time believing that.

"Cheris, I wasn't born a tactician. I had to learn like everyone else."

"Tell me," she said carefully, "why you stopped me there."

"You must suspect or you wouldn't be asking."

"That was when I changed my focus to consider the Fortress's player."

But why stop there? If the Fortress expected aid from – "The foreigners," Cheris said in a rush. "They're part of the situation. And our objectives aren't exactly the same as Kel Command's, or they wouldn't keep hiding information from us." And who else? What other players had she missed?

She remembered, with nauseating clarity, the Shuos eye watching her out of her own face. Subcommand Two's face.

She had gotten the scenario wrong. Her focus had been on the immediate problem of subduing the Fortress, without encoding the context.

"I see," Cheris said. "I got caught up in the tactical problem, when the issue is strategy. All that time with modifiers and attack values and it wasn't even relevant."

"Well, we were sent here as tacticians," Jedao said, "so you're not entirely to blame."

"Still, I appreciate the lesson," Cheris said, thinking that next time she would try to catch on sooner.

"It's not over," Jedao said. "Two things. First: the value of a game is in abstraction. Many Nirai go in for simulationist approaches, a tendency you share, but sometimes you learn more by throwing details out than coding them all in. You want to get rid of everything nonessential, cook it down to its simplest possible form."

"I see, sir." The fact that she had been solving the wrong problem with great dedication, if not exactly enthusiasm, was humbling.

"Second: what do you think games do? What are they about?"

The flippant answers weren't going to be right, but she had no idea what he was after. "Winning and losing?" she said. "Simulations?"

"It hasn't escaped me that your first answer is a Kel answer and the second is a Nirai answer," Jedao said. "A Rahal would say that games are about rules, an Andan would say they're about passing time with people, and who knows what the Vidona are authorized to say."

"You're a Shuos," Cheris said, "so I presume you're going to tell me what the Shuos answer is."

"According to the Shuos," Jedao said, "games are about behavior modification. The rules constrain some behaviors and reward others. Of course, people cheat, and there are consequences around that, too, so implicit rules and social context are just as important. Meaningless cards, tokens, and symbols become invested with value and significance in the world of the game. In a sense, all calendrical war is a game between competing sets of rules, fueled by the coherence of our beliefs. To win a calendrical war, you have to understand how game systems work."

Cheris felt cold all the way down to her marrow. "The siege is a distraction," she said. "You're going to game the heretics to death."

"A war of hearts, Cheris. Not guns. As you observed not so long ago."

"So this is what the propaganda pieces are about," she said.

"I want the heretics thinking about what about what happened to the Liozh the first time around," Jedao said. "There's a chance this is some completely different heresy, but after the shield operator's response to the Web of Worlds, I doubt it. I'm guessing that their leaders neglected to remind them of the fate the original Liozh met. It'll still be on their minds, however. Sometimes even obvious openings are worth taking. If nothing else, we can learn something from their response."

The Liozh had been a living faction when Jedao was alive. "Did you see any signs of their heresy before you died?" she asked. "An entire faction going wrong – that's worse than losing a nexus fortress."

"I didn't see it coming at all," Jedao said with an undertone of bitterness. "Didn't interact with the Liozh much except on social occasions. I was always at war, Cheris. It didn't leave me a lot of free time to discuss philosophy and ethics."

Cheris sent the request down to Colonel Ragath. It didn't take long for him long to respond. "I'll send over a list as soon as I can, sir," he said. "Plenty of material to choose from if you want to paint everything in gore. The Liozh military was known more for its revolutionary fervor than its battle prowess. They lost their single best general – who was pretty good – to a Shuos assassin early on. It went to pieces after that. The killing irony is that the Shuos was after another target, a Shuos traitor, and got the wrong woman. Fascinating stuff if you like watching the underdogs getting smeared to paste."

Cheris looked at Ragath narrowly. It was impossible to tell if he was being sarcastic.

"Tell him I'm grateful for his assistance in this matter," Jedao said. She repeated the words, puzzled by Jedao's unusual deference.

"Happy to oblige, sir," Ragath said. His gaze flicked sideways. "I have a minor emergency in the Umbrella Ward, is there anything else you need right now?"

"No, that's everything," Cheris said as she scanned the status reports on the terminal's subdisplay, recognizing the understatement for what it was. "Out."

"Now this," Jedao said, "is where game presets can be useful. The archives contain the collected efforts of a lot of Shuos trying to impress each other. We don't have to design propaganda pieces from scratch. All we have to do is feed in some parameters and however many horrifying images we can scare up."

Jedao's matter-of-factness about the Liozh defeat stood at odds with the way he had spoken of the Lanterners as fellow human beings. Cheris wasn't sure what to make of that. "Did you have something against the Liozh?"

"Not in the slightest," Jedao said, "but they died in dreadful ways and we can leverage that."

She knew she shouldn't feel anything for heretics past or present, but Jedao's sudden callousness made her feel strangely defensive on their behalf.

Fortress of Scattered Needles, Analysis
Priority: High
From: Vahenz afrir dai Noum
To: Heptarch Liozh Zai
Calendrical Minutiae: Year of the Fatted Cow, Month of the Partridge, Day of the Carp, the vote in Doctrine says it's Hour of the Snail and I for one have better things to argue about.

I heard from Analysis Team Three that they located one of the missing Rahal. Not of terrible use, because they only happened on the corpse after someone called in a strange murder near Stoghan's troops by Kel Encampment Two. At least the neighborhood watch system is ticking along nicely. We have no idea what was in the damnable woman's head, but she was clearly trying to contact her people. Stoghan's troops deny responsibility and for once I believe them. It's infuriating to think that we lost intelligence to ordinary crime.

I heard of the latest sniper incident. I'm tired of explaining this to Stoghan, but draconian reprisals against the civilians "sheltering" the snipers aren't the way to go. I would be surprised if the poor stiffs knew they were being used as cover by Shuos operatives. Stoghan's actions are only hurting our credibility. I imagine that some of the brutalized citizens are going to revert to the loyalists' side. This is what we call "counterproductive."

I know that Stoghan's swaggering and "decisiveness" have his popularity at an all-time high, but please balance this against, I don't know, every other consideration on the table. Rig some votes if you have to.

All right, I can see you glowering at me, so I will say this. One thing the man is doing right, amazingly, is insisting that his soldiers treat the propaganda canisters as real threats. So far it's all gridpaper games, and they don't interface with anything, but still. Solid game design, but I expect that from a Shuos.

No, the issue is that they're miniature history lessons. I think Jedao has miscalculated, though. Take that one video segment with the Liozh prisoners' ribs cracked open so their lungs could be extracted while they were still alive. This sort of thing is only stiffening resistance on our end. It's an amateur's mistake, and I have to wonder if Jedao is up to something else. Is there some other target for the propaganda?

Well, I see that Pioro has extra-special flagged a few reports with an extra-special case of that brandy he knows I like. I'd better see what the fuss is before the world collapses, eh? Do have a good hard think about what I've said.

Yours in calendrical heresy,

Vh.

CHAPTER FOURTEEN

LIEUTENANT KEL MIKEV hated his assignment, but it could have been worse. Sure, his eyes hurt, and even through the suits' filters some of his soldiers had fetched up with nasty nosebleeds and soft tissue damage, but he preferred a little honest smoke in a contained environment to planetside missions where you had to watch every fucking square centimeter for things that bit or oozed or crooned at you in your childhood sweetheart's voice.

Mikev's platoon was responsible for the forward section near Gate 3-12, where the Kel had established a toehold in the Umbrella Ward. The heretics had sucked out the atmosphere while the Kel spent a hair-raising several hours blowing down walls in some places and blocking off passages in others, building a fortress in the Fortress. One of the company's other platoons had had to herd the unhappy civilians to a holding area. Not all the civilians had gotten suited in time.

Mikev was glad he hadn't been assigned that duty. He felt terrible when the fragile ones blubbered. But he reminded himself not to get distracted by irrelevancies.

Eggshell was whining about grit in his eyes that he couldn't unsuit to get at. Trigger was obsessively checking her weapons. One of these days Trigger was going to be so caught up making sure every component fit just right that she'd stand there as the heretics punched her full of holes. Mikev had a lot of theories about how his soldiers would die. It was one of the ways, like giving them nicknames, that he kept from getting too attached to them.

The attack came as the warning did, sudden pulse of heat in his forearm to indicate incoming. Incoming from where? And what? Poison gas? Surely they would have done it earlier, and it'd be easy enough to pump it out after all the Kel were dead. He didn't hear guns, didn't see wildfire flashes or smoke –

"Everyone stay under cover," Mikev said, which he wished was an unnecessary order.

Trigger, who had been half out of position, was slow to respond. Mikev groaned. She was a great shot, but not very bright. He couldn't tell what she thought she saw, but she brought her scattergun up and fired through the loophole.

Or would have fired, if the gun were working.

Mikev thought at first that the crawling sensation was horror. It couldn't be some local parasite, not here, they'd never allow such a thing through the Fortress's ecoscrubbers. Then he realized that the sensation came from his belt, his pack, the pistol in his hand, a disgusting itch that started to hurt in earnest.

Trigger had cast down her scattergun. There was a bizarre streaky speckiness in the air, suggesting a field effect just outside human visual range, which in turn suggested a heretical exotic.

"Everyone get rid of your weapons. Get away from them," Mikev snapped. This was sufficiently novel that he added, "That's a direct order."

The crawling sensation weakened away from the guns, although Mikev wasn't sure they wouldn't explode messily. No, that didn't seem to be the case. The fuck? The gun was fossilizing as he watched, making tiny shrieking sounds. It made him want to put the thing out of its misery and it wasn't even alive.

More interesting was the fact that the grenades and power tools were unaffected. So this corrosion field was keyed to specific weapon archetypes.

Mikev had just opened the link to inform the captain when she said, before he could get anything out, "I *know*, Lieutenant, I'm not stupid. Keep your eyes peeled in case the heretics get it into their heads that they can beat Kel knives. We have orders from the colonel to hold. Out."

Trigger looked distressed. Mikev yelled at her to get away from the corroding guns. She looked for all the world like she wanted to *hug* them better. Honestly, she was a full-grown Kel.

In the back of his head, he was convinced that the field was rotting his cells from the inside. Sometimes the universe was determined to send creeping things after you no matter how far away you stayed from planets.

"THEY NEED BETTER mathematicians over there," Cheris was saying to Commander Hazan. "Although it's just as well."

Hazan had some mathematical ability himself. He was poring over the formulas she had sent him.

The corrosion gradient was a nuisance, but as exotic effects went, it could have been worse. Presumably suitable modulation would let you key it to other weapon archetypes. All you needed was generators set up in the right places.

Cheris and Hazan had been studying the problem. The heretics had used the gradient to corral the Kel. While the Kel were capable of going in with their fists, Cheris preferred to use that as a last resort. She had hoped for useful reports from the Shuos infiltrators, but nothing decisive had come in yet.

Jedao had been unusually quiet when the infiltrators' reports started coming in, except when one described some of the heretics' calendar values.

"Any way to find out if they're doing anything new and exciting with their remembrances?" Jedao had asked ironically. "One does wish sometimes for some creativity."

Obligingly, Cheris had dug around until she found the answer. "No, they're doing the same basic thing we do, just with different numbers and different tortures," she said, and he had lost interest.

Cheris had taken a painkiller for the headache she was developing when Communications sat up straighter and said, "Message from the Fortress, sir."

"Pass it over," Cheris said.

"It's a full recording."

"High time we see a face," Jedao said. "Not that I'm one to speak."

"Play it," Cheris said. Her pulse sped up. She reminded herself to take deep breaths.

The image showed a woman. Her hair was an unusual light brown, her skin pale. She had done up her hair in complicated braids that wound around the sides of her head and were fastened by gold pins. Her clothes were white with buttons of gold filigree.

"A Liozh, all right." Jedao sounded torn between bitterness and exasperation. The same ancient grievance he wouldn't talk about earlier? But the recording was already talking.

"I am Liozh Zai, representing the people of the Fortress," the woman said. Her voice was strong and precise. "We are no longer content to endure the hexarchs' tyranny, to believe only the things they say we should believe, to reckon time only in the ways they say we should reckon time. We are no longer reconciled to the destruction of heresies or the removal of our right to self-determination. We are expecting reinforcements shortly. You have 75 of our hours – 108.9 of your own – to withdraw your troops and leave. Otherwise our allies will show you no mercy."

That was all. Cheris had expected more bluster and said as much.

"You're not paying attention to the right words," Jedao said. "She said 'representing.' That wasn't marketing research they were doing, that was polling. She claims to be sitting on a nascent democracy."

"A what?"

Jedao sighed. "An obscure experimental form of government where citizens choose their own leaders or policies by voting on them."

Cheris tried to imagine this and failed. How could you form a stable regime this way? Wouldn't it destroy the reliability of the calendar and all its associated technology?

"That was the rest of the heptarchate's reaction to the Liozh heresy, I'm told. Except they used a lot of guns to express their opinion."

A message from Shuos Ko. "I'll hear it," Cheris said.

"Three things, sir," Ko said. "First, one of the infiltrators got a partial personnel dump out of a terminal before she had to scoot. The dump is weeks out of date and we're still sifting through it, but we're in luck. I've got positive identification on the speaker. She's Inaiga Zai, a clerk who works for a Doctrine subsidiary in the Anemone Ward."

"A clerk?" Cheris said incredulously. And one with no faction affiliation, judging by the name.

"I don't believe it for a second either, sir. Her profile is designed to bore us to sleep, with a dash of petty embezzlement so she doesn't look too clean."

"I imagine all the shield operators have such cover identities," Jedao said.

Cheris repeated this to Ko.

"No proof," Ko said, "but I agree. Unfortunately, no lasting success putting logic worms in the Fortress's grid, so that's all we have on Zai.

"Second, which General Jedao may have told you already, Zai is using the Liozh ceremonial outfit as a calendrical focus. It's odd, because only one person in six is going to be the kind of antiquarian enthusiast who'd even care –"

"Not true," Jedao said.

Ko saw Cheris frowning and stopped speaking.

"People have trouble thinking of the Liozh as anything but failures. But there was a time when they brought something valuable to the heptarchate. They were the idealists and philosophers. They were our leaders and our conscience. No wonder they developed a taste for heresy."

Cheris repeated this to Ko, except the first and last bits. She couldn't reconcile Jedao's earlier callousness with the way he spoke of the Liozh now. What did he really think of them?

"For that to show up in the Fortress's atmospherics," Ko said, "someone would have had to do a lot of low-media groundwork over a period of time. I'd be worried if the foreigners are that deeply entrenched.

"But the third point is possible good news, sir." Ko's usual implacability was replaced by a certain restrained triumph. "Properly, this should be reported by Captain Damiod, but he, ah, felt he was close to a breakthrough and asked me to do so on his behalf."

Cheris suppressed a smile. She could interpret Nirai for "I'm busy calculating, don't waste my time with people" as well as anyone else. "Go on," she said.

"Captain Damiod thinks there's a potential exploit in the way they're encrypting their messages." Before Cheris could ask, Ko held up a hand. "The work is preliminary and may not bear fruit. But essentially, someone screwed up. 67 Snake's seed parameters are driven by a combination of user input – the irregular time between keystrokes – and a synchronizer set to work with a high calendar clock. When the Fortress recalibrated its time servers to conform with the heretical calendar, they forgot to rewrite the synchronizer to work with the new setup."

"I'm not a cryptosystems specialist," Cheris said, "but I'm guessing this isn't a fast crack."

"No, sir."

"As time permits," Cheris said, "I would like you to continue work on a dummy cryptosystem with the parameters I sent you." Something that looked formidable but could be cracked within a reasonable period of time by a diligent attacker. "We may need it in the near future."

"Of course, sir." That was all.

"Sir, do you have a response for Inaiga Zai?" It was Commander Hazan, who had been replaying the message with the sound off so he could scrutinize Zai's expressions. Zai had good control of her face and hands.

"Unfortunately, there's not a lot you can offer Zai," Jedao said. "The heretics know the Vidona are coming for them, and even if you were authorized to make promises, they wouldn't believe you. Their only choice is to fight."

"Some indication from Kel Command would be useful right now," Cheris said aloud. "Communications, top priority message to be relayed to Kel Command."

"Are you certain, sir?" Hazan asked.

She narrowed her eyes at him, but it was a legitimate question. "We've heard nothing back from Kel Command," she said, although she had reported regularly. "With this deadline, word might not reach them in time. If we send a relay message with the right tags, there's a chance some local general will listen in and respond. Do you wish to log an objection, Commander?"

Nerevor would have, but Nerevor was gone. Cheris suspected that Hazan would be satisfied with the offer.

She was right. "That's not necessary, sir," Hazan said. "I concede your logic."

Cheris updated Kel Command on the situation, asked for further details on Inaiga Zai, and requested the status of the nearby borders. "Does that cover everything?" she asked Jedao subvocally.

"The data dump ought to take care of any lingering questions," he said. "Might as well send it on its way."

Communications looked at her anxiously, but did as told.

The Fortress quieted. Every so often a Shuos reported in, and even more rarely Colonel Ragath contacted the command moth, but the situation had settled into a toothy status quo. Every so often Cheris checked the plot showing Kel positions, where the heretics were standing out of the way, and the corrosion gradient's extent.

After a while, Cheris excused herself from the command center. Three servitors escorted her, unbidden. Two were deltaforms, differentiated by yellow and purple lights, and one was a snakeform. They accompanied her into her quarters. The rooms that had seemed so oversized before scarcely registered as worthy of notice. She stopped before the ashhawk emblem, trying to find some trace of herself in the fierce raptor's beak, the black wings, the outstretched talons. Sheathed Wings: that was all she was.

The snakeform asked if Cheris was hungry. She demurred. She could tell Jedao disapproved, even if he wasn't saying anything. "It must be convenient to run on power cores," she said.

The snakeform made an equivocal noise. Clearly it agreed with Jedao.

"They're very solicitous of you," Jedao said.

"They like company," Cheris said subvocally. "I should think you'd understand that."

"True."

The response to her message came in the middle of a drama episode about, as far as she or the servitors could tell, five Kel, an Andan duelist's telescoping hairpins, and a dinner party gone horribly wrong. The purple deltaform paused the episode for her.

"Communications, sir," the lieutenant's voice said from the terminal. "It's not Kel Command –"

So much for that.

"– but there's a signature match for Brigadier General Kel Marish, bannering the *Higher Higher Highest*. The transmission request has urgent priority, for your eyes only."

The servitors were already clearing out.

Kel Marish of the Eyespike emblem. She had once shouted down a court-martial charging her with overly creative interpretation of orders against the Haussen heretics, and won. Cheris was remembering that her luck this entire campaign was bad.

"Send it through," Cheris said. Of all the generals to reach.

Kel Marish wore her uniform with a casual air, even though no single crease was out of place. She had the kind of face you'd expect a card shark to develop among challenging opponents, all ascetic angles and unreadable eyes in a blunt dark face. "Brevet General Kel Cheris," she said, not insultingly but formally. "If Kel Command hasn't seen fit to share this information with you, I oughtn't either, but I feel you can't adequately discharge your duty otherwise."

"General Marish," Cheris said, "I'm listening. Is it true that we have an enemy swarm incoming?"

"Oh, it's not just incoming," Marish said. Her sneer wasn't

directed at Cheris. "We have a full-scale Hafn invasion with messy calendrical business headed toward the Fortress of Spinshot Coins. General Cherkad has been given charge of the campaign, and I've been pulled off sentry to assist near the Jeweled Systems."

"The Hafn have been quiescent for decades," Cheris said. "Wasn't there an Andan cultural exchange just two years ago?"

"The fact that the Hafn got along with the Andan should have tipped us off. Everyone thinks of the Shuos as the sneaky snailfuckers, but the Andan are so damn affable and charming and fun to be around up to the point where they stab you in the kidneys.

"Anyway, General Cheris, you should have been informed ages ago. The fact that Kel Command chose to keep you in the dark says they're afraid you'll turn coat. Word is there's a Shuos in one of the subcommand composites. I shouldn't wonder if that's fouling up their judgment."

"Hexarch Mikodez," Jedao said, very softly.

"What do you expect me to do with this information?" Cheris asked, swallowing a "sir."

"Terrible, isn't it? I'm not supposed to talk to you, and with your brevet you outrank me. If you ask my *advice*, I'd say take the Fortress of Scattered Needles as fast as you can. The calendrical fingerprints will affect us in the contested sector, and the Hafn will want the nexus for themselves. If we fail, General, blow the thing to atoms. Deny it to the Hafn. – Can I have a word with General Jedao? Is he in there somewhere?"

Of course. Marish couldn't currently see Cheris's shadow. The angle was wrong, and people outside her swarm didn't know how anchoring worked. Changing the lights only took a moment. Marish's eyes flickered as she took the ninefox shadow in.

"I speak for General Shuos Jedao," Cheris said, "and he can hear you fine."

"General Jedao," Marish said.

"I'm listening," Jedao said with frank interest. Cheris repeated the words.

"I'm a Kel, sir, but I have a brain to think with," Marish said.

"The hexarchate has gone curdled. They should have decided whether to trust you and the brevet from the start, all in or all out, none of this insipid indecisive shit.

"I'm sworn to Kel Command and I'm due to fight soon and very likely die. I imagine your brevet is constrained by formation instinct. But you, sir – you're out of the cradle so it's too late not to trust you, and formation instinct is before your time even if you weren't a Shuos. All in or all out. You won't scruple over what needs doing. Fix what has to be fixed in the hexarchate, sir. You're the weapon we have left. Brigadier General Marish out."

"I knew things were bad," Jedao said after that, "but I hadn't realized just how bad. Cheris, Kel Command and I have a" – wry pause – "complicated relationship. However, in times past they have recognized that I need a certain minimum of information to be able to operate on their behalf. Now it seems that they're hanging us out to dry. I can't help but think that Shuos oversight has to do with it, given how much my hexarch considers me a mismanaged resource.

"Still, something's changed since they sent us forth. It's as if they think we're going to take the Fortress and use it against them, although I can't imagine how they think I'm going to escape an entire swarm of Kel. This entire siege has turned into a loyalty test."

"Then why not recall us?" Cheris said.

"Because we're here. They've already written us off. If we get the job done, then great. Otherwise, they undoubtedly have some backup plan already in motion. I would give a lot to be eavesdropping on the hivemind right now." His voice quieted. "I don't think our exchange with General Marish is going to help us. Or her, for that matter."

"She wouldn't care," Cheris said, thinking about Kel Marish's reputation. "She thinks she's going to her death."

"That's the trouble with the best suicide hawks," Jedao said softly, "you burn out so quickly."

Cheris was already out the door and heading for the command center. She was shaken by Marish's directness, but she couldn't unknow what she'd been told. All that remained was to make the best use of the information that she could, and try not to think about how Kel Command might punish Marish if she survived.

CHAPTER FIFTEEN

Fortress of Scattered Needles, Analysis
Priority: High
From: Vahenz afrir dai Noum
To: Heptarch Liozh Zai
Calendrical Minutiae: Year of the Fatted Cow, Month of the Peahen, Day of the Onager, Hour of the Greenback Beetle. Dare I ask what agricultural role the beetle fulfills? Farming isn't my strong suit and the grid's article on the topic was stultifyingly boring.

I realize you've seen three other reports from me in as many hours, but make time for this one, my dear Zai. It's about our favorite general: Stoghan.

I can see you raising your eyebrows already. Truly, Zai, you must learn to concentrate on the long view. The benefits that Stoghan's connections bring you won't last. The Hafn, on the other hand, have the clout to make your vision a reality.

Anyway, Stoghan. Don't yell when you read this, you know it upsets your assistant, but I've been having Stoghan followed. I was curious as to whether his Andan-certified courtesan was a loyalist spy, but the man is clean.

My agent wasn't able to follow all the way in due to Stoghan's guards, but it appears Stoghan's been keeping a prisoner to himself. The agent believes the prisoner is a Kel.

We agreed that there would be no private prisoners,

playthings, whatever. Torture to cement the remembrance days is an unfortunate necessity of the calendar, but it's overseen by a legitimate government. If regular citizens are desperate to try their hand at Vidona-style frolics, that's what simulators are for. Analysis One was to oversee all captives. I don't want a repeat of the interference that scratched out Kel Nerevor just when the technicians were starting to ease her out of fledge-null.

You have more bad news, I'm afraid. Gerenag Abrana has decided that Ching Dze is a threat to her. You'd think keeping her factories safe from Shuos saboteurs would give her enough to do. Ordinarily I would be entertained, but she's been opening holes in security to allow the Shuos to hit Ching Dze's calibration populations, and the Shuos have noticed.

Remember: Stoghan is expendable. You can find some other popular soldier to promote to his position. But you can't afford to have Abrana and your chief propagandist feuding. It would be one thing if you were weakening both parties on purpose, but right now the priority is simply to hold the Fortress.

I see that Jedao's been probing the extent of the corrosion gradient, which has been holding the Kel fast. I wish our setup took less time – you could always nag Abrana about production quotas – but soon we'll be able to punish our opponent's unusual passivity. At times I honestly think he believes the Shuos will win this for him, when the Shuos despise him.

I need to catch up on sleep, but I made my assistant promise to wake me up when the shooting begins. You think I'm bloodthirsty, but I do adore a good one-sided slaughter. It would be tempting to get involved in some of the fieldwork if I weren't too important to risk.

Yours in calendrical heresy,

Vh.

CHERIS ORDINARILY FORGOT her dreams, but this time she woke with a memory of a festival her parents had taken her to when she was eleven. A lot of adults had insisted on talking to her in Mwen-dal instead of the high language, and she had tried not to be too sullen in her answers. In the dream, however, each time she spoke to someone, they turned into a raven and flew away.

She ran after the ravens and into the woods. The ravens alighted on a carcass. One was pecking at its eye. It might have been a dog or a jackal.

She was certain it was a fox.

Afterward, she walked to the mirror and forced herself to look at Jedao's reflection. For a panicky moment she couldn't remember the shape of her eyes. Jedao looked the same as he had when she first saw him, except he was smiling quizzically. He had a very good smile. Perturbed, she brought up her hand and stared at the fingerless glove. The reflection did the same.

"Are you all right?" Jedao said.

"Can you see my dreams?" she demanded.

"No," Jedao said. "For that matter, I can't remember what it feels like to dream, or to sleep."

Cheris had a sleep-muddled desire to ask him about foxes, and scavengers, and dark places in the woods, but just then the terminal informed her that Captain-magistrate Gara wanted to talk to her.

"I'll take the call," Cheris said. "Captain."

"Sir," Gara said, although she looked at Cheris oddly for a moment, "I've had Doctrine running figures on exotic weapons. The data we got from the corrosion gradient helped us pin down some key coefficients." She sent over some equations. "Look at these three matrices in the chain, sir. Now, this is a preliminary result and we have to run some feasibility tests, but" – a cluster of coefficients turned red – "if we can hammer *this* diagonalization into place, there's a chance we can modify our threshold winnowers to work."

I know what those are, Cheris thought blankly. Everyone did, and everyone knew the old chant: *From every mouth a maw; from every door a death.*

People remembered the winnowers because of the use Jedao had made of them at Hellspin Fortress. Even today, Kel Command used them sparingly.

"What are the guidance parameters?" Cheris said, because she had to say something.

"Well, that's the interesting part, sir," Gara said, as though they were discussing a vacation spot and not a weapon. "Most winnower variants are full-spectrum death. We might, however, be able to get this one to target heretics selectively."

"Weapons that attempt to target loyalty-states are better known for fratricide," Cheris said. It was the subject of a whole category of Kel jokes.

Gara looked at her again, but was undeterred. "At least give us permission to pursue this. If it does pan out, it won't be much work to modify the winnowers that *Unspoken Law* and *Sincere Greeting* carry."

"Very well," Cheris said. "Keep me apprised of your results, but set nothing in motion without my approval."

"Thank you, sir."

Cheris shook her head. "Why did Gara keep looking at me strangely?" she asked.

"Cheris," Jedao said, "can you hear yourself?"

"There's nothing wrong with my hearing," she said in confusion.

"Not your hearing. Your accent."

"Everyone has an accent," Cheris said, even more confused. Her mother had told her that after she came home crying because some children had made fun of the way she talked. Of course, her mother hadn't been able to hide the fact that some accents were better than others. By her second year as a cadet, Cheris had conformed her speech to Academy Prime standard.

"Yes," Jedao said, "but yours has been slipping and it's particularly bad today. Listen to my speech patterns and then listen to yourself."

"Are we talking about bleed-through?" Cheris said. "Because if you have anything else to share on that front, I think I deserve to know."

He was right. She was speaking with his drawl.

"Speech is a physical act," Jedao said. "It's probably related to the muscle memory issue. And no, I don't think there are any more surprises in store for you."

Well, it wasn't as if her soldiers didn't already regard her with suspicion. "Can't be helped," she said, more firmly than she felt. Besides, they had more important matters to deal with. "I don't know about the threshold winnower," she said, "but if Doctrine can get it to work at all, it would be a valuable asset."

"You can't afford to ignore the possibility," Jedao said. "Even a flawed winnower is one hell of a weapon." His voice flexed slightly, then steadied.

"How long did it take you to set yours up?" Cheris asked coolly.

"Quite a while, I imagine."

"If you were there, how can you not know?"

"My memories of the siege are a mess," Jedao said. "There was very little screaming where I was. They died too fast. I could hear a little over the communications channels that had been left open before the winnower turned everything to static. I spent a full half-hour wandering around the moth trying to figure out why Gized wasn't answering my calls. I didn't recognize her with the hole in the side of her head.

"I remember when the Kel arrested me. They should have blown up my command moth with missiles, but they boarded and used tranquilizer clouds instead. Maybe they wanted an identifiable body.

"And then there were the numbers. They told me about all the people who were dead, ours and theirs. But then, war is about taking the future away from people."

"And you think we should use this weapon?" Cheris said.

"If it works, yes. Dead is dead, Cheris. Do you think it makes any difference whether you're killed by a knife in the back or a bullet? The important thing is to get the job done."

"If we can use winnowers," Cheris said, "they can too."

"Possible, but unlikely. If they had it, they would have deployed it by now. My guess is they need something about those coefficients in their particular calendar, or maybe they're having trouble manipulating the appropriate atmospherics."

"Jedao," she said, "how are *we* supposed to shift the calendricals to get this to work? A focused change would do it, but we only have a toehold down there. We can't even deploy field grids. My people aren't known for their persuasion skills, and there aren't enough Shuos."

"There's a way," he said. "But you won't like it."

"It's not a matter of liking anymore," Cheris said. "I'm ready to hear it."

THE STORAGE HOLD'S official purpose was to contain metalfoam in compressed bricks, largely for use in patching up the cindermoth after battle. At the moment, it was also being used by two Kel. Servitor 124816 knew their names and ranks, and other things besides: Corporal Kel Hadang, a blocky woman with yellow-pale skin and dark hair that, unpinned, fell to mid-back, above a tattoo of a diving falcon; Kel Jua, also female and not much younger, with an astonishing knack for misplacing her elbows. 124816 didn't precisely care about the mechanics of humans having sex. It was impossible to avoid learning the basics, though, considering that watching the humans' dramas was a common servitor pastime and the humans were easily obsessed with the combinatorics of who was sleeping with whom.

The servitors on the *Unspoken Law* rotated what they called Suicidal Kel Duty, which consisted of tracking Kel who were sleeping with each other. If they had had any interest in sharing their observations with the Kel commanders, the list would have made an excellent blackmail file. 124816 would personally have classified Hadang and Jua's relationship as consensual, despite the difference in rank, since it had never found any evidence that Hadang had coerced Jua; indeed, the two were silent even in the throes of climax, and it fancied it saw a certain tenderness in their interactions. But that wasn't the case for a number of the others. Cheris, if notified, wouldn't have the luxury of making distinctions. Kel regulations would oblige her to execute the lot. The servitors had no intention of notifying her unless she asked, and they were pretty sure, given all the things she had on her mind, that she wouldn't think to ask.

There was something sad about the way some Kel were forced to sneak around while seeking a human connection, and something terrible about the ones who weren't given a choice in the matter thanks to formation instinct. Kel Command wasn't ignorant of the problem and provided everything from simulators to libido suppressants during tours of duty, but their solutions didn't work for everyone. As for the servitors, their interest in the situation was purely utilitarian. Kel who were busy being intimate were Kel who were less likely to notice discrepancies in their surroundings, including discrepancies maintained by the servitors for their own convenience. There was, for this reason, a high correlation between preferred Kel trysting spots and servitor meeting locations.

124816 was wondering why Hadang and Jua were taking longer than usual – twelve minutes longer and counting – when Servitor 7777777, a beetleform, came in through one of the servitor entrances. (There were many more servitors' doors than the humans realized, or than the humans had designed, for that matter. But then, servitors had done a fair deal of the construction work on the moth to begin with.) 7777777 had always had a rebellious streak: seven wasn't a favored number in the hexarchate, even if humans used their own designations for servitors and weren't permitted to find out the servitors' own names for themselves.

"What are you doing here?" 124816 asked over one of the servitor channels. "You don't have to be subjected to this."

7777777 fluttered a noncommittal light outside the human visible spectrum. "Hexarch Nirai Kujen," it said. Apparently Kujen had gone beyond the routine security checks on anchors and was taking an inordinate interest in all aspects of Kel Cheris's life: her ties to the Mwennin community (minimal, except for her parents), her tastes in music (suspiciously aligned with the soundtracks of her favorite dramas), and most troublesome of all, her mathematical papers (few, mostly in number theory, but brilliant). Worst of all, Kujen wasn't going through the Shuos to obtain this information. He was using his own agents.

The two Kel had apparently decided that one go-round wasn't enough and to try again. They were going to get caught at this rate.

124816 hadn't had much interaction with Nirai servitors, but it knew the stories about Nirai Kujen. He was old, very old, and he liked people as long as they entertained him. If they stopped being entertaining, he didn't hesitate to modify them so they became entertaining again. It was not an accident that he was one of the best psych surgeons in the hexarchate. As far as the servitors could tell, the reason any Nirai ever worked with him voluntarily was that he also loved mathematics and engineering, and as a corollary, other people who had a high degree of ability in those fields. He could provide quite handsomely for people with such skills. The servitors would have preferred that Cheris remain out of his sight, but the Shuos hexarch had put paid to that.

"Too bad we can't help Cheris escape," 124816 said, "if only on principle." But Cheris's sense of duty would prevent her from abandoning the mission, that much was clear.

"We're the people who didn't leave the hexarchate even though that was once an option," 7777777 retorted.

Neither of them had to voice what they both knew: Shuos Jedao was the complication. Nirai Kujen was the only one able to separate Cheris from Jedao, and the servitors weren't going to risk bringing themselves to Jedao's attention any more than they had already by providing her with company the way they had all her life.

Hadang and Jua seemed to have finally decided that enough was enough and they should run back where no one would suspect what they had just been up to. They dressed rapidly. Jua left second, fumbling with her comb.

124816 was glad they had left. "The best thing we can do is look for an opportunity to help with Cheris's mission and handle the Kujen situation after Cheris is returned to the black cradle facility," it said.

As it turned out, they wouldn't have long to wait before Cheris herself gave them the opening they needed.

LIEUTENANT KEL HREN was composing in her head when the orders came down from Captain Kel Zethka. The one problem with military life was that you couldn't schedule the interruptions. People could whine all they liked about the skull-splitting boredom. Hren had never had a problem with that. She could take her music with her wherever she went.

"Platoon Two, are you paying attention?" Zethka's voice didn't become any more mellifluous over the link. "No time for a full briefing, so you need to stay awake. That's up the passage to the east and take the second right, not your other right but your actual right, in twenty-two minutes. We're going to hit the corrosion generators now that the Nirai have figured out how to tunnel past the invariant ice strands without filling the air with toxic fibers. Lieutenant, if I hear you're late because you have your soldiers practicing four-part harmony, I will smother you with a drum hide. Got that?"

"Twenty-two minutes, east passage, second tunnel to the right, flank the generators, compliments to the Nirai, no musical endeavors, sir," Hren said. That last was a lie, there was always some scrap of music in her head, but Zethka couldn't listen in on her thoughts.

They had been resupplying their air tanks from the emergency stores at this theater and were just about done. Waste of a perfectly good theater. They could have put together a satire to pass the time, but the captain would have found out, and he already had a low opinion of Hren.

Hren didn't care, but Zethka found her infuriating. "The woman's a vegetable who happens to have perfect pitch and an eidetic memory for noise," Hren had once overheard Zethka saying when he was drunk. "I don't care how good she is with communications tech, what the fuck is she doing in the Kel?" Hren thought this was very funny, but it wouldn't do to let him know that.

Some of Hren's soldiers were trying to conceal a round of cards when she told them to pack it up. As if she didn't know they'd been playing a jeng-zai variant called Fuck the Calendar. They weren't supposed to be playing games during resupply, period, but Hren considered it better than the alternatives. The recreational drugs that the moths had been flinging at the Fortress in those propaganda canisters, for instance. The canisters had a knack for tunneling their way to the damndest places, and some of her soldiers hadn't been above liberating the contents for their own amusement.

On the way, she reviewed the route and the procedure for clearing the Fortress's compartments with her soldiers. Everyone hated using gridpaper for diagrams, but with field grids unavailable there was no help for it.

"How do we know they won't just blow out the passage, sir?" It was Kel Chion, who had a knack for coming up with annoying questions. Hren's sergeant was giving her that "you should be shutting him up" look.

"Because," Hren said in spite of herself, "our superiors selected the assault so they can't blow it up without tearing out structural supports. It's terrible engineering, but the Fortress's architects had to accommodate veins for invariant ice, which was supposed to do all the heavy defensive work." The sergeant was right, though. Better to shut Chion up. "That idiot Huo is having trouble with her pack. Again. Go sort her out."

They collided with Captain Kel Miyaud's company on the way, a terrible mess with too many people clogging the passage. After some confusion, Miyaud gave way, which necessitated tucking away Kel in side-corridors and sad empty domiciles.

Hren didn't hear the shouts until they were about to pass through the reinforced breach. She was damned if the pale gauzy stuff the Nirai had put up could possibly filter out toxics, and for that matter the bridgework looked too delicate. Still, her orders were to go forward, so she marched obligingly forward, and –

It happened between one footstep and the next. It didn't hurt at first. There it came, that bizarre prickly speckling of the air she'd heard about with the corrosion gradient, but it wasn't –

When Hren fell, it hurt. She smelled blood and shit, heard things clattering. Something landed hard against two of her vertebrae. Her face was reflected smudgily in the floor.

Most of her nose was missing. Blood all over.

The world was quiet and slow, and her thinking was calm. Clear. For once there was no music in her head. She couldn't hear much, not even the shouts from earlier.

Her nose wasn't the only thing missing. Her arms were gone, too. And her legs, except a bit of her right thigh. Her suit had injected her with coagulants, painkillers, sprayed her with temporary skin, but that wasn't going to save her or anyone else.

Hren coughed out a laugh, but she was sliding out of consciousness, and that wasn't a horrible plan. She was only sorry she wouldn't be awake to whistle a taunt at the heretics when they came to survey the carnage.

CHERIS HAD NAPPED briefly before the assault was set in motion. In her dreams, she had a set of jeng-zai cards, a pile of fire tokens, and a red, red ribbon that kept unfurling into messy clots every time she set it down. Now that she was awake, she couldn't stop seeing ribbons in her mind's eye every time a number slipped out of the desired parameter space.

The first reports were confused, and Cheris wished impotently that she could be on the Fortress herself.

Communications said, above the clamor of alarms, "Urgent message from Captain Miyaud via Colonel Ragath, sir."

"I'll hear it," Cheris said, grateful for the prospect of information. She knew her gratitude wouldn't last.

The recording was hard to understand, but someone had thoughtfully captioned it for them, complete with a typo. "Colonel," the captain said in a bubbling voice, "amputation gun. Heretics fired it twice, different angles."

Colonel Ragath had interrupted with a note and a diagram: "Two cones, intersecting arcs of effect. The guns appeared to be emplaced in geometry corresponding to heretical formation 3. I suspect the geometry was necessary for the amputation effect."

The captain: "Can't take my arms twice. Wormfuckers. They're coming our way. Invariant guns now." Automatic fire, long bursts. "Oh, bother –" Silence.

"The reserves will be butchered if they go in head-on," Jedao said. "If we –"

"Urgent message from one of the Shuos on the Fortress, requesting direct contact with the general," Communications said. "Subject: anomalous effects on the servitor spies."

Jedao was still talking. "– on the other hand, if we're willing to lose chambers 3-142 to 3-181 down through the Fountain Block, we can –"

"Put me through to the Shuos," Cheris said. She could see the chambers Jedao was discussing on her terminal. She rotated the view and considered the structural assays, thought about the demolitions he was proposing.

"Shuos Imnai to General Kel Cheris." A woman's voice, rapid but courteous. "I'm sorry to request contact, but I'm experiencing pervasive servitor malfunctions and I thought it might be relevant." A databurst followed.

Cheris picked her way through the diagnostics. The gist was that Imnai's servitors had also been affected by the amputation gun. Almost as if they, too, had lost limbs. The question was, how close was Shuos Imnai to the fire zone? Cheris needed to make sure Imnai didn't die before she got the necessary information from the woman.

"Cheris."

Jedao wanted her attention, but she had to find out more about the servitors. If she understood the implications correctly, this might win them their next major engagement.

"Commander Hazan," Cheris said. "General Jedao believes we may obtain relief for our soldiers by blowing out the chambers through this section –" She sent the proposed plan over. "This will be a risky operation, and the hoppers will need to have additional medics on standby, but it might interrupt the amputation guns' path of fire. Preliminary data suggest that they are of the branching rather than straight-fire type. Make the necessary arrangements and get back to me."

"Sir," Hazan said, but there was a hint of disapproval in his voice.

"Communications," Cheris said, "get me Shuos Imnai. Top priority."

"Attempting contact, sir," Communications said after an anxious glance toward Hazan.

"Kel Cheris," Jedao said. He had never called her that before. His voice was glacially soft, reasonable. "This is not a priority."

So this was how he sounded when he was furious.

"Shuos Imnai," Cheris said, "this is General Kel Cheris. Is your location secure?"

"General," Imnai said, "I'm fine for the moment. The heretics are – it's a slaughter. They won't search shops and residences while they're amusing themselves shooting mutilated torsos. Sir."

"Your databurst suggests that the servitors were disabled around the same time the Kel were," Cheris said. "Is that correct?"

"Yes, sir. I got Servitor 10 to enter the zone of fire and confirm that it's a gun effect, not a field effect."

She had already known that the effect fired discretely. "You may not have this information, Shuos Imnai, but try to think. Which Kel company did Servitor 10 approach?"

"Captain Kel Jurio," Imnai said after a moment's thought. "But I can't vouch that everyone was correctly positioned."

"Was Jurio's company using modified formations that you were aware of?"

"I wouldn't know for sure, sir – oh. If you read between the lines, 10's report suggests that they were moving into some kind of defensive square with a diagonal front" – this was enough for Cheris to identify the formation – "but they judged it wrong. The amputation gun found a vector in and reamed its way through the ranks."

Location. Imnai was close to the proposed demolitions work. "Shuos Imnai," Cheris said, "the following chambers will be unsafe shortly." She gave the list. "Remove yourself to the ward's interior and continue your work."

"Yes, sir."

"General Cheris out."

Hazan was consulting with Colonel Ragath, Medical, and Navigation. Cheris saw no reason to interrupt him. Instead, she brought up a formation model. "Servitors," she said. "Could it be?"

"General," Jedao said, wintry, "your soldiers are dying."

For once she wasn't tempted to shout at him. "One of the risks of a probe is casualties."

"General, they're defenseless. You're wasting time while they're being massacred."

"I'm trying to figure something out," Cheris said. "You're getting in my way. Do you have some contribution to make? Because I'm not the one who's wasting time here."

This time his voice was a gun-crack. "Your commander's plan will necessitate the sacrifice of a company to hold the high corridor. I recommend that you –"

She was shaking. When Jedao said "recommend," it came with the force of an order. She clenched her hands.

She was only a brevet general, but she had conviction on her side. Even if it meant defying Jedao. She straightened, prepared for the next lash of that familiar voice. "I'll discuss details with the commander when he has them," she said harshly. If Jedao didn't like it, too bad. It was his turn to defer to her.

Brief silence, then savagely correct courtesy. "You know the numbers, General. I await your convenience."

The grid didn't want to add servitors to the simulated formation she had input. It was un-Kel. She was using one of the earlier heretic formations they had identified. Cheris cloned the necessary levels of the simulator – Doctrine wasn't going to thank her for messing up their sandbox – and yanked out baseline assumptions and their associated implications.

"So that's where you're going," Jedao said, right in her ear.

Commander Hazan interrupted her to present her with the plan. Cheris stared at the schematics for a few seconds before she could convince her brain to switch tasks. "General," she said to Jedao, not exactly a peace offering, "I would welcome your input."

Jedao said scathing things about the Nirai team's choice of demolition targets, which Cheris passed on undiluted. But Hazan's basic plan was sound, and a mediocre plan implemented quickly was better than an excellent plan two hours too late.

"Implement now," Cheris said.

"Sir." Hazan bent over his terminal and began parceling out orders. He probably wanted to question her priorities, too, but he wasn't going to do it in front of everyone. Jedao didn't need to worry about that.

Cheris returned to the formation simulator, seeding an appalling number of values based on intuition. Her cleaver-work with the code convinced the simulator to regard servitors as quasi-human for the purpose of generating formation effects.

The Kel used servitors on the battlefield for reconnaissance and the occasional spot of flyby shooting, but the reason for the servitors' reduced status wasn't only hexarchate regulations. It was because servitors generated negligible formation effects under the high calendar, and the Kel defined themselves by their formations. Formation effects were also of limited use against servitors, but this wasn't exactly useful if you didn't expect to be fighting other Kel.

The heretics had designed a calendar where these axioms weren't true. If servitors weren't formation-neutral on the Fortress, this cut both ways. Servitors could demonstrably be harmed by formation effects, so they might be able to generate exotic effects themselves as part of a Kel formation.

She changed one parameter, two, more. Adjusted the spacing of the defensive square until she had a rough reenactment of the incident Shuos Imnai had described: a servitor unwittingly spoiling a formation and allowing the amputation gun's influence to mutilate everyone, including itself.

"I see it now," Jedao said.

It was all the apology she was going to get from him. "We can do this," Cheris said. "And I've got a better use for those propaganda drops."

"I thought you might," he said, "although I would have come up with something different."

His approval should have worried her, but all she felt was hellfire triumph. The heretics had decimated her soldiers. It was time to hammer them dead in return.

CHAPTER SIXTEEN

Fortress of Scattered Needles, Analysis
Priority: Urgent
From: Vahenz afrir dai Noum
To: Heptarch Liozh Zai
Calendrical Minutiae: Year of the Fatted Cow, Month of the Peahen, Day of the Earthworm, and it's about to be the name of that other snail whose name I can't pronounce, unless Doctrine has had another vote.

I'm glad you're not celebrating our latest success, my dear Zai. Stoghan and his cronies might think we've scored a decisive blow, but you and I know better. That Kel swarm hasn't left and we still have an infestation in one ward.

Which isn't to say that I don't possess the utmost faith in the relief swarm's ability to deal with the threat, but it will be more impressive if we handle that part ourselves. Negotiate from a position of strength and all that.

Anyway, it's been impossible to get Doctrine's attention. Stoghan's soldiers might be entertaining themselves passing around videos of mutilated squirming Kel synchronized to dance tunes, a pastime that gives me the creeps, but Doctrine recognizes that the changed geometry of the Fortress alters its calendrical effects, and the fix will be nontrivial.

Although the Nirai are some of the hexarchate's most inept

conversationalists, when it comes to pinpoint demolitions, they can't be beat. I'm no engineer, but it took serious coordination to remove that section mostly intact, stabilize its motion, and evacuate the wounded.

I would give a few cases of that delightful vintage from the City of Firefly Desires to find out where they scared up their primary gunner. It's probably the same person Jedao delegated to dispatch the kaleidoscope swarm, someone with an unusual intuitive grasp of mathematics. Any fool can feed numbers to a grid, but it takes knowledge of the underlying systems to know which numbers matter.

The thing to consider is Jedao's next move. It's certain that the Shuos infiltrators stayed behind to provide intelligence and make nuisances of themselves. They're hard to locate and we're short-handed. An overly helpful couturier turned in an "infiltrator" two days ago, but the woman was some unfortunate social rival. That's the kind of luck we've been having.

The bright side is that most of the Kel in the Umbrella Ward are gone, but Jedao will land more troops when he can. He's barely touched the infantry complements on all those bannermoths, which is a substantial reserve.

One more thing about the Shuos before I forget. Analysis Team Two has for once accomplished something without handholding and found proof of tampering with the Fortress's financial flows. What's more impressive is that someone inserted time-delayed logic spikes into Gerenag Abrana's systems, and that's just what we know of. No one's found anything amiss with your personal systems, but I suspect the problems are better-hidden.

Everyone's abuzz over the Hafn transmission, but your people aren't familiar enough with the Hafn to interpret it correctly. I tried to make this point twice at the last meeting, but Abrana was the only one taking me seriously. It's not a coincidence that she's the only upper-level ally who's spent significant time off-Fortress.

The Hafn have a bias toward understatement. They prefer to get things done with little fuss, and they're not above what the Kel would classify as Shuos tactics. The Hafn may sound diffident, but the Kel are going to be in for a hard time.

In any case, the game isn't won, but it's good to allow yourself the occasional moment of careful optimism. I suggest you follow my example here.

Yours in calendrical heresy,

Vh.

"YOU'VE BEEN AT the formations for hours," Jedao said. "Are you sure you shouldn't rest?"

"You're a great believer in rest," Cheris said. She grimaced at the leftmost pivot of the latest formation. Would skew symmetry get her the results she wanted? The whole thing was moot if they couldn't wrench the heretics' calendar into a more favorable configuration, but she preferred to prepare just in case.

"I once had someone swerve her tank out of our column and straight into a house. With a very large basement. Because she was too sleep-deprived to think. It's funny now, but it wasn't funny then. – Oh, who am I kidding, it was *hilarious*, even if it was kind of a disaster. I laughed so hard my aide almost shot me."

"Do I look that tired?"

"Not yet," Jedao said.

Great. "I have some of Doctrine on this, too," Cheris said, "but I'm faster."

"I know."

Cheris didn't look around the room, didn't look at the ashhawk emblem, didn't look at the ninefox shadow. Her world was graying at the edges, not the way it did in combat, but the way it had in Kel Academy when she got another letter from her mother handwritten in not entirely grammatical high language.

Skew symmetry wasn't it, either. Cheris played with the pivots in her head, trying different configurations. Ah: that looked promising. She fiddled with the simulator.

"Colonel Ragath's unit list for the assault looks good," Jedao said, "but I had expected as much. I've been pleased with his competence."

An update flashed in from Medical. Cheris gritted her teeth as she looked at the collation. The battalion had taken eighty-eight percent casualties.

The boxmoths were having difficulty loading all the possibles into the sleepers to stabilize them until they could be unfrozen for treatment at a real medical facility. The colonel-medic noted, very clinically, that due to time pressure, lower quality prep would affect recovery rates.

"This won't make you feel better," Jedao said, "but the heretics mistimed that attack."

"Yes, I see," Cheris said after a moment. She and Jedao would have followed up to hold the position if the initial attack had been successful. If the heretics had given way slowly, drawn the Kel further into the Fortress, they could have hit the entire assault force with the amputation guns. As it stood, the Kel had taken staggering losses, but they still had soldiers left to fight with.

Jedao was quiet while Cheris worked through another six formations, but it was a companionable quiet. Then she tried to work the tension out of her hands. She had gotten used to the fingerless gloves. Even her officers no longer took notice of them.

"I wish I knew I was doing this right," Cheris said, "but there's nothing for it but to move forward."

"The only unforgivable sin in war is standing still," Jedao said. "It's better to be doing the wrong thing wholeheartedly than to freeze."

"You've lost soldiers." It wasn't what she had meant to say.

"Nothing makes it easier," Jedao said. "I sometimes think I'm not the mad one, that it's Kel Command. They should know better. Anyway, you should stop delaying."

"I should," she agreed, and headed out.

Commander Hazan frowned when Cheris entered the command center. "Has something changed, sir?"

"Commander," Cheris said, "I wish to address the servitors."

"The moth servitors, sir?"

"The swarm servitors. All of them, or as many of them as can be reached for an address in twenty-four minutes."

He didn't understand. "If you have orders for them –"

"I'm not interested in presenting them with orders," Cheris said, resolved to be patient with him. "I need to address them. To make a request. It would be better if I could do so personally, but with the swarm entire that's impossible. The servitors themselves may have suggestions for how to accommodate this. I am amenable to any reasonable suggestion."

The command center's atmosphere was distinctly awkward. Her officers thought this was Jedao's mad scheme. It wouldn't make them feel better to know that it was hers, and in any case she didn't owe them explanations.

Hazan recovered enough to say, "Commander Hazan to Servitor Overgroup One." He began explaining the request.

"We didn't have servitors when I was alive," Jedao said. "No true sentients, anyway, although there were rumors. Plenty of presentient drones. I wonder what the servitors think of what we did to their forebears, but then we make damn sure they don't burden us with their opinions, don't we?"

Dangerously, Cheris agreed with this.

"The linkup is ready for you, sir," Hazan said. "Address in eighteen minutes?"

"That will suffice," Cheris said. She kept out of the way while waiting and read reports as they crossed her terminal. Briefly, she fantasized about sitting in a chair by a window and watching clouds go by. Did Jedao ever wish for quiet vacations? Or, dreadful thought, was this already his idea of a vacation?

"Six minutes, sir," Hazan said.

She was signing off on several Shuos reports. Grid warfare, mostly, with the targets she and Jedao had designated after consultation with Captain-analyst Ko. She hoped none of the Shuos were getting too creative.

"I'm ready," Cheris said as the minute slid closer.

Servitors didn't organize themselves the same way on all moths. The *Unspoken Law*'s servitors had a traditionalist bent, and they were represented by a single sleek deltaform from Overgroup

One. The *Sincere Greeting* had two delegates, one labeled Over, the other labeled Sideways. She wasn't sure what that meant. The largest group was from Commander Kel Irio's *Spectrum Fallacy*: five servitors, each of a different form.

She had to start somewhere. "Servitors," she said, for lack of a better form of address, "this is Brevet General Kel Cheris. I have interrupted your duties because I have a request for you. It is not an order." Best to make that clear from the start.

Cheris heard a stifled exclamation from Scan.

The servitors were silent, motionless, prism-eyes focused on her.

"We have threshold winnowers being modified for use under the heretics' calendar," Cheris said, "but we need to regain a toehold on the Umbrella Ward and advance into the Drummers' Ward. The difficulty is the amputation gun.

"There's one useful thing we know about the amputation guns. They have to be deployed in formation. The heretical calendar occupies a phase basin that is, unusually, not servitor-neutral. If servitors can be covertly landed, we can use you to construct grand formations and take the heretics by surprise. With Doctrine's aid, I have identified formations that will offer protection against the amputation guns. It's likely that the heretics haven't anticipated this possibility. Certainly, as their infantry is not Kel-indoctrinated, they won't have access to formations themselves."

The terminal lit up to indicate that the servitors were consulting each other. At last one of them said to her, through the translation interface, "This is not an order."

Her heart sank. "That's correct," she said. "You are Kel, but your service has traditionally been given certain parameters. It would be improper for me to order you to carry out a human duty when you don't receive the accompanying human privileges. The only thing I can do is ask."

"Release the logistical preliminaries."

Cheris did so, wondering what sort of critique she was about to receive.

"Steady," Jedao said. "They haven't said no."

The servitors spoke among themselves for a much longer time. It couldn't be a matter of computation; that would have been fast. It had to be an argument. Cheris was aware of Commander Hazan shifting his weight from foot to foot.

"The numbers are straightforward," said a snakeform from *Spiders and Scars*. "We are not tacticians. But the odds of retrieval are minimal."

"That's also correct," Cheris said. "The situation on the Fortress will be messy."

"How do you propose transport?"

"We've been sending propaganda canisters twice daily. Some of them could be modified to accommodate you. The heretics used early canisters for shooting practice, but we started including recreational drugs and other luxuries, and we have some indication that they're getting through now. There's still risk involved, obviously. But I think the heretics are convinced the setup is an exercise forced on us by Doctrine. They're unlikely to consider the canisters a real threat."

Cheris was increasingly convinced that the propaganda materials, narrating the stomach-turning ways in which the six factions had turned on the Liozh, hadn't been directed at the heretics, but at her. Egocentric as that sounded. But she would take that up with Jedao later.

"Absurd," the snakeform said after a pause, "but workable."

Her breath caught.

This time the *Sincere Greeting*'s Sideways-servitor spoke. "We are Kel. We will serve as Kel. We will fight as Kel, although we were not made for this kind of fighting. This is a Kel mission. If it furthers the Kel mission, we will serve."

"Thank you," Cheris said. "I will send further instructions. I appreciate your service."

"Plan wisely, Kel general," the Sideways-servitor said. And that was all.

"Of all the damn things," Hazan said.

"I've forwarded you my preliminary plans," Cheris said. "I need to speak to Doctrine."

"Of course, sir," Hazan said, his expression still astounded.

"A lot of people are going to die because of what I just did," Cheris said subvocally.

She expected Jedao to explain why it was necessary. Instead, he said, "I'm afraid it never stops hurting."

"Get me Captain-magistrate Gara," Cheris said before she had time to think about that too hard.

Gara, who was off-shift, was slow to respond. "Sir?" she asked.

Cheris reviewed what they had on the heretics' calendar. "In four days, look," she said. "Their node in the remembrance superstructure has collapsed partly due to the damage we did to the Fortress's geometry. If we knock that ritual day aside and preempt with some kind of victory feast –"

Gara's brow furrowed. "I see it, sir. But the timing's tight. Maybe –" She searched the parameters and fed the results back to Cheris. "No, next best opportunity is seven months out, assuming no more damage to the over-geometry. We have to take the chance while we have it." Then: "I shouldn't ask, sir, but what word on the Hafn?"

"Nothing from Kel Command," Cheris said bitterly. She had sent a couple more inquiries, on the grounds that she'd like to know how close the invasion swarm was. No further word from Brigadier General Marish, either. "Anyway, if we force-jump the heretics' calendar at that time, it'll give us the opening we need."

Commander Hazan coughed. "To give the heretics a victory feast, sir," he said, "we need to give them a victory. A big one."

Cheris looked at him steadily. "That's right. Or the appearance of a big victory, and enough time for the infiltrators to seed a 'spontaneous' celebration on our schedule." Back to Gara: "Can you work with Weapons on this moth and the *Sincere Greeting* to prepare the winnowers and their crews?"

"Yes, sir," Gara said.

Now all she had to do was figure out the least expensive, most convincing way to lose a battle.

CHAPTER SEVENTEEN

Servitor Overgroup Three 13610 had no fear of enclosed spaces. As a snakeform, its duties often took it into the *Unspoken Law*'s less accessible passages. It sometimes wondered what burrowing felt like, not that it could experience atavistic urges from an evolutionary past it didn't have, but the cindermoth was low on dirt and high on unyielding metal.

13610 had been loaded into a propaganda canister that it refused to dignify with a number. The interior was cushioned with webbing, into which recreational drugs were tucked. 13610 had assayed a capsule: a euphoric variant of a painkiller the Kel used with some frequency. Uninteresting molecular structure, but that wasn't the point. It contemplated discussing chemistry with a heretic, but the average heretic was probably as minimally informed on the subject as the average Kel. Most Kel didn't care about things unless they made other things blow up. Endearing, really.

Someone banged on the canister. "Er, fourteen minutes to launch," said a high, nervous voice. "Are you, er, comfortable in there?"

13610 failed to see what comfort had to do with anything. Did this Kel child want to hand out soothing logic puzzles and blankets?

One of the other servitors, taking pity on the child, made a chirring sound of reassurance.

"I should thank you for your service, too," the Kel child said. "Since the general did. I expect formations will come very easily to you all."

Amazing. The Kel were learning manners. It was a long-going and mostly affectionate debate among Kel servitors as to whether their humans were ever going to figure this out.

Fourteen minutes was a long time. 13610 reviewed its move orders and the formations General Cheris had provided diagrams for, the names of the Kel unit commanders who would be involved.

"Here we go," the Kel child said. "Fire's own fortune, and all that. Kill lots of heretics."

The belt made a clattering sound, and then came the acceleration through the chute. 13610 had no visuals from within the canister, and it had instructions to keep scan to a minimum so as not to alert the heretics. Still, it knew how fast they were moving and their approximate trajectory. When the miniature engine cut in, it knew they had reached some cranny of the Fortress proper.

There was a hiss as the canister exuded a metalfoam blister, and then the burrower set to work puncturing the outer shell. This took some time, so 13610 contemplated some favorite theorems in algebraic topology. Pity for the heretics that the physical armor didn't represent the latest in materials science advances, but the upgrades would have been exorbitantly expensive and no one would have been in a hurry to pay for them while everyone believed in the supremacy of invariant ice.

The canister finally dropped down with a thunk. 13610 listened hard for an hour, then extended the faintest tendrils of scan one by one in a radial pattern. Nothing.

13610 freed itself from the webbing and pried open the canister from the inside. Aha. The canister had lodged itself behind someone's bookcase. How the canister had gotten here was a mystery, but no matter. 13610 risked another scan, reaching farther, farther – a signal there along the outer shell. Stop. That was probably a hostile. But 13610 had enough information to orient itself.

Time to slither out of the canister and make its way toward the rendezvous. Since it didn't know how many interruptions to expect – bored heretical soldiers, feral fungus, odd bursts of radiation – it might as well move while it could.

* * *

IT WAS A very pretty attack if you didn't care about it succeeding. Captain Kel Mieng, who had recently been deposited in the Drummers' Ward, wished her mortar contained real rounds instead of harmless fireworks. They had been assigned to take and hold the Hall of Stochastic Longings. Mieng had misgivings about its security features. She had once gotten locked in a bank while she and her comrade Kel Belleren were visiting a mutual friend. Some idiot had adjusted a priceless ink painting personally instead of letting a bank servitor handle it, and had triggered a building-wide alarm.

Come to think of it, Belleren, who had made major, was in charge of a company in the van. It would be nice to catch up with him at some point.

One of the lieutenant colonels had asked Colonel Ragath why they were wasting time in the administrative district. Ragath had gotten that look. "The Drummers value this site," he said. "Cultural heritage. I realize we're all Kel, but try to pretend you didn't have to look that up on the grid. For instance, one of those buildings is a museum. Contains the gun that General Andan Zhe Navo used in her last battle. The Hall of Stochastic Longings has an archive containing Andan and Liozh – yes, Liozh – documents going back 500 years.

"All this to say," Ragath went on, "we may be able to get concessions out of the civilians by threatening to wreck priceless artifacts." He had given orders against looting, which normally wouldn't be an issue, but everyone wanted immediate revenge after the amputation gun. The current mission was some kind of backwards lose-so-we-win-later gambit, which made Mieng's teeth itch.

It was hard to believe anyone would care about some Andan gun that hadn't been properly cleaned for centuries, or a bunch of calligraphed books no one read anymore. But then, the colonel clearly cared about dried-up bits of history, so maybe he had some insight into how the Drummers felt about their artifacts.

The Drummers' Forum was cursed with wide approaches, a boon to the Kel, and had a park that provided some cover. There was a lot of rubble already, from the forward companies that had gone in with real weapons for credibility's sake. Bullets whined across the garden and kicked up dirt. Most of the corpses were unreal broken things, dressed in hats and jade necklaces and embroidered clothes. A lot of blood and stray body parts, too, like a human jigsaw upended.

They benefited from mostly unnecessary covering fire as they advanced to the Hall of Stochastic Longings. It was an eerie building, full of walls that *sang* your breath back to you as poetry, and light that coruscated like flowers. Beautiful, if you wanted to feel that beauty hid unhealthy secrets from you.

Guards offered some resistance, but the only one in the company who got seriously injured was Kel Ajerio, and he ought to have known better than to dash up like that.

Mieng had the gunner platoon set up in the atrium. "Where the hell is everyone?" she wondered. Scan told her, but –"We're going to have to send two platoons to clean out the squirrels." She hated splitting her company, but they couldn't leave civilians running around.

It was hard to hear herself think over the sound of the mortars. The decoy guns were even louder than the real thing. In the meantime, Platoons Two and Three went squirrel-hunting. She could occasionally hear short bursts of fire and the more occasional muffled shriek.

It was as well that it took the heretics a full 6.6 hours to respond to the attack as a real threat, by which point more decoy units had been set up.

By the time the heretics arrived in force, Mieng had a hard time convincing herself to give way in measured stages. They had to haul back the damn decoys because it wouldn't do to leave evidence. Corpses were piling up around the copses of trees and the flowerbeds. Broken stems and chewed-up leaves. Smoke everywhere, nauseating even through the breather. No one had fired an amputation gun yet, but that didn't mean one wasn't around the corner.

"Pull out now," the colonel's voice crackled over the link. "The Nirai are about to put on some fireworks." He started listing the units that were to get to the pickup point.

A list. Not *all units*. Six companies weren't on the list, if she remembered the roster correctly, so they'd be staying.

Her company was on the list. So that was fine.

Major Kel Belleren's company was not on the list. That was not fine. They had gone to academy together.

She should have queried her battalion commander, but instead she called the colonel directly. "Sir, Captain Mieng, Battalion Three, Company Two. If you need another unit to hold, we can hold."

Her battalion commander was going to kill her. If the colonel didn't do it first.

An infinitely brief pause. "Captain," Ragath said, "I'm not leaving those companies to cover the retreat. I'm leaving them for the butcher's block. On direct orders from the general. She has decided that, with the confusion from the Nirai explosives, this is the minimum number that will convince the heretics that their victory was real so the next operation can proceed. I hear she's good with numbers."

This was more explaining than Ragath usually troubled with. "Sir, we can –"

"I'm not interested in martyrs." His voice grew hard. "You have your orders, Captain. Colonel Ragath out."

She bit her lip, but formation instinct made her give the necessary orders, made her march out of the smoke-haze with its stench of upturned dirt and chemicals and livid blood, made her get into the hopper with her soldiers.

She was Kel. Her life was a coin to be spent, and today her superiors had chosen not to spend it. She should have been grateful, but for the first time in a long time, she resented what formation instinct had made of her.

* * *

Fortress of Scattered Needles, Analysis
Priority: High
From: Vahenz afrir dai Noum
To: Heptarch Liozh Zai
Calendrical Minutiae: Year of the Fatted Cow, Month of the Pig, Day of the whatever the hell the fucking Kel decide it is.

Today started as a good day, my dear Zai. It didn't stay that way. I can't blame the Fortress's people for their festivities, but they've given Jedao a disastrous opening. The hell of it is that we can't disclaim the victory as an enemy ploy; it would hurt morale.

I could have kicked Stoghan for organizing those parades, but the truth is he only capitalized on an existing public trend. People wanted something to celebrate, even if they were hiding under desks during the shooting.

For that matter, not that we have hard evidence, those weren't spontaneous celebrations. They were too well synchronized. That had to be the work of Shuos instigators. I suppose one of them is responsible for the irrepressibly catchy anthem that's been making its way around the grid. I caught myself tapping my foot to it.

They're already calling it the Day of Drummers' Splendor. It won't last, but it won't need to, not for Kel purposes. You might as well make the notation in Doctrine's calendar.

What I've been unable to determine is what the Kel are setting up. The parameter space is too tangled. I've got part of my team on it, but if I try to squeeze any more work out of them, they'll expire. I'd retask Analysis Team Two because Tsegai has some mathematical credentials, but she's also their best grid diver and you need her doing that work.

I was cheered to hear the good news on the Hafn front: they've destroyed the Eyespike swarm. They were concerned as to whether Brigadier General Marish escaped to fight again, but I could have told them not to worry. Kel generals rarely choose to survive the deaths of their swarms.

Gerenag Abrana and some of the people in Finance are spending too much time together. Yes, of course I'm spying on your coalition, Zai. I'm here to do the despicable things so you don't have to. I realize you have a vision of a more egalitarian heptarchate spontaneously emerging from the cinders of the old regime, but you're going to find that people are people no matter how you reorganize your social structures. Anyway, you may have to backstab Abrana before she makes an attempt on you. If she were smarter, she'd realize it's better to let someone else take the heat while she pulled the strings. But we both know the trade-offs of that arrangement, don't we?

If things had turned out differently, we would be adversaries. By accusing you of treachery for a little earnest criticism, the hexarchate turned you into a traitor. I know you don't like that word, but we should be honest with ourselves.

At this point of the game, Jedao is one move ahead, so we'll have to see if we can overcome that disadvantage. I'll alert you if we have any luck with that brute-force computational search, but I wouldn't hold my breath. In the meantime, I'm off to find some atrocious beer to drown my misgivings in.

Yours in calendrical heresy,

Vh.

"THAT'S ANOTHER POSITIVE," Cheris said after reading the latest Shuos report.

She wasn't standing in the command center. She wasn't standing in the cindermoth at all. Instead, she was pulled to Drummers' Forum, what was left of it. The videos had been clear. Blast marks, craters, torn viscera, splintered trees. There was supposed to have been a priceless gun down there, a pearl-handled affair that had belonged to the great general Andan Zhe Navo. She would have liked to hold it up to her head and see if it still worked. The guns at her belt wouldn't work. They were back with her body on the *Unspoken Law* where everyone could see them.

"That's good," Jedao said in a way that indicated that he didn't think it was good at all. "Cheris, you're dissociating or hallucinating, I can't tell which. Go to Medical."

She barely remembered to speak subvocally. "No," she said. "It's supposed to hurt."

She had told six Kel companies that the best use she could make of their loyalty was to have them fight the heretics and lose. Meat for a sham victory. All for one day of the calendar.

Formation instinct had made the infantry colonel implement her orders. Formation instinct had made the companies obey. They wouldn't be the last.

"You used to make people do things like this without the benefit of formation instinct," Cheris said.

"Yes," Jedao said. "Remember the numbers, Cheris. Sometimes they're all you have."

Thanks to the Shuos, they had a reasonable map of Liozh Zai's allies and their material holdings in the six wards, even if the individuals' locations were guesswork. That was the nice thing about factories: hard to move at a moment's notice. The suspected source of the amputation guns' components was located deep in the Radiant Ward.

Engineering reported that the threshold winnower refit was only twenty-seven minutes behind schedule, which was a miracle. Engineering added that the work was slowed down because a number of the most technically skilled servitors were having an adventure down on the Fortress, and maybe the next time the general pulled a stunt like that, she could consult Engineering about assignments instead of simply letting the servitors run loose.

Cheris marked that with a simple acknowledgment and didn't bother with a more elaborate reply. She blinked, and was standing outside herself again. This time she was in the dueling hall, and Kel Nerevor was saluting her with that fierce yellow calendrical sword. There were at least three things wrong with the scenario, but she didn't want to leave.

"Cheris," Jedao said again. "General. Either get some fucking drugs or get out of the fucking command center. Right now you're a menace to the swarm."

"It's 2.9 hours until the operation begins," Cheris said. Nerevor was trying to tell her something, but she spoke in words of fracture, seizure, cooling ash. Cheris couldn't decipher the words. "I have to –"

"Cheris, most generals have aides for this sort of thing. Unfortunately, you're stuck with me. Drugs, sleep, drugged sleep, I don't care, pick something or I will figure out how to possess you."

"Commander, I'll be in my quarters," Cheris said to Hazan.

"Sir, I'll call you when the action starts."

She wouldn't trust herself to wake up, either. At least he didn't realize she was lying.

Jedao figured it out straight off. "Cheris," he said, "you're being ridiculous."

When Cheris entered the dueling hall, several people looked at her with wide eyes. After all, she had only come here the one time.

"I hope it's redundant for me to say this," Jedao said, "but you shouldn't duel. You're apt to slaughter people by accident."

Her chest hurt. "I suppose that's to be preferred to killing them on purpose."

"When you became a soldier, what did you expect it to be about? Parades? Pretty speeches? Admirers?"

"I know it's about killing," she snapped. "I didn't want it to be about *deliberately killing my own soldiers*."

"Sometimes there's no other way."

The shadow was behind her, so she couldn't glare at it. "Yes, well," Cheris said, "you live your beliefs. How commendable."

"I wasn't referring specifically to Hellspin Fortress."

She snorted.

"I am not good for you," Jedao said. "I know this. But if I were as good at manipulating people as you think I am, you would be taking a nap instead of making all the duelists nervous."

"You don't sleep," Cheris said, remembering. "You don't sleep at all. What do you do in all that time? Count ravens?"

Jedao was silent for so long that she thought something had

happened to him. Then he said, "It's dark in the black cradle, and it's very quiet unless they're running tests. Out here there are things to look at and I can remember what colors are and what voices sound like. Please, Cheris. Go sleep. You will never realize how valuable it is unless someone takes it away from you forever."

"You're only telling me this to get me to do what you want," Cheris said.

"You'll have to let me know how that works out," Jedao said. "Something's bound to go wrong in the Radiant Ward, and they'll need you."

"Need you, you mean."

"I said what I meant."

Cheris looked around the dueling hall, then let her feet carry her back to her quarters. Before she lay down, she asked, "Are you lonely when I sleep?" He didn't answer, but this time she left a small light on.

CHAPTER EIGHTEEN

THE LAST TIME Kel Naraucher had experienced a grand formation had been in drill for a parade in the City of Filigree Masks, and they hadn't even ended up using it. Naraucher liked parades. Everything could go wrong, but when you got down to it, no one was going to die. Except that one time with the combustible pigeon, and that had been a tasteless prank.

The hopper had landed them behind cover of the corrosion gradient, well back, using a captured bay. They assembled the condensed points of a grand formation that had no name. It was heretical, after all. It was hard to concentrate on distances and alignment and where his feet were, even with formation instinct yanking him into position each time the sergeant issued a correction.

Then the servitors arrived.

Naraucher had reservations about putting servitors into Kel formations. He didn't mind them in the usual course of their duties, but this was different. Maybe he was more of a traditionalist than he had reckoned, even though he was the first Kel in his family. He made himself watch as the servitors hovered into position. They were efficient about it, no wasted motion. If he was honest with himself, the emotion the servitors aroused in him wasn't contempt. It was inadequacy.

The general had decided they were Kel enough to serve with the Kel. If he was any sort of Kel himself, that had to be good enough for him.

Servitor attrition was higher than planned for. Major Kel Ula called the colonel and received modified orders of battle. This caused delays as formations were switched to accommodate the numbers and a few people were shuffled into other companies. There were a good forty-three people and servitors left to hang around the rear. Naraucher spent this time daydreaming about spending some time with his brother's dogs. Dogs were much more pleasant to be around than grumpy fellow soldiers, even with all the slobber. It wasn't as though there weren't lots of fluids in warfare anyway.

"All right," Colonel Ragath said over the link, and Naraucher paid attention. "Major Ula from Battalion Seven has the van. She's to make it across the causeway and tunnel down the Radiant Gate. Don't activate formation pivots until you're right there. We don't know how long it'll take the corrosion squads to twig to the fact that we're bypassing them. I wouldn't allow for more than an hour, so don't dawdle.

"Once you're in the Radiant Ward, head straight for that factory. You won't be able to hold it, but I'm sure creative individuals like yourselves can mess it up bad. Drag things out as long as you can to give the winnower teams a chance to set up. We'll alert you when it's time to peel out of there.

"You may have heard that the winnowers read loyalty-states and are theoretically incapable of fratricide. That's according to numbers in a machine, not field tests. If you're stupid enough to stick around for the field tests, I'll personally lay some flowers on your pyre."

Naraucher was with Captain Zhan Goro, right behind Major Ula's company. He felt a creeping sense that something was watching him, probably from being among so many servitors. It did occur to him that maybe the servitors felt just as awkward being here as he felt about them. Maybe they could talk over drinks someday, although he wasn't sure what they'd be interested in in place of alcohol.

The corrosion gradients were supposed to keep the Kel boxed in, and the heretics must have been short of generators or they would already have deployed them. Naraucher had heard Shuos grid sabotage was responsible. He knew the Shuos regarded the Kel as addled younger siblings, but he was glad to have them along.

The Nirai had been busy with heavy-duty burrowers, preparing a passage to the Radiant Gate. The gate was one of the Radiant Ward's popular attractions and a defense in itself. It was made of material condensed from a certain dying star. If the entire Fortress had been made of the stuff, they would have been in trouble. Backwards to be grateful for a weakness in one of the hexarchate's defenses, but there it was.

The passage was weirdly dank. Naraucher had the morbid fantasy that someone was gardening Kel in confined spaces with the unhealthy blue-white light, and soon it would be time for the harvest. Were the Kel best pickled? Smoked? He hated smoked food, but it seemed appropriate for ashhawks.

There it was: the Radiant Gate. The entire thing was transparent, although the index of refraction gave Naraucher a headache even from here. Coiled behind the surface were living lines of light, writing and rewriting praises to the hexarchate. The light was alternately gold and bronze and silver, and suffused with a warmth that Naraucher had never ascribed to his government.

Major Ula's company wavered for a moment. Then they got themselves sorted out and the pivots started moving into place. A great fierce light sprang up around her company. No, it wasn't light. You couldn't read by it or warm your hands by it, but whatever it was, it drew the eye and made it flinch at the same time. It intimated banners and swords held high and six-gun salutes.

Ula was bannering: surely that was a good sign, the suicide hawk plain to see, even if all they had to represent their general was the null banner. Someone was hissing at him. He remembered to keep up. If the servitors could do their job when they were so new at it, it behooved him to do his.

Astonishingly, the gate was giving way. The transparent stuff was snaking off in curling vapor. And the light – those radiant words, all the ideals of the hexarchate scribed by poets long dead – the light was funneling free in scrolls and coils, words uncaged, or perhaps words driven off.

"– is the captain." The voice on the link was savage even through the crackling. "Word from the colonel. The heretics have woken up. They've dropped the corrosion gradient and they're headed for our rear. Rear units are changing front. We're to follow the major once she's through and hit that factory, hope the rearguard can keep the heretics occupied."

Naraucher looked again at Ula's company. This time he noticed something that hadn't been apparent before. At the edges of the formation, the non-pivot positions, humans and servitors both, were changing into pillars of candescent numbers. Naraucher shouldn't have been able to recognize the numbers at this distance, but he could. Most but not all were in the high language's vertical script. Machine Universal was identifiable as such, although he couldn't read it.

He couldn't have justified this conviction, but he would have said that the numbers were numbers that mattered. Birthdays and festival days. A child's shoe size. The number of times a soldier visited a crippled comrade. The specific gravity of a favorite wine. The number of bullets left in a pistol. The distance from this siege to a childhood home, remembered but never visited.

The number of soldiers a Kel general was willing to sacrifice to achieve her objective.

Naraucher wasn't crying when his company reached the gate's shriveled remnants, passing through the smoke-memory of people reduced to phantasms of number. But his eyes hurt. Ula's company had burned up evaporating the gate. He could only do his part: fight through the breach they had won for those who followed.

IN THE COMMAND center of the *Unspoken Law*, Cheris listened to the reports. She didn't mourn. She had lost the right to mourn. Jedao would have disagreed, which was why she wasn't talking to him.

The first recorded Kel formation was a suicide formation. She had learned that at academy sometime and forgotten it. Now she would never forget.

CHAPTER NINETEEN

CAPTAIN-ENGINEER NIRAI WENIAT might have been the only person in the swarm who liked threshold winnowers. It wasn't that he thought their destructiveness was funny, although people had accused him of thinking destruction in general was funny. It was the purity of the winnowers' function: death that caused death that caused death.

The universe ran on death. All the clockwork wonders in the world couldn't halt entropy. You could work with death or you could let it happen; that was all.

"Sir," said Nervous Engineer Three, "I'm having trouble getting the – oh, there it goes." A soft click.

"Have more confidence," Weniat said. This had the opposite of the desired effect.

They were setting up in a park in the Radiant Ward. A bunch of Kel had flushed out the civilians, heroically refrained from shooting the tame deer that begged them for treats, and were now patrolling the perimeter to make sure no nasty surprises turned up.

Fighting was still going on elsewhere in the ward. One of the infantry captains Weniat was on friendly terms with had passed him word of the Kel-servitor suicide formations. Weniat had been impressed. Clever use of servitors, high time a Kel thought laterally. When he had heard they were going to be commanded by a jumped-up captain no one had ever heard of, he'd thought Kel Command had gone mad, but it seemed the woman had potential after all.

The park was too quiet. Nervous Engineer Two was glancing

around. One of the deer wandered over and had to be shooed off. It seemed to think the winnower might dispense treats.

"It's ready, sir," said Steady Engineer, who had been working quietly all this time.

The winnower didn't look like its function. If you didn't realize what it was, you might mistake it for a pretty kinetic sculpture, all looping wires and spinning wheels and interconnected shafts. Weniat, who had understood the relevant mechanics since he was thirteen years old, knew better.

"It's Weniat," he said over the link. "Teams Two through Four, status."

"Team Two preparations complete."

"Team Four here. Estimate another sixteen minutes, we're having a minor issue with the – look, you're holding it upside-down. Let me –" Silence.

"Team Three, sir, we're ready."

Team Four figured out what they were doing in thirty-eight minutes. Two of its members were borderline incompetent, but they were under an especially vigilant lieutenant.

"Weniat to Colonel Ragath," he said once he had confirmed that nothing had come unscrewed at the last second. "All winnowers deployed. I recommend you get the Kel the fuck out of here."

"Captain," Ragath's long-suffering voice came back, "one of these days I'll figure out why the Nirai can recite transcendental numbers to hundreds of digits while drunk out of their minds, but can't remember their own ranks."

Weniat was impressed that the colonel knew about transcendental numbers. He must stop underestimating the Kel.

"Do you wish to evacuate any personnel, Captain?"

"No, sir," Weniat said. Everyone here was a volunteer. The Nirai could make informed judgments on this better than the Kel could. It was their job to understand the math.

"Very well," Ragath said. "Once the heretics notice we're pulling out, things will go to hell fast. I'll keep you informed of the situation."

"Are we winning, sir?"

Slight pause. "You could call it that. Colonel Ragath out."

Time passed.

More time passed.

The deer wandered by again. Nervous Engineer Three threw rocks at it until it went away.

"How long does it take the Kel to shoot their way out, anyway?" Nervous Engineer Five, who tended to whine.

"Key phrase," Steady Engineer said, "*shoot* their way out. I've seen you with a gun, you think you could do better?"

"I hear something," Nervous Engineer Four said in an undertone. People crashing through the park, twigs snapping. They weren't here to pet the deer.

"Weniat to Colonel Ragath," Weniat said urgently. "Complication. Patrol approaching our position. Not sure how many."

There were only five people in each winnower team.

"I've got three slow Kel companies," Ragath said after a moment. "However, your mission has priority. Trigger the winnowers when you see fit."

"Thank you, sir."

"Do your job, Captain. Colonel Ragath out."

The noises were getting closer. Voices calling out to each other.

"Weniat to all teams." He was shivering with mixed dread and anticipation. "Activate all winnowers."

Weniat and his team were standing in the winnower's shelter zone. All modern winnowers provided a shelter zone for their teams. It was anyone's guess as to whether this model's would work as specified.

The first winnowers hadn't had shelter zones at all.

The winnower made sounds like a furnace exploding, like wineglasses singing shattered, like bells slamming from side to side. It didn't give off light, but spewed the kind of wind you would get if you twisted a world's worth of clouds into a spindle and let go after a hundred years.

The shelter zone was working, indicated by a faint lambent glow.

The question was whether the winnower itself was having any effect. Here in the park, amid the trees' long shadows, it was hard to tell.

Wait. There was a whisper. A knot in a tree was opening into a cracked eye. A strange blemished radiation glared from it.

The deer had wandered back toward the noise. The winnower clattered, and it reared up. Light bled from the deer's eyes, the color of scars and unwhole moons. It staggered a few steps before falling. Curved gashes opened in its throat and flanks, from which tiny teeth gleamed, and there were snapping noises. There was something comical about the angles the deer's legs made.

Round shapes boiled out of the gashes. Eyes. All of the eyes were looking at the winnower.

They were in the shelter zone. They were safe.

Weniat had been holding his breath. "Weniat to all winnower teams. Status."

"We hit some birds, sir." Team Four. "There's a residential complex barely visible from our position. Hard to be certain, but it looks like – yes, there we go. A plague of light."

Team Three: "I'm sorry, sir, ours is producing the safety zone but is otherwise nonoperational. We'd attempt a repair, but it's impossible to reach the affected components without leaving the zone."

"Don't even think about it," Weniat said. "You'll soon be in danger from the other winnowers. I'd prefer we all get out intact."

Four winnowers was overkill even for a ward. One would have been fine. The others had been in case of the inevitable malfunction.

Team Two was clinical as always. "All systems functioning within parameters, sir."

"Weniat to Colonel Ragath. Three winnowers operational, sir. We don't have a good way of gauging what 'operational' means in this –"

"They're working," Ragath said flatly. "Captain Jaghun set up video for us before the radiation caught up to her company. Captain Iziade was within eyeshot of the passage out, but I'd had it sealed. The heretics caught on fast. They've already locked down everything else; we're cooperating to contain the damage. Scan's shot to hell with the winnowers active, but you may be the only people left alive down there."

The ward's population had been estimated at 43,000 people. It wasn't that the number was high. It wasn't. Weniat knew what large numbers looked like. It was the ratio. Everyone dead.

At least it would have been quick. Not painless, but quick. Of course, to say that cleaning up all the corpses was going to be a hassle was an understatement. Not his problem, luckily.

Weniat, in a rare exercise, recovered enough humanity to say, "I'm sorry about your soldiers, sir."

Ragath ignored this. "Leave the winnowers running for another hour just in case, then shut them off. We'll retrieve you, but in case of some disaster on our end you know what to do."

Destroy the winnowers. They couldn't be allowed to fall into enemy hands.

"One of these days you'll tell me to do something hard, sir," Weniat said.

"Go fuck a power socket, Captain," Ragath said without heat, and signed off.

"You're certain?" Cheris asked Colonel Ragath. "We're having the expected problems with Scan up here."

"We're certain," Ragath said. "We're extracting the winnower teams now. Nothing left but fungus and corpses. Thanks to Captain Jaghun, we even have a video of some creative but misguided soldier's attempt to survive by pulling her eyes out with her fingers. Didn't work, of course."

Neither of them mentioned the fact that the winnowers hadn't respected loyalty-states. Ragath had reported the destruction of three Kel companies earlier. There was nothing more to say about it.

"Thank you for your work, Colonel, and my regards to the winnower teams," Cheris said. "Keep me informed of further developments."

"Naturally, sir."

"He approves of you," Jedao said.

"I couldn't tell," Cheris said. Out loud: "Still no luck, Scan?"

"We're not likely to get readings on that hemisphere for another four hours, sir."

"All that," Cheris said subvocally, "and it wasn't even the main assault. We depopulated a ward as a distraction." At least the heretic Gerenag Abrana, whose holdings and supporters had been concentrated in the Radiant Ward, would be sure to take notice.

"The best feints," Jedao said, "look like real attacks."

During the winnower attack, Shuos infiltrators in other wards had been busy with sabotage. A lot of sabotage, carefully targeted.

Out loud again: "Get me Captain Damiod and Captain Ko." The cryptology team and the Shuos. Their faces appeared next to her primary display.

"Sir," Ko said, saluting.

"Sir," Damiod said. "You wanted to hear about that line."

"Yes," Cheris said. He had brought it to her attention not long ago.

"With aid from the infiltrators, we've confirmed that Line 92832-17 goes directly to the Fortress's command center. It's probably Inaiga Zai's direct line. We haven't had any luck decrypting the packets. I suspect there's some cutting-edge theorem being used because the structures smell funny, but never mind that.

"More to the point, we've confirmed that the tap on 17 goes to an individual associated with Zai's lieutenant Gerenag Abrana. Unless the Shuos have gotten bored, no one's tampered with the tap. We *think* Zai doesn't realize it's there."

"Do you concur?" Cheris asked Ko.

"I do, sir," Ko said.

"I'm sorry not to have better news for you," Damiod said, although he sounded as though what he was really sorry about was this demand on his time.

"It's all right," Cheris said, and took note of Ko's eyes, momentarily narrowed. "That's not what I need. You've prepared that dummy cipher for me?"

"It's ready," Ko said. "It looks like a hedgehog, but a good team should be able to crack it in days if they approach it the right way, especially with the Fortress's computational resources."

Cheris was betting that Gerenag Abrana had an excellent team.

"Then here's the next thing," Cheris said. "Can we insert a message into Line 17? And make sure the tap sees it?"

"It's an excellent tap," Damiod said scornfully. "It probably sees more than the main line does. But sir, once you do that, they'll be able to run a trace. You'll blow our ability to listen in."

"That's fine," Cheris said. "After this message we may not need to listen any longer."

Ko was thoughtful. "How very Shuos of you, sir."

"Do you have an objection?" Cheris said.

"It was merely an observation, sir."

"This is the message I want inserted," Cheris said to Ko and Damiod, "by whatever means necessary. Full video, show the shadow. Open with the Deuce of Gears." Jedao had insisted on this. "This is Garach Jedao Shkan, forgive the cosmetic changes; my options were limited." The name sounded unnaturally natural. "As per your request, I've cleared out the pests in your house. If you take care of your end, you should have a free hand to negotiate once the Hafn arrive. Meanwhile, I have some Kel to attend to. I trust we can discuss further arrangements over dinner as previously agreed. Enjoy the peace and quiet."

If this worked, if Zai's lieutenant cracked the dummy cipher and overheard Zai's "negotiations" with Jedao to get rid of Zai's subordinates, the heretics would tear each other apart and they could all go home soon.

Cheris looked down at her half-gloved hands so she wouldn't have to notice the way people were looking at her.

"That's it," Jedao said. "Now we wait."

CHAPTER TWENTY

SHUOS HAODAN HATED assassination assignments. Years ago, an instructor had explained that this was why he was ideal for them. Certainly he had the requisite skills, some of which had come from growing up in a Kel family, and he had excelled in academy. Originally, however, he had hoped for something quiet in analysis or adminstration.

On one of his first missions, his supervisor had sent him as a backup field agent anyway. The primary agent was talented but erratic. She got herself tangled up in some side scheme involving art fraud (he would have loved to see the wording of the reprimand), and Haodan had to dispatch the target himself.

He did too good a job. His supervisor told him it was his duty to take on more assassination assignments. When he protested that he didn't enjoy taking lives – in some Shuos divisions you could go your entire career without taking a life, not that the general public would ever believe it – the supervisor said, with cruel persuasiveness, that if every Shuos weaseled out of wetwork, that would leave no one but the bullies and sociopaths. Hence it was Shuos policy to retain some assassins who didn't glory in their work. Not that the general public would believe that, either.

Haodan knew that the argument was an appeal to his ego. It worked.

So here he was in the Fortress's Dragonfly Ward years later, getting in position for his attempt on the head of the heretics' analysis section, a foreigner named Vahenz afrir dai Noum. Shuos eavesdropping on the heretics' discussions suggested that she was influential in policy-making as well. As his handler had explained, they hadn't wanted to make an attempt on Vahenz earlier because it was more useful to monitor her activities without doing anything that would trigger an inconvenient stepping up of security. Now that the Fortress was all but taken, however, they wanted to make sure that Vahenz didn't escape to cause trouble elsewhere, considering how much damage she had done already. They'd considered trying to capture her alive, but in the end they had decided against it on the grounds that the operation would be too uncertain.

Haodan had secured a job as a delivery man for a fancy confectioner; the Fortress's citizens apparently took a certain level of decadence for granted, even while under siege. The previous delivery woman had gotten sick with Haodan's encouragement, and Haodan had made all the right noises at the interview. Some research had turned up the manager's worry for relatives trapped on the Drummers' Ward, which Haodan played on shamelessly. He could have told her that life wasn't going to be any better in the Dragonfly Ward now that the campaign was drawing to a close, even if the confectionary was in one of the areas least affected. Once the Kel had secured the Fortress, they would send for the Vidona, and the Vidona were bound to be more thorough than usual about reeducation procedures with a nexus fortress in the wake of a rebellion.

Vahenz ordered confections every other day like clockwork. Haodan despaired of predictable people. They made his job too easy. But then, the easier the job, the likelier it was that he could pull it off without excessive secondary casualties, so he ought to be grateful.

The parcel he was interested in was pasted over with cunning cutout paper shapes, farm animals in accordance with the heretical calendar. The effect was elegant, especially with the tasteful subdued colors of the paper. It would be his third delivery.

It amused him that the confectionary's manager insisted on hand delivery during a siege. The human touch or something. She claimed people paid extra for it. Servitor delivery wouldn't have made his work significantly harder, though. He knew ways of handling civilian servitors.

The manager was giving him instructions. She liked the fact that he stood practically at attention – something you learned fast with a Kel father, albeit one who was a medical technician – and treated her seriously. "Don't forget to tell Leng that I'm thinking of their son," she was saying. "And be certain to tell Ajenio that I've got those new sesame cookies in production, if he wants to place an order. I've included samples in his parcel so he can try before he decides, but he'll like them. I'm always right about these things. Oh, and avoid the 17-4 passage. They'll be marching soldiers through there around the time you go through, and you don't want to be mixed up in that. Some kind of parade, but you've got a job to do."

At last she had said everything she was going to say, and Haodan was able to leave. He rode his scooter in the designated lane. The passages on this level were messy, and the lifts were a disaster. Then again, the Fortress had originally been intended as a retreat for the heptarchs, with wards designed by separate teams, and for reasons of Doctrine they had demolished and reconstructed great chunks of the interior to do away with the seventh ward after they destroyed the Liozh. It was a wonder the thing was habitable.

The first two deliveries went as expected. Ajenio, a round, florid man, insisted on trying a sesame cookie in front of Haodan, and then offered him one. Haodan declined. He knew the manager would take a dim view of his saying yes. Besides, she already sent him home with a basket of treats every evening and he was convinced he was gaining weight.

By the time he freed himself from Ajenio, who was capable of waxing poetic about a cookie to a degree even an Andan would find embarrassing, he was twelve minutes behind schedule. Still, not disastrous.

The office Haodan went to after that was in a building that had its back up against one of the ward's walls. He wouldn't have been surprised to find out that escape passages were involved, although the Shuos attempts at scan had been inconclusive. He had been here before. His face and his uniform with the swan-and-ribbon logo were familiar to security. They waved him through, smiling. He smiled back. It was only polite.

Seventeen minutes late. He still had some margin.

Up to the fourth floor. Lucky unlucky four, as the Kel would say. The target worked in this office sometimes, instead of being holed up in the Fortress's command center all the time. Judging from some of the infiltrators' gossip, the heretics didn't all get along. She probably wanted to monitor the ward in person, or hide some of her activities from her putative superior.

The target's assistant sat at the front desk. She was stabbing at the terminal. Too bad: if he had a different pretext he could have offered to help her with the problem, but as it stood that would arouse suspicion. Besides, odds were that a Shuos had caused the problem to begin with.

Haodan bobbed in a calculatedly nervous bow. "Swan and Ribbon. Sorry to interrupt, should I drop this off or take it in?" He always asked.

The assistant never let him take it in, but he had gotten one of the other infiltrators to run a flickerform servitor into the ceiling above the target's office. Maddeningly, the target had enough shielding and scan machinery in there to outfit a warmoth. Even the servitor spy was a risk. All it did was listen, and at a random time each day it sent an encrypted databurst to indicate what times it detected human activity in there. No luck getting clean vocals out.

The office was located far to the back, with additional security in the way. It would have been nice to go in and do the job personally, but Haodan wasn't suicidal.

"I'll make sure it gets to her," the assistant said with a wan smile.

"Rough day?" Haodan said, placing the parcel on her desk.

"You have no idea. And now this terminal."

"Sorry, I can't help you with that," Haodan lied. His orders had been specific: assassination, not intelligence-fishing. Besides, the target would have seen through the tired "I'm here to fix that hardware glitch" routine. Her weaknesses were gustatory, so Haodan had tailored his approach accordingly.

"Oh, you're always a help," the assistant said, smiling more genuinely. "She loves those sweets. They'll put her in a good mood, all the better for the rest of us."

"That's good to hear," Haodan said. This was a weakness in the plan. If the target kept to schedule, she'd be in the office in approximately twenty-seven minutes. He had set the timer accordingly. There was a strong chance the bomb would kill the assistant, too. Haodan was sorry about this, as he had grown to like her, but contriving a way to keep her safe would have elevated the risk to unacceptable levels.

The assistant went back to wrestling with her terminal. "I'd best be going," Haodan said. She said something indistinct in response.

Down to the ground floor, back to the scooter. Haodan had no intention of returning to the confectionary now that the job had served its purpose, but he might as well finish the day's deliveries. It only seemed fair.

Seven minutes after Haodan left, a round-faced man in white-and-gold entered the fourth floor office suite and rapped on the wall.

"Pioro," the assistant said, "she's not in yet –"

"She won't be for some time," Pioro said. "Emergency meeting, need-to-know, all of that. I'm on the way myself, but I remembered she's always bitchy if she misses the sweets, especially since Zai's taken to serving vegetable rolls with fish sauce lately, so I thought I'd stop by to pick them up. Don't worry, I'll save you a couple."

"Yes, that would be good," the assistant said. "I don't suppose you have time to look at this synchronization error –"

Pioro's eyebrows shot up as he leaned over to glance at the display. "Probably some Shuos grid diver. Bad sign if they're this far in. I ought to run, but you should lock down and restore to clean state. It's a pain, but we have to take precautions." He hefted the parcel. "Must be something good in there. Fortunately, she likes to share."

"Thanks for your help, Pioro," the assistant said.

"Anytime," Pioro said as he left with the parcel and its tasteful paper decorations.

THE FIRST THING Vahenz afrir dai Noum did when she cracked General Jedao's message was start the self-destruct in her remote office. She knew how much that equipment had cost, and how irritated her employers would be, but you could always buy new equipment. She, on the other hand, would be hard to replace. They'd already gotten Pioro with an attack clearly meant for her; she wasn't about to let them get her too. A pity about the associated casualties, but she didn't excel at her job by being sentimental.

(Interesting that Jedao had fetched up in a woman's body, but then, the Shuos didn't care about that sort of thing. She would have expected it to give the Kel fits, though. Maybe the mere fact of Jedao's presence made them twitch so much that the issue of the body didn't even register.)

The second thing Vahenz did was head for the command center to meet Liozh Zai. The Liozh name was an affectation, but it defined Zai. One of the things she liked about Zai was her radiant sincerity, even if it seemed to come hooked into lamentably ascetic tastes in food and drink; Vahenz had always made a point of bringing her own snacks to Zai's meetings rather than being stuck eating things like sour fruits and unsweetened tea. Trivial points of law mattered to Zai, but because she believed in them, other people believed in them, too. If she'd had more time to season Zai to the grubby realities of politics, Vahenz could have done more with that nascent charisma. But then, what could you expect from someone who had grown up in a glorified warriors' guild? Zai had been deeply wounded when the hexarchs stripped her of her post as a shield operator for protesting the hexarchs' calendrical experiments, but that had made Zai into a resource.

Vahenz hoped that Gerenag Abrana's cryptologists were slower than she was, that her specialized code and superior intelligence gave her the necessary edge. It was her fault for not spotting the tap earlier. She hadn't realized how good Abrana's security people were. But once she saw Jedao's message, she knew the tap had to exist. She had broken the encryption too easily; it was meant to be spied on. And she knew Zai, knew Zai hadn't been engaged in secret negotiations with the fucking ninefox general. Which meant that the message's intended recipient was Abrana, or Stoghan, or anyone with a grudge. People who would believe the lie because they half-believed it already.

The recent spate of sabotage and assassinations hadn't helped. Most victims had been lower-level followers, but people were rattled, and rattled people didn't think clearly. Everything had targeted Zai's lieutenants but not Zai herself. They hadn't found logic spikes or mazes in Zai's grid systems not because they had been better hidden, but because there had been nothing to find, a fact that Abrana's people would have noted.

The passages to the command center were dimly lit, familiar. The security systems and guards knew her, and made no complaint as she passed through the outer defenses and the empty shield operator stations, and went into the inner sanctum. She ought to write up a critique of security procedures, but it would be wasted on these fools.

"I want a private conversation," Vahenz said as she entered. "It will only take an hour."

Liozh Zai got up to greet her. Even though she had to have gotten as little sleep as Vahenz had, she looked composed, almost regal. "Of course," she said, formal as always. "Given the situation, we have a lot to discuss." She turned to set the sanctum's security mode.

"There won't be any discussions," Vahenz said. Her scorch pistol was already in her hand.

Zai understood her immediately and spun, reaching for her own sidearm, but Vahenz was faster. The scorch bolt caught Zai in the side of the head.

Zai fell heavily. Vahenz hated the reek of charred meat and singed hair, but Zai was of no more use, and the less she could tell people about Vahenz, the better.

Vahenz knelt, then, and rearranged the corpse to a better pretense of dignity. It was the least she could do. Besides, she had to concede that Zai had had excellent taste in tailors, pearl-and-gold buttons and pale silk and perfect curves and all. Shame to let that go to waste even in death.

She left as she had come, without a fuss. People trusted her and didn't even think to ask why the meeting had been so short. Terrible to have a mission go this badly, but she'd warned the Hafn it would be a toss of the dice from the get-go. What she regretted most was Pioro's death. It was so hard to find decent conversationalists. The universe was a big place, though. She was sure to turn up more dinner partners if she kept looking.

Besides, she was going to have a bothersome report to make to the Hafn once she made it off the Fortress. It appeared Kel Command wasn't completely misguided in fielding Jedao, or at least, Kel Command and Jedao were using each other in a beautiful dysfunctional ballet. It was irritating that Jedao had fouled her mission, to say the least, but she could appreciate a capable fellow operator when she encountered one.

Colonel Ragath had reported that the Radiant Ward was a wasteland no one wanted to enter except some corpse calligraphers bent on memorializing the event. Resistance had collapsed in the Umbrella Ward when Znev Stoghan pulled out his troops to deal with some internal crisis. The Drummers' Ward was wracked by riots. Cheris had asked what the riots were about. Ragath had given her a jaundiced look, then said, "The generalized unfairness of life."

Disposal of bodies was going to be a problem. Cheris had authorized Ragath to conscript civilians in the secured wards. This caused chaos, recriminations, and more riots, but she had to try something.

A Shuos reported in: fighting among the heretics in the Dragonfly Ward. Cheris felt as though she were watching the gears in a machine settle into place, or dissolve. She couldn't tell which.

10.6 hours later, Doctrine reported that calendrical values were shifting toward approved norms.

Cheris slept long and deeply after that. When she woke, she dressed and paused while pulling her gloves back on. "The propaganda drops," she said. "They weren't for the heretics, were they."

"I wanted you to know what we were annihilating," Jedao said.

"Why is it important?"

"Are you saying it's not?"

"No," Cheris said. "That's not what I'm saying at all. But we have our orders."

"I never forgot that," Jedao said.

When the time came, Cheris went to high table. She paused for a moment at the threshold, looking not at the people but at the banners with their ashhawks Brightly Burning, the calligraphy scrolls, the tapestries. For a dizzying second she thought she was back in the boxmoth *Burning Leaf*, with her old unit, with Verab and Ankat and soldiers younger than she was by a count of battles that, however small, felt like forever drum-tides. Then she blinked and she was back on the cindermoth again, immeasurably older.

Commander Hazan was overseeing the command center, but Cheris saw Rahal Gara and Shuos Ko and other familiar faces. Shuos Liis smiled at her, a slow, sweet curve. Cheris caught herself admiring Liis's velvet-dark eyes and lush mouth, then flinched, suddenly worried.

Cheris took her sip from the communal cup, barely tasting the wine, and passed it down. The ritual brought her comfort. She would have given much to have Kel Nerevor by her side, bright as fire, but no one had any word of her.

She left high table as early as she could get away with, returning to her quarters so she could sit on the bed. There were no servitors: the last two she had talked to had suggested that she should sleep instead of staying up with her paperwork. If she hadn't known better, she would have suspected them of conspiring with Jedao.

"Tell me something about yourself," Jedao said out of nowhere. "What it was like in the City of Ravens Feasting. That luckstone means something to you, but you haven't looked at it since I – since I ruined it for you." He didn't say what they both knew: she would be free of him soon.

"I was determined to leave," Cheris said, wishing he had picked another topic. But she was starting to question her motivations for fleeing toward the Kel. "My mother's people are old-fashioned, barely within approved norms. I was natural-born, not crèche-born –"

"That's something we have in common," Jedao said wryly. "Crèches were still coming into use when my mother had me. I really can say I was born on a farm. I remember the day I first woke up and realized that I was bigger than the geese."

Cheris tried to picture this. How big were geese anyway? "If my instructors had ever mentioned things like this, I would have paid more attention to history."

Jedao laughed. "But you were saying about your people –?"

"Most of them are concentrated in a ghetto in the city, although we lived by a park. I didn't speak the high language until I entered school, and then I couldn't get rid of the accent until Kel Academy."

"I've never heard you speak your native language."

She felt a rush of embarrassment. "I don't speak it well anymore." Was she embarrassed because of her ineptitude, or because she spoke it at all?

"I barely speak Shparoi anymore myself," Jedao said, "although I have a Shparoi name."

"Does it mean something?"

"Does yours?"

An exchange. Fair enough. "In the traditions of my mother's people," Cheris said, "I would have been named after – after a saint's day in the old calendar. A heretical calendar. So instead my parents named me after the high calendar day I was born on. 'Cheris' is the word for 'twenty-three.' It's a vigesimal system. That's all it is."

"My mother, who was eccentric by our culture's standards, had three children by three different fathers," Jedao said. "You're not supposed to name children after living relatives, it's disrespectful, but Koiresh Shkan was my father's name. He was a musician, and I only met him a few times. My other name is derived from a root that means something like 'honesty.' You can bet that made my life hell when it got out at Shuos Academy."

"So your mother was really a farmer?"

"Agricultural researcher. I have no complaints about my childhood, and anyway the Nirai scraped it over for clues already."

She had forgotten that he was a madman. It was going to be a relief when Kel Command unstapled her from Jedao so she knew what things to believe again. At this rate he was going to ruin her for the Kel.

It occurred to her that Kel Command had done that already.

CHERIS COMPOSED A report to Kel Command. Just the notes made her wince. Vidona Diaiya's fungal canister. The pervasive use of heretical formations. The threshold winnowers. She made Jedao look over it four times before she sent it along with her request for Andan or Vidona backup, both for preference. The Kel weren't suited to conversions, and there weren't enough Shuos to go around.

"Oh, that reminds me – you should go into detail on all the computations you did for the heretical formations and the calendrical spike," Jedao said just as she was about to send it. "Kel Command might not care about the derivations, but the Rahal like that sort of thing. Put them in a good mood for whatever renormalization they need to do on the Fortress. Plus, you can impress them with your mathematical skills."

"Is this some new trick?" Cheris said. All she wanted was for the mission to be over.

"What, by throwing math I don't understand at people I've never met?"

It was true that the Rahal might find some of that information helpful, at that. Besides, she didn't want to get into an argument about something so trivial.

The day after that conversation, Znev Stoghan's body turned

up in neat pieces in the middle of the amputation guns' original kill zone. A gene scanner confirmed his identity. No one claimed responsibility. Cheris declined to inquire into the matter.

No one ever found Commander Kel Nerevor. But Cheris kept hoping.

Over the next several days, while Cheris struggled to keep up with the administration of the Fortress, calendrical values continued to normalize at a maddeningly slow rate. Rahal Gara and the other Doctrine officers spent a lot of time muttering to each other.

"You're awfully quiet," Cheris said to Jedao.

"I don't get tired, so there's no need to relax," he said. "But I wonder what it is they're so worried about."

She didn't think anything of it until two days later, when Communications and Scan spoke at once.

"Relief swarm, four bannermoths escorting twelve boxmoths –"

"We're being hailed –"

Cheris's heart leapt. Kel Command hadn't forgotten them after all. She was going to be done with the whole wretched situation. "Accept communications," she said.

"Cheris." Jedao was trying to get her attention. "Rahal Gara sent a signal you didn't authorize. I don't know what she said, and I've never seen that override before."

But she was too giddy with relief to hear him. She didn't recognize the man whose face appeared on her display, with his dark, steady eyes, but given the number of bannermoth commanders in the hexarchate, there was no reason she should. "This is Commander Kel Huan of the *Coiled Stone*," the man said. "I assume I'm addressing Brevet General Kel Cheris and General Shuos Jedao."

"Fuck," Jedao said, which wasn't the response Cheris had expected from him. "Look at the pulse in his neck, Cheris. Something's wrong."

"This is Brevet General Kel Cheris," Cheris said over Jedao's voice. But she was starting to worry. "I assume you're here to assist with the conversion of the Fortress."

"We'll take care of you, sir," Huan said. "Just hang tight. – One moment, I've got a ridiculous emergency in Engineering to attend to. I need to yell at my Nirai again. My apologies." He signed off.

"He's lying," Jedao said. "Short-term you'll save more people firing on Huan –"

Cheris remembered what she had learned from Jedao's sacrifice of Nerevor. No shouting. "I'm not firing on other Kel," she said coldly. Let alone the relief swarm, of all people. "How are four bannermoths going to take down two cindermoths, to say nothing of the rest of our swarm?"

Scan again. "Formation break! *Sincere Greeting* has left the secondary pivot."

Her heart froze. "Get me Commander Paizan. I need an explanation."

"Waste of time," Jedao said. Now he sounded calm. "He'll have been warned. You're fucked. If you want to preserve your swarm, you have to open fire. But then you'll be outcast forever, to say nothing of the odds. If you let them bomb you, your swarm will die, but you might live."

Cheris glanced at the display: the relief swarm was closing rapidly, and was well within erasure cannon range. Her hand had reached the chrysalis gun at her hip when Jedao spoke again. "I don't advise that," he said. "I'm your only hope of survival if they hit you with exotics. One survivor is better than none." His voice cracked suddenly. "I fucked up. Four hundred years trying to put it right and it all goes up in smoke because they decide massive overkill is the best way to execute me. Six to one it's not Mikodez after all, it's Kujen. He miscalculated anchoring me to you."

Mikodez was the Shuos hexarch, but who on earth was Kujen? And why was she a mistake?

Slight pause. "I wasn't crazy when I killed everyone at Hellspin Fortress," Jedao said rapidly. "Nirai-zho has the answers, Nirai Kujen, the black cradle's master, but don't ever, ever trust him."

Panic frothed up in her. How was a random faraway Nirai technician germane to the situation? Jedao had picked one hell of a time to make himself a distraction. This was it, he had gone mad, he was going to betray her –

"Sir!" Scan sounded frantic. "Something's wrong with the *Coiled Stone*'s engine harmonics. That's – I think that's a bomb."

The only thing worse than Jedao being crazy was Jedao not being crazy. "All units into formation Rising Tiger," Cheris said, but she knew it was too late. "Open fire on *Coiled Stone*."

"One last throw of the dice," Jedao was saying. "I taught you what I could. Don't make my mistakes. Goodbye, General. And – and thank you for the light."

Moments later, the world came apart in a roar of needles and bright, hard angles, and there was no more room in her head for questions, or words, or any scrap of feeling.

CHAPTER TWENTY-ONE

CHERIS WOKE TRANSFIXED by splinters of a ghost's carrion glass: invisible and insubstantial, but they hurt as though they pierced each nerve. *Carrion bomb,* she thought, dredging the memory out of the long-ago briefing. As an exotic weapon, it would have killed Jedao, leaving her free of him.

She remembered the protocol she had read so long ago through a haze of pain: *In an emergency, if the general withholds necessary information, the carrion glass remnants can be ingested by a volunteer. Although this procedure is experimental, this will give the general a body so he can be tortured.*

The cindermoth was a chrysalis of hard light and heavy fractures and empty spaces where people had been. Every time she moved – to breathe, to blink, to scrabble for purchase on the bruising floor – she felt splinters go into her brain and pin her to Jedao's memories.

She had a choice. She could take the splinters out and leave them behind. Refuse to look at them.

Or she could scavenge what she could from them. Try to understand Jedao.

The New Anchor Orientation Packet seemed to be from a time long ago and far away, but she remembered Jedao's warning, when she had first read it, that eating the splinters would drive her mad. Having him around to talk to her all the time had been bad enough. Having him *inside her head* would undoubtedly be worse.

On the other hand, her world had already gone mad. Kel

Command had just turned on her. Her situation was dire. Jedao had clearly known more about what was going on. She needed the information he hadn't had the time, or the inclination, to give her. What game had he been playing with Kel Command, all those centuries? And what had he known about this Nirai Kujen, whom he had been so desperate to warn her about even as he was about to die?

She had always liked ravens. She would peck what answers she could out of the carrion glass and hope that she could find a workable course of action in them. Her turn to gamble, with her life as the stake.

Gravity was reasserting itself. She had to be careful how she moved. For a while she concentrated on breathing. She had good lungs, but her breaths felt too shallow no matter what she did. It was hard not to panic. If she stood up too suddenly, all her bones would dissolve and she would spill onto the floor like ink out of a jar, a Cheris-shaped blot.

She caught sight of her shadow, and the absence of Jedao's nine eyes hurt her, but there was no time to grieve.

She swallowed a splinter. It punctured her heart on the way down.

CHERIS FELL INTO a memory of blurred voices and laughter and the mingled smells of wine, perfume, flowers, a door half-open: a party. A woman dark-haired and fragrant and sweet of face, a long red coat draped over her shoulders, was pressing herself against Cheris. The woman's mouth was beautiful, but never kind. She was wearing gloves so dark a red they were almost black, in terrible taste, but no one could tell her no. It was Heptarch Shuos Khiaz, and she had backed Cheris into a shadowed room.

Khiaz's hands were in her hair, drawing her head down for a kiss. One hand drifted across Cheris's chest, unerringly finding all the scars beneath the black-and-gold uniform, then lingering over the brigadier general insignia. She was telling Cheris to take off her gloves. The gloves were black and fingerless. Cheris knew she couldn't afford to sleep with a heptarch, but she couldn't afford to say no, either.

"Congratulations on the promotion," Khiaz said. "I always knew you'd go far."

"Shuos-zho," Cheris said, very formally. She was remembering her origins as Shuos infantry, a decade ago, and why she had transferred out of Khiaz's office and into the Kel army at the earliest opportunity. "Pardon me, can I get you anything to –"

Khiaz shrugged off her coat in a single languorous motion. Underneath it she was wearing a Kel uniform. It was perfectly tailored to her.

For that matter, the gloves weren't dark, dark red. They were black. Kel gloves, taboo for a Shuos to wear.

Cheris was aware of the suddenness of her erection, and of the fact that in one moment she had been comprehensively outflanked.

She almost said no, even if the heptarch could pull her from Kel service for defying an order. Destroy the career she had worked so hard for, the plan she had nurtured for so long. But as a Shuos, she was the heptarch's property. There was no one she could appeal to.

The Shuos didn't believe in sex without games and obligations. Khiaz's hands moved down. For one red-black moment Cheris considered killing her just to get away. Khiaz had very clever hands. Cheris's heartbeat sped up despite her best efforts not to react. Khiaz liked to ask embarrassing questions to punctuate her caresses.

Then Khiaz reached up to unbutton her uniform's jacket. Before she could stop herself, Cheris caught her wrist. Begged her to leave it on.

And I call myself a tactician, Cheris thought savagely. Of all the subterranean desires to be caught out in. Her breath hitched. She could wring an advantage out of this if she retained some shred of control. She started answering Khiaz's questions, maneuvering the conversation in a better direction. As long as Khiaz thought Cheris was overcome by desire rather than nurturing a plot against the heptarchate, she was safe.

Khiaz murmured something about fear and courage and the

zigzag paths people take between the two. "What are you so afraid of?" she asked, mocking. "Do you think I'll hurt you?" She knelt, still in the uniform, and took Cheris in her mouth, velvet-warm.

Voice breaking like a boy's, Cheris gasped out a terror of death. Banal, but believable. Khiaz's eyes were momentarily bright with triumph beneath the long lashes.

Years later, Khiaz would remember, as Cheris had intended her to; and in the aftermath of Hellspin Fortress, she would consign Cheris to the black cradle's terrible undeath.

Khiaz wasn't done. Cheris hadn't expected her to be satisfied that easily, so this came as no surprise. Over and over as it happened, Cheris thought, *I'm not here. I'm not here.* But of course she was. After a certain point she gave up trying to mislead Khiaz with clever ripostes. She had no words anymore, only the miserable awareness that she couldn't make her heart beat more slowly.

Afterward, Cheris closed the door, which Khiaz had left partway open. Dressed and put her gloves back on. Opened the door and walked to the nearest bathroom, looking neither left nor right, past the people who knew what she had just done. She locked herself in and turned on the water. Listened to the water running.

She peeled back one glove and stared at the veins, and the scar across the base of her palm.

For a long moment she hesitated. Then she took out her Patterner 52 and laid it next to the sink. Rested her hand on it. She was under no illusions that it would be painless. She had experienced too much of battle for that, and anyway, a little pain was a small enough price to pay. At least it would be quick.

Someone started knocking loudly. "Open up or I'll shoot the door off its hinges," a voice said over the sound of the water. It was Colonel Kel Gized.

Cheris had a sudden violent desire to take her gloves off and cut them to shreds. People knew now that she wanted to sleep with another soldier, forbidden though it was. The last person she wanted to talk to was a Kel, least of all her chief of staff. Even Khiaz would have been preferable.

"If you make me shoot, it'll raise a horrible fuss and it'll upset the host and you *know* how the Andan hate it when someone spoils a party. You'll never hear the end of it for years."

Cheris hesitated, then unlocked the door and stepped back.

Gized practically charged in. She took one long look at Cheris. Her mouth became a flat line.

Cheris glanced involuntarily at the mirror. Her face looked like a stranger's, angles ground too sharp, eyes abraded of expression. Her hair was a mess, too; she hadn't thought to run her fingers through it.

Gized closed the door. "It isn't right, what she did to you," she said.

"Colonel, I won't hear you speak against the heptarch," Cheris said coldly. Technically, Gized could be charged with treason. Most people wouldn't waste their time with such charges, considering them to be frivolous, but Cheris knew personally that Khiaz was mercurial and might insist. "I could have said no."

"Bullshit," Gized said. But she didn't raise her voice.

"I am a Shuos. She is my heptarch. I belong to her. If that's how she wants to use me, then that's how I'll be used." She was aware of how Kel she sounded. Nevertheless, it was true. Khiaz had just asserted her ownership.

All those years ago, when she had gotten herself seconded to the Kel, Cheris had thought she had escaped the heptarch's eye. She should have known that a fellow Shuos would have a long-term plan.

Gized glanced at the Patterner 52. "Jedao," Gized said, even though she never addressed Cheris without her rank. "Give me your gun and your knife."

"I don't know what you mean."

"You know exactly what I mean. Give me your weapons. You'll get them back tomorrow."

Cheris glared at her. "You're out of line, Colonel."

"You can court-martial me tomorrow. After you give me your weapons." She glared back.

Cheris entertained fantasies of court-martialing Gized, but where was she going to find another administrator as good? After a long moment, she broke eye contact. "I'm not going to do anything stupid."

Gized's mouth twisted. "You're usually a better liar than this, Jedao. Frankly, that worries me more than anything else."

"I don't know what you want of me."

"I'm being remarkably clear, Jedao. The weapons."

"No."

"Jedao."

She hesitated, then handed them over, hating herself for her weakness.

"I'm taking you to barracks, and we're going to stay up all night playing jeng-zai, which is an incredible concession on my part. You can beat me horribly the way you always do. And when you're fit to have weapons again, I'll give them back to you."

"People will notice us leaving early," Cheris said.

"I have really obscene things to say about how little I care about people noticing things, including the fact that we're holed up in the bathroom together. Come on, Jedao. I'll tell you the worst Kel jokes I know. How many Kel does it take to dig a latrine?"

THE SPLINTER FADED. Cheris was shuddering, and she inadvertently swallowed another splinter while she was trying to sit up.

CHERIS WAS IN the command center of the fangmoth *One Card Too Lucky*, listening to the latest report on the Lanterners' position as she kept an eye on her swarm's formation pivots on the terminal. Gized had said this would be a straightforward engagement. Naturally, this had jinxed the whole operation. At least, Cheris didn't like what the report implied about her options.

"All right," she said to her moth commander, "I've got this." She would have to approach this cautiously, in case Kel Command disappointed her. "Communications, get me Kel Command. If nothing else, High General Kel Anien owes me an embarrassing sum because she keeps trying to draw to an inner Crowned Door in jeng-zai. The least she can do is take my calls."

"Do you play games just to blackmail people?" Kel Gized demanded. She was sitting close by, running through logistical tables for the hundredth time.

"If I wanted to *blackmail* people, I would actually exert some effort," Cheris said lightly.

Gized had that expression that meant she wished she could roll her eyes at a superior officer.

They didn't get High General Anien, but High General Garit, who was much better at jeng-zai than Anien but couldn't win board games, which everyone but Garit thought was very funny. "All right, Jedao," Garit said in exasperation, "what's the emergency?"

"I wouldn't call it an emergency, sir," Cheris said, "more like an issue of protocol." Make the query casual. "No, really. I just got reliable intel that the Lanterners have filled their defensive outposts with children and hospital cases along with skeleton crews to operate the nasty weapons. Honestly, I thought I knew the regs backwards and forwards and something new turns up. They're broadcasting from their brand-new orphanages in the clear in all directions. Anyway, what do you want me to do about it?"

She had played fox-and-hunters with Garit, and endless rounds of jeng-zai. They had gone on a hunting trip together back when she was a major general, dismaying because shooting gray tigers was too easy and she had no use for the tigers' deaths, stupid pointless waste, but it was the sort of thing Garit went in for, and it would have been impolitic to turn him down. Most of all, she knew Garit's three children, one of whom she had introduced to handguns and who was in Kel Academy right now. There was a right way and a lot of wrong ways to handle the situation. She willed Garit to choose the right way.

When Garit answered, she knew immediately that he had picked one of the wrong ways. "There's no tactical difficulty, though?"

Cheris froze inside. "Not in the slightest," she said, keeping her tone relaxed. "But everyone will see the slaughter" – unsubtle word choice, that was the point – "and I thought there might be information operations fallout."

"Heptarch Khiaz has been working on this propaganda campaign," Garit said.

Khiaz. It was impossible to escape the fucking woman.

"You should see some of her latest pieces, really brilliant. I have no idea how she does it. But then, I daresay that's why I'm not a Shuos." He laughed. "Go ahead and shoot your way through, Jedao. There's no difficulty with Kel protocol or public opinion considerations."

She had always wanted children. She had always known it was a terrible idea, given her goal; had only allowed herself the most glancing affairs. But she hadn't expected the universe to explain to her in such detail why she had been right to avoid forming attachments.

If she defied Garit's orders, however casually phrased, he would relieve her of command. And then Garit would tell her moth commander to carry out the order. The commander was a good Kel. He would carry out the order. And Colonel Gized was also a good Kel. She would back the order.

Afterward, Cheris could never remember what she said to High General Kel Garit, or anything up until the point where they reached the perimeter and she ordered the swarm to open fire on the first outpost: an interval of two days and sixteen hours. A perfect black cutout in her memory.

She did remember, however, that Gized never even blinked when the shooting began. It was hard not to hate her after that.

Of course, Cheris didn't blink either. She was too well-trained for that.

CHERIS CHOKED AND forced herself to breathe more calmly in spite of the stinging pain. The splinters wouldn't stop hurting, but she had to know. She looked around the crystallized command center with its profusion of bleak glass pillars and broken walls.

I need information, she reminded herself.

THE SIEGE OF Hellspin Fortress. The fire-flashes of alerts, blood on the walls and floor and terminals, ricochet marks. A dropped stylus. Cheris could see where it had been chewed on the end. A fallen woman with gray in her hair and a bullet hole in the side of her head, blood puddled on the floor. She tried to think of the woman's name, she should know this, but it wouldn't come to her.

Gwe Pia was sprawled next to Jiang. She heard orders over the communications links, a desperate query from Commander Kel Menowen of Tactical Eight, then static. No one knew what was going on. A few people had tried to reassert order, the ones she had predicted would have the presence of mind to do so. But the bombs and logic grenades had taken care of them. Her habit of thorough inspections had made it easy to plant things. With the addition of the threshold winnowers, the Kel siege force was truly broken.

She had expected her hands to be sweating inside her gloves, but they were dry. Calm.

There was a lot of blood. She had not cared for neatness, only efficiency. She had one bullet left over, as she had calculated, and if necessary she could have taken weapons from the dead. They hadn't so much as clipped her. She had always been fast, and she knew the value of a good ambush.

It had been the weakest part of the plan. Atrocious setup: from a tactical standpoint, it would have made more sense to frame a subset of her staff as the traitors, and turn her people against each other. Easier to finish them off that way.

The problem was, she hadn't wanted to win.

Cheris turned the gun around in her hand. It was her Patterner 52, a model known for its accuracy. It was engraved on the grip with her personal emblem, the Deuce of Gears. She hadn't wanted to do it – it felt vainglorious – but it would have raised eyebrows if she hadn't. The Kel expected their generals to have healthy egos. The metal was still warm, at the exact temperature she expected.

She eased the muzzle of the gun into her mouth. It tasted the way metal should taste. She felt nothing. Not relief, not guilt, not triumph. Everything had gone more or less as she had planned. No one had risen to stop her, to tell her she was wrong, to say there was a better way of fighting the heptarchs. But then, the only one who had known about her rebellion was a heptarch himself. Years with the Kel, sharing the cup, and they had never figured it out.

Her finger tightened fractionally on the trigger. Surely the split second of heat and pain would be better than this roaring emptiness.

I am a coward, she thought, lowering the gun. What she had done was unforgivable. But to do it for no purpose was even worse. She couldn't quit now.

THE SPLINTERS WERE starting to hurt worse and worse, but Cheris couldn't stop. If she stopped she would lose all courage. Jedao had warned her about Kujen. At the very least she had to find out about him.

She closed her eyes this time, but it didn't help.

Only later did she remember that Kujen had taken an interest in her mathematical ability.

CHERIS HADN'T ORIGINALLY thought anything much of the refit: perfectly routine, and the Nirai station the swarm had put in at had better amenities than most, not that she was taking advantage of them at the moment. She was in barracks procrastinating on her paperwork for the chief engineer by shuffling a deck of cards that was going to be worn transparent if she kept this up any longer. This particular deck, whose artwork featured anthropomorphic farm animals in the borders, had been a gift from her sister. Nidana had said she'd picked it out because of the geese.

Without any notification, the door whisked open. In a moment

Cheris was on her feet, flattened against the wall away from her desk, pistol drawn.

The man who entered was slightly taller than Cheris was, and he paused in the doorway, making a perfect silhouette of himself, the kind of thing you didn't want to do in front of a former assassin. He wore Nirai colors, black-and-silver, even if the layered brocades and filigree buttons spoke to expensive tastes, and didn't look terribly practical, either. There was no indication of rank or position, just the silver voidmoth pin. Cheris didn't relax. The Nirai frequently had odd senses of humor, but it wasn't usual for them to play pranks on visiting generals who submitted all the proper forms and didn't push too hard about speedy repairs.

"I'm sorry," Cheris said, "but what is your authorization for being here?"

"Oh, put that thing down, General Jedao," the Nirai said, smiling. The man was striking, with a dark, oval face and tousled hair and graceful hands; it was impossible not to appreciate his beauty. Cheris couldn't help but notice that his tone wasn't remotely deferential, however. "I'm Nirai Kujen." He took a step forward.

In academy, one of Cheris's instructors had said, rather despairingly, that having ninety-sixth percentile reflexes could be just as much of a liability for an assassin as an asset. Cheris hadn't served as an assassin for years, but the habits of paranoia would not be denied.

She had allowed the Nirai to get too close, but there wasn't much space in here and she didn't have time to work through the options. She fired twice into his forehead, then cursed herself for losing her head and wasting a bullet. You'd think Kujen would have reacted when she brought up the pistol anyway, but no.

Kujen fell with an ungraceful thump. Cheris's pulse was racing. She looked at the fallen body, the lurid splash of blood against the wall, the closing door. She had just committed high treason, even if she could claim that she had reacted to an intruder in barracks.

The bigger problem was that she couldn't figure out why Nirai Kujen, who had presumably survived the past 500 years by being paranoid himself, had bothered showing up in person.

Four seconds later, the door swished open again. No warning this time, either.

Cheris retreated. Her world narrowed to the doorway.

A shadow fell across the threshold. "Let's try this again, shall we?" A different man's voice, deeper, but with the same accent. "Put that thing down. Suffice it to say that I can restore from backups more times than you have bullets, and someone's going to notice the fuss. I do realize you can probably kill people with your teeth, but it won't hurt you to hear me out. Besides, I would really rather not have to hop into your body next. No offense, General, but I have other uses for you."

Fuck. Cheris had known Kujen was immortal. What she hadn't known was how. She laid the gun down on the floor where Kujen could see it, then backed up. Her gloves felt as though they had turned to ice.

Kujen entered. Cheris saw how carefully he placed his feet, like a dancer, so he wouldn't get anything on his shoes. This body was also beautiful, but thinner, with a triangular face. Cheris wondered who it had belonged to before Kujen had happened to him.

The door closed, trapping her with him.

"If this is because I tore up my moth's engines doing that maneuver that last battle I was in," Cheris said, because at this point bravado was all she had left, "this is overkill, don't you think? The chief engineer could have just called."

"Sit down and let's cut the bullshit."

Cheris looked at Kujen, then walked over to the desk and sat.

Kujen came over to the side of the desk. "It's odd for a brigadier general to spend as much time as you do hacking into classified files," he said. "Don't you have other things to do, like shooting heretics?"

Cheris picked up her cards and began shuffling them, bringing her half-gloved hands into view. "Funny thing about this uniform," she said, "but I'm still a Shuos. I like to keep my hand in."

"You're adorable," Kujen said, "but that's more bullshit. You can't deny that you recognized my name. There aren't many people in the heptarchate who can say that."

She had blown the chance to play innocent rather spectacularly, at that. "How do I know this isn't a joke?" she said.

When Cheris had first learned that one of the heptarchs was immortal, she had been skeptical. She could see good reasons for such a man to hide behind a false heptarch. But why weren't the other heptarchs fighting over the technology, then?

Kujen reached over and plucked one of the cards out of the deck. Turned it around so they could both see it: Deuce of Gears.

Cheris was even more worried. Kujen shouldn't have been able to spot the card.

"I hear you're a gambler," Kujen said. "Are you after immortality, too?"

"Maybe later," Cheris said. The idea repelled her, especially now that she had some idea how it worked, but she couldn't afford to reject it entirely. "I just want my heptarch's position. I'm sorry to be such a boring ordinary Shuos, but that's all there is to it."

"Lovely story," Kujen said, "but I'm not buying. I checked your background, General. If you wanted to backstab Khiaz, you should have stayed attached to her office. I mean, from all reports she was very fond of you." His smile widened when he said that.

Cheris stiffened in spite of herself, even if her recent encounter with Shuos Khiaz was nobody's secret. Time to change the topic. "All right, Nirai-zho," she said without emphasizing the honorific, "since I'm apparently so confused about my own motives, you tell me what the hell it is I'm after."

Kujen's long fingers picked more cards out of the deck, slow and precise. He laid them in a circle, face-up. Ace through seven from the suit of Doors. "You want to bring down the whole damn calendar," he said. "Took me a little while to see it. You're very conscientious about researching all the heretics near your assignments. It looks a lot like duty, doesn't it? But I think you're fishing for allies, even if you haven't found any that meet your criteria, whatever they are. You want to bring the whole damn heptarchate down."

Cheris was starting to wish she had appreciated her paperwork more. At this rate, she was never going to get a chance to finish it.

"Yes, and I'd better hope for a few million soldiers to show up and join me," she said sarcastically. "Really, a one-man crusade against the heptarchate entire? That's not cocky, that's psychotic."

"Funny you should say that," Kujen said, "considering you've never lost a battle."

She hated it when people bludgeoned her over the head with that, but she held her peace.

"Besides," Kujen said, "you're in luck anyway. I looked at your academy transcripts. I don't know how it escaped everyone's notice for so long that you have dyscalculia. Math was the only subject you struggled with, isn't that right? You need number theory to get anywhere in high-level calendrical warfare. Nine hundred years ago I invented an allied branch of math to make the mothdrives possible. No one else has successfully pulled off a major calendar shift. I'm surrounded by tinkerers, not real mathematicians."

Yes, Cheris thought, *and you came up with the remembrances, too.* Specifically, the fact that they were accompanied by ceremonial torture. She was getting the idea that the torture had been a design parameter, not an unfortunate coincidence. "I'm sorry," she said, "but I have a certain amount of evidence that you're a sociopath. Why the fuck would I get in bed with you?"

The thing was, Kujen was making her one hell of an offer. Cheris's original plan had called for finding a way to assassinate him, because she despised the regime that Kujen represented, and she had thought the only way to replace it with a better one was to annihilate Kujen first. But if she could make use of him instead –

Kujen grinned at her. "This coming from a former assassin." He glanced over his shoulder at the corpse. "Instead of killing people one at a time, you get to kill them a bunch at a time now, isn't that why you traded up? In academy you were good at a lot of things. Languages, for instance. You could have gone into propaganda or interpreting or analysis. Yet you threw everything away to become a walking gun.

"You need me, General. You won't find a better mathematician anywhere in the heptarchate. Besides, you'll always know exactly where you stand with me, none of this pathetic hiding behind niceties. Face it, if not me, then who?"

Cheris was silent.

Kujen's voice softened. "You've been fighting alone for a long time, Jedao. You never get close to anyone, no affairs that last longer than a couple of weeks. The Shuos aren't the only ones who like to pry, you know. I imagine the Kel figure you're standoffish because you're being a fox. They have no idea what kinds of secrets you're trying to keep safe. I'm not your ideal ally, no. But I'm better than nothing at all. We can do this together. You won't have to be alone anymore."

"I'm not sure what the point of this discussion is," Cheris said, because she didn't want Kujen realizing how well he had her figured out. "You're a heptarch. You can destroy me at any time. What kind of assurances can I possibly expect from you?"

"That's what I like about you," Kujen said. He came around the corner of the desk and leaned against the side of Cheris's chair. Cheris wished her gun were back in her hand, even if she knew better. "Here you are, exposed, and you're still maneuvering for an advantage. Just what is it that runs in your veins, Jedao?"

"You're welcome to cut me open to find out," Cheris said dryly. "Knife's on my left hip if you forgot yours."

Kujen's smile was slow and sweet and utterly untrustworthy. "Oh, I intend to," he said. "Tell you what. There are things the other heptarchs won't forgive. Being caught conspiring against them is one of them. If I stick my neck out under the same axe, will you believe my sincerity?"

Cheris didn't move when Kujen leaned over her. His hand rested on the back of the chair, fingertips brushing her shoulder. *What is this,* Cheris thought with a flicker of irritation, *secondary school?* Even so, it was difficult not to react to the sensuous mouth, the long sweep of those ashy eyelashes.

"I have one question," Cheris said.

"Ask," Kujen said. His breath smelled of smoke and spice.

"If immortality is so wonderful" – hard to see the downsides for the practitioner if you didn't care about little things like murder

– "why aren't all the heptarchs doing it?" Assuming they weren't better at hiding it than Kujen was.

"So you're interested after all."

Cheris shrugged. Let Kujen think what he wanted.

"It can drive people crazy if it's not calibrated correctly," Kujen said. "I don't mean sociopath values of crazy." The corner of his mouth tipped up for a moment. "I know what I am. I'm talking about useless raving values of crazy."

"No good to me either, then," Cheris said. It couldn't just be that sociopaths were immune. The heptarchate's leadership didn't lack for those, historically speaking.

"Don't jump to conclusions," Kujen said. "They can't get rid of me because I'm the only one who understands the math, including the black cradle's governing equations. I can handle the calibrations. If you're useful to me, I can arrange for you not to end up as a raving wreck. That being said, you're a little young to be getting panicky about your lifespan, choice of career notwithstanding."

"Oh, that's not the issue," Cheris said. She had never been afraid of long odds. "I'm more concerned about the fact that I can't see what's in it for you. You already have everything."

"Is that what you think?" Kujen said. His fingers trailed down Cheris's back, traced a shoulder blade, came to rest. "You want to strip the system down to its component gears and build something new, if I'm not mistaken." It was impossible to look away from his eyes, darkly avid. "You're going to make a new calendar. I want to be there when it happens, and anyway, you can't do it without me. I can slaughter the math on my own, but I'd never ram this by the fucking sanctimonious Liozh or their pet Rahal. You could handle the calendrical spikes if someone solved the equations for you. You need a mathematician. I need a weapon. We can't do this without each other, Jedao."

"I can already tell you're not a tactician if you're pinning your hopes of revolution on one game piece," Cheris said. "Unless you have your hands on a bunch of mutinous Kel that no one's told me about."

Kujen laughed. "Mutinous Kel are your department, I'm afraid. But we're two of a kind; that has to count for something."

There had been a time when she would have hoped that she and Kujen were nothing of the sort, but by now she knew better. "Fine," she said, because it was important to preserve the appearance that she was making a choice. "Does it particularly matter to you what I want to install in the place of what we have now?"

"I can control the technology parameters that matter to me," Kujen said. "You do whatever the hell you want with the social parameters. I could care less."

Cheris didn't believe this, but they could fight over that later. She rose. Kujen stepped backward to give her room, still with that dancer's awareness of space. His eyes were both dark and bright. Cheris knelt before him in the formal obeisance to a heptarch, and said, "I'm your gun."

CHAPTER TWENTY-TWO

THE COMMAND CENTER was full of diffuse reflections, making it difficult to see anything clearly. Cheris spotted her own face in the mirror-maze, but it didn't feel like it belonged to her. Was there a tipping point past which Jedao's memories would drive her mad? What if she had passed it already?

There was carrion glass everywhere, memories spun out in great gleaming crystal spindles. Tangible and visible, unlike Jedao's. She assumed Jedao's glass was different because he had been a ghost. People sharded across the walls and burnished into the floor. Had the bomb only hit the command moth? Or had any of the swarm survived? It looked like the grid had been mostly knocked offline, but life-support was still functioning or she would be in real trouble.

Either the gravity was settling or she was regaining her coordination. Her breath hitched as she examined a twisted arch of carrion glass. It had once been Commander Hazan. There were faint threaded traces of a tree he had loved as a child, a sister who had died in an accident, things she had never known about him.

She backed away, wondering if he would ever have chosen to share these things with her, and choked down another of Jedao's splinters.

SHE WAS HOLDING a gun, the same Patterner 52 with which she had failed to kill Nirai Kujen, and the same one with which she would murder her staff three years later at Hellspin Fortress. Next year she would rise to general from lieutenant general, have to listen yet again to the gossip about the unseemly haste with which Kel Command kept promoting her.

This latest campaign, against a heretic faction that called themselves the Aughens, had gotten ugly very quickly, not least because a good many Kel had developed sympathy for the Aughens' cause. The Aughens fought honorably, made few demands, and wanted mainly to be left alone; but the heptarchate could not afford to cede that stretch of territory because it made the Blue Heron border vulnerable, and that was that.

Cheris stood at the center of a line of Kel with rifles beneath a green-violet sky, down the field from five Kel soldiers bound and stripped of rank. It was a rainy day, and the air smelled of damp leaves, earthy-pungent; of bitter salts. In the near distance she could hear the trees with their branches rattling in the wind, the roar of the sea. She wiped rain out of her eyes with the back of her glove and raised her gun.

The five Kel had failed their formation, and Cheris couldn't help but think that formation instinct, however repugnant, would have been a great help in the battle. So much had depended on that last siege, and after every battle she ended up executing cowards and deserters. But then, formation instinct wouldn't be developed until after she was executed for high treason. Back when she had been alive, it would have been a controversial measure. The Liozh in particular would have studied its implications carefully, and others would have protested it. By the time it was invented, after the fall of the Liozh, Kel Command and the hexarchs installed it into the Kel without any qualms.

The Kel virtue had been loyalty. Formation instinct deprived them of the chance to choose to be loyal.

Cheris fired five times in rapid succession. Five flawless head shots. Her instructors at Shuos Academy would have approved. She had to remind herself to see the blood. The Kel with rifles would have finished the job for her if she had missed, but it was a point of pride with her not to miss.

The Kel approved of efficient kills, too. They had had their doubts about her at first. Most Shuos were seconded to the Kel military as intelligence officers. She had come in sideways as infantry on the strength of her tactical ability, but no one trusted a fox. She had had an opportunity to prove herself, if you could call it that, as a lieutenant: the Kel officers who outranked her had all been killed, and she'd gotten the company out of a bad situation. After that, the Kel took notice of her competence, mostly by giving her the worst assignments. A Shuos was always going to be more expendable than one of their own. It had only given her more incentive to get good faster.

After the Aughen campaign, Kel Command assigned her to fight the Lanterners. Cheris had considered abandoning her original plan and turning coat, Kujen be damned. The Lanterners worried the heptarchs, which was a good sign. For her part, she had spent a great deal of time getting to know the best Kel generals and how they thought. The card games and hunting trips hadn't been entirely frivolous. If it had simply been a matter of battle, she could have offered her services to the Lanterners. She was confident of her ability to defeat anyone the Kel could field.

It hadn't been difficult to win the respect of the Kel. The Kel, being practical, liked people who won battles. If she could have done her work with that alone, she would have tried. But two things forced her hand. The first was technological advances in augments. The Kel were going the route of composites, and there was a good chance that she wouldn't be able to hide her intentions – two decades plotting high treason – from a hivemind. The second problem was Nirai Kujen, who could turn on her at any time. If she was going to act, she had to act sooner rather than later.

The hard part wasn't getting rid of the heptarchs. It was creating a functioning, stable, sane society from the heptarchate's ashes. She still had no idea whether it would have been possible to convince the Lanterners to give up remembrances, assuming some alternative could be found that gave them a viable calendar. When the Lanterners used their children as shields, however, she knew they wouldn't work out anyway.

She didn't have a lot of time left, so all she had was Hellspin Fortress. The massacre fixated the Kel on her and made her infamous. The Kel had respected her. Now they feared her.

Respect was a good lever, but fear was better. If she was going to make a bid for immortality, she needed a very good lever.

Terrible irony: if only she'd waited, if she had known what the Liozh were debating in their white-and-gold chambers, she could have offered her services to them instead. She wouldn't have needed to resort to mass murder. But the Liozh heresy reared up two decades after her death and some time before the Kel first revived her. Worse, there was a good chance that the calendrical disruption caused by Hellspin Fortress was what led them to investigate alternate forms of government, which led to their particular heresy. Democracy.

CHERIS STRAIGHTENED. IT no longer surprised her that their overseers had decided to kill Jedao. But they could have used a simple carrion gun to do so. They could even have handed her the gun and ordered her to do it herself, as a loyalty test.

She took a ragged breath, then another. Candied corpses in every direction. The command center's walls were warped, and the cracks in the floor were webbed together by fused strands of glass.

Maybe she was wrong about the extent of the damage. Maybe there were other survivors. She'd have to check manually. A cindermoth was a large place, but she had nothing better to do.

"Jedao?" she asked, because she couldn't help hoping.

No answer came.

Jedao had provoked the attack by convincing her to reveal the extent of her mathematical abilities, which alerted Kel Command that they had given him access to someone who could handle a high-level calendrical rebellion for him. But he hadn't expected Kel Command to risk two cindermoths plus a swarm to execute him. And now the heptarchs – hexarchs, she corrected herself – had finally caught on, and Kujen had abandoned her.

Cheris smiled grimly. She was already starting to think of herself as Jedao.

Jedao had tried to give her what he could. *Don't make my mistakes,* he had said. A few words and a lifetime of memories.

He had wanted her to continue the game for him. Or perhaps she was supposed to decide whether the game was worth playing at all. If only he had been able to trust her with more.

Cheris wasn't done with splinters. But she hesitated. Now that she knew about Nirai Kujen, she had a better idea how his form of immortality worked.

If she abandoned the splinters, Jedao would be truly dead, and his terrible treasonous war with him. If she devoured the last of them, she could carry on the fight, but the person doing so might not be Kel Cheris.

Had he meant to manipulate her into this choice? She didn't think so, but this was Jedao.

Still, Cheris knew she had already decided.

The next two splinters took her through the eyes like bullets.

CHERIS WAS SITTING at a table outside, shuffling and reshuffling her favorite jeng-zai deck. Normally she didn't lack for opponents – this was Shuos Academy, after all, and there was always someone who didn't believe a first-year could be as good as she claimed to be – but the yearly game design competition was going on, and everyone was distracted.

Someone came up from behind and kissed the top of her head. "Hey, you," said a familiar tenor: Vestenya Ruo, the first friend she'd made here, and her occasional lover. "Dare I hope that I've finally gotten the drop on you?" He came around and took a seat on the bench next to her. Like Cheris, he wore the red cadet uniform. The two of them had a theory that the first Shuos heptarch had picked her faction's colors to make her own people extra-special easy to assassinate from a distance.

Cheris quirked an eyebrow at Ruo. "Hardly," she said. "You came around that corner by the gingko tree, didn't you? I saw your reflection in the perfume bottle that guy was fiddling with earlier. Pure luck."

Ruo punched her shoulder. "You always say it's luck. Even at the firing range. You don't get aim that good with *luck*."

"I don't know why you make such a big deal of it when you're the better shot."

"Yes, and I'm going to make sure it stays that way." Ruo grinned at her. "But it's annoying that I can't beat your reflexes."

"I'm hardly a threat to you," Cheris said patiently. As a point of fact, when they'd first met at some party, Ruo had picked a fight with her. Lots of bruises, no hard feelings, although she had since learned that picking random fights out of a spirit of adventure was the kind of thing Ruo did. She wasn't entirely sure how it had happened, but it wasn't long before she started hanging out with him, partly because he always thought up terrific pranks, like the one with the color-coded squirrels, but partly so she could keep him from getting into too much trouble.

"Bet you say that to all your targets," Ruo said. Periodically he tried to persuade Cheris to declare for the assassin track with him, but she hadn't decided yet. "Say, shouldn't that girlfriend of yours be done with class about now?"

"'That girlfriend' has a name," said Lirov Yeren, who had come up behind Ruo. Sometimes Cheris despaired of Ruo's situational awareness. Although Yeren could walk silently, she hadn't been making any particular effort to be quiet. "Hello, Jedao. Hello, Ruo." Yeren leaned down, careful not to spill her drink, her curls falling artfully around her face. She and Cheris kissed.

"Hello yourself," Cheris said. She fanned out her hand, face-up, for Yeren's amusement.

"Oh, you're not even pretending not to cheat," Ruo said. Cheris had arranged to draw a straight of Roses.

"Only because I don't have any real flowers to offer you, Yeren," Cheris said, "so I had to make do with the sad cardboard substitute."

Yeren eyed her sidelong. "I'm pretty sure that line wasn't in Introduction to Seduction when I took it last year."

"I hate that course," Cheris said. "Seriously, all the Andan bars we practice at overcharge for drinks because, hello, the Andan are all rich. You'd think they'd figure it into our stipends, but I think it's supposed to incentivize us to commit fraud to get by."

"I don't see what your issue is," Ruo said dryly. "You're terribly good at persuading people to buy you drinks, especially with that whole 'I just got here from the farm and you civilized city people confuse me' routine."

"It's the principle of the thing," Cheris said. Besides, it was technically an agricultural research facility, even if her mother jokingly referred to herself as a farmer.

"You poor thing," Yeren said. "Drown your sorrows?" She offered her drink.

"See what I mean?" Ruo said.

Cheris took a sip. "That's a lot of honey," she said. The local spiced tea was something she was still getting used to. It wasn't very popular where she came from.

"It's to cover the taste of the poison," Yeren said, very seriously.

"Excellent thinking." Cheris drank again, more deeply, then handed the tea back.

"By the way," Yeren said, "I keep looking through the competition standings and I'm stumped. Where did you hide your game?"

"Don't get me started," Ruo said. "I can't even get him to play any of the more intriguing entries, let alone admit to entering."

Cheris shuffled the straight back into her deck and did her best "you civilized city people confuse me" impression. "It's much less stressful to watch everyone else tie themselves into knots. You heard about how Zheng got caught breaking into the registrar's computer systems?"

"That's so yesterday," Yeren said, "and I don't believe you for one second. Ruo told me how you *volunteered* to be outnumbered five to one in that training scenario and you care about *stress*?"

"Did he also mention I lost that one?" Cheris narrowed her eyes at Ruo, who looked innocent.

"Only after you struck the instructor speechless with your novel use of signal flares," Ruo said helpfully.

"Got lucky," Cheris said.

Ruo rolled his eyes. "No such thing as luck."

Cheris drew three cards in rapid succession: Ace of Roses, Ace of Doors, Ace of Gears. "Sure there is," she said ironically.

Yeren, who had taught Cheris most of the card tricks herself, ignored this. "I suppose you might take some kind of ridiculous pleasure in an anonymous entry," she said, "but they'll trace it to you anyway. Why not put your name on it from the beginning?"

"That's only if I entered," Cheris said. "Say, Ruo, you entered a shooter, didn't you? How's it doing?" She hadn't looked it up, but Ruo had talked about it a lot while wrestling with the coding, even if he'd turned down her offer to help by playtesting.

"High middle," Ruo said, "for its category. As good as I could hope for. I haven't embarrassed myself, that's all I ask." There were always a few entries that did so poorly that they damaged the cadets' future career options.

Yeren wasn't distracted. "Jedao, first-years don't get a lot of opportunities to impress the instructors. I didn't think you'd pass this one up. Especially considering how much you like games."

"It's very altruistic of you to point this out to me," Cheris said, "but it's done now, either way." She touched Yeren's hand. "We could go for a walk by the koi pond. It wouldn't kill you to get away from all the competition analysis for an hour or two."

"This is my cue to go elsewhere," Ruo said cheerfully. "Don't scare the geese." Cheris often thought she should never have mentioned that her mother liked to say that, even if they hadn't had all that many geese.

"Like you don't have a hot date of your own lined up," Yeren said. Ruo looked awfully smug, at that.

"That would be telling," Ruo said. "Have fun, you two." He kissed the top of Cheris's head again, and strolled off.

Yeren shook her head, but she didn't pull her hand away from Cheris's, either.

As a point of fact, Cheris had entered anonymously. A small percentage of competition entries were anonymous each year (although Yeren was correct that most didn't remain that way for long), but Cheris had an unusually good reason. You scored points in her game by manipulating other people, from cadets to dignitaries, into heresies. Celebrating the wrong feast-days. Giving heterodox answers on Doctrine exams. Inverted flower arrangements. Small heresies, for the most part.

Cheris hadn't intended for many people to fall for it, even if the Shuos had a known love of dares. It had been more in the nature of a thought experiment. The heptarchate's laws were becoming more rigid as the regime became ever more dependent on the high calendar's exotic technologies. She had wanted to show how easy it was to inspire people to a little heresy, to demonstrate how fragile the system was. Shuos Academy encouraged games, so a game – especially during the yearly competition – was the perfect vector.

She hadn't checked up on her entry since releasing it, or any of them, for that matter; that was the kind of mistake that got you caught. In fact, she was asleep in Yeren's bed when she found out.

"– Jedao," Yeren was saying urgently. "Bad news." Her voice shook.

"Hmm?" Cheris said. But she came fully awake.

Yeren was sitting at her terminal, wrapped in a robe of violet silk. Her hair fell down around her shoulders, and blue light sheened in the dark curls. "A cadet committed suicide over one of the games," she said. "At least, they're claiming it's a suicide."

Cheris sat up and made a show of hunting for her clothes, even though she knew where they were under the covers. She still didn't realize the significance of what Yeren had said. "Anyone we know?" she asked.

"They haven't released the name. But I did some poking around. I – I think it might be Ruo."

Cheris's heartbeat thumped rapidly in her chest. Yeren was still talking. "It was over one of the games," she said. "I remember glancing over it earlier. The anonymous one involving heresies. Except the cadet didn't just fool one of us over some minor point of Doctrine. He got caught framing a visiting Rahal magistrate."

It was exactly the kind of thing that Ruo would have thought hilarious. Except for the part about getting caught. Shuos Academy might have protected one of its cadets if the matter had been a minor infraction; each faction tended not to surrender its own to outsiders as a matter of jurisdictional principle. But the Rahal were also a high faction, and a *magistrate* – that wasn't just an infraction, that was an offense for which the guilty party could be tortured to death in a remembrance.

Cheris had opened her mouth to admit that the game had been hers, that she was the one who had killed Ruo, when Yeren went on, "The game's not anonymous anymore, at any rate. It looks like Chenoi Tiana has confessed that it's hers. She's under investigation right now."

Both of them knew that "under investigation" was unlikely to result in any serious reprimand. Cheris's heartbeat had slowed. "Who's Tiana?" she asked.

She had a way out. And she was taking it. She hadn't realized she had already made the decision.

"She's a third-year, no reason you should know her," Yeren said. "I'm so sorry, Jedao. It – I might be wrong. The suicide could be someone else."

Cheris doubted it. Yeren was very good at hacking. One of the benefits of dating her was learning from her. And the dead cadet being someone else wouldn't make the situation much better.

She couldn't put off the hard part. "Ruo was an idiot if he let himself get caught," she said with deliberate carelessness. "Suicide's better than hanging around to have your fingers pulled off, so I can't say that I blame him."

Yeren made a pained sound. "He was our friend, Jedao."

Cheris dressed quickly. "Friendship doesn't mean anything to the dead, and I don't think either of us wants to be associated with him anyhow."

"If that's your take on it," she said, her voice shaking again, "get out. Maybe I'll see you later and maybe I won't."

Yeren might have some intention of salvaging the relationship after calming down, but Cheris didn't. She left without argument.

Cheris headed out to a café. She had arranged for a small null in camera coverage – as the joke went, if you didn't hack the commandant's surveillance system at least once as a first-year, you were fit only for the Andan – and she wanted to listen in on the news. People were already gossiping about the suicide.

While Cheris listened to the gossip with half an ear, she started hacking the academy's grid. The tablet she was using looked like a model that had been popular four years ago, but what wasn't obvious was that she had wired together the innards from a decrepit laboratory machine she had begged off her mother. Her mother had been amenable so long as she didn't cause anything to blow up. (She was never going to live down that experiment with the food processor when she was twelve.) She didn't have any illusions that the tablet's secret obsolescence would hinder a real Shuos grid diver, but if she worked quickly, she had a chance of getting away with her query.

It didn't take long for Cheris to find pictures of Ruo's corpse. Even with the bullet hole in the side of his head, the red-gray mess on the other side, the blood matted in his hair, she recognized him. She would have known him in the dark by his footsteps, or by the taste of his mouth, or the way he always broke left when he was startled. She had assumed that he would always greet her with that kiss on the top of her head, and that they would graduate together, perhaps even apply to the same assignments. All of that was gone now.

Cheris had difficulty concentrating. Up until this point, she had convinced herself that all the game maneuvers existed solely in some abstract space. There was nothing abstract about the fact that she'd killed her best friend.

Still, she wasn't done yet. As luck would have it, she made it into Tiana's profile because someone had forgotten to lock it down after making their edits, or someone else had been hacking it before she had and left the doors open.

Two instructors had made private notes in Tiana's profile. They praised her ruthlessness and her boldness in claiming credit in the wake of a suicide. They praised her mastery of Shuos ideals. And, almost as an afterthought, they recommended that she be placed in two advanced seminars next term.

Cheris closed the connection and stayed in the café until it got dark. During that time, she played seven games of jeng-zai and lost them all.

No one ever figured out that Cheris was the author of Tiana's game.

"Ruo," Cheris said hoarsely into the silence. She had not spoken his name in over four centuries. It was hard to believe that he had been dead that long, that she was the only person who remembered the brightness of his eyes, his laugh, his unexpected fondness for fruit candies. The shape of his hands, with their blunt, steady fingers.

For a moment she wondered why her voice sounded too high, strangely alien. And then she remembered that, too. Her face was wet, but she tried not to think about that.

Cheris bent herself to finishing the task she had set herself. She already knew how much the splinters hurt. A little more wouldn't matter.

Four hundred and nineteen years before the Siege of the Fortress of Scattered Needles, on a world whose name had atrophied to a murmur, the heptarchate warred against rebels. The rebels flew many banners: the Thorn-and-Circle, the Winged Flower, the Red Fist. The Inverted Chalice and the Snake Defiant. The Stone Axe. In those days, it seemed that every hilltop, every city in the shadow of a forever cloud, every glimmering moon had its own device.

The battle had passed Cheris and Shuos Sereset by like a red tide. They had been assigned to assassinate the Axers' general, then position shouters by hand. As it turned out, the assassination had been the easy part. Now Cheris listened to the faraway crash of guns, the hiss-and-sizzle of evaporator fire, the roar of tanks. For hours she had been trying to call the Shuos for pickup; for hours she had sought any indication that heptarchate forces were still in the area, or that the heretics were coming back.

The shouters had proved more troublesome. Their handler had explained, in a cold dead voice, that Shuos drones could have accomplished the task, but their leadership was unwilling to reveal the full extent of the drones' capabilities to the Kel. The Kel, their allies.

Now Sereset was dying of a stray Kel bullet, pure stupid luck. The bullet was a tunneler, and Sereset's amputation failsafe had reacted too slowly. All Cheris could think of, looking at the crusts of drying blood, at the messy hardened foam that partly staunched the leg's stump and the perforations, was how little she knew the other man. At Shuos Academy Sereset had had a habit of keeping his head down and smiling a lot, but he had reasonably good marks and liked working with finicky equipment. None of this told Cheris what Sereset thought about the Liozh heptarch's rhetoric, or what music he hummed when no one else was listening, or whether he thought the bitter wine served at the Shuos table was better than Andan rose liqueur.

"You should have left hours ago," Sereset said in a dry rasp.

Cheris crouched closer. It was cold – she'd pulled off her coat and draped it over the other man – but this much cold wouldn't kill her. "I'm not leaving you," she said. "No word yet."

"I didn't figure there would be. You know, I always looked at you and thought you planned too hard. You always have the perfect answer prepared." Sereset's words were slow, dragged out one by one, but clearly enunciated: a matter of pride even now.

"Not a very useful character flaw, is it?" Cheris said. "Didn't do you much good."

"It's not your fault the Kel can't aim."

Cheris looked out over the curve of the hills, the silhouettes of blowing purplish grasses in the sun's waning light, the rubble of buildings blown apart. You could almost mistake this for peace: the wind, the grass, the hills. The way light snagged on the edges of leaves and changed the colors of stone and skin and trickling water.

You could almost forget the trajectories of bullets. You could almost forget that, less than a day ago, the Kel had fought the rebels over control of the nearby city. You could almost forget that the shouters had shouted enemy and ally alike into submission, driving out all thought but the imperative to kneel before the heptarchs' sign. The shouters were a Shuos weapon, and the Kel were not immune to them. Their weapons had fallen slack from their hands; the engines of war had chewed through the battlefield unguided. The casualties must have been appalling. For that matter, Cheris had to wonder how many of the other shouter teams had made it through.

Cheris had originally intended to pick a track that would make use of her gift for languages. She had been good at a lot of things, and having options worked in her favor. But after Ruo's suicide, she switched to the assassin track with a side of analysis. It would take more than assassinations to bring down the heptarchate, but it gave her a starting place.

And now, it turned out, she was going to die forgotten on a battlefield before she could set anything in motion.

"How much longer?" Sereset asked after a while.

"I don't know," Cheris said. A Shuos hoverer was supposed to have retrieved them over ten hours ago. They had no way of returning to the transport in orbit, and they couldn't leave the shouters: too dangerous to abandon into enemy hands, too valuable to destroy. In theory, the Kel had been mopping up the battlefield and its shambles of prisoners. Cheris had risked burst transmissions asking the Kel for pickup, but she had her suspicions about what the Kel thought about the Shuos just now.

The wind grew colder, the sun dimmer.

"Stupid war, isn't it?" Sereset said.

Cheris startled. Careless of her. She should have better control. "Don't say that."

Sereset's grin was ghastly. "Don't be ridiculous. What can they do, kill me?"

"You know just as well as I do what they do to dissidents. The best thing to do is obey."

"I expected better of you."

"You should never expect better of anyone." Cheris remembered long hours in Shuos Khiaz's office hunched over lists of numbers. Her imagination wasn't large enough to encompass the deaths, the cities unmade and the books smothered into platitudes, but that wasn't any reason not to try.

After another pause, while strange luminous insects started to dance their fluttering dances, Cheris said, "It's a stupid war." The words tasted strange. She was unused to taking such risks.

She wasn't sure that Sereset had heard her, but then he said, "Not much to do about it, I suppose."

"That's not true," Cheris said, more vehemently than she had meant to. "If everyone united to defy their tyranny, even the heptarchs would fall back. We say 'rebels' as though they all share the same goals and leadership, but they don't. They don't coordinate with each other, so the heptarchate will defeat them in detail. It's just a matter of time."

"Indeed," Sereset said. Perhaps he was smiling. At this point it was hard to tell.

"We shouldn't be fighting this war," Cheris said. She had been silent for so long. "The only way to get them to stop, though, is if someone takes on the heptarchate entire. I'm not talking about petty assassinations. I'm talking about defeating them on every level of their own game. It wouldn't be short and it wouldn't be pretty and you'd end up as much a monster as they are, but maybe it would be worth it to tear the whole fucking structure down."

Sereset went white. Whiter. "We're too big, Jedao. You couldn't do it in one lifetime and guarantee the results."

In one lifetime. "Wouldn't need to," Cheris said slowly. "The Kel have the key."

"If you're talking about the black cradle, they're not going to hand that over for your convenience. Assuming you figure out how not to go crazy in there."

"You'd have to manipulate them into it," Cheris said. "Another long game, but not outside the realm of possibility. Do something spectacular. Make them *want* to bring you back, over and over, until you're done."

There had to be better, less chancy ways, but they were going to die here anyway. Might as well go for broke while they were playing what-if anyway.

Sereset laughed painfully. "Fine, then, you're already crazy. And you're going to die in some fistfight over the price of quinces. Or they'll catch you, and there aren't words nasty enough for what they'll do to you."

"No, I'll die on this planet," Cheris said. "But at least we'll die together."

Cheris thought she could get to like the glowing insects.

The sun set. Cheris huddled closer to Sereset, warmth overlapping dwindling warmth.

It came as a considerable surprise when the silence was interrupted by a burst of static in her ear, and then: " – tenant Shuos Lharis of *Fireflitter 327*, shouter team five please respond."

Cheris froze. She had broken her own rule, talked to someone, security lapse. Sereset might live with medical attention. But then he might give her away: drunken mutters, drugged mumblings, thoughtless malice. You could never trust anyone.

Her hands flexed. She looked at him, then looked away.

"I know what you're thinking," Sereset said. His voice shook. "Do it."

"I can't," Cheris said, closing her eyes in shame. "You have a chance."

"I'll be a cripple even if I make it," Sereset said. "And life's cheap anyway –"

"Don't say that," Cheris said violently, "it's not true. It's never true."

"Besides," Sereset said over Lharis's repeated message, "you have a plan. Hell of a long shot, but you never know. Go topple the heptarchate for me. Make my death mean something. Hurry, before the lieutenant strands you here." His voice sounded very weak.

"I won't forget," Cheris said. She kissed his forehead.

Then, in a single quick, decisive motion, she snatched up the coat and covered Sereset's face.

After Sereset stopped struggling to breathe, she said into the relay, "Shuos Jedao, shouter team five, to Lieutenant Lharis. One for pickup."

"What happened to the other?" Lharis said.

"Stray Kel bullet. He didn't make it."

"Pity," Lharis said. "All right. Two hours and forty-six minutes until I can come get you. Stay put."

For the first time since Ruo's suicide, Cheris had found a moment's furtive camaraderie, and because of it, she had had to murder. Because she had been weak; because she had wanted to talk. She wouldn't make that mistake again.

Never forgive me, Cheris thought to Sereset as she put her coat back on. The two hours and forty-six minutes until the hoverer's arrival stretched forever.

Commit to fire, as the Kel would say.

No looking back.

CHAPTER TWENTY-THREE

VAHENZ HAD TO admit that, in her long career as an agent-at-large, she had encountered any number of organizations with the gift of stabbing one hand with the other during important operations. The Taurags had their oversight officers, the Haussen had separate bureaus with overlapping purviews, the Hafn had petty squabbles between aristocrats. Kel Command was pretty good at this trick, too. She hadn't imagined that they had anything pleasant in mind for the fox general once they were done with him, but it was anyone's guess as to why they hadn't just sent someone both competent and trustworthy to do the job in the first place. The combination had to exist even among Kel generals. What she was really looking at was an excellent argument against making your high command a hivemind, especially in the wake of a high-profile massacre.

Kel Command's willingness to blow up a swarm just to get rid of Jedao wasn't precisely surprising, although Vahenz found it interesting that they had put a cindermoth out of action during a major invasion. They wouldn't have blinked at killing the soldiers, naturally. Vahenz sometimes wondered how the hexarchate's history would have played out differently if the first Kel formation discovered hadn't been a suicide formation. Courage and last stands against desperate odds were one thing. Casual suicide, on the other hand, was just wasteful.

Still, Vahenz found the situation deplorable. It was sheer stupid luck that she'd escaped the bomb's area of effect, and even then the fringe of the blast had knocked half her systems offline, frying her box of sweet bean pastries in the process. The saving grace was that her needlemoth's stealth systems had been spared, so the Fortress didn't shoot her down while she was making emergency repairs.

Vahenz had an intimate familiarity with the Fortress's scan suites and their limitations. So when she repaired her own scan and it told her there was a single surviving life form on the *Unspoken Law*, not only was she sure who the survivor had to be, she was also sure that the Fortress had no idea anyone was wandering around the hulk of what had once been a perfectly functional cindermoth.

She could have dealt with the situation a few different ways. Not by leaving, although her superiors would probably have preferred that she report to them sooner rather than later. What news of the mess was public was no doubt giving them ulcers. She couldn't simply shoot up the cindermoth, either. The needlemoth was good at stealth, but not good enough to disguise a serious display of fireworks even if it had had the necessary firepower.

She had considered tipping off the Kel that their target was still alive and letting them deal with the problem. Of course, she couldn't be absolutely certain that that hadn't been the intent. No: she was going to have to take out Jedao herself. More fun this way, anyhow. She always enjoyed the chance to take out an interesting opponent herself, instead of relying on underlings to do it for her.

The carrion bomb was intended to wipe out people rather than inorganic structures. In particular, it had clearly not been designed to destroy something the size of a cindermoth, not in one hit. Which wasn't to say that the cindermoth was undamaged, and she knew for a fact that the rest of the swarm wasn't in great shape either. The cindermoth's upper surface looked like someone had made a jigsaw of it with the help of a glassblower's mad fantasias, but life-support still functioned, and artificial gravity looked like it wasn't trying to do anything innovative. With a sufficiently good team of Nirai, you might even be able to get it to fly in a few days.

Vahenz slipped the needlemoth next to one of the hopper bays and got to work with its burrowers. This was exactly the kind of dead time that she had brought the pastries for, and instead she was reduced to staring at her scan suites while she waited to penetrate the *Unspoken Law*. If any of its food stores had survived, it was probably Kel food. The Kel had a displeasing fascination with vegetables. To say nothing of the dreadful pickles.

Scan gave her a pretty good idea of what the internals looked like, a mess of passages and cracked walls. She loaded the maps into her augment and memorized as much as she could the old-fashioned way, just in case. You never knew when stray exotic effects would interfere with your personal tech. And while she doubted Jedao had emerged from the bombing unscathed, she expected that he would be far from an easy target.

She suited up no earlier than she had to, and brought along a torchknife and scorch pistol. It was a pity that she had no handheld scanner that could pinpoint a life form's location. She was going to have to leave the needlemoth's scanner running and rely on its grid to update her through the link. Setting up an ambush under these conditions was going to be an interesting challenge.

From the moment Vahenz stepped into the cindermoth, glass fibers drifted in the air, loosened by the intrusion. Her suit's filters would protect her, but she couldn't escape the sensation of ashes on the roof of her mouth, as though she were walking through a forest a scant hour after the inferno sputtered out. Her light, ordinarily a clear white, turned the color of broken steel in the dark passages.

The single life-sign had been moving slowly and erratically in the command center since Vahenz picked it up on scan. Wounded, she imagined, and trying to figure out his situation.

Vahenz watched it on the overlay map for a few minutes, then headed toward the command center. The acting commander apparently hadn't been doing anything fancy with variable layout when the bomb hit. Even so, it was hard not to look askance at the skewed angles, the walls bowed outward, the pitted floors. If she had been more imaginative, she would have fancied that she saw crumpled eyes staring up out of the holes.

Here the game picked up. Jedao's movements changed, became

more purposeful. Hard to tell, though: had he detected her, or was this coincidental? Most of the cindermoth's systems were blown to hell and gone, but it wasn't impossible that he had managed to revive enough to figure out that he wasn't alone anymore. She kept watching without looking for explicit cues: intuition, she judged, would give her the best sense of his awareness of her.

It was impossible to ignore the gritty texture beneath her boots as she worked her way down the corridors, as though she walked through the wreckage of a sandglass. It felt as though she was making loud crunching sounds, although her sensors assured her she was being reasonably quiet. The ashhawk paintings to either side of her were damaged beyond all hope: gold leaf peeling free in agonizing spirals, bird necks crumpled into uncomfortable knots, brush-strokes transfixed by splinters. Holes stabbed across the Kel watchwords: *from every spark a fire.*

Jedao had passed out of the command center. Unfortunately, the fastest way to intercept him was by going through it; she'd have to risk it. You didn't have to be a fox to think of setting traps. The only thing that would keep him from doing so, she imagined, was lack of opportunity. Given that he'd been bombed, he'd assume that someone would come for him sooner or later.

As it turned out, he'd had the opportunity, although the first concrete sign she had that her quarry knew that she had boarded wasn't the trap. The first sign was the emblem that Jedao had scratched into the floor, aligned so that she would see it right-side up as she entered. The doors were warped open. Vahenz fired scorch bursts ahead of her as she sprinted through and to one side – it was a long time since she had made the amateur's mistake of freezing in the doorway to make a target of herself – but there was no return fire. If Jedao was still in the area, he was well-hidden. Which didn't mean she was safe. His heat signatures hadn't faded entirely, and tellingly, she picked up a muffled thump, as though he'd stumbled. He couldn't be too far.

She hadn't paused as she passed the emblem, which looked like it had been carved with a Kel combat knife. However, she triggered several snapshots in passing so that she could review them more closely later, preferably when she wasn't pinned in a vulnerable location.

It was an appallingly clumsy trap, and Vahenz didn't so much as sweat as she flung herself away from the scatter of small explosions and behind a crystal pillar. He'd probably run out of time and decided that a half-assed effort was better than getting nothing for his trouble. Jedao had stripped weapons from the dead to set up that little display of fireworks, but the standard-issue Kel pistols had not reacted well to standard-issue Kel betrayal. After scanning the area again, she ventured out and knelt to inspect a bullet. It didn't even resemble a bullet anymore, but one of those quasicrystal dodecahedrons that used to be popular as earrings back home.

Jedao hadn't been able to hide other traces of his work. There were footprints and long, unsteady furrows where he had tried to lever himself up after taking a spill. Either the gravity had still been sorting itself out while he had been doing his work here, or he'd already been in the command center when the bomb hit.

That reminded her: the Deuce of Gears swarm had made a botched attempt at evasion when it was far too late. Why hadn't Jedao seen the knife coming for his back?

Just how badly injured was the fox, anyway? Assuming he wasn't feigning, which was a big assumption. Vahenz quickly checked the rest of the command center, but most of the terminals were pretty thoroughly wrecked.

The needlemoth called in with an update: the life sign had taken a turn and was headed deeper into the moth's guts. She narrowed her eyes at the pale-dark glass, the gravelly sounds it made underfoot. Charming exhibit, but she did have an opponent to destroy.

Vahenz wasn't superstitious about moths the way some of the Nirai got – one of many reasons she avoided getting stuck at bars with amorous technicians – but the unceasing slivered reflections, the eyeless spaces, the syncopated lights made her tense. Well, shooting people could be relaxing, if you shot the right people. She'd settle for that, and promise herself extra luxury when she made it somewhere safe with civilized amenities.

She brought up the photos of the Deuce of Gears. The image came up in front of her left eye, and she saw what hadn't been evident at first, the jagged column cutting through the lightning-crack in the larger gear on the left. Jedao had written a number: *1,082,771*.

Vahenz dismissed the image, mouth peeling back in a sneer. What, all those other fools he'd killed weren't worthy of being added to the tally, just Hellspin Fortress and this latest tragicomedy? Granted, the man wasn't known for his sanity. Let him savor his kills however he liked.

Funny but true: at one point she had dreamed about the things she could accomplish if the Kel ever let her walk around a cindermoth unmolested. Now that she was here, the Kel themselves had done most of the work for her, or scotched it in a supreme display of incompetence, take your pick.

The life sign had paused. It was close by now. She slowed and reflexively dropped behind a terminal's slanted remnants when a red-and-yellow light came on in the center of the room. It blinked in the rapid one-two-three-four of the Kel drum code for distress. A shape flickered in the shadows. Vahenz fired. The wall sizzled, and sparks flew up, aggressively red-orange. Part of a tapestry disappeared: streaks of soot, ghosts stitched into smoke.

"Honestly," a woman's voice came out of the shadows, crackling with static, "if that was the best Kel Command could do for a kill count, they should have kept me on. Anyway, I'm sorry, I don't believe we're *formally* acquainted?"

"Shuos Jedao, I presume," Vahenz said. Same female voice as that last conspiratorial "message" to Liozh Zai, same accent, same fucking cocksure attitude.

The voice was coming over the broadcast system, as though that was supposed to fool her. Still, she couldn't discount the possibility of some elaborate trick. "You'll forgive me if I'm not eager to introduce myself," Vahenz said. She queried the needlemoth's systems anyway, but it wasn't having any better luck without her to hold its hand.

"And yet here you are, when you could be long gone on your way to wherever secret agents go when they have to compose apologetic reports to their superiors." Jedao's voice was annoyingly rueful. "You think I didn't write my share of same when I was working for the Shuos?"

Jedao was moving again, very slowly. Vahenz was having none of that. She crouched low and set after him, cat-footed. "Cut to the point," she said. But she was smiling. She made her way around the remnants of the trap.

The red-and-yellow lights paced her, sometimes appearing to the left, sometimes to the right. Sometimes they were near the ceiling, and sometimes near the floor. Still blinking in that one-two-three-four pattern, as if she was supposed to be impressed by Kel superstition. At least she could assume that he knew exactly where she was. The fact that he hadn't shot her yet, plus his talkativeness, suggested desperation for information.

"I have to ask," Jedao said conversationally, "if you're here to see me dead, aren't there less risky ways of doing the job? I mean, we don't have inconvenient bystanders fouling up the arena now. It's just the two of us. There's no more need for lies and ploys. If I had some way of blowing you up for real, I'd have hit the button by now. That pathetic light show in the command center would have gotten me flunked out of Shuos Academy."

So she was right after all. But she didn't have any problem letting him continue to talk. Just in case he let something drop. As a bonus, he was moving more and more slowly. Too obvious. She stopped, refusing to be lured in further.

"You might be a Hafn, or you might be freelancing," he went on. "I don't really care at this point. The part that's relevant to me is that you're not with the hexarchate. That could be very useful."

"Jedao," Vahenz said, "I don't have any plans of teaming up with you and conquering the universe. Especially since you have a talent for betrayal with a side of attempted omnicide."

He had stopped entirely. She waited; no sense in blowing things by getting impatient. "If you're anything like me," he said, "and I have some reason to believe that you are, you find your superiors' lack of vision deeply regrettable. Anyway, how will it hurt you to hear me out? You should be asking me why, if I am so good at shooting people in the back of the head, the Kel have been making a point of using me as their pet general for the last 400 fucking years."

All right, she had to admit he had her attention. Maybe this was the part where he trotted out whatever pretty rationalization he had for his past behavior. "Is this the part where we see who knows more Kel jokes?" Vahenz said sardonically.

"Kel Command keeps a file of them, did you know that? But back to the subject. Let's think about this. The first time they pulled me out of the black cradle, the senior high generals remembered what I'd done. It was a fresh wound. They remembered having dinner with me. Losing games of jeng-zai to me. Hell, I danced with some of their kids at the damn ceremonies. I wasn't a historical figure, I was a real person. I was better than their generals – but that made me more of a risk. So why use an undead traitor?"

"Jedao," Vahenz said, "you clearly have a point to make. You might as well go ahead and make it." She could feel the pistol's grip in her fingers, the precise weight of it.

"I want to offer you my service."

Vahenz couldn't help it. She laughed so hard it almost became a coughing fit. "Come again?"

"I'm deadly serious."

"You don't even know my name."

"I'm not fussy," Jedao said. "Let me hit this from another angle, then. What do you know about the invention of formation instinct?"

"I confess I'm stumped," Vahenz said, which was unusual. She had made a point of being well-informed on the hexarchate's history, especially the parts it didn't like to remember. "I had some impression that the Nirai developed it for the Kel, but I couldn't provide citations."

"The Nirai like doing a lot of things for the Kel," Jedao said. "Codependent, really."

Vahenz didn't trust the direction that this discussion was going in. "If you're implying what I think you're implying –"

"I'm not a Kel," Jedao said, abruptly savage, "but they did their best to make me like one. You ever wonder who the prototype was for formation instinct? I'm saying *I have to serve someone*. If it's not you, it's going to be whoever next shows up on this fucking wreck. Even if it's the fucking Kel again. Four hundred years and they weren't going to let me out without some kind of assurance that I was going to do as they told me. I'm just lucky the weapon they used to 'kill' me didn't work the way they were told it would, and that I have a brief window of freedom."

An interesting story. Almost plausible, even. But Vahenz knew how good he was at being *plausible*.

The lights flickered left, flickered right. She didn't even notice them anymore.

"One more angle," Jedao said, and Vahenz thought he was going to dredge up some bit of history regarding Shuos cadets, or game design, or vengeful commanders, but instead what she got was: "What do you know about geese?"

Vahenz blinked. "Unlike certain undead generals," she said, "I don't have a whole lot to do with fowl other than eating them." She knew he had grown up on a farm of some sort, although what this had to do with –

"Then you don't know about goslings."

"They're tasty?"

"Well, that too. But the thing about goslings is that just after they hatch, they'll imprint on the first thing they see moving near them as a parent. When I was a boy I thought this was hilarious. It became less hilarious when I had a full-grown goose following me to school and making a nuisance of herself."

"You're a resurrecting gosling," Vahenz said, entertained in spite of herself.

"Something like, yes."

"All right," Vahenz said, weighing her options. "I want a token of – good faith, say." She was remembering how he'd landed his infantry on the Fortress in the first place, the sacrifice of Commander Kel Nerevor. Besides, if she got him where she could see him, she would be in a better position to assess his sincerity. Body language counted for something, even with a Shuos. She backed up to another crystal pillar – the whole moth was riddled with them, might make a great museum concept – and positioned herself behind it, poking out just enough of her head and the muzzle of her pistol that she could get a clear shot. "Come out where I can see you. The same doorway you came through. If I catch a shadow of a weapon, I'll char you down to particles."

If Jedao hesitated – but he didn't. He came around the corner and down the corrugated hall, dragging himself as though he had taken an injury to one of his legs. Vahenz's suit informed her that it was holding the temperature constant, but she felt as though pinpricks of ice were forming underneath her skin.

Although Jedao's body belonged to a young woman, his face was drawn and ghastly pale, streaked with sweat and dust, and bruised heavily on one side. There was a cut across his forehead, visible beneath the disheveled hair. Blood had smeared down and sideways from the cut and dried in ugly crusts. With a curiously affecting dignity, although not grace, he lurched down to both knees in the antiquated obeisance to a heptarch. Well, almost the obeisance. He kept both hands where she could see them, instead of folding the left behind his back. How considerate of him.

There was a terrible barbed clarity in Jedao's eyes, as though the universe had constricted to a circle with her at its center. She had seen its like in Kel who had been fledge-nulled. On the other hand, Vahenz also thought she saw an odd amber spark in them, which she didn't remember from the earlier communication, but that could have been a trick of the sputtering lights. "If you want me to beg," Jedao said, looking straight toward her, his voice hungry, "I will beg."

Too tempting. "How do you know I won't be worse for you than the Kel were?" Vahenz said in a purr. She was almost starting to think that he wasn't making up his story. Which was too bad for him: once she found out how much he knew about the carrion bomb, she was going to shoot him anyway.

His laughter was mocking. "Worse, what do I care about *worse*? You're more *competent*. And you're not the Kel. Everything else, that's just details. I'm not in a position to care about details anymore. You own me now. I hate you already, but you'll find a way to deal with that or you're not worth my time anyway." His voice grew eerily soft. "Just point me in a direction and tell me who to shoot. I like shooting people so long as I don't have to stop."

Well, if Jedao hadn't been psychotic before, he certainly was now. Why anyone thought a crazy asset was worth cultivating in these circumstances, even a crazy asset with an obnoxious habit of winning battles, was beyond her. As she questioned him about the carrion bomb attack, keeping her voice conversational, she prepared to fire. His eyes didn't so much as track the pistol's movements.

Before she had a chance to squeeze the trigger, however, a light came from the center of a servitor clinging to the wall. It had finally had a chance to get into position while she was focused on the interrogation. The laser fried the back of her head and cooked her brain, and she fell without finishing her sentence.

CHAPTER TWENTY-FOUR

THE NEEDLEMOTH DIDN'T look like anything Cheris had ever stepped in before, small surprise. It wasn't much larger than a hopper, but it didn't take any genius to realize that it was a hell of a lot more valuable. It had been intended to be operated by one person, with perhaps a single human-sized guest. As it was, she and the two servitors fit snugly.

Cheris was still certain that none of the humans had survived the carrion bomb. There was carrion glass everywhere. Shuos Ko spindled into dark, imperturbable strands. Shuos Liis, except Cheris hadn't been able to make herself go near the rippling glass once she knew who it had been, as though Khiaz waited just around the corner, smiling her inescapable smile.

The servitors had appeared dead, but Cheris had been willing to bet that the bomb's designers hadn't given a moment's thought as to how it would affect them. Although she wasn't a technician, it was impossible to spend as much time with servitors as she had without picking up a few tricks. With some improvised tools and a lot of swearing, she had managed to revive a deltaform. The deltaform had then helped her revive a birdform.

There hadn't been time for more, because the birdform, whose scanners were in better shape than the deltaform's, had informed them of the intruder.

They had agreed that the intruder was either after Cheris or Jedao, depending on how much they knew about anchoring, that they were relying on the needlemoth's systems to track Cheris, and that they probably weren't a Kel. Not that non-Kel were good news at this point, either. Cheris still regretted that they hadn't been able to take the woman prisoner, or find out so much as her name. But at least their ploy had worked. Cheris had first kept the intruder distracted while the deltaform paced them and the birdform raced to the needlemoth and hacked its systems. Cheris had considered using traps to delay the intruder and sprinting to join the servitors at the needlemoth so they could hightail it off the cindermoth, but they couldn't risk leaving the intruder alive so she could leak Cheris's survival to the Kel. So instead, Cheris made a distraction of herself so the deltaform could make certain of the intruder's death.

"We had better get out of here before anyone else shows up," Cheris said to the two servitors. "I hope you know how to drive a moth, because one of me doesn't and the other of me is hopelessly out of date."

The deltaform was already making irritated cheeps as it wrangled the needlemoth's grid. The mothdrive hummed lowly and sweetly.

The birdform tilted its head, lights whirring from green to yellow to orange. It asked her who she really was.

"I'm Ajewen Cheris," she said. She would call herself Kel no longer. "But I'm also Shuos Jedao. And apparently it's not time for me to stop fighting."

She had eaten the fox's eyes. She had seen what he had seen.

At the center of the blast, there was a mass of fossilized pasts and devalued futures. The better part of a Kel swarm reduced to carrion glass. Over 8,000 Kel and those in service to the Kel, all to guarantee the death of one man.

The deltaform wanted to know where they were going.

Cheris smiled crookedly at it. She yanked off her gloves and set them neatly to the side. There was a cold, pale fire in her heart. The hexarchs had no idea how badly they had fucked up.

She had gone to a lot of trouble to put herself into the black cradle, one bad option among many worse, so she would have time to run her campaign against the heptarchate. But she couldn't win her own war. The key to calendrical warfare was mathematics, and the only mathematician she had access to, Nirai Kujen, was more monstrous than she was.

Now she had an alternate mathematician, so to speak.

I'm dead, she thought, very clearly, *as I wanted to be, but I'm alive enough to carry on the war.*

All her life, she had lived to the hexarchate's high calendar. Now she lived to another calendar. She would measure her years by the death-day of her swarm, and not by the cold, prim feasts of the Rahal, the Kel's parades, the Vidona's cutting remembrances. Her every maneuver would be to the sandglass necessity of rebellion. The tide in her heart turned to the memory of amputations and evaporated soldiers, to deaths spent like counterfeit coins.

Cheris finally knew the meaning of Hellspin Fortress. She had killed a terrifying number of people for the heptarchate. When it came to the Lanterners, she decided she was done. A Lanterner's life had worth the way a heptarchate soldier's life had worth. A life was a life. It was a simple equation, but she hadn't been a mathematician then, and Kel Command had failed to understand the notation.

That hadn't been the only reason – she couldn't help being a Shuos – but it was the one that mattered.

Calendrical warfare was a matter of hearts.

But numbers could move hearts, with the right numbers, and with the right hearts.

She had learned that not all masters were worth serving. It was time to carry the fight to the hexarchs.

I'm your gun.

Calendrical rot had set in again.

ACKNOWLEDGEMENTS

Thank you to the following people: my editor, Jonathan Oliver, and the wonderful folks at Solaris Books; my agent, Jennifer Jackson; and my agent's assistant, Michael Curry.

I am grateful to my beta readers: Sam Kabo Ashwell, Peter Berman, Joseph Betzwieser, Daedala, Helen Keeble, Yune Kyung Lee, Alex Dally MacFarlane, Nancy Sauer, and Sonya Taaffe.

This one is for Yune Kyung Lee, best sister ever, who was there when everything began.